D1329806

Extraction Point!

By Travis S. Taylor
and Stephanie Osborn

Twilight Times Books
Kingsport Tennessee

Extraction Point!

This is a work of fiction. All concepts, characters and events portrayed in this book are used fictitiously and any resemblance to real people or events is purely coincidental.

Paladin Timeless Books, an imprint of
Twilight Times Books
P O Box 3340
Kingsport, TN 37664
www.twilighttimesbooks.com/

First Edition, May 2011

Library of Congress Control Number: 2011927070

ISBN: 978-1-60619-005-0

Cover art by Darrell Osborn

Printed in the United States of America

Chapter 1

Ray wasn't quite sure where the music was coming from, but it was loud. The second time he managed to force his head above the murky brown and gray water in the hubcap-deep tire buster of a pothole, he could hear the music pounding even louder than his heart AND the pouring rain–which was saying something. It was a remake of the old Guns 'n' Roses tune *Perfect Crime*–and from what he could tell, IT ROCKED.

The rain and the music and a chance to catch his breath gave him a quick burst of adrenaline to fight against the force of the two knees in his back, the hand grasping tight at the nape of his neck, and the fist beating into his left ribs. Ray flinched from the repeated jabs of pain pummeling into his side and could feel the adrenaline—and his hold above the water—slipping. So he took a deep gulp of air just before his face was slammed forward into the puddle, his nose bashing hard against the gravelly, broken asphalt at the bottom. The automatic gasp of pain that came next was inevitable. So was the water that filled his mouth.

Instinct engaged, and his body thrashed in wild desperation as he fought to avoid inhaling the filthy water. Despite his best efforts, he began choking, which in turn brought on a cough/gag reflex. Drowning, he realized, triggered bodily responses that were not only hardwired, but damn difficult to overcome.

I'm getting my ass kicked, he thought, verging on panicky despite himself. *I've got to do something! Something Goddamned quick!*

Using every ounce of willpower he possessed, Ray let his strength go and relaxed so that the man on his back could force him down and therefore be baited into a false sense of dominance–even, maybe, the notion that Ray was dead. Then he gritted his teeth and threw his right elbow up with all the strength he had left.

"Get OFF me!!" he yelled, muddy water gurgling from his lips as his elbow hit something hard–just when he lost his balance with his left hand, causing him to slip full face forward into the murky pothole… again. But the grip around his neck was gone.

Maneuvering both of his hands under himself push-up style, Ray managed to roll his body to the right, forcing his attacker off his back while continuing his roll over and then flipping backwards onto his feet. Ray shook the rain, mud, and blood out of his eyes, hacked slimy water from his windpipe, and made ready for an attack, but soon realized that his elbow had caught the man that he had been fighting square on the nose.

The man was standing, briefly stunned and temporarily blinded, with bright red blood mixed with rain pouring profusely down his face. This gave Ray only long enough to catch his breath and scan the area for his handgun. He didn't see it anywhere. *Shit. I liked that gun. Ok, hand to hand it's gonna be then,* he thought to himself, easing into a shallow horse stance while really wishing he hadn't let the guy get the drop on him and knock his pistol out of his grip earlier.

Just as the thought occurred to him, the man regained his poise and his vision, and rushed at him wildly–at least it seemed wild, at first. So Ray sidestepped and attempted to Judo throw him. But the man countered the move with an Aikido circular motion that flung Ray around a full three hundred and sixty degrees and then downward and forward, sliding belly first and hydroplaning in the several inch deep rainwater. His belly slide splashed a double rooster tail of water out behind him. Ray tucked his right arm under his body—ignoring the pain caused from the street pavement peeling skin from his forearm—and used his momentum in a Judo roll to bring him back up to his feet just in time to be tackled from behind mid-back. *I'm not doing too well with this guy,* he thought, rueful. *Jesus, this son of a bitch is fast.*

Ray twisted and squirmed free, tossing the man backward, and barely missed him with a spinning back kick. In a flurry of elbows, backward head butts, punches, and blocks, the two men ended back in the exact same spot they had been a few moments before. Ray was face down in the same pothole struggling for his breath as his would-be assailant ground knees into his lower back and pummeled him from behind. But this time, to Ray's surprise, the man's grip let go sooner–much sooner.

As Ray forced his head up above the water again, he understood why. He could hear the semiautomatic weapon's fire splattering off the alley-way wall in front of them. The rain of bullets was obviously fired overhead as a warning, spraying yellow sparks and shards of brick ubiquitously, but it still startled the man and the break was all Ray needed to throw him forward. At first Ray covered, afraid of friendly fire, but the man he'd already chased for two solid freakin' miles into this alley entrance had bear-crawled his way to the turn in the alley and was getting away.

"Hold your fire," Ray heard someone call over the music and the rain and his pounding chest. With that, he lunged to his feet with all the strength he had left and headed forward in pursuit of the man, lungs burning, dredging endurance he didn't expect from some unknown, here-tofore untapped place inside.

"You are NOT going to get away from me, dammit!" He sprinted around the corner in time to see the man climbing a chain link fence crossing the alley. "Shit!"

Over the fence, Ray said determinedly to himself. Ignoring various protesting bodily parts, he scrambled up to the top of the rusty fence and leaned over it, grabbing the other side of the fence with his hands, and then let his body weight flip him feet over head. He splashed down on the other side, already in a full sprint. *Come on! Push it!*

Ray was gaining on the larger man, but his heart was pounding at least two hundred beats per minute and felt as if it would explode at any instant. *If only I hadn't dropped my damn pistol, I'd have him now!*

Ray turned the corner and nearly slammed face first into a brick wall, stopping just in time to scratch his right elbow up a little more on the rough brick as he caught himself against the wall. *Ow. Really needed THAT.* Quickly he scanned around for an exit. There was only one—a primer-coated metal staircase up the side of the building—and the man had a full story and a half head start on him. It was almost as if the man knew the route he was going and had known the staircase would be there.

Shoving his way through the pain and exhaustion, Ray threw himself up the staircase, keeping his pace steady and the man in sight. Twice he saw the man slip on the wet metal steps, and each time Ray made a slight gain on him, his treaded boots proving a better grip on the metal than the man's street shoes. Pushing harder than he thought he could, Ray closed the gap to only half a story behind the man as he went out of sight over the rooftop of the ten story building.

Ray crested the rooftop cautiously and there was the man, sitting on the edge of the rooftop barely a couple of meters away, looking over the edge at the street below and then at his watch–or one of them; for some reason, he was wearing two. Different ones, at that. His pale blond thatch, cut short enough to stand in upright spikes but not short enough to qualify as a buzz cut, wilted a bit in the rain.

"You... you are rather good," the man offered, wiped blood from his aquiline—though now slightly misshapen—nose, gasped for breath, and looked at his watch again with bright blue eyes.

"Listen, I've got backup right behind me. There is no way down and I can keep you busy long enough for 'em to catch you. What d' you say we just sit down, take a breather, and wait on 'em?" Ray panted and smiled at the same time, hoping to stall long enough that he wouldn't have to fight the guy any more before backup arrived.

"I've got a better idea." The man looked at his watch one last time and then leapt over the side of the rooftop, pushing off with his hands as he slipped gracefully from the lip of the ledge. There was a brief flash of white light—Ray assumed it was lightning—that caused him to flinch and cover his eyes for a moment. And the man was gone.

"NO!" Ray rushed to the edge of the building, peered over, and... saw... nothing. "What the hell!?" *No blood on the street below, no screaming passersby, no squished and maimed body—nothing.*

"Ray! You all right?" a voice from behind him gasped.

Ray stood there, confused—no, flabbergasted—peering over the edge of the building, visually searching every nook, cranny, alley, and pavement all the way down. Nothing. The man had simply vanished like a ghost. No body, no visible escape route, no sign.

The rain continued to wash the red blood from Ray's broken nose and swelling lip down the front of his already stained and ripped shirt and he could still hear the music off in the distance somewhere. He stood in a contemplative calmness, surveying the volume of space off the side of the building, and gasping for air as his heartbeat slowed. *How in the. Bloody. Damn. HELL did he get away? This time, is it... nah, can't be.*

"Your pistol, Ray." A young man in his late twenties with a blond military haircut and an athlete's build scanned the rooftop as he offered Ray his weapon.

"Huh? Oh, thanks, Jay." Ray took his favorite handgun, checked the magazine and safety, and slipped it in the clip holster on his waistband at his back. When he did, cold water squished from the holster, down his back and into his already soaked underwear, giving him a severe chill. He shivered violently for a second. He was still more than a bit dazed by what had happened moments ago—and the beating he'd taken—oh yeah, and the running.

"Uh, Dr. Brady?"

"What? I know, he got away." Ray panted, still having a hard time talking between breaths.

"Uh, no sir, uh, Ray, you've been shot." Major Sampson pointed to the bloody mess on his left shoulder. The young Army major said it nonchalantly as if he had seen the same situation before.

"Oh, that. It's just a flesh wound," Ray waved his hand in dismissal—right before he collapsed backwards onto the rooftop.

"Man down! Medic!" Sampson called over the radio.

Chapter 2

"Uh huh, right, flesh wound. Orders?" Army Major Jay Sampson looked down at the dark haired physicist—the one degree, among many, that Ray principally associated with himself—in concern. Their medic, Staff Sergeant Ernie Travers, rubbed Ray's bloody nose with smelling salts, once more startling Ray, making his eyes burn and water even worse; but it did wake him up. Boy, did it wake him up. A hot coal shoved up his nostrils wouldn't have felt worse.

Ray tried to raise himself up, but the major and the medic both put hands on his chest, forcing him back down to the rooftop. Ray tried not to blink as the medic held his eyelids open and shone a light at his pupils. But rain continued to fall on his face, forcing him to squint his eyes shut despite his best efforts. He squirmed beneath their hands, trying to get his eyeballs out of the downpour.

"Now hold on, Ray. Let's make sure you're not concussed TOO badly." There was a hint of a Latino lilt in Ernie's voice.

"Whatever," Ray pushed their hands away and pulled himself upright. His head throbbed a little, but he'd been hit in the head before. Hell, he couldn't figure out exactly why he'd passed out anyway. "Sweep the block and see what you can find and, uh, what time is it?"

"Forget it, Ray. You've already missed your flight." Major Sampson laughed.

"Aw shit! The boss ain't gonna like that." Ray rubbed gingerly at the bloody wound on his shoulder, then winced at the pain that lanced down his arm. "Well, get me a charter. I have to get home."

"Right. How about a doctor?"

"Sure, why not? Just as long as he looks at me on the plane." Ray still puzzled over the odd ending to the chase; finally he shook his head and chalked it up as either majorly weird or really well planned. "How did he get off here? Must be a rope or something down there. In all this rain, I just couldn't see it. And… he was leading me rather than me chasing him. Damn. I thought I had him running scared, but he knew exactly what he was doing and where he was going. Shit!" Frustrated, he kicked a pipe protruding from an air conditioning unit.

"Chief Master Sergeant Holmes." Sampson motioned to his men taking station around the building.

"Yes, sir?"

"Sweep this block and this building VERY carefully. Have Chief Olson sweep for fields and get Mr. Donaldson and Specialist Hamilton up here and have them run me a full MASINT analysis. I want to know how that man got off this building. Oh, and get Doc up here too; Dr. Brady's been shot. Among other things."

"On it, sir." The sergeant nodded and set about communicating orders to the group of very specialized soldiers that were assigned to Ray. The team wore no insignia, identification, or rank patches, only solid black battle dress uniforms and light armor vests. Of course they were heavily armed and ready for anything–anything except people jumping off the roofs of buildings and vanishing into thin air. Chief Master Sergeant Holmes had seen some weird shit since he had been assigned to Dr. Brady but he'd never seen a man disappear into thin air before.

"Thrift, call Dime in for an evac to the airport," Holmes spoke into the radio attached to his shoulder harness. Then he turned his attention to Dr. Brady.

"Uh, okay Ray, let's get you down from here."

"Huh? Oh, right, down." Ray shook his head and wiped the rain and the blood from his face again. The rain tickled his swelling nose, forcing him to sneeze. An aerosol spray of blood flew everywhere. "OW!! Shit! That didn't feel good. Woah…" He staggered, and Jay grabbed for his good shoulder.

Ray was woozy for a few seconds after the sneeze, and saw stars. Lots of stars. All different colors of stars. And for the first time he noticed the Empire State Building in the skyline in the distance. He paid it little attention.

⁎◕⁏

"No, sorry honey, I'm not gonna be home in time tonight. You'll have to give the baby her bath, I guess, and deal with the briefing to the Old Man." Ray talked into his headset; on the other end was his wife back in Kingstowne, Virginia.

"Are you ok?" Samantha asked her husband.

"Uh, well, I'm all right. A little banged up but all right. The doc is stitching me up now and he gave me another tetanus shot even though I told him he gave me one only three weeks ago. I'm gonna change clothes then get outta here and head off to the airport. I'll be into the airport there about 10:06 or so and I'll see you before eleven."

"Stitches!"

"Oh, yeah, no big deal, just a scratch on my left shoulder."

"You sure?"

"Sam, I'm fine."

"Reagan?"

"Yes, Sam?"

"Did you catch him?"

"He got away."

"Shit!"

"Yeah, sorry. I'll debrief you when I get home. Love you. Bye." Ray tapped his BlackBerry and pulled the specialized bluetooth out of his ear, placing it in his pocket. *There, that's done.* The lack of distraction now left his mind open to tactile sensation, however. "Shit, Doc! You using a wood screw to put those stitches in?" Ray flinched.

"Sit still, Dr. Brady, and I'll give you another local." The team doctor frowned and went back to his work, mumbling. "He doesn't even know he's been shot, but he complains about my stitching. Hmmph."

"Well, Doc, you know's well's I do that Reagan Brady is never in pain unless there's somebody around to feel it with him. Big drama queen." Jay stepped around the edge of the helicopter and laughed as he lightly patted Ray on the back, making sure to avoid any gunshots, road rash, or similar injuries in the doing. The physician paid the U.S. Army soldier little attention, as always.

"Jay?" Ray merely raised a questioning eyebrow at his teammate. He was too tired and beat up to cuss at the major's jokes. He thought about sticking his tongue out after the "drama queen" remark, but decided that might only prove Jay's point. Jay was really more of a right hand man to Ray—the closest thing he had to a best friend, if men so deep undercover as they were dared HAVE best friends—and oftentimes Ray felt as vulnerable without Jay around as he did without his wife Sam. The three of them had worked together on their "special projects" since the major had been a lieutenant.

꧁꧂

"Nothing there, nothing anywhere, Ray. It's like he plain damn vanished. Sarge and the boys tore that entire city block to bits and didn't find a damn thing." Jay shrugged and took a seat in the evac chopper across from him. The rain had finally moved through the area and the Moon was coming out overhead, shining silver through the breaking clouds. The added light helped him see how haggard Ray really looked, which was pretty haggard. *Damn. He ran a record speed marathon AND got beat to hell and back this time. And DIDN'T come out on top.* He internalized the sympathetic wince.

"Then how the hell did he get off that rooftop?" Ray frowned and flinched again as Doc put in the final stitch. "Shit! We about through yet, Doc? It's only a nick. I'd like to get us off the ground sometime in the next day or so."

"Not quite, Dr. Brady. By the blue lines on the side of your nose I'd say you've once again broken what I'd just fixed. Hold still, this is gonna hurt... a lot." Ray knew Doc was irked with him because he was calling him "Dr. Brady," not "Ray." Doc grabbed Ray's nose between his fingers and squeezed it and yanked it to the right. Ray's nose crunched and then popped and a slight trickle of red oozed out of his right nostril.

"YEEOOW! SHIT, Doc!" Ray swatted the doctor's hands away and grabbed at his nose. Reflexive tears ran freely down Ray's cheeks, mixing with the blood. Ray blotted at it with his hand until Doc shoved a roll of cotton gauze up his nose. "HEY! Dhad doesd't feel ady bedder!"

"Jesus, Ray, that had to hurt," Jay laughed and turned a little pale at the same time. Had it been the first time he'd seen something like that, he'd probably have lost his lunch—had he eaten any lunch. Or dinner, for that matter. Days like today, meals tended to take a back seat.

ଔଔଔ

"Leave this splint on there for a week and ice it several times a day for about fifteen minutes at a time. You know the drill by now," Doc said while placing a plastic splint over Ray's nose and taping it down. "Here, use this for the time being." Doc cracked a chemical ice pack against the deck of the chopper and then shook it up, squishing and kneading it a couple of times in his fingers. Ray could feel it getting cold already by the time he took it from the team's sawbones.

But "Doc" John Fields was more than just the team's trauma and first aid guy. He was also a research physician specializing in nasty bugs and chemicals and other extremely hazardous pathogens that could be proliferated as chemical or biological weapons. He'd even become an expert in nuclear weapons biological effects somewhere along the way. But, lately, Ray had done his level best to keep Doc's emergency room skills up to par, at least to hear the physician tell it.

"Ok... NOW can we get in the air?" an impatient Ray asked him.

"I suppose so, but this I.V. stays in until we get you home in one piece. You lost a lot of blood, judging by your shirt, which was bloodied front AND back—"

"The back, too? Oh, that wasn't mine, then. I busted the other guy's nose, too." Ray started to gesture with his elbow, then thought better of it; it was the one Fields had just finished stitching.

"...And we need to get you an MRI in the morning to look at that brain bucket of yours. It IS concussed. The only question that remains is how badly so." Casually Fields injected a strong, broad spectrum antibiotic into the I.V. line, to prevent possible pneumonia and any other nasty pathogens that had managed to enter Ray's body through the numerous injuries.

"So we're evac-ing him all the way?" Jay asked.

"Either that or he waits till tomorrow to go home."

"Not doing that. I wanna get home." Ray nodded, only half listening to Doc's orders. He twirled his right index finger around and nodded at Major Sampson.

"Got it." Jay jumped up and stuck his head out of the chopper. "Sarge, get the men back to the office. I'm gonna see Ray home in the chopper."

"Got it, Major. Any other orders?" Sergeant Holmes asked.

"I'd say we've done enough damage for tonight, Sarge. Just get the team home and be in for debrief tomorrow afternoon."

"Sir."

“”

"She looks so peaceful when she's sleeping." Ray leaned over the crib to kiss his tiny daughter good night. The sight of her little fuzzy blonde head almost made him forget about the pounding in his own skull, which increased when he leaned over. He patted her chest ever so lightly and smiled as she cooed softly at being disturbed, but didn't wake up. He sighed and held back the tears of despair, unaccustomed tears it was true, but all too near the surface in his battered condition. "You'd never believe she was such a sick little baby."

"Shhh! If you knew how much trouble I had getting her to sleep..." Samantha whispered and elbowed her husband. In the right side, Ray realized thankfully.

"We've gotta face it sometime, Sam," Ray managed to choke out around the swelling lump in his throat, his weariness temporarily breaking down the emotional wall he'd erected against the truth. "Most children with cystic fibrosis don't make it past twenty, twenty-two."

"Not ours," Sam insisted. "We've got the best team in the world. And you know you and Doc Fields are working on that. You'll do it. I know you will."

Ray smiled, feeling his spirits lift at his wife's confidence in him, and eased over the giant Legos and around the plastic Roll-Arounds scattered about on the floor as Sam ushered him out of the nursery. Ray stopped for a moment, staring down at a giant stuffed caterpillar, tempted: The caterpillar was called Alphabet Pal. Each of the caterpillar's feet, when squeezed, said a letter of the alphabet, followed by the letter's sound. If they were squeezed quickly and in the proper order, the caterpillar would crudely enunciate words. Ray and Sam had had a running game for some time to try to make it say curse words and other rude things, but the manufacturers had evidently taken such a notion into consideration, and the caterpillar would only giggle, its cheeks lighting up red, as if in embarrassment. But Ray had recently had a new idea, and wanted to try it out. Doped on pain meds as he was, now seemed as good a time as any. Sam saw the direction of his gaze.

"OH, no. Not tonight, Mr. Gutter Brain. She's only gotten to sleep, you're beat to shit, and we still have things to do. Come on."

Obediently, Ray allowed himself to be ushered out of the room. Samantha eased the door closed and sighed.

"You look tired, Sam."

"Yeah, well, you don't look so hot either, Dr. Brady."

"Yeah, I could use a nap, a cup of coffee, and a GOOD woman," Ray said wryly at his wife, cocking a suggestive eyebrow at her as he raised his wrist and looked at his watch. It was pushing midnight. Raising his arm had been a bad idea, however, as it sent a nasty, tight feeling up the stitches in his shoulder. So was raising his eyebrow, as his nose splint tugged, putting pressure on that broken facial protrusion. He winced, which also hurt his nose. *Shit. Can't even flirt with my wife without it hurting like a son of a bitch.*

"Not yet," she replied, ignoring him. "Come on. We've got to see the Old Man tomorrow and I want to know what happened in New York."

"It can't wait 'til morning?" *So much for flirting.*

"No."

"You da boss," Ray shrugged.

"Stop saying that," Samantha frowned at her husband.

She led them downstairs to the basement hallway. Sam spun the combination lock on the door a few times and pulled the door open. Quickly she punched in her code number on the security alarm; it beeped twice in a shrill tone and "unarmed" appeared on the display screen.

"Step into my office, sir," she said, while scribbling the date and time in the *Opened* line of a form on a clipboard hanging by the alarm keypad.

"Like I said, you da boss," Ray goaded her with an affectionate smirk. She stuck her tongue out at him.

The basement of the two story dwelling in one of the newer suburbs of Kingstowne had been converted to a secure office before they ever moved into the house. Sam was the official "leader" of the clandestine government team, one of the deepest, if not the deepest, Homeland Security teams in existence. Although in the field, the team usually followed along behind her husband, the brilliant scientist/operative Dr. Reagan Brady, as swiftly as they could while trying to keep up and cover his ass. Sam was a good leader and knew when to put her foot down and when not to. On the other hand, Ray, despite his intellect and multiple degrees in several different hard sciences, had always been at the mercy of his own wild and free will and he performed best when left mostly to his own recognizance. His own recognizance, however, usually was analogous to something along the lines of a bull in a china shop—on one of the bull's clumsiest and orneriest days. Pamplona, his colleagues declared, had nothing on it. Sometimes, Sam had to lay down a swim lane or two to keep him going in the right direction. They were really broad swim lanes, big enough to drive a barge through, but she did lay down the boundaries every now and then. And, even though the team jumped when Ray told them to do something, they literally defied gravity and flew if Sam gave them an order. There was no doubt in the team as to who was really in charge. As far as the Old Man was concerned, the two of them had carte blanche permission, but "his girl" was the unquestioned head of the team. Sam was indeed "da boss lady."

Things only got more complicated when she and Ray decided to have a child. They knew she would have to work from home or retire. Hell, she wasn't even thirty yet, so retirement was absolutely out of the question. Working from home at least temporarily was the only option, and said work required a top secret/sensitive compartmented information, or TS/SCI, facility. So the Director authorized the Chief of his most effective "hard problems" team the "home office" solution.

Sam sat down at her desk and tapped a few keys on a computer wearing a green label on its side claiming *This Computer Is Not Authorized For Classified Material.* An infrared webcam image of the baby's crib came into view. She turned up the volume a little until they could hear the baby's light breathing. Both Sam and Ray smiled from the inside out. Light blue eyes met golden hazel ones for a moment, shining happily with love. The baby continued to snore softly, a habit she'd acquired after nearly continuous respiratory infections over the last six months, which had ultimately led to the diagnosis of cystic fibrosis, a systemic genetic disease that caused progressive disability, frequent illnesses, and often, early death. *At least Abby's not sick right now*, Ray thought. *Maybe the diagnosis is wrong, anyway. It's still early in the game.*

"Ok?" Ray plopped down in a chair on the opposite side of Sam's desk and tried to get comfortable while not getting so comfortable that the pain meds and the events of the day took their toll on him, forcing him to doze off. Ray fought back a yawn and straightened up in the chair. "Why couldn't this wait until the morning?"

"Hold on for a second." Sam rolled her desk chair over to a two drawer Mosler safe against the wall, spun the combination a few times and then pulled the handle of the lock down with a loud clank. Sam pulled out a laptop red-labeled *This Computer Is Authorized For TS/SCI* and plugged it into a power cable which was sitting on her desk. She flipped a little magnet over on the front of the safe with the red side out saying that the thing was "open."

"What's this all about, Sam?" Ray watched the baby monitor with more interest, thinking that the little one looked just like her mother. There was no way he could tell that from the low image resolution of the IR camera, but he knew it was true. They both had the same pale blonde hair and light blue eyes, while he had dark brown hair and hazel eyes. She'd gotten Sam's cheekbones, too, Ray supposed; it was hard for him to remember anymore what his own used to look like.

"This." Samantha booted up the computer and tapped a few keys. Ray had to fight trained instincts not to snoop her password as she typed it. "Let's see…" she tapped the touchpad and pad keys again. "Here, look at this." Sam turned the laptop around for Ray to see the screen.

"What's this?" Ray looked at the image on the screen. It looked like a security cam image from inside a laboratory of some sort and the image had been labeled *Top Secret/SCI* at top and bottom.

"This is a security cam shot from inside… INSIDE… the Y-12 enriched plutonium rod machining facility at Oak Ridge. Recognize anybody?"

There were three men and one woman in the poor quality gray scale image. Ray looked closer at them, then did a double take. He clicked the touchpad pointer on the zoom for a closer view of the faces.

"No shit?"

"That's him, isn't it?" Samantha asked, but judging from the expression on her face, she already knew she was right.

"Yep, that is definitely the guy that jumped off the building tonight." Ray looked closer. "When was this taken?"

"Zoom in on his face a little further," Samantha replied. "Oh, never mind. I already did that and ran the enhancement algorithms on it. Toggle to the next slide."

Ray clicked the slide viewer to move to the next slide. And there was an enhanced image of the man's face—the same face that had sneered at him in the alley in New York. It was a little fuzzy, but there was an obvious black line under his right eye and his hawk-like nose appeared swollen. He looked like he'd recently taken an elbow and maybe even a backward head butt to the face. But his pale blond hair was dry—and spiky, in the modern fashion that had come from anime.

"No way. When was this taken?"

"About five minutes after you called me tonight. How long was that after you lost him?" Samantha leaned back in her chair, subconsciously looking over at the baby monitor screen. Ray did the same. Abby was comfortably cooing in her sleep.

"It couldn't have been an hour at the most. No way he could've had enough time to get from New York to Tennessee on any aircraft I've EVER heard of. And how would he get into the Y-12 facility? I mean, that's where they machine the enriched plutonium and uranium rods for nuclear reactors." Ray pointed at the screen, then ran the fingers of his right hand through his short brown hair. "A twin?"

"With the same black eye you gave his brother? Barring some sort of strange phenomena like the Corsican Brothers, I don't think so."

"Well, that's just it. It's not exactly the same black eye, Sam." Ray gestured at the image. "It looks about a day old, not 'less than an hour' old."

"What?? You sure?!"

"Hell, yeah. Trust me, I got experience, ya know. Either it's a day old, or the son of a bitch heals faster than Wolverine."

Sam studied the image closer. "Hm. You're right, at that. Still, if he can pop from New York to Oak Ridge inside an hour..." Sam hesitated and then said, "Think about his clothing. Is it the same?"

"Uh, I dunno, let me think." Ray closed his eyes and focused on what the man had looked like. Ray had a good recollection of what the knuckles on his right hand looked like up close and personal, but as far as clothing went, he couldn't be sure. Most of the rest of his memory of the conflict consisted of muddy water that stank of diesel, and on the rooftop he'd been too winded, and too intent on delay tactics, to pay attention to such details as clothing. Dark. He remembered he'd been wearing something dark. And loose. But that was it; as much as he could dredge up past the jackhammer in his head. He opened his eyes and studied the image. *Dark, with an open overshirt. Hm.*

"Maybe? You should ask Jay. He got a look at the man too, right before he gave us the slip. But he'd be bloody. And wet. I mean, it was raining cats and dogs on us."

"He could've dried off and changed clothes. You did." Sam shook her head. "I have no idea how I'm gonna get all the blood out of those clothes. Smears and clots and all kinds of nasty shit. What a mess. At least they're black."

"Yeah, true. On both counts. Sorry."

"I think we need to tell the Old Man that we have a possible anomaly." Sam waved off the apology.

"I was afraid you were gonna say that. Let's see if Jay agrees too before we tell the Old Man that. What kind of anomaly? Santa Claus or Easter Bunny?"

"You're the expert. You tell me." Sam held her hands palms up and shrugged.

"Shit, Sam, my nose is throbbing too hard for me to think straight and I'm worn out and groggy as hell from the pain meds. Let me think on it."

"That's fine, honey. Your subconscious works better than most people's consciousness anyway," she grinned. "We've got until the briefing tomorrow for you to decide that. Besides, I don't think we have enough information yet, but this could be the one we've been looking for, for the last eight years." Samantha seemed excited.

"Well, ok, but, there has to be another explanation. Remember how excited we got over Quebec and you KNOW how that turned out."

"Don't remind me," she replied, scowling.

"Right. You da—"

"And STOP saying that."

஑௸

Ray drifted in and out of sleep. Pain meds typically did that to him. He would either be zonked out of his gourd like a zombie, which wasn't very restful sleep. Or he'd be in and out of sleep with fitful dreams, which wasn't very restful sleep. Either way, Ray wasn't getting very restful sleep. Every time he rolled over one way, he bumped his stitched-up arm, which sent a shriek of pain up his shoulder and down his spine. That would make him jump, which, in turn, made the throbbing in his nose increase, which dominoed into a pounding head. Every time he rolled over the other way, the bruising in his ribs slammed into his side, which made him jerk back... which made the throbbing in his nose increase, which dominoed into a pounding head. Never mind the substantial patch of missing hide on his "good" forearm. The scab on it turned into a jelly-like goo if he happened to rest it against Sam's moist bare skin in his sleep. Then, when he pulled away, the jelly went with her and he had an oozing, raw wound again, which felt like somebody had turned a blowtorch on it. He wished Fields had at least slapped some gauze on it. Sleeping on his stomach with a broken nose was flatly out of the question. He sighed, and stretched out on his back.

His mind raced over and over the events of the day. His dream sequence continued to run the interview with the genetics research scientist at Columbia University. The guy had written several papers on some extremely dangerous bio-agents and methods of making them viable weapons by inserting their DNA into airborne viruses. The problem—depending on your point of view—with most of the nasty bugs was that they weren't easily spread like other, more common viruses. A common virus, such as an influenza or a rhinovirus, would have to be the delivery mechanism for the really bad one, for the simple reason that it could be spread more readily and rapidly. This research had been nothing new except for the fact that some of the scientist's more recent work was with viruses that spread quickly but took a long time to incubate. This way the people infected with it wouldn't die off before they had a chance to infect others with it. So when the NSA and the DHS computers got a hit on this guy as well as a very large deposit of money in an offshore account with his name on it, certain people immediately became decidedly interested in the particulars of this fellow's lifestyle. Rather quickly Ray's team at the Department of Homeland Security Directorate of Special Research Projects and Operations, or DSRPO, was alerted and brought into the mix.

The DSRPO, pronounced "dee-surp-o" by the very few people who knew it existed, was put in place by executive order not long after the creation of the Department of Homeland Security. Only the Secretary of Homeland Security, the Assistant Director of Homeland Security—or ADDHS—over the directorate a.k.a. the "Old Man," the President, Secretary of Defense, the Chairman of the Joint Chiefs of Staff, the chairman of the House Permanent Select Committee on Intelligence (HPSCI), the chairman of the Senate Select Committee on Intelligence (SSCI), the Director of the FBI, and the Director of National Intelligence (DNI) were briefed on the existence of the organization.

The executive order gave the DSRPO "full Patriot Act authority" as well as "global initiative" to protect the security of the United States. What that meant was that they could pretty much do whatever the fuck they needed to do, in order to get the job done. That didn't mean they couldn't get in trouble if they crossed the line. It just meant that their line was somewhere way the hell out there with James Bond's. Which fit, considering their job was somewhere way the hell out there with Star Trek. Protecting the country against the consequences of alien or futuristic tinkering wasn't exactly your everyday job anyway.

All members of the Directorate had been, and continued to be, hand picked by the ADDHS, Robert Kruger—the "Old Man"—from civil service and active duty branches of the military. So far no civilian contractor types had found their way in, but that didn't mean it couldn't happen one day; it just made it harder, was all. Since the existence of the organization was way the hell above Top Secret, the active duty military were transferred under the Office of the Secretary of Defense (OSD), while the civil servants were moved to DHS as staff to the Office of the Secretary of Homeland Security. But the Directorate they ended up working for didn't "exist" and the executive order placed heavy penalties and jail time on any breach of security about the organization. There were a LOT of "men in black" jokes in the organization, especially after the movies came out.

Ray's dreams always bounced around and usually seemed to include the day he was briefed into the DSRPO. That had been a defining moment in his life. After all, it had also been the day he met Samantha. It was a good day, a good couple of weeks, right up to the first mission. He often dreamed with that memory as the basis of the dream, but not tonight. The day's events had overpowered his subconscious mind and were replaying over and over.

ಶಲಃ

The office at Columbia University where Dr. Gupta sat was within a genetics lab. Beyond the office and the first room was a hazardous materials lab that was sealed off with a negative pressure airlock. The existence of that lab in such close proximity to Gupta's office told Ray a lot as soon as they walked in. Ray leaned against a wall and scanned the equipment in the room while Jay questioned the scientist, which was proving fruitless. After realizing that Gupta wasn't going to cooperate, Jay showed him a printout of an offshore bank account, the numbers and access codes for it, and the record that a large sum of money had just been placed into it. Links between the scientist and that bank account were quite clear.

"So why were you given this money?" Jay questioned the scientist, towering menacingly over him. The scientist was short and a recently naturalized citizen from India. His accent was strong, but he'd picked up some of the local New York vernacular on top of it. He raised an eyebrow and adjusted his tie.

"Go fuck yourselves," he spat. "I'm not saying shit to you without my attorney. You can't come in here and push me around. I know my rights, so piss off."

"Look pal, this can go easy or hard. Who paid you and for what?" Jay replied.

"Maybe he won't mind us looking through his things," Ray said, wandering back over and tugging at a filing cabinet drawer that was locked. He pulled out his .45 caliber pistol, chambered a round, and then pointed it at the cabinet lock. "You want to open this thing or shall I?"

Jay looked over at Ray with a grin on his face. Gupta seemed nonplussed and not a little disbelieving, and merely nodded for Ray to go ahead.

"What do I care? I've got nothing to hide. I'll just bill you for the damage. Now get the hell out of my office!" he snapped.

ഇ✆ᏸ

An unconscious Ray rolled over in bed again in an attempt to find a more comfortable position but it only aggravated his stitches. The pain woke him out of his dream. He squirmed a bit and, after several minutes of being unable to get comfortable, decided to get up and take another pain pill. He squinted at the alarm clock on the nightstand and the faint red numbers told him that there were still a few hours of good sleep time left. He eased out of bed, trying not to bother his wife, but he was too groggy and stiff to be graceful; he nearly fell out of bed on his first try. He stumbled into the bathroom on legs that felt as flexible as ramrods and ached about like rats gnawing on them, and rummaged through the medicine cabinet for his meds. He took two of them though he wasn't really certain what Doc had said the dosage was. At the moment he didn't really give a shit either. He chased the pills with water and then sluggishly found his way back to the bed.

"You okay?" Sam asked without moving as he crawled back in bed.

"My nose hurts."

"It'd be better to duck next time. Now get some sleep."

"It wasn't a matter of ducking, Sam. The guy—"

"Ray, sweetheart, just go to sleep." Her tone of voice said Sam's sleepy patience was wearing thin.

"Wish I could. I'd sure like to."

"Then do it."

"You try it."

"Okay—right after you try shoving a baby out between your legs."

"...Right."

So much for sympathy. He sighed and silenced. Ray closed his eyes and finally dozed off again. This time the pills kicked him into zombie sleep.

Even when the sun peeked through around the heavy curtains, he was still out, and he didn't rouse until he heard the front door downstairs open and close. That brought him to. Adrenaline kicked in, and he immediately rose straight up, one hand extending toward the nightstand, and reached over to nudge Sam. She wasn't there. Realizing who had come through the front door, he flopped back down into the pillows, closing his eyes, content to lie however he'd fallen.

"Uhhg. I feel like crap," he breathed to himself right before the bedroom door creaked open. It was Sam.

Sam tiptoed across the room and began removing her shoes and clothes, trying to be quiet. She was doing a good job of it right up until she stubbed her toe on the corner of the bedpost.

"Ow! Goddamnit!" she grumbled under her breath.

"You can turn the light on. I'm awake," Ray told her in a bleary tone.

"You couldn't have told me that ten seconds ago?!" She sat at the foot of the bed, pulled her socks off, and began rubbing her toe.

"Been running?"

"Yeah." She stood up and crossed back over to the doorway to flip the light switch. Sam was wearing a lime green sports bra and dark blue spandex running shorts. A t-shirt, soaked with perspiration, had been discarded on a corner of the bed. Her long, pale blonde hair was pulled back in a ponytail; sweaty tendrils stuck to her neck. From the looks of her hardened, muscular body nobody would ever believe that she had had a baby girl barely over a year before. "I'm so out of shape."

"How far 'd you go?"

"Ten miles."

"Hmm." Despite having to restrain himself from drooling—and other things—Ray didn't want to say anything about her being out of shape because he knew that Sam had superhuman ideas of fitness. She had run the marathon and competed in Tae Kwon Do in college at an elite level. Ten miles was just an easy short jog for her when she was at peak form.

"'Hmm,' what?" she raised an eyebrow at her husband. Ray was afraid she'd taken it the wrong way.

"Most people haven't run ten miles in their lives, Sam."

"Yeah, how far did you run yesterday?"

Ray's first thoughts were, *with or without gunplay?* Knowing that this particular line of conversation was not going to lead to anything short of disaster for him, Ray suppressed that notion and changed the subject, levering his stiff body into a sitting position with some effort. "Where's Abby?"

"She's with Teresa today. Frank's got the front."

Teresa Mathers was the live-in nanny slash bodyguard they had hired onto the team. When Sam and Ray decided to start a family, the two of them had used all the resources at their disposal to conduct background checks and to dig into anybody that had applied for the job. Teresa turned out to be the cream of the crop. She was an active duty Army Specialist medic having been "attached to" the 82nd Airborne in Iraq for two years. Teresa had fired her M4A2 on more than two dozen occasions because she had been shot at first. Several times she pulled wounded men to safety while under fire and on two occasions brave young men died in her arms while she did everything she could to keep them alive–while still under fire.

After coming home from Iraq she had reached the rank of Staff Sergeant and ended up at a dead end career path at a VA hospital in Arizona, topping out as the ER's head nurse. Teresa had applied for training in forward recon but had been turned down because of her gender. It was the applications for combat intelligence training that brought her to the Assistant Director's attention. He pitched the idea to Sam and Ray when Sam was only three months pregnant. Sam immediately flew to Arizona to meet her. Not long after that, Teresa was transferred to the Office of the Secretary of Defense and moved in with the Brady family. Teresa had no idea then what she had gotten herself into. She did now.

Staff Sergeant Frank Grayson was their household security guard. With the SCIF "home office" in the basement, his presence was required. Ray had no idea where he'd come from, except that the Old Man had expressly assigned him to the Brady household. His cover was as Sam's brother. There WAS a slight—only slight—resemblance. Frank was a little darker complected than Sam, though.

"What is that?" Ray noticed a dark bruise on Sam's left shoulder as she turned toward the bathroom. He pointed a lead-weighted index finger in its general direction as Sam turned to see what he was referring to, before letting it—and the rest of his abnormally heavy hand—fall back to the bed.

"Oh, I got that yesterday, I guess, sparring with Frank and Teresa." Sam waved it off and pulled the bathroom door closed behind her.

"Yeah, well, maybe it'd be better to duck next time," he said under his voice with a grin as the door shut. If she heard him, she never acknowledged it, which was probably good for him. Seconds later Ray could hear the shower start.

At first he thought of getting up and joining his lovely wife. Then he glanced at the clock and realized it was only eight forty-five. They weren't due into the office until after lunch. "Why did I tell her she could turn on the lights? Shit." He plopped back onto the pillow and didn't move because he was too tired to worry with the damned lights. For a fleeting instant he imagined pulling his pistol out of the nightstand drawer and shooting the bulbs out, but images of Sam, Frank, and Teresa bursting into the room with their weapons at the ready deterred him. Besides, squeezing his eyes shut tighter and pulling Sam's pillow over his head took less effort.

Chapter 3

"Yes, I get that you were interrogating the man, but that still doesn't explain to me how you got into a shoot-out with some completely unrelated individual, yesterday." The Old Man looked more than a little impatiently across the gray metal conference room table at Sam, Jay, and Ray later that morning in the debrief. "Major, would you mind skipping the fluff and getting to the point?" That last was more of a command than a question, and directed specifically at Jay.

Jay seemed a little flustered at first and Ray considered stepping in and helping his teammate out, but Jay recovered quickly. Sam sat quietly and calmly, saying nothing. If she felt things were going in the wrong direction, Ray was certain that she would speak up.

"Uh, yes sir," Jay replied awkwardly. He was always a little bit uncomfortable around the Old Man. Something to do with legends of Odin, he'd once muttered to Ray. "Well, he wasn't unrelated, per se. You see after we got zilch out of Dr. Gupta we tagged him. While Dr. Brady pumped a couple of rounds into the man's filing cabinet with his .45, I slipped a transmitter on him—"

"Ray did *what*!?" the Old Man shouted in Ray's general direction. Suddenly feeling sheepish, Ray gave a wry grin and decided it would be best to say nothing at this point.

"Uh, he shot up the lock on Gupta's filing cabinet," Jay repeated uncomfortably.

"How the hell did he do that without drawing half the university down on you?"

"Silencer," Ray interjected, succinct. "It did get some attention from Security, though."

"Don't think they'd realized what we'd done to it until later," Jay added. "As soon as they burst in, Gupta pointed to us and yelled, 'OUT!' They grabbed us immediately. Not that we resisted; it was what we wanted at that point. But we sorta got, um, 'escorted' off the premises."

"Well it is a Goddamned good thing that neither of you two assholes exists or I'd be doing some serious explaining up on the Hill." The assistant director laughed and scowled almost simultaneously. He'd had his days of hard work in the field and Ray could sense that in reality the old man kind of got a kick out of their good-cop bad-cop routine; he just had to act pissed for the sake of protocol.

"Anyway, about a half a second after Gupta was certain we were out of his hair and the campus security buffoons had reached the misconception that they had thrown us out, he got on his blackberry and text messaged somebody for a rendezvous. When he left for it, we followed."

"I see." The Old Man nodded. "And at some point Gupta made all of you, got the upper hand, and then got away?"

"No sir," Jay corrected, "he met the other guy, handed over something—Ray thinks it was a flash drive—and part of our team followed Gupta back to the university and the rest of us followed the new guy. We'd gotten maybe a couple blocks before this other guy made us, and the OTHER guy was the one who launched in like a buzz saw."

"So the OTHER guy whupped your ass."

"Well, boss," Ray couldn't help but interject a protest at that point. "It wasn't THAT easy. He was one tough son of a bitch! He hit like a God-damned elephant. And he tossed me around so easily that I damned near got whiplash, and I'm NOT a small man. He was fast as blazes and stronger than any man I've ever seen. I'd sure as hell love to spend a month or two with HIS martial arts instructor."

"I gotta agree with Ray on that," Jay averred. "I've never seen anybody fight like that dude. It was one helluva thing to watch, those two going at it. You coulda sold it on pay per view, easy."

"And you didn't back Ray up during the fight because…?"

"Uh," Jay began.

"Because I doubt they could've shot this dude without hitting me," Ray rescued his second in command. "We were all over each other. They did try some overhead shots, and that helped. Got him off my back, anyway."

"Literally," Jay added.

"Dog pile?" the Old Man suggested, wry. Ray shook his head.

"Moved too fast. Like a Matrix Agent on crack."

"And half the time he had Ray's head in a pothole fulla water," Jay noted. "That's how he got his nose broke, when the dude slammed his face down in it. If we'd 'a dog piled this guy, he'd 'a drowned Ray, for sure." Sam shot Ray a hard look. Ray ignored it as best he could.

"So I take it we don't have any further leads on this guy?" the ADDHS asked. He tapped his fingers impatiently on the table, continuing to grow more and more unsettled with the outcome of the events in New York City the day before.

"Well, Sam has something." Ray raised an eyebrow toward his wife and team leader, who promptly dropped the scowl and slapped on her business face.

"Samantha?" the Old Man never referred to his number one pupil as Sam.

"It is the damnedest thing, Robert." Sam nodded to Jay to toggle the screen into the briefing she had put together the previous night. The slides of the man Ray's team had fought the day before popped up on the flat panel on the wall at the end of the conference room.

"What is this?"

"This is an image captured by a street camera near the building in New York where Ray's strong guy gave him the slip. And here at the bottom is the time stamp. This is an image of the same man, we believe, inside the Y-12 plutonium rod machining facility at the Oak Ridge National Laboratories near Knoxville, Tennessee about forty-three minutes after Ray's team confronted him in New York City. Again, note the time stamp."

"No doubt that's him, sir," Jay added. "I'd recognize him anywhere."

"Yeah, I gave him that broken nose and that black eye," Ray chuckled and then rubbed at a streak of pain in the stitches in his shoulder as he laughed. The rubbing hurt worse than the jab of pain, so he stopped. Laughing made his head pound like jackhammers so he cut that short as well. *Humor isn't too funny today*, he decided.

"And he reciprocated," Sam fired back in annoyance. "Half drowning you in the process. Was the shoulder shot from him, too, or was it friendly fire?"

Ray and Jay exchanged bemused glances, a hint of dismay in them. Both shrugged uncertainly.

No, definitely forget the humor today, Ray concluded.

"You're telling me that this person vanished off of the side of a building into thin air and then somehow materialized inside a Top Secret highly secured facility, several hundred miles away, just forty-three minutes later?" The Old Man got the discussion back on track, leaning all the way forward in his chair to get a better look at the images on the slide. He looked over the top of his glasses and then paused for a long moment as he studied the images.

"It's—" Ray started to say something but Sam held up an imperative hand, implying that now would be a very good time to keep quiet.

"Okay," the Old Man finally broke his long pause. "What's the catch?"

"I think we've uncovered an anomaly, Robert," Sam said confidently.

"An anomaly?" he frowned and leaned back in his chair as if he didn't really want to hear what was coming next. "Okay, Samantha. I'm all ears. All I've got to say at this point is that this had better not be Quebec all over again."

Ray winced. *Quebec.*

"Well, sir," Sam began, "there is no known method of transportation that would have gotten this man from New York City to Oak Ridge in such a short amount of time. That means that a technique of unknown capabilities was implemented. I can't say what type at this point." Sam stopped at that and waited for the Old Man to size up her statements. Ray watched closely as the play between the ADDHS and his wife resembled more of a father-daughter relationship than that of a boss and an employee. And he wasn't the only one on the team who noticed it either. But if any of them made the mistake of asking about it, Sam would likely say nothing and ignore the question—or she might get upset. And nobody, NOBODY, was dumb enough to go there. Especially in her current mood.

"Little gray aliens, I'd guess?" the Old Man asked, completely serious. "Or The Time Tunnel?"

"I didn't say that. But I believe we should invoke the Anomaly Protocols and treat this as such a priority." Sam opened a Top Secret file folder that was sitting in front of her and recited from it. "Under suspicion of activities only explainable by unconventional means, said activities are to be labeled as anomalous and to be treated following the protocols herein…"

"Yes, yes, I know the Protocols. I know the damned things backwards, forwards, and sideways. You know I do, as you helped me write them. That wasn't my question. Give me a best guess or a gut feel about what this is." Kruger turned from Sam and looked at Ray. "Dr. Brady, you're the mega-scientist here. I'm sure you have a theory?"

"If I were gonna go for the Sci-Fi Channel answer I'd say he beamed up to his ship and then beamed back in to Oak Ridge a few minutes later. Obviously, he "beamed in" SOME way, because there was no sign of forced or manipulated entry into the Y-12 machine shop. And, according to the security records I accessed this morning, no list of him coming in at the gate, either. He just showed up at the Security office and got a badge. Well, I take that back. The scanned-in, handwritten list from the guard shack didn't show him. The electronic gate file did. Which is telling." Ray thought for a second and then continued. "We should take our own look at that facility. Did he take anything?"

"That's precisely the point," Sam added. "As far as all preliminary investigation indicates, they—he, rather—took nothing. He was right there, in with the nuke rods, and took nothing."

"Well… that IS anomalous." The Old Man leaned back in his seat and frowned. As he did, the long scar, across where his left eye had once been, stretched as if he'd raised an eyebrow that hadn't been there for years. Ray sometimes wondered how he compensated for the lack of parallax data; he'd never seen any indication that the Old Man had a problem with depth perception. "So… what kind of anomaly? Santa Claus or Easter Bunny? Or do we have enough data to determine that, yet? And is he a national security risk, or not, either way?"

All eyes turned to Ray, and he sat back and pondered some more. He'd known this question was coming ever since his debrief with Sam the night before, and he'd been thinking about it pretty much ever since, but he still hadn't made up his mind. *Santa Claus* had been the code name used by Mercury astronaut Wally Schirra and Apollo 8 astronaut Jim Lovell, when they'd supposedly seen unidentified objects outside their spacecraft. The DSRPO had co-opted the phrase as their anomaly code for an alien entity, alien as in extraterrestrial. Correspondingly, they had snagged *Easter Bunny* for their other type of proposed anomaly, a time traveler from the future. Nobody had yet dared think about a combination of the two; or if they had, they hadn't expressed the thought. Personally, Ray would've voted for "Doctor Who" as a code name, but that was probably much too obvious. *Maybe the Great Pumpkin*, he considered. *Or Cupid. Or something.*

"Hard to say, sir," he finally decided. "Insufficient information, in my mind. His ability to pass as human argues for Easter Bunny. But the way he slung me around like a rag doll indicates Santa Claus. In fact, I'm inclined to think Santa Claus at the moment. Maybe masquerading as human."

The Old Man pondered that in silence for a few minutes, then nodded. "So. Next question. No, make that plural–questions. What was he doing in New York, why was he doing it, what did he want in Oak Ridge, what's his goal, and how the hell did he get from one to the other?"

"Well, he was connected with an office at Columbia University, in the bio-med department, specifically cellular protein research," Jay pointed out, "so I think we c'n safely say he was interested in that."

"He'd sure as hell have access to some interesting buggums," Sam observed. "They're doing some work on bio-agents there. And cell protein research might let him bio-engineer something..."

"Something nasty," Jay added. "So security risk, yeah."

"Maybe..." Ray murmured, eyes distant as he dredged his memory for something... a puzzle piece that he'd seen recently, something that might factor into the equation.

"But what's the connection to the Y-12 plant?" the Old Man wondered. "Assuming he's building something nasty as the major says—and given Ray's physical condition, I think it's safe to assume he's not exactly friendly—either it's a bioweapon, or a nuke. It can't be both."

That triggered the memory, and Ray sat up straight. "Maybe it can, in a way," he decided. "I just remembered reading something recently, an article on a bacterium that lives in radiation. Lemme think... what was the name... dino... radiodino... no, that wasn't it... aw hell." He broke off and frowned in thought, raking his hands through his brown hair, trying to dredge the information from his aching head stuffed with facts, as the Old Man turned to the corner, where an unclassified laptop with wifi rested. "Streptococcus... Deinococcus. Got it. Deinococcus radiodurans. Latin for 'radiation resistant terrible berry,' or some such shit. It's one of those extremophile bacteria, you know, like the ones that live around the black smokers at the ocean bottoms, or in the hot springs at Yellowstone? Only this little bugger loves radiation. Well, I dunno that it loves it. But it can resist it, at least."

The Old Man was typing quickly as Ray spoke. "Here it is," Kruger noted in satisfaction, pulling up a file on the laptop. Then he stared for a long moment. "Dear God," he said blankly. "'Extremophile' is right. This little bastard can not only survive more radiation than you can imagine, it's resistant to acid, vacuum, dehydration, and cold. Among other things. Get this—it can withstand an instant dose of five thousand Greys of radiation and remain perfectly healthy, compared to humans, who croak at ten Greys." A chuckle escaped him despite himself. "Its nickname is 'Conan the Bacterium.'"

"I believe it," Jay muttered, eyes wide. "Shit."

"So, maybe we have the answer?" Samantha wondered. "Is this guy making a superbug?"

"Using radiodurans as a base for bio-engineering the ultimate germ, you mean?" Ray replied. "Or maybe he's trying to create an übertoxin from it. Dunno. Could be either. Could be both. I need to do some re-search…"

"Then do it," the Old Man commanded. "And yesterday."

"But we debrief first," Sam added.

ഇഀ

Doc Fields was waiting for Ray in the hall when they got out. "Debrief," Sam told him.

"Not yet," he replied firmly, taking Ray's semi-good arm on an area that still had skin. "Right now it's MRI time."

"Oh… yeah," Sam said, a worried crease forming between her brows. "Okay, debrief in two sound all right?"

"That'll work," Fields said, towing Ray off. "We'll see you then."

ഇഀ

Ray would have liked to sleep during the MRI; after all, all he had to do was to lie there and be still. But the incessant clacking of the instrument prevented that, even if the noise hadn't slammed into his pounding head like a rock drill; and he couldn't wear headphones to drown it out because they would get in the way of the scan.

So he lay there and stared at the top of the MRI recess, closed his eyes, and did his damnedest to ignore the racket, as well as the throbbing in his head. Finally the scan ended and blessed peace descended. Ray's whole body almost instantly relaxed. He was nearly asleep by the time Doc got into the room with the results.

"Well, it could be worse," Doc commented sourly. "You're concussed a little, of course. But your faint was more due to being unable to suck air fast enough than being knocked upside the head, I'd say. But dammit, Ray, quit leading with your nose. You're gonna end up worse than a punch drunk prizefighter at the end of his career."

Ray sighed and eased out of the MRI machine. "I didn't exactly mean to, Doc," he pointed out. "The other guy had… SOMEthing… on me."

"Yeah, I guess I can't really blame this one on you," Doc admitted, quirking his lips. "But be careful, buddy. I really hate having to patch you up at least once per mission."

"Yeah," Ray agreed, sober. "I suppose it WOULD be better if I didn't get myself killed before I get to," his voice cracked, "walk Abby down the church aisle."

"There ya go," Doc said softly. "Remember that baby girl of yours next time. And we ARE going to get her to that church, I swear, old friend. C'mon, we've got a debrief waiting on us."

"Uh…"

"Yeah?"

"That machine makes a helluva lotta racket…"

"Meds are waiting in the other room. Let's go." Doc laughed.

༄༅

The team Sam oversaw wasn't incredibly large, but it was impressive. Besides herself, Ray, Jay, and Dr. Fields, there was Chief Master Sergeant Randolph "Randy" Holmes, head of their field security force; Chief "Skip" Olson, an expert in electromagnetic fields and shielding; Mr. Don Donaldson, Measurement and Signature Intelligence and Imagery Intelligence expert; and Specialist Josh Hamilton, who assisted Donaldson. Staff Sgt. Ernie Travers was the medic who worked alongside Doc.

Major Paul Sussens was the top sniper in the Army—or he had been, until an "enemy grenade" took him into DSRPO. There was also Captain Peter Hansen, munitions expert; playing off Sussens' recruitment, a "sniper" had taken him down in the field. The sniper in question for the choreographed scenario had, in fact, been Sussens.

Lieutenant William "Billy the Kid" Hargrove was their information technology expert. He could hack the Pentagon itself, and if he didn't know about it, it hadn't been invented yet. Captain Payton Thrift was their communications expert, and often worked in conjunction with Billy.

Captain George "Dime" Tanner—Dime as in "land on a"—was their pilot, capable of flying cargo aircraft as well as anything with a rotor. His copilot and navigator was Eric "Straightedge" Liststrom. Danny Wilson was their "eyes," a human/signal intelligence expert, experienced in surveillance and covert ops, pulled from deep inside the CIA, only to go even deeper by entering DSRPO.

They met down the hall from the Old Man's office in a secure conference room for their debrief. No one had much to say that added to Ray's and Jay's tale, until they got to Straightedge.

"Yeah," he said. "We saw something. We were flying backup, stealth mode between the high rises. Dime had the stick, and I was keeping one eye on the video monitor and the other out the windscreen, so we could keep up with the chase. We got… REALLY interesting video."

"What?" Sam barked, nanoseconds before Ray could.

"The guy jumped off the roof right as we passed behind a building. He wasn't obscured a second before I had a view again—and he was gone." Straightedge shook his head. "No greasy spot, no rope, no sign of a zip line, nothing. Just like Randy's guys said. But," he added, "the live infrared got something. Watch this."

Straightedge cued the video player, and they all watched the split screen: visual on one side, infrared on the other. Just as he had said, the perp jumped, was obscured briefly by a building, then was gone.

But the IR camera showed something different. A bright humanoid form—brighter than any of the others on the roof—leaping into space, vanishing behind the building... then being replaced by an irregular, rapidly fading blob of heat.

"Shit," Skip said, eyes wide. "That sure as hell wasn't there by the time I got my instruments in place."

"Us too neither," Donaldson agreed, as Hamilton nodded.

"No, it's dissipating fast," Ray observed. "If Dime and Straightedge hadn't been right there at that moment, I doubt they'd have gotten anything either." The others stared at him, questions in their eyes. Ray shrugged. "Whatever it is, I'd say it has to be how he got away without making a greasy splot."

"Okay, I want all our fields and signature people on this," Sam ordered, looking directly at Skip, Don, and Josh. "Get me a profile, a spectrum, whatever data you can pull from this video. I want to be able to spot one of these... things... again."

"On it," the three nodded.

"Good. Team dismissed."

ಬಿಂಚಿ

Ray spent most of the next twenty-four hours with his head buried in the internet. That didn't prevent him tending the baby when it was his turn, and Sam tried to hide her affectionate smile when she saw Ray. His nose was still in a splint, shoulder bandaged; his sleeping daughter was in the halfway good arm, the other hand one-fingered the laptop keyboard, and his hazel eyes were glued to the screen. If Abby so much as grunted in an unhappy fashion, Ray immediately began rocking in the desk chair, his focus never straying from the computer. Only when it was feeding time did he experience difficulties: he lost his typing hand to the baby food. Sam also noted that, between the baby and the computer, he'd completely forgotten about his nose, his concussion, his ribs, and the stitches in his shoulder.

"How's it coming?" she wondered softly at one point.

"Mm. I have a suspicion I know what our anomaly was after, although as yet I don't know why."

"That's good. Want anything?"

Sam had half expected Ray would ask her to take the baby so he could have both hands on the keyboard, but she saw his arm tighten slightly around Abby, possessive. "Nope," he answered, if a bit absently. "I'm fine."

No wonder I love that man, Sam thought with a grin, before going about her own business.

Later that evening, when Sam had the baby, however, not even the research could keep the effects of the fight from taking its toll on Ray. Twice she found him asleep at the computer, an energy drink and his bottle of pain medication on the desk beside the laptop. The drink, she noted, was one of the highest in caffeine on the market, and well more than half consumed, yet Ray was still asleep. The third time she found him nodded off in his desk chair, she brought him just far enough out of his exhausted, drugged slumber to get him upright and help him stagger back to the bedroom, where she eased him onto the bed. Removing his clothes, she pulled the covers over him and let him sleep.

It's nearly bedtime anyway, she thought with a tender smile, turning off the light.

He never knew when she put the baby down and came to bed herself.

℘つℂ℘

Ray dreamed all night. Only this time, they were coherent dreams, his subconscious working at putting multiple puzzle pieces together. But by the time he woke, he was somewhat confused again. He eased out of bed before daybreak, careful not to wake Sam, threw on some lounge pants and a t-shirt, and returned to the computer to continue his research.

℘つℂ℘

Sam woke a couple of hours later, finding him missing from bed. Pulling on a robe, she went in search of him. When she found him, he was feeding their baby—which, Sam considered, should probably be called a toddler now, given Abby's predilection for wandering when they didn't expect it—while deep into an internet paper on extremophile characteristics. His short, slightly wavy, deep brown hair was still rumpled from sleep, and he hadn't shaved. *Not,* she decided, *that shaving is gonna be fun around that nose anyway. How does it always manage to be a target? It's so cute. Even if it IS plastic surgery. Handsome, girl, handsome. Ray will kill you if you ever forget and call him "cute."*

But it's still cute, another part of her brain thought defiantly. She decided to drop that line of thought.

"I smell breakfast," Sam murmured, not wanting to startle him.

"Mm. Yeah." He sat the empty baby bottle on a corner of the desk and picked up a mug of coffee, waving it vaguely at Sam before taking a sip. "Frank's on duty and Teresa is up. She's in the kitchen. I told her I'd feed the baby."

"You're a sweetheart. I love you."

"Hm. Love you, too." He sat the cup back down.

"Give Abby to me so you can concentrate, and I'll go see how breakfast is coming."

"Have to?"

"Don't even try to tell me that you don't want breakfast." There was more than a hint of argumentativeness in Samantha's tone.

A dusky flush crept up Ray's face, and he finally looked at his wife. "No, I meant the baby."

"Well... but..." Sam was flustered. "Don't you need to concentrate?"

"Yeah." Ray's flush grew deeper. "And a fuzzy little head on my shoulder, snuggling in, helps." He grinned sheepishly.

Sam gave him a tender smile. "Okay. Breakfast here, or at the table?"

"Here. I guess you'll have to take the baby, at that point." Ray knew better than to suggest he skip breakfast after having gotten the shit beat out of him only two days before, but his reluctance showed all the same.

"Okay. I'll bring you a plate when it's ready, and exchange it for the baby," Sam smiled again. "Will you have something pulled together in time for the meeting?" She nodded at the computer.

"Oh, I've already got lotsa somethings," Ray admitted. "I've come up with a complete dossier on our little bacterial suspect. It's the 'WHICH something' I'm still not sure about." He shrugged. "I ought to have it figured out by the meeting, though."

৪০৫৪

"It's the repair system," Ray told the Old Man as he, Sam, and Jay sat in Kruger's office again. "It's got to be. It's the only really interesting tie I can find between cellular protein research and radiodurans."

"What do you mean?" the Old Man wondered.

"He's either trying to locate the proteins that enable the various environmental resistances—probably all the same, judging from experimental results on extremophiles—or he's trying to duplicate the DNA repair process," Ray explained. "The two are connected. There are two families of proteins in radiodurans that either don't exist, or are much smaller, in other bacteria. They seem to be part of the repair process, insofar as we can tell. Those are the MutT and DinB protein families... both of which appear to be induced to act by DNA damage."

"And major DNA damage would be caused by high radiation doses," Sam realized.

"Exactly, honey," Ray nodded vigorously, then wished he hadn't as his head threatened to explode, his nose throbbed, and his stitches pulled. "And a significant amount of research into this little buggum is going on at... ta-daaa–Oak Ridge. Seems it grows somewhat prolifically in the spent fuel pools there."

"Hence the anomaly's visit," Kruger realized. "He wasn't after the plutonium at all."

"Yep," Ray agreed. "That would be my guess. Information jaunt."

"But why?" Jay asked.

"Well, that's the kicker." Ray sighed. "I don't know that yet. There are several possibilities–one of which includes inverting the ability, to magnify radiation damage. Another is to make a bug that can't be killed. Radiodurans isn't infectious on its own, but if you modified it through genetic engineering to force it to become an infectious disease..."

"And there wasn't a way to stop the disease," Jay added grimly, understanding.

"Of course, that also means getting around its own repair systems to MAINTAIN the engineered genes, which is another reason for studying the thing," Ray pointed out.

"Dammit," the Old Man muttered.

"Not good," Sam agreed.

"Get this to Fields immediately," the Old Man ordered.

"Yes sir," Sam said, extracting an extremely special palm computer and punching in the information.

Ray shook his head–very gingerly this time. "I don't know, guys. I'm still not convinced, and I sure as hell haven't figured out what direction to go in from here. All I can say for sure is that, if he was out to help, I wouldn't be wearin' this damn thing," he tentatively fingered the splint on his nose. "I think I need to see what else he got—if anything—at Oak Ridge. I'm still not convinced he didn't pinch something else. Something besides information."

"Let me see what I can arrange," the Old Man said, reaching for the phone.

ಬೊಂಆ

While the Old Man was arranging matters, Jay, Ray, and Sam met with their field and signature experts.

"What have you got for us, boys?" Sam opened the meeting.

"Well, we fine tuned the resolution a bit, with some help from the Kid," Don, their signature expert, noted.

"It's an interesting picture," Skip, their EM specialist, declared, "but damned if I know what to make of it."

"That makes three of us," Josh Hamilton, Don's colleague, piped up.

"Lemme see," Ray demanded.

Don Donaldson floated a paper across the glossy tabletop to the scientist. A negative gray scale image was imprinted on it. Ray studied it curiously.

"Huh," he said in some surprise. "That's different."

"But do you recognize it?" Sam asked.

"Well, I've never seen a real one in three dimensions before—not that this thing would really be three dimensional—but it sure looks like a Klein bottle."

"Klein bottle?" Skip wondered.

"A manifold," Ray explained. "Sort of like a next generation Möbius strip."

"Elaborate," Sam ordered.

Ray drew a deep breath and prepared for a detailed explanation.

"The concept of manifolds comes from mathematics. Geometry, specifically. They're surfaces that, on a small scale, appear Euclidean in geometry, but taken as a whole, depart from Euclidean, sometimes radically. There are different families of manifolds, and some of them pertain to spacetime. If this thing started out as a Lorentzian manifold, and sort of collapsed down through successive dimensions as it disappeared, then this guy may have figured out how to bebop around Minkowski space."

"Minkowski space?" Josh asked.

"The four dimensional spacetime of general relativity," Ray elaborated. "It could even get into M theory, which looks at even higher dimensions."

There was a long silence.

"Well, it would sure explain what happened on the roof," Jay decided.

"Yep," Ray agreed.

"You guys get anything else out of the images?" Sam wondered.

"Not yet," Don admitted, "but we're working on it."

"Good. Keep it up." She paused, turning to Ray. "So... Santa or Bunny?" Sam asked.

Ray shook his head. "Still not enough information," he insisted. "Could be either. Could be both."

"Santa Bunny," somebody at the table muttered, too low to be identified.

Ray quickly aborted the snort that tried to form and chuckled gingerly instead, on account of his nose. "I'm still leaning toward Santa," he admitted. "After all, if you could change location almost instantaneously, it would LOOK like Easter Bunny, but really wouldn't be."

"All right," Sam sighed. "Well, let's see what Robert worked out for us."

Chapter 4

The next morning Dan Wilson, John Fields, and Ray headed to the Oak Ridge National Labs, just outside the town of Oak Ridge, Tennessee, under cover as government auditors for an unscheduled inspection.

"Hello there," Dr. Michael Chung, their hastily assigned liaison, smiled as he greeted them in the security office. "Unexpected, but then, that's the point."

"Exactly," Ray chuckled, clipping on his unescorted visitor badge for the government facility. "Dr. Raymond Chase, and these are my colleagues, Dr. Sherman Peters and Dr. James Meyers. Sorry for the, uh, facial ornament; I ran into the doorframe in the middle of the night, the other night." He gestured at the splint still on his nose.

"Ow," Chung winced. "Fun. Anyway, pleased to meet you. I'm Dr. Michael Chung." They all shook hands. "Now," Chung continued, "do you have anything specific, or is this a general inspection?"

"We'd like to verify your fissile materials accounting, first," Meyer, really Fields, DSRPO's chief medic slash nuclear, biological, and chemical weapons effects expert, said. "Then we'll see where to go from there."

"Ah," Chung said knowingly. "Let's go, then."

"Dr. Sherman Peters" reached into his trousers pocket, fingered a tiny device, and hit a small button on it.

෨෬

Dr. Gupta was hunched over his computer, frantically backing up data, when he heard the genial voice behind him.

"Hello, Doctor Gupta."

Gupta's blood went cold. An icy hand seemed to grip his guts. Despite the friendliness in the voice's tone, Gupta could have sworn the temperature in the room seemed to drop forty degrees in an instant.

"H- hello, sir," Gupta said, turning around slowly to meet brilliant blue eyes beneath a spiky thatch of straw colored hair. The owner of those eyes was dressed decidedly oddly for a university office: he had on a pressure suit, the spherical helmet held casually under one arm.

"Abhu, you did a bad thing," the man told Gupta, as if reprimanding a child. "The question is, did you do it deliberately, or accidentally?"

Gupta paled.

෨෬

"But that's not unusual," Chung noted in his office several hours later. "As much as we have around here, the error bar on one batch, plus the error bar on another, and another, and another… It makes it look like a bunch is missing, when it's not. We're still well inside the overall error bound. The amount varies from audit to audit, depending on the size of the batch and the accuracy of measurements."

The three DSRPO agents avoided glancing at each other. "Of course," Fields replied smoothly. "We understand."

"We've encountered it before," Dan agreed, not missing a beat. "We just like to make sure."

"Good. Now what?" Chung wondered cheerfully.

The other two turned as if in tolerance to Ray, who slapped on a sheepish grin. "I was wondering," he began. "I've been reading about this radiation super bug, and saw where some of the research came from Oak Ridge. Lessee, what was it called… I was, uh, never good at Latin…"

"You mean Deinococcus radiodurans?"

"Yeah, that's the stuff! I was hoping… could I see some? Just out of curiosity?"

"In situ or in the lab?" Chung grinned broadly.

"Ooo, in situ first," Ray seemed to practically drool.

"C'mon," Chung laughed.

⁊ᴑᴑᴣ

"…Accidentally!" Gupta blurted, desperate to make the other man believe him. "I thought they were gone, sahib! I swear! Campus security practically dragged them away! I was going to rendezvous with you per our schedule, then disappear so that they could not find me!"

"Then what are you doing now?" The unknown man waved a gauntleted hand at Gupta's computer, which had just spit out a CD.

"Still trying to disappear!" he exclaimed frantically, gesturing. "Look at my document safe! He SHOT it! The madman actually shot it! I did NOT want them to come back and… I saw part of the fight from a hiding place, Doctor. You were magnificent."

"But so was my opponent." The space-suited man paced restlessly. "It makes me suspicious of him, of his origins. No, no, I did not expect YOU to enter the fray," he waved off Gupta's protest aborning. "You would have been killed in seconds."

He paused and stared into Gupta's dark, wide eyes. "So… you were going to disappear."

Gupta nodded vehemently.

"So they couldn't find you."

Another emphatic nod.

"Did it occur to you to let ME know how to find you?"

Gupta looked shocked. "N- no, sahib. I... I thought, with your abilities, you would... would know how." His eyes dilated.

"Now you're lying." The blond man raised an eyebrow.

"I expected you to... but I hoped... I mean, I..."

"You mean you were afraid of them AND me."

"Y- yes. I knew as soon as I saw them that I'd inadvertently led them to you, and I... well, I..."

"Wanted to get away before either of us found you."

"Y- yes, sir. I swear to you, I used every ounce of stealth I possess. I do not know how they followed me. Please believe me, I would not have come had I known. I would NEVER have come—I would have contacted you and rescheduled instead. I knew as soon as I saw them, you would be angry—but it WAS an accident!—and I hoped to give you the time for your anger to cool." Gupta's expression was pale and desperate.

ജഇ

They found themselves passing through the very machining facility where their suspect's image had been obtained. Ray and Doc glanced at each other behind Chung's back, knowing looks that spoke volumes without a word being exchanged.

"This way, gentlemen," Chung said, leading them through the facility, down a corridor, and through a series of containment doors. They found themselves standing beside a spent fuel pool. "In there," Chung pointed at the pool.

"There? Where?!" Ray babbled, swiveling his neck as if it were made of rubber.

"Far side," Chung said, handing him a tiny pair of binoculars. "Spent rods are stored in the opposite corner of the pool, in the racks near the bottom. New rods are the brighter ones right next to 'em; we're getting ready for a swap. Look for the red patches on the racks. You might see some scrape marks in some of the patches; a researcher from Columbia University came by a couple of days ago to get a sample."

"Yeah, I see it," Ray said, glasses held lightly to his face so as not to press on his tender nose. "Cool." He handed the binoculars to Fields. "Wanna see?"

"No thanks, Ray," Fields chuckled, playing his role to the hilt as he waved the glasses away, "that's your latest big thing." Truthfully, he could have gotten samples through his own channels had he wished; but that wasn't the purpose behind this visit anyway.

"Wanna see the little buggers up close and personal now?" Chang offered.

"Oh hell yes," Ray declared, vehement, handing the binoculars back to Chang.

"Okay. That's in a different building."

"We're right behind you."

જીભ્ય

"I see." The blond man nodded calm understanding at Gupta. Gupta relaxed slightly as the man continued. "Are you finished there?" He pointed at the computer.

"Yes, sir," Gupta averred. "That was the last disk."

"And the data is now erased from the computer?"

"Just a minute." Gupta turned and executed several commands, waited a moment, then popped in the operating system disk. Minutes later the computer had been reformatted, effectively erasing all prior information. "It is now."

"Good. Give those to me; I'll take care of them," the other man ordered, gesturing at the stack of newly burned CDs.

Gupta gathered the stack of CDs and handed them to the other man, who enclosed them in a cargo pocket of his pressure suit, velcroing it shut. Then Gupta watched as the blond man with the vivid, piercing eyes raised his helmet, donning it and locking it in place and initiating oxygen flow as well as an external speaker.

"Come with me, Abhu." He glanced at one of his two watches, special versions that could strap over his pressurized gauntlet.

"Where are we going?" a trusting Gupta rose immediately and moved to the man's side.

"Someplace where you will be entirely safe from our team of adversaries."

"Praise Krishna!" Gupta exclaimed, relaxing. "I did not know where to go, or how best to flee the bastards. Thank you for your help, sahib! But why are you wearing that space suit?"

"Because," the blond man smiled blandly through the helmet, sounding vaguely like he was speaking in an electronic barrel, "I will need it." He rested a light hand on Gupta's shoulder. Gupta failed to notice the tightness of that hand's grip.

"But…" Gupta's face, which had begun regaining some color, paled again. "I do not have a space suit."

"I know," the blond man's grin was wolfish, and a wild, almost demented light suddenly glowed in the blue eyes. Fingers dug into Gupta's shoulder.

Panic washed through Gupta's gut, and he tried to dart away—

—Just as a blazing white light flared in the office.

When it faded, both men were gone.

‮ঙ‬ওপ

The radiodurans looked exactly like what Doc and Ray expected: little berry-red quad colonies living happily under almost any conditions to which the Oak Ridge researchers could subject them. What the investigators were heretofore unaware of was that the bacteria were already being gene engineered for bioremediation of radioactive waste sites.

"Yes," Dr. Stevie Patterson, a cute, petite brunette and the head of the study, informed them. "You see, the more we look into it, the more it seems that it isn't the genes that are most susceptible–it's the proteins. Bacteria sensitive to radioactivity, desiccation, infrared, and the like sustain serious damage to the proteins before the DNA. The more of the DNA sequencing we work out on radiodurans, the more of the DNA possibilities we eliminate. It seems to be all about protecting the proteins of the cell. Specifically, its own special variety of RecA, the protein that repairs any DNA breaks, and certain other proteins called MutT and DinB, that help control replication and cleanup. It helps," she added, "that, unlike other bacteria, radiodurans keeps multiple backups of its DNA, and keeps them all hooked together in parallel in one place in the nucleus."

"So the techie doesn't have to go looking for the backup drive," Wilson chuckled.

"Exactly," Patterson grinned. "And as long as the techies are around, the hard drive stays properly maintained."

"So if it's so resistant to DNA modification, how the hell do you mutate it to experiment with it?" Ray wondered.

"Radiodurans' mutation resistance is a function of natural environment," she explained. "Expose it to an UNnatural environment—like a manmade mutagen—and presto! You can make whatever change in its DNA you like."

"What might some of these mutagens be?" Fields inquired casually.

"The hands down favorite is N-methyl-N-prime-nitro-N-nitrosoguanidine."

"Da wha?" Wilson expostulated.

"That's why we usually call it MNNG. It's a helluva lot easier." Patterson laughed.

"What she said," Wilson decided. "I'm down with physics. But this is startin' to get a little over my head."

"So…" Ray was thinking fast, dredging up his knowledge of genetic engineering from beneath the deep layer of overlying physics and engineering, and trying hard to make it look like he was merely concentrating to understand, "you could make it susceptible to radiation. Could you make it more than usually susceptible?"

"Susceptible is susceptible. I mean, humans are about as susceptible as it gets. You can't go much lower than ten Grays. Well, I guess you could, but what's the point? Even E. coli is six times more radiation resistant than humans." Patterson shrugged.

"Speaking of which: What about making it infectious?" Fields asked point blank.

Patterson studied him for a moment, sizing him up. "You're an NBC expert, aren't you?"

"…Yes," Fields responded, "they sent me along for a safety check. Nuclear, biological, chemical. I wasn't expecting to use the 'B' part of the expertise, though," he lied with a grin. "Not here."

"Right," Patterson nodded comprehension. "Good idea, that, and I can understand your curiosity on finding out about this. To answer your question, I suppose you could," she decided, "but we don't do that here. We're more interested in what makes it tick. I'd have to sit down and think awhile before I could come up with a compatible 'merger.'"

"Meaning what infectious bacteria would have genetic characteristics compatible with radiodurans?" Fields followed up.

"Right. Our little red berry there," she nodded at the microscope, "is pretty special. Elitist, you could say, if we're personifying it. It doesn't 'mate' with just anybody."

"But it could be done?" Ray wondered.

"Theoretically, I suppose," Patterson agreed. "But my team hasn't worked on it. I don't know anyone who is. Even on the weapons side of the house." She glanced at her watch. "Excuse me, gentlemen, but I've got a team meeting coming up in about fifteen minutes. Do you have any other questions I can answer for you?"

"No, ma'am," Ray said, slapping a shit-eating grin on his face. "Thanks a lot for letting us have a look. When I read that article, I was like, 'DAY-um! I have got to see this thing when I go there next week!'"

"And now you have," Patterson smiled. "I'm glad I could help. Not many people have seen Conan in his native environment, so you're lucky. I enjoyed our little conversation."

"So did we," Wilson agreed, and they followed Chung out.

ಶೂಲ

On their way back home in the plane, with Dime in the pilot's seat, the three DSRPO operatives discussed their visit.

"How much of the radiodurans did he get, Ray?" Fields asked.

"Oh holy shit, more than any five university studies would EVER need," Ray said, disgusted. "And considering how easily the stuff is cultured, he's got a lifetime supply, now."

"NOT good," Wilson muttered. "And the amount of fissile material that fits into their current 'error bars' is disturbing, too."

"Yeah," Ray agreed. "Almost exactly the right amount for about two bombs in the last six months, as long as you primed 'em with tritium."

"Did any of you get a look at PREVIOUS audit data?" Fields wondered.

Brady and Wilson shook their heads in the negative.

"It gets worse," Fields said glumly. "Over the last five years, enough material fits into those error bars for close to a dozen fusion enhanced bombs."

"SHIT," Ray said, with feeling. "Danny, you get anything with your little ninja stuff?"

"Chung was telling the truth, insofar as he knew," Wilson, their HU-MINT/SIGINT specialist, declared. "Patterson was delighted at getting so much interest in her research—especially in a matter of days."

"So our anomaly talked with her?" Fields asked.

"That's the way I read her reactions, yeah," Wilson averred. "Her research isn't classified, so there was no harm, no foul, as far as she was concerned."

"And we got the answer to how to get around radiodurans' automatic repair systems, to modify its genetic structure. So our anomaly probably did, too. You get anything else, Dan?" Ray wondered.

"Nope. Not according to my sweeper." Wilson pulled a small device from his pocket and double-checked its readout. "No. No bugs. Nobody was lying, nothing. Whatever this guy is, he's trusted, and he's doing it all as clean as a whistle."

"This Columbia U. guy was recently over from India," Ray pondered. "You suppose he's a Muslim extremist, maybe slipped across the border from Pakistan into India, then here? And our marathon runner is a Muslim terrorist?"

"How the hell did he get the clearance to get into the Y-12 plant, then? Besides, he didn't look it. Light blond hair, blue eyes, pale skin, judging by the picture and your and Jay's descriptions. That sure ain't typical Mideastern. Thor wouldn't be any more Caucasian than that; all he needed was Mjolnir and a helmet. So he'd hafta be a homegrown," Wilson pointed out. "And how would Gupta have gotten a post at Columbia, if he was an extremist? Well, I take that back; can't say about Columbia, but given some universities' political policies, maybe my question oughta be, how did he get into the States?"

"Dunno. I think we need to dig into Gupta further personally, but regardless, if Runner Guy managed to get out with as much fissile isotopes as we think, AND the radiodurans, he's got enough for one hell of a jihad," Fields riposted.

"How did he know whether he was getting too much fissionable junk, if he really did get any?" Wilson fired back. "Whether he'd exceeded the error bars?"

"Bloody hell, guys, how did he get into and out of the Y-12 plant to begin with? How did he get away from me?!" Ray pointed out. "Whatever 'beam me up Scotty' device he's got would make it a cinch to get in, look at records, even modify records, and get out, unnoticed. He could have ten TIMES the amount of fissile materials we're estimating, for all we know."

The other two silenced, shocked, as they considered the ramifications of Ray's statement.

"We've got a real issue here," Fields finally said.

"Oh, shit, yeah," Wilson averred.

𝔰🙰𝔠𝔰

It was dinnertime when they got back home. But they still met with their MASINT and EMF specialists.

"What have you got for us, guys?" Ray asked the three men.

"Well, we've got down the sequence of—what d' you call 'em? Manifolds?—that Straightedge caught on instruments," Don Donaldson noted. "There was something right before the Klein bottle, but we can't really tell what it is. Something like a Möbius strip came after, just like you said.

Then it sorta… sorta unfurled, or maybe it rolled up… shrank to a point, and faded out."

"Let me see," Ray demanded.

Josh Hamilton handed him a palm computer, keyed to a video sequence. Ray hit "start," and the enhanced video played. It was a short sequence, and when it was over, Ray crossed his eyes.

"Uh, yeah," he said with a sheepish grin. "Well, looking at four dimensions is hard enough. Whatever it was, I'd say we were looking at five or more dimensions collapsing down to zero."

"And how do we manage that?" Fields wondered. "Or rather, how did HE manage that?"

Ray leaned back in his chair and put his hands over his head, ignoring the pull in his shoulder stitches, not to mention Fields' raised eyebrow. "Five or more dimensions takes it beyond Minkowski space," he decided. "More and more, I'm leaning toward M theory. Cosmic strings and membranes. Probably the branes. Did we get anything else?" he asked, before anyone could ask what the hell he'd just said.

"I got a decay spectrum," Skip Olsen noted. "Or part of one, at least. You said in the debrief you got blinded by what you thought was a lightning bolt. Blue-white?"

"Yeah."

"Uh huh." Skip nodded, lips pressed together. "Figured. From what I was able to pull, between the visual video and the IR video, I got a blackbody spectrum whose initial peak was indeterminate, since we didn't actually record it. But the peak decayed rapidly in intensity and frequency, down through the visible, into the infrared and finally off into microwave. That would normally correspond with a temperature drop…"

"You don't know the initial peak, but it was past visible?" Ray paled slightly.

"Yeah."

"Wow." Ray paled further. "I was far and away closest to it, other than our anomaly. Have I been irradiated?"

"Unlikely," Fields interjected then. "No sign of burns, and no indication of radiation sickness."

"He could be a 'dead man walking,'" Wilson pointed out hesitantly. Brady turned almost white, thinking of Sam and Abby.

"No," Fields shook his head firmly. "No nausea, no vomiting or diarrhea, and his shoulder is healing fine. Not even a tan. He did NOT take a radiation dose of ANY significance. Later, Ray, if you want me to, I can double check for DNA damage and sterility. But I doubt our perp would be stupid enough to use something that irradiated him every time he used it. That's assuming he's human—but this interest in radiodurans makes me think he understands irradiation enough to play it safe. I think we can assume that the initial peak was what Ray saw, in the far blue visible to UV near visible, spectrum. Hell, if it had been very intense, he'd have been blinded. Sunburned. Per my rundowns after the incident—which were damn thorough, considering it's Ray we're talking about—he's fine except for the observable injuries and mild concussion."

"Agreed. But... Doc, I'll still take those double checks, if you don't mind," Ray said, subdued. "And guys, don't say anything about this to Sam for now. If Doc's checks turn up anything, I'll handle it."

The other men nodded solemnly, in complete comprehension.

"So, we've got a probable peak in the far blue portion of the spectrum, maybe slightly into the ultraviolet, and a smooth decay in intensity and frequency with time," Skip noted. "Like I said, that should have corresponded with a temperature change. Did anyone feel any heat?"

"No," Ray said. "If anything, I was cold."

"That was probably shock from your injuries," Fields pointed out.

"Mm, okay, fair enough. Then you need to talk to Jay and your medic. They were soonest on the scene."

Doc pulled his cell phone.

⁜⁝

"Ummm," Jay said, slightly confused. "We sprinted a marathon, laid down cover fire, then sprinted another marathon up the side of a building, and you wanna know if we felt any heat, Doc? Hell yeah, I was hot, but I couldn't tell you if it was from me or our anomaly. I just know I had steam comin' off me in the rain."

"Damn," Fields muttered in frustration. "Ernie?"

Ernie Travers, the medic, shrugged. "After being in the rain for so long, I did notice that the roof seemed a little warmer than I expected, especially considering the winds were higher up there. Felt good."

"How much warmer?" Skip queried, leaning forward. "And how long after the event did it take you to get there?"

"He was there about a minute after Ray collapsed," Jay interjected, "and Ray collapsed within about fifteen to thirty seconds, I'd say. I saw the blue-white flash myself as I was topping the stairs to the roof. But not the perp. So between a minute, minute and a half, make it."

Skip was jotting notes as fast as his hand would go. "Good, good," he muttered to himself. "That fits the timeline. Now, Ernie, back to the question of how warm it felt?"

"Eh," Travers shrugged, his Latino features matching the gesture in a dismissive expression. "Not a whole lot. Enough to cut the wind chill."

Skip was scribbling furiously now. "Wind chill... and distance... inverse square..." Even upside down across the table, Ray recognized the equations emerging under Skip's hand.

He must have the entire layout memorized, even to dimensions, Ray realized, impressed. *And who knew he could calculate wind chill? We got ourselves a helluva team.*

"Yeah, it fits within the data spread," Skip looked up. "More confirmation for the radiation spectral decay."

"So at least we have something recognizable to go by to find these things," Ray declared.

"Looks like it, Dr. Brady," Donaldson agreed.

ଚଠଔଷ

"Now," Wilson changed the subject, "wanna explain this brain shit to us?"

"Huh?" Ray said, confused. "You talking about my concussion? I'm fine."

"I'll be the judge of that," Fields retaliated, "and he means that crap you spouted earlier about branes and M theory."

"Oh, that," Ray said. He leaned back, folded his arms, and let his eyes defocus. "You guys heard of cosmic strings?"

"Yeah," Donaldson nodded.

"Sorta like that franchise movie some years back, where the starship captain was presumed dead, but he was really living in another universe inside that string thing?" Hamilton suggested.

"Sorta," Ray tried not to grin. "Same general idea, but they wouldn't look like that. I'm not sure they would 'look' at all, really. Anyway, different scientists took string theory in different directions, and each one managed to explain certain observations, but not others. M theory is an attempt to unify these five different theories into one coherent theory. It requires at least eleven dimensions, and then looks for commonalities between them. Take the string and... and sorta stretch it into a p-dimensional membrane, I guess you could say. Where p is a number, but a number we don't know yet. Could be five, could be fifty. Thus the concept of membranes, branes for short. Following me so far?"

Nods went around the room, some more hesitant than others.

"So far, Ray. Keep going. We'll yell if you lose us," Fields noted.

"Well, the fact that we've got five or more dimensions appearing in our manifolds," Ray gestured at the palm computer, "suggests we're working with M theory, since it 'rises above' string theory, dimensionally speaking. Also, at low energies—as the decaying spectral peak indicates—strings appear as point objects, not as extended ones."

"So that's why the thing eventually crumpled to a point and then winked out," Skip grasped. "It got so low on energy it went bye-bye."

"Well, it probably didn't cease to exist," Ray decided, "it probably just moved elsewhere–or when."

"When?" Fields echoed. "You saying this guy might not even be from our universe?"

"Well, one version of M theory says that you can't have parallel universes or be changing the timeline by time travel. Or well, you can, but whatever happens, happens anyway BECAUSE OF the time travel. You know, 'world lines are straight, they don't branch off at decision points.' That's how they avoid chronal paradoxes. But it's all a bunch of mathematical abstractions anyway, so who the hell knows?" Ray explained. "I, personally, could see a completely separate universe—multiple universes—being in the mix, totally unrelated to ours. Universes that aren't branches of our world lines, that aren't even connected. If we're working with that many dimensions, why not?"

"What do you mean?" Ernie asked.

"Well, let's say our universe normally occupies dimensions p_1, p_2, p_3, and p_4," Ray suggested. "But maybe somebody else's occupies p_6, p_7, p_8, and p_9. Complete universes, totally separate and unrelated. Or maybe not. It's just an idea of mine that I never got around to working out details on."

"I'm gonna get a headache," Jay complained. "Never mind, too late. I've already got one."

"Doc'll take care of it," Ray quipped, shooting a mischievous glance at the physician. "Now, if what we saw was our anomalous person using, say, a membrane to hop around, we'd expect to see a multidimensional manifold form during the full 'intersection' of the brane with our reality, followed by the manifold degenerating through fewer and fewer dimensions as the brane 'moved away.' Follow me?"

"Yeah," Skip said eagerly. "And the latter sounds like exactly what we DID see. That would mean we," he indicated himself, Donaldson, and

Hamilton, "need to go back through the video BEFORE the guy jumped, to see if we can identify the reverse process, as the... brane... contacted our reality."

"Hm. There's an idea," Ray's eyebrow rose. "I like. Yeah, guys, get hold of Straightedge and get as much of the copter imagery as you can, then see what you can find."

"All over it, Dr. Brady," Skip grinned, suddenly excited.

The meeting broke up.

ঙ০৫৪

Outside the meeting room, they split up. Skip, Don, and Josh went off together in search of Straightedge. Jay headed for his office, and Sergeant Travers walked off toward the elevators, headed for Medical. Ray started for home, until a light hand fell on his shoulder.

"Thought you wanted to be checked out," Fields reminded him.

"Oh. Yeah," Ray said, face falling. "Let's go."

ঙ০৫৪

Back in Fields' domain, Ray allowed himself to be put through a number of tests, some of which were rather personal. In the end, Doc concluded that, other than the bashing he'd gotten, Ray was about as healthy a male specimen as could be found. Ray tried not to sag in relief.

"Feel better?" Doc asked gently.

"Yeah," Ray admitted. "I kept thinking about—"

"Samantha and Abby," Doc finished for him. "I would, too, in your shoes. Don't worry. Abby can have normal siblings if you two decide on it, and you aren't going to leave them alone anytime soon–unless you keep running headlong into battle." He deliberately avoided the mention of possible cystic fibrosis in said siblings.

"Okay, okay, point taken, Doc," Ray sighed. "I'll try to ease up."

"I'll do my damnedest to hold you to it."

"Yeah, yeah."

ঙ০৫৪

By the time Ray finally got home, the household—except for Frank, of course—was already asleep. He slipped into the kitchen, where he grabbed a protein bar and wolfed it down with several slugs of milk straight from the container, before tiptoeing into the nursery, past a lightly sleeping Teresa stretched in the recliner in the corner. There, he leaned over the crib and planted a butterfly kiss on Abby's forehead. She cooed in her sleep, and a voice behind him said, "You better watch that, Dr.

Brady. I almost made your concussion a hell of a lot worse."

"I doubt it, Teresa. You know my footsteps as well as you do your own." Ray chuckled softly.

"You and Mrs. Samantha both. But that still doesn't excuse you scarin' a body half to death." Teresa giggled in return.

"Sorry. I was trying not to wake the baby."

"I know. I'm just gettin' on your case. Go on and get to bed. Mrs. Brady stayed up late for ya, but finally threw in the towel."

"Headed that way now, Teresa," Ray said, tearing his attention from the tiny body in the crib. "I just wanted to see my princess first."

"You better not be talkin' about me."

"God forbid," Ray grinned at the nanny in the low light. "The day I call you princess is the day you take my head completely off."

"Damn straight. Off with his head, and off with you now," Teresa grinned back. "Your missus is waiting, if she isn't already asleep."

Ray slipped out of the room and down the hall. The bedroom was dark, and he eased in, trying to keep the door from squeaking any more than he could help, and disrobed. *I gotta remember to oil those hinges one 'a these days. We'd both sleep better for it, given the weird shit hours we keep.* He slid under the covers and settled into the softness of the mattress with a faint sigh.

"Mmph," emerged from the body beside him. "'Bout time."

"Sorry, hon. Auditing that much uranium, plutonium, radium, ad infinitum, ad radioactum, isn't a quick job to begin with. And then we had to figure out what we found out."

"I know," Sam murmured, turning over. Suddenly Ray realized he had a very female, very naked body pressed against him. And it was very ready for his. "I'm not griping. I've just been waiting."

"Thank God for that," Ray breathed, taking his wife in his arms and pulling her close as their lips met and parted.

⊱⊰

Sam nestled close, hooking her upper leg over Ray's thigh. She wrapped her sinuous arms around him and kissed him deeply.

How does she do it? he wondered. *Go from tough hardbody and tougher mind to soft and warm and sensuous, all in a matter of seconds?* He arched slightly, allowing their bodies to come into intimate contact as he grew aroused. "Mm. Mrs. Brady?"

"Yes, Dr. Brady?"

"You are utterly awesome."

"I could say the same." She pushed him onto his back, rolling onto him, straddling him, and sitting up. He found himself engulfed in her warm body, and he moaned softly. "Like that, huh?"

"By this time, you shouldn't have to ask, hot stuff."

She leaned forward and licked a white scar on his right deltoid. "Your shoulders will match soon."

He chuckled, meeting her thrust for thrust. "I suppose."

"This is the one you got in Afghanistan, right?" Her lips locked onto the weal and sucked gently. She rocked her hips, then undulated. Male fingers briefly dug into her hips in response.

"Yeah. I got that, but we got bin Ibrahim and all his lieutenants," Ray declared, beginning to pant. Suddenly an image appeared in his mind: a blue eyed, blond Army officer sitting in on the pre-briefing for the Afghan mission, and bumping shoulders with him on the way out the conference room door. The bright blue eyes haunted him.

But that was years ago, he thought. *And this guy looked the same age as that guy. No way. Distant uncle or cousin or something, maybe. Or just coincidence. I hope. Maybe.* He mentally shook his head. *Gotta get away from shop talk, especially now.*

"Hell, Sam, if you're gonna do this," he thrust upward by way of meaning, "come up with some more pleasant pillow talk, honey."

She released his shoulder for a moment. "You gotta tell me about it SOMEtime."

"I will. Just not NOW."

"Okay." Samantha ramped up the intensity. Ray promptly forgot everything else.

Damn. This lends a whole new meaning to six degrees of freedom, Ray thought in a kind of erotic whimsy, as Sam's hips rocked back and forth, side to side, up and down, before rotating in circles of various sizes. She smiled mischievously, as if reading his thoughts.

"Ohhh..." Ray groaned, squirming slightly.

"How about bangin' my brains out for a topic?" she breathed in his ear.

"Perfect subject."

"Apropos, I thought."

"Jus' one problem."

"What's that?"

"Don' wanna talk right now..."

Ray's body began to tense in expectation. He slid his hands over his wife's warm, fragrant skin, caressing breasts and hips, lavishing special affection on her nipples and the structures hidden in the downy juncture of her thighs. Her beautiful blue eyes fluttered closed and she smiled dreamily.

I love that expression on her face, floated through Ray's brain. *Love everything about her. My wife, my lover, the mother of my daughter, the center of my world. Right here. In my arms.*

Suddenly the center of his world was thrashing wildly, mewling and moaning. A jolt seemed to leave her body and enter Ray's through their joining, and promptly defied physics by instantly and simultaneously searing every cell of his body with pleasure. He let out a cry and allowed himself to become totally vulnerable to the one being on the planet he trusted with… *Everything, Sam. I give you everything.*

Then they were slumped in each other's arms, completely and utterly limp.

After awhile, Sam wiggled about enough to pull the covers over their naked bodies, but otherwise remained atop her husband as their respiration and pulse slowed to normal.

They drifted off to sleep together, still entwined.

Chapter 5

The next morning, Sam woke Ray in the same wonderful way she'd put him to sleep. Eventually they got up and began preparing for the day, and Samantha scanned him up and down before he finished getting dressed. "Good," she remarked succinctly and somewhat sharply. "No more additions to the wound tally this time."

"Why should there be?" Ray raised an eyebrow. "We were only going to Oak Ridge to check a few things out."

"Yeah, and a couple of days ago you were 'only' going to Columbia University 'to check a few things out.'"

"So?"

"So, Ray, it gets old, your coming home busted up every time you go on a mission. I worry about you, sweetheart."

"The day we met, Sam, you knew who and what I was. You know this face isn't the one I was born with, even if it is somewhat close. You know the name you took as my wife isn't the name of my father. You, of all people, hot stuff, know every scar on my body, even better than Doc."

Conversation ceased for a moment, and Ray knew both of them were remembering the day the Old Man had brought her in to the hospital to see him, the day the bandages from the plastic surgery came off. *Damn,* he remembered. *I sure as hell thought I'd bit it that time. Bomb got me, and I still didn't manage to rescue that Marine. And hell just wouldn't end after that. Wish I could remember how long it lasted. Or maybe not.*

He winced unconsciously. Sam saw, but said nothing, recognizing that he was working through old memories.

ಸಂ೮ಐ

Ray had been leading a covert mission deep into Iran, high into the mountains, in an attempt to determine if their nuclear program had yielded functional weaponry as yet. His small team of six had managed to get into one of the facilities and ascertained its status—though Ray remembered little of it now, save that it was active and in production.

They'd gotten in, gotten their data, and gotten out. A ground based extraction team was to meet them in a mountain valley fifty klicks from the target site at midnight the next night—it was the closest they dared come to the security around the facility. It had, and the infiltration team was glad to finally get out of native wear into desert camo BDUs and off their feet.

"Long hike," Ray had remarked, settling into his seat in the humvee. "Glad it's over."

"Smooth sailing from here," he remembered his second, a certain Lieutenant James Samuels, had remarked. "On to the aerial extraction and we're gone."

Everything had proceeded normally until they'd driven squarely into the mine field about an hour after dawn the next morning. It wasn't supposed to happen: the new vehicles were supposed to be shielded on the bottom, but Ray watched in slow motion horror as the vehicle ahead of him blew up from below, spewing fragments of humvee and human flesh everywhere. His own driver simultaneously slammed on the brakes as a splatter of blood sprayed the windshield. Part of a hand bounced off the hood.

One single Marine flew, relatively intact, through the air, a trail of bright red blood arcing behind him, to land hard on the ground a few yards away. Miraculously, his landing didn't trigger a secondary explosion. But he wasn't moving, and a puddle of blood was starting to form in the dirt under him.

"ALL HALT!" Ray barked as loudly as he could into his radio. "ALL HALT! MINE FIELD! MEDIC! MAN DOWN!"

"Medic's in the back, sir," came a reply over comm. "If you've got a mine field up there, how you want us to get him to you?"

"Carefully," Ray ordered into the radio, thinking fast. "Have him climb from vehicle to vehicle. We do NOT need him biting it, too."

"Smith's not gonna last that long, boss man," his XO noted over Ray's shoulder, nodding at the wounded Marine.

"I know, Jay. Gimme the sweeper."

Ray's second in command dug the detector out of the back and handed it to his superior, then got another out. "What do you think you're doing?" Ray wondered sharply.

"Helping."

"Hell no. Stay IN THIS VEHICLE. The unit needs one of us to keep going."

"But sir…"

"NO BUTS. Stay in the vehicle. That is a direct order, Lieutenant Samuels."

Jay stood firm. "Sir, I HAVE to protest. You're the brains. You're the one that's got EVERYTHING from the mission in your head. I've got most of it, but you've got all of it. If you won't let me… let someone else do it, then."

That had made sense. "Driver's gotta stay here," Ray had mused, "to get ready to get us outta here."

"True," Jay agreed. "He's out."

One of the other two soldiers crammed in the humvee had raised a hand. "Sir, volunteer to retrieve comrade."

Ray drew a deep breath, realizing every second's delay was costing the vital blood of one of the unit. They'd already lost three in the blast, and undoubtedly alerted every hostile in the sector. It was only a matter of time before the Iranians descended; the covert op was blown to hell and back, literally. It was only a matter of time.

"How much training have you had with these things, soldier?" He waved the detector at the volunteer.

"Standard training, sir."

"You?" Ray turned to Samuels.

"Training plus two weeks' duty."

"I've got you beat by a full month of solid duty assignment, Samuels," Ray noted. It always came down to time, he mused. Time always seemed to allow for things to happen and time right then wasn't a commodity they had lots of. "Just because I'm not precisely 'military' doesn't mean I haven't done military work. I'm the logical one for the retrieval. Stay put. I'll be out, throw him over my shoulder, and follow my footsteps back, in two minutes." Those two minutes could be life or death.

In less than a minute he had made big progress. He'd gotten to the side of the wounded Marine, managing to grapple him up and over his shoulder, with the detector over the other, before starting to walk in his own footsteps back to the humvee. He'd glanced up long enough to see the medic, climbing from vehicle to vehicle in their convoy—

—And kicked a pebble. Time slowed down in his mind as he watched the pebble skitter across the road and bounce, once, twice, a third time... Time always allowed for things to happen...

He remembered a roar like all the cannons in the history of the world firing at once, and searing pain, and then blackness.

೮つಣ

He woke up in the covered back of a dusty and blood-soaked humvee. And it was hell. It was a hellish time that seemed to last forever. A pain filled fight with death that was hell. Time moved so slowly it might as well have stopped.

Gunshots and mortar explosions rattled and boomed about them. He tried not to flinch from the noise.

He felt like most of his skin was missing. It wasn't by a long shot, but damn, did it feel like it. And significant chunks of the rest of him had been carved up pretty good, too. A glimpse of his head in an overhead lamp shield made him look away quickly. A bloody, mangled remnant of a cheek, bone protruding, nose laid open, with two hazel eyes peering back at him out of a sliced up face and a thickly blood-caked thatch of dark brown hair on top, partially detached. 'Oh God. Half of my face is... gone.'

"Oh geez! Dear God! Madre de Dios! Somebody get me some more gauze!" the Latino medic was shouting. "Yes! The whole damn supply! NOW! This is the one guy we have GOTTA get outta here!" He'd bent back over Ray, mopping bright scarlet blood with a handful of gauze that was already sopping in it. That was when he realized Ray was looking up at him.

"Smith..." Ray managed to croak through a throat that felt as shredded as his face, worried for the wounded Marine. "How's Smith, Ernesto?"

"He... he didn't make it, sir. I'm sorry; you almost had 'im, too. The mine took his head off. Nearly took yours with it. We must've still been too close, or maybe we're nearer another sensitive site than we realized, Samuels said."

"Jay... is Jay here?"

"Right here, sir." Samuels leaned over Ernesto's shoulder, a bandage on his own arm. "And I'm not goin' anywhere without you, I swear. Ernesto and me, we're gonna get you out of here. Ern, get him ready. The team's shot to hell and back. We're gonna make a run for it, as soon as the last Marine squad cuts us an opening. How much time has he got?"

"There's time, sir."

"Who's left?" Ray managed to force out a whisper.

"Us." Samuels disappeared forward in the humvee.

The medic reached for something. Ray saw a bright metallic flash out of the corner of his eye, and within seconds grew groggy. "Relax, sir," the medic told him. "We're less than a klick from rendezvous with the evac chopper. We're gonna get outta this."

৪০০৪

The evac chopper didn't show; the damned Iranians chased them off with surface to air missiles. Ray, Jay, and Ernesto were the only ones to even make it that far. By that time Ern had gotten Ray numbed, bandaged, and stabilized enough to take part in the decision making. The three decided to head for the Iraqi border, hoping to find U.S. troops there and get out. As far as the medic could tell Ray's vitals were stable but the longer they waited, the more time it took them to get to a hospital, the more likely complications and infections could take hold that Ray couldn't fight off. There was time, but it was ticking away rapidly.

They took the humvee as far through the mountains as they could get, until it ran out of fuel, then they hid it under a rock outcrop, draped in a camo tarp. Jay had had the presence of mind to grab several sets of the native clothing. He had also gotten all the ammo and weaponry he could reasonably—or maybe unreasonably, Ray had decided—load onto the humvee; it had been how he'd gotten the bullet in his shoulder, darting from vehicle to vehicle with the supplies. Ray figured he'd been lucky only to take the bullet, running around a mine field like that.

They ditched the BDUs in three "graves" near the humvee, to make it look like some locals had taken them out and hidden the hummer for parts, then donned the ragged garb of mountain country dwellers, hiding substantial firepower in the loose trousers and folds of the garments. They gave Ray the homespun cloak with the hood, and tugged it down over his face, hiding—and protecting—as much of the damage and bandages as it would cover. Ray wore an IV on his back like a CamelBack drinking bag and ran it down his arm. Ernesto taped the needle in well and also added another dose of morphine to ease Ray's pain. Ray watched as Ernesto also hid as much of his precious medical supplies as he could in the same fashion. Jay loaded himself down with canteens of water, and hacked a walking staff from a nearby scrubby sapling for Ray to use to stay upright. Then they began the long, arduous hike through the mountains, following herding and animal trails for the most part, headed southwest toward the Iraqi border.

They foraged as they went, eating the native nuts and berries, the occasional clutch of grubs, and whatever they could kill, usually raw. Jay and Ernesto mashed it all up for Ray, who had a hard time eating, between the condition of his face and the bandages that covered it. Mountain springs and streams had eked out their precious supply of water. But Ray remembered little of it; between the pain of his injuries and the narcotics Ernesto gave him, all he could recall was Hell. He thought he recollected one or two close calls, where Iranian patrols had stopped them as they crossed major roads, but neither Jay nor Ern would talk about it afterward. Time continued to tick away.

ഇൻ

Ray thought he vaguely remembered the crossing into Iraq, but not much changed when they did: that part of Iraq was still mountainous, and still potentially enemy territory. He did recall finally coming down out of the mountains and eventually crossing a large river. Later, much later, he managed to reconstruct that it had been the Tigris. They bypassed Baghdad in favor of Fallujah, which had been one of the most peaceful cities in Iraq as of their last briefing.

But time had allowed that status, unbeknownst to them, to change.

They arrived just in time for Operation Vigilant Resolve.

If the mountains of Iran had been a moment in Hell, Ray decided, Fallujah had been a lifetime of it.

೪つಅ

Stumbling through a chaos of street battle for over two days, narrowly avoiding grenades, rebel insurgents, and small arms fire from both sides, the three men searched for and finally located a 3rd Battalion Marine unit and approached it in relief. Still clad in mountain villager clothing, however, the three had been mistaken for insurgents, especially when Ray had staggered under the influence of his narcotics and accidentally exposed one of his guns.

"Rebels!" Ray could barely recall the unit commander with the brilliant, almost glowing, blue eyes shouting. "Lay down smoke! Surround and capture! Lethal force authorized!"

The white phosphorus grenade hadn't been intended as anything other than a smoke screen to confuse the three men, but intent and reality didn't coincide. A nearby crate on the sidewalk just inside an alley turned out to be a real insurgent's munitions cache, and Jay and Ernesto were caught in the blast when the WP ignited it. Ray, far enough away to avoid the worst of the blast but still close enough to be knocked down by it, blacked out.

೪つಅ

The next time Ray had awakened, it was in a hospital. State-side, he had presumed, and been correct. There were more bandages on him than a living body ought to have, in his opinion, from what he could see. An IV dripped all kinds of fluids into his neck. He sighed despondently, remembering Smith and his failure to save him.

"You're awake," a man observed in response to Ray's sigh, and a face matching the voice appeared in his field of view. Ray assumed he was the doctor, since he had on scrubs and a lab coat. "That's a good sign."

"Did Jay and Ern make it?"

"Your two friends? They did. Better than you did. Not that that's saying much."

"H- how bad?" Ray managed to get out through oddly stiff, thick lips, and the doctor sighed.

"*Humpty Dumpty,*" *he decided, "all three of ya, but we had all the king's horses and all the king's men, and then some. So you're together again, all major parts attached and working, and believe it or not, you're gonna come out of this okay. You got buckets of blood, though, and I'd have to count on your chart to see how many surgeries you've had." The physician waved a thick clipboard. "I sure didn't know the military had that many, or that good, plastic surgeons, though."*

"*Why is my whole face bandaged?*"

"*They had to rework your entire face to make it look right. Your right cheek and nose in particular were in bad shape.*"

"*Oh. Is it... will I...?*"

"*Look normal? The plastic surgeons said ninety to ninety-five percent chance you'll look completely normal when it all heals. Not like your high school photo, of course, but not like you got caught in a bomb blast. Or two, from the scuttlebutt I heard.*"

The statement was an obvious invitation to elaborate, but Ray ignored it in the face of the percentages he'd been given. 'Ninety to ninety-five percent... not like your high school photo.'

Ray knew what that meant: 'My old face is gone. My own mother, if my parents were still alive, might not recognize me. And there's a five to ten percent chance of coming out looking like Frankenstein's monster.'

"*They took your dog tags,*" *the doctor had added, "you're patient P-1 to us, as in Priority One. Your friends are P-2 and P-3, respectively. Who the hell ARE you guys, anyway? The President himself wouldn't get any better treatment."*

Grasping the significance of the confiscated dog tags even in his condition, Ray didn't have an answer he could give, and he couldn't shrug, so he just lay there.

৪০৫৪

He'd been there a long time, healing slowly, when the Old Man and Samantha had finally showed up. Not all the bandages and stitches were gone, but his semi-new face had been revealed to him only that morning, and he was surprised at how well they'd done. Even his old friends weren't going to recognize him, let alone casual acquaintances, but he looked like a normal person instead of a scarred wreck, and his bone structure had remained more or less intact. Even his scalp had been reattached. 'Not a bad looker,' he'd decided. 'Damn if I don't think they might have made an improvement here or there.'

Which had proven convenient as soon as he'd laid eyes on Sam. Time always seemed to allow things to develop. Sometimes good things and sometimes not so good, but time always kept moving things along.

ᏮᏙᏣᏸ

Ray came back to the present—almost. The entire memory had played on his mental movie screen in a matter of seconds, but he was still tied to that past in a bizarre, macabre sort of way.

I'm a dead man walking. I died. Even though I lived, I died. The man I was born as no longer exists. That mission was bloody hell, literally and metaphorically, he concluded. *Yea, though I walk through the valley of the shadow of death…*

He knew he still flinched mentally whenever he woke up after a fight to see Ernie Travers bending over him. He suspected sometimes the flinch wasn't just mental, either. If he did, Ernie had never said anything about it.

But for the sake of his morale and his emotional well being, he tried to put it all in perspective. *Well, historically, that whole area has been a valley of death for… damn, over a century, off and on, I guess. Probably millennia, if you look at the archaeological data. But I still lost Smith, not to mention an entire Marine Special Ops unit. How do you manage to LOSE an ENTIRE Special Ops unit?! It's a wonder they let me do ANYTHING else after that mission, let alone be field commander of a team like this one. And hell, but did that mission turn me into hamburger.* Unaware that he did so, Ray shook his head.

ᏮᏙᏣᏸ

Sam knew her husband as no one else on Earth knew him. And she knew what he was thinking, during that protracted silence.

And suddenly for the very first time, she understood. Understood why he was so focused. Why he was so intense, so determined. Why he fought like hell on a mission, and took each one so seriously. Why he often took the point when he didn't have to; why it was so important to him that he bring all of his team back intact.

He's atoning, she realized, a flash of comprehension like a lightning bolt going off in her mind. *Subconsciously trying to make up for surviving, and maybe trying to do his job and theirs, too. And not lose another one, let alone an entire team.*

Still, Sam could tell from the look on his face, Ray didn't regret what he'd tried to do, those years back. And the Old Man had heard about it, seeing to it that he got the best of treatment, that he got some semblance of normalcy back in his life, before introducing Ray to himself and Samantha. Sam herself remembered the pink scars Ray had had running around the edges of his face and down his chest as he lay in the hospital bed. Remembered, too, that even then she had wanted to finger them lightly, to tell him that it was all right, that they meant he'd survived. They'd faded into invisibility now, of course; the best plastic surgeons in the country, maybe the world, had worked on his face. And body, for that matter. But she still knew exactly where they were by memory. And, to some small extent, by touch.

ಬೂಗ

"Look, Ray," she said quietly. "I know it's just who you are. And I know you're single minded when you're on a mission. And... I know why. At least I think I do. And that's good; there's nothing wrong with your reasons, or your heart. But now we've got Abby..."

"I know, Sam, I know," Ray murmured, as his mind drifted back to the tests Doc had run on him the night before. "Better than you realize. And I remember we talked about a brother or sister for Abby, too, a couple weeks back. I'll do my best. That's all I can say. It's just that... well, after all the training and field history I've got... When somebody comes at me, I go into the moment and it's kind of hard to..."

ಬೂಗ

Sam watched him, comprehending that something had happened to cause him to think about the subject more than usual; never before had she elicited more than a grunt from him on the matter. Worry gripped her gut. "Ray... is everything all right? You're not...?"

Ray gave her a genuine smile.

"Everything's fine, sweetheart," he told her, and she recognized his sincerity. "Let's just say Doc climbed on my ass and proceeded to chew most of it off, and he used the same arguments you're using. And leave it at that."

"You're a strong man, Ray, physically, mentally, and emotionally," Sam said, coming to him and wrapping her arms around him. "I'm betting there's only one real chink in your armor."

"And what would that be?"

"Abby."

"Then you'd be wrong."

"WHAT?!"

"I have two. Abby... and you."

And he kissed her soundly.

ଽଠଔ

After breakfast, Sam took Ray down to her basement office again. "While you guys were off to Oak Ridge," she explained, "I was doing a bit of research on my own. Let me show you what I got." She began booting the computer. "Meanwhile, tell me what you found out."

Ray gave her a brief, but detailed, sketch of their discoveries. He explained about the amount of fissile material that could be missing, and the possibility that the accounting records had been tampered with, given the level of technology with which their target seemed to be operating. Then he told her about the ability to mutate radiodurans, and the discovery of both a spectral and a manifold decay sequence corresponding to the vanishing point of their anomaly.

"That's not good," she muttered, as she opened the media player on the computer.

"Echo... echo... echo..." Ray gave her a humorless grin. "Every last damn one of us said those exact same words at various points yesterday."

"All right, then, let's combine it with what I've found. Look." Sam opened what was evidently a very long montage of video from various locations and times.

ଽଠଔ

Ray watched the video as a string of bank vault robberies took place on it. Most were in color; some, black and white.

"I started looking for other anomalies," Sam explained, "based on using the same modus operandi with unrealistically short time spans in between. In the last two years, I found a slew of mysterious bank robberies, all across the world. Nobody could figure out how the robbers got in or out. But not even Interpol seems to have connected them via M.O. yet, so they're not investigating them as a series.

"So I got video from the vault security cameras and took a look, then spliced them all together in chronological order." She gestured at the screen. "This one was in New York... this one in London... here's Brussels... back to New York... over to Tokyo... Toronto... Hong Kong... New York again..."

"Shit," Ray interjected.

"Bombay, Frankfurt, Madrid, Johannesburg. You name it, if there's a major stock exchange, or financial center with lots of banks—it's been hit," Sam declared. "Some, multiple times. Paris was hit only an hour before a big bank in Chicago, which was hit less than thirty minutes before a bank in Hong Kong. Two days later, Tokyo, Brussels, two banks in New York, and London were all hit in the span of six hours."

Ray drew a deep breath.

"Notice anything about the security video montage?" Sam asked.

"Yeah–you could've edited it better," Ray pointed out. "You got the guys robbing the vaults. You don't have the entries and exits at all."

"That's just it, Ray–there weren't any!" Sam expostulated, mildly irritated that he, of all people, had failed to grasp the significance. "That's what drew my attention to these in the first place! I've looked at these sequences frame by frame. One frame, there's nobody in the vault; the next frame, they're all there, ransacking it."

"Why haven't we heard about this?!" Ray stared at her, shocked.

Sam shook her head. "Security and publicity," she remarked. "The banks are not gonna want it publicly known that somebody waltzed in and waltzed out with that much in… GOLD. And never so much as elicited a peep from all their vaunted security during the waltzing. Besides, like I said, no one but us has pieced together the connection. Look at the robbers, Ray. Really LOOK at them."

Ray carefully studied the humanoid images flashing onscreen for several long minutes.

"Dammit," he cursed abruptly. "They're masked, but, judging by the postures and body language…"

"It looks like the same people, over and over." Sam nodded.

"Yeah…"

"And look at this one coming up," Sam instructed. "Wait a minute. Let me back up to the beginning of the sequence." She jogged the video timeline toggle back a few millimeters. "There. Now watch."

There was a brief instant of black screen, followed by a bank vault suddenly full of four masked men–and one other. They spread out and began gathering up stacks and bags of money, some in paper, some in gold coin. The unmasked man stood in the center of everything, next to a large dolly with a hand truck handle, and looked on calmly, arms folded. He had spiky blond hair and bright, sky blue eyes. He was tall, long and lean, but muscular, and in contrast to the uniform-like jumpsuits the others wore, he was clad in dark trousers, a black t-shirt, and a dark long sleeved shirt, open down the front.

Ray's eyes widened, then narrowed. "Marathon Man. And not even masked. Cocky son of a bitch."

"Keep watching."

Onscreen, one of the masked henchmen inadvertently tripped a laser alarm. "Marathon Man's" face suddenly contorted in a near-maniacal rage. He grabbed the man by the throat and lifted him into the air with one hand like a puppy, slamming him back against the vault door. Seconds later, the man's throat was crushed, windpipe collapsed, with blood pouring from his open mouth, and a panicked, desperate look in his dying eyes. The unmasked man threw him aside as if he were no more than a used paper napkin. He spun to his remaining henchmen, rotating his finger in the universal "hurry up" gesture, then checked his watch as placidly as if his unbalanced, homicidal attack had never happened. The lackeys scurried to his side, loading the dolly with sacks of gold coin and cash–and then the entire lot was gone, saving one very dead body. Ray sucked in a sharp breath.

"Was he in any of the others?"

"A few," Sam noted. "Seems to be the ringleader–of course."

"Of course," Ray murmured, thinking. "Shit. Talk about extremophile…"

"In more ways than one," Sam agreed, tapping her temple with meaning.

"Yeah. He's like… I dunno, like a human version of an extremophile. You know, I used every trick in the book, every move every sensei I've ever had taught me, and a few I made up myself, when I was fighting him," Ray remembered. "But the son of a bitch still kept getting the better of me, no matter what I did."

"And you're one of the top combat fighters in the States, maybe the world," Sam observed, "or Robert wouldn't have picked you for the team. Maybe he's where the extremophile bacterium is going to."

౸౦౧౩

Ray shook his head, pondering the theory. Suddenly a horrific idea hit.

"Honey–have you checked Fort Knox?"

"Yeah. They're clear. At least for now. Security there seems to be something they don't want to fool with at the moment."

"What about the body of the dead cannon fodder?"

"I'm not sure," Sam admitted. "That was one of the most recent robberies, maybe two days before your encounter. I notified Robert, and I think he's trying to get hold of the body and personal artifacts for us."

"Good," Ray said. "Maybe it'll tell us something. Meanwhile, I wonder if Skip and the guys should go over this, look for a spectral trail or something."

"Not a bad idea," Sam decided.

හ෧

Skip took a good long look at Sam's videos. "There's not a lot to see," he pointed out. "These are low-res visible light cameras. We can probably get a nice portrait of our anomaly guy using some enhancement algorithms. But note how some of the videos do have a saturation frame for either the 'beam in' or the 'beam out.' In some cases, we have both."

"So that's what those are," Sam muttered. "I thought the cameras were just staticky."

"No," Skip verified, "that's part of the anomalous entry and exit, according to our research and Ray's and Jay's observations. Now, what we really need to see, at this point, is some non-visual data. And, since most vaults also have infrared cameras, let's see what we can find, shall we?"

"All over it," Sam grinned.

Ray, for a change, leaned back and watched as his wife and his teammate went to work, pulling up infrared camera footage from any of the robberies they could find. *Makes for a nice rest*, he decided. *I still feel beat to hell, but I can just sit here, watch, and kinda zone out. Feels good.* He got a long rest, dozing off once for a few minutes, but jerking himself back to consciousness before anyone else noticed. *Or I start snoring, with this nose.*

"Excellent," Skip declared after about an hour and a half. "Burn it to CD for me and I'll add it into the mix. Ought to have an answer for you on this," he pointed at the computer screen, then turned to Ray, "and the pre-jump footage by tomorrow."

"Good," Ray said as Sam burned the CD.

හ෧

Later that day, the Old Man called on the secure line to inform them that the henchman's body and personal effects were being shipped to Fields.

"Then Ray and Doc can both have a good look," he remarked.

"Excellent," Ray said. "I have the feeling that the search won't be fruitless."

"Be patient. It'll be a couple of days, at least, before it arrives," Kruger warned.

"Like all beaurocracy," Ray shrugged. "We've got plenty of stuff to work on in the meantime."

"Yes, I saw Samantha's report about the robbery videos," the Old Man said. "Sounds intriguing. Keep me posted."

"Always, Robert," Samantha smiled.

"By the way," Kruger added, "I've got some of the team off looking for someone of your acquaintance, Ray."

"Oh?" Ray wondered.

"Yeah. The guy whose filing cabinet you shot up. Dr. Abhu Gupta has gone missing."

"Don't blame him after Ray got done with him," Sam chuckled.

"No, Samantha," the Old Man corrected. "Not into hiding. Missing. Vanished. As in, we can't find a sign of him. Suitcases still in the trunk of his vehicle, which was abandoned in the parking lot at the university, no call for a taxi, no airplane tickets, subway tickets, train tickets... nothing."

Ray and Samantha stared at each other.

"I hate mysteries," Ray muttered.

"Wrong line of work then, honey," Sam responded.

"Hell if I don't know it."

&OCB

Later that evening, when both of them had had enough of staring at robbery videos and pulling nothing in particular from them other than the fact that their mystery man was constantly checking his watch, they decided on some family time.

Ray sat in the floor and played ball with Abby while Samantha watched in delight from her prone position on the sofa, occasionally joining in. Abby was still too weak from all her illnesses to fully sit up on her own as yet; she tended to get out of breath from laughing and topple over. This, they'd learned quickly, instantly turned playtime into crying time with a bumped head. But Ray had a bright idea: he propped her up in a nest of pillows and rolled the big red ball across the floor to her. She didn't really catch it so much as stop it with her legs, if Ray rolled it properly. Abby had only recently learned to roll it back, although her aim was not exactly what could technically be termed accurate. In fact, it was nowhere close. But she let out a happy squeal and hoarse cackle each time she rolled the ball, and that made both Sam and Ray laugh. Ray spent most of the game crawling around the floor retrieving the ball, backed up by Sam, who caught a few strays that reached the couch and tossed them back.

Then it was bath and bedtime, which, once again, they shared. Teresa was waiting in the nursery when they put Abby down, and as usual, the nanny sat in the recliner until she was certain the little one was soundly asleep.

&OCB

As Sam and Ray left the nursery, Ray gave his wife a suggestive glance. She smiled coyly in return.

"Shall we turn in a little early?" Ray wondered innocently, but his eyes were heavy lidded.

"Oh, I suppose," Samantha replied in mock indifference.

But Ray had seen the lustful sparkle in her eyes.

৪০৫

They wandered casually into the bedroom, and Ray closed the door firmly behind them. Then he turned to Samantha and pulled her close, kissing her fervently. Powerful yet deft male fingers found the buttons of her blouse, and seconds later it was off, followed immediately by her bra.

He was surprised to realize that his own shirt was gone by that time, and his belt unfastened as well. *Quick little minx,* he thought, amused.

Toes pried off shoes and socks, and jeans dropped to the floor. "Commando today, huh?" Samantha noted, scanning her husband's strong, muscular body from head to toe.

"Yup."

"Left over from this morning?"

"Might say that."

Ray peeled his wife's panties off, wrapped his arms around her, and proceeded to mold the entire length of her softening body against his hardening one as he kissed her again. "Mmph. Feel good," he muttered gruffly against her lips as his palms skimmed across her skin.

"You too." Delicate fingers traced patterns on his back, and he knew she was following the outline of scars, faint though they were by now.

She likes them. Heaven only knows why, but she actually likes them. In the wrong light I look like a damn jigsaw puzzle—but not to her. She loves every inch of me, the same way I do her.

And with that, he scooped her up and carried her to the bed.

Moments after that, he was on her, in her, pressing her into the mattress as she sighed her pleasure. He brushed an annoying stray curl of dark hair out of his eyes, and Sam giggled.

"What?" he asked.

"I love that curl."

"Damn cowlick. Been there ever since the scalp surgery. Must not have reattached right, somehow."

"Shush. You already had a buzz cut, and they had to basically shave *it* for the surgery. They did the best they could. Besides, I like it," she reiterated. "It's your Superman curl."

"Oh, Lord. You gotta be kidding me, hot stuff." Ray rolled his eyes, and Sam giggled again, then kissed him on the nose. "I musta got into one helluva batch of kryptonite then, to be as chewed up as I am."

"Hush," she whispered, pulling him down into her arms as they made love. "Every scar on your body is a message, did you know that?"

"Saying what? 'Ray's a klutz'?"

"No. They say Ray is a survivor. He's tough. He's unafraid. He fights for what he loves, and he's a helluva fighter. He does what needs to be done, regardless of the cost." She shifted position under him, and he gasped at the sensation. "And that's one of the many reasons why I love him."

Hazel eyes abruptly filled with emotion—love, gratitude, amazement, humility, adoration. A shuddering breath left his body, and he tucked his head into her shoulder. "I... Sam... hot stuff..."

"Ssh. Don't say anything," she whispered. "Show me."

So he did. Ray pulled out all the stops, kissing, caressing, suckling, thrusting, determined to prove to this woman what she meant to him. Soon they were both glad that the nursery was at the other end of the hall, because Sam was all but screaming in pleasure. Ray smiled down into her face, panting as his own excitement grew.

"Hurry up, baby," he told her breathlessly, "and make sure you're... ready, because I'm not... gonna make it much... longer."

His answer was her arms and legs being flung about him.

Ray fairly roared his ecstasy.

&OC3

Later, they lay snuggled together. Ray's good arm hugged Sam close, and she rested her cheek on his good shoulder, her hand on his chest. The tip of her index finger traced designs on his skin; he wasn't sure if they were scars, or just random patterns, but at that moment, he didn't care.

"Sam?"

"Yeah, Ray?"

"We both adore Abby."

"We do. And we both adore each other."

"You wanna have another baby?"

"Yeah, I think Abby needs a baby brother or sister eventually. We already discussed that."

"No... I mean..." Ray's voice faded out, as he struggled to express a deep desire he didn't fully comprehend. "I mean, you're still relatively young, but I'm not getting any younger, and... well... I mean now. Like, take out the birth control implant and let's start trying to make another baby."

"Right away?!"

"Uh… yeah."

୫୦୧ଓ

"Ray, I think that's too soon," Sam protested gently. "We'd be up to our eyeballs in dirty diapers." She wrinkled her nose in distaste. "Let's wait a year or so, at least until we get her fully potty trained, and just enjoy Abby."

"I…" Sam felt Ray's body slump. "Okay."

She pushed up on one elbow, worried. "What's wrong, honey? What brought this on? I thought you said you were okay. Is… you're not…?"

"No, no, nothing like that. I'm fine. I dunno. I just… It feels like, if we're going to, we need to hurry and do it." Ray shook his head, a crease forming between his dark brows.

"Why?"

"I don't know why. I just… do." He gazed at her with confused but sincere and urgent hazel eyes.

Sam shook her head, and stared at him, puzzled.

୫୦୧ଓ

The next day, Samantha and Ray, after cuddle time over breakfast with Abby, met in the basement office with Skip and Don.

"Bingo, boss peoples," Skip crowed. "We got it."

"All videos?" Ray pressed.

"Most of them," Don verified.

"Got what?" Sam wondered.

"Remember I debriefed on the manifolds and the spectral deterioration, hot— uh, Sam?" Ray reminded her.

Don and Skip successfully hid grins. *Guess last night went well,* Skip thought fondly. *They make a great couple as well as great team leads.*

"Oh yeah, I remember now," Sam recalled, not so much as blushing at Ray's slip of the tongue. "So you got the reverse manifold appearances and blackbody spectrum at the beginning of the copter video sequence?"

"Exactly," Don noted. "Not on all of the bank videos, and of course those were only the IR parts of the sequence, but—"

"Why not on all of the bank videos?" Ray demanded, sitting forward, his usual intensity literally coming to the fore.

"Some of the cameras were set up to pan," Skip explained. "They just weren't looking at the right place at the right time."

"Oh, okay," Ray eased up, leaning back. "And the rest?"

"We got a pretty clean reversal of sequence on the copter vid," Skip elaborated, "minus a few building sides. Point, Möbius strip, Klein bottle, n-dimensional doomiewhatchie, another n-dimensional doomiewhatchie, for around three or four values of n all told as best we could estimate from their shapes, along with the increasing blackbody radiation peak."

"Which does seem to max out in the deep indigo to near ultraviolet range," Don added. "Oh, and some nice headaches from staring at n dimensions." He handed Sam one of the hard copy images of a multidimensional manifold, then he and Skip gave Ray a questioning look as Sam bent her head over the photo. Ray accurately read the looks of concern, and gave them the high sign. They nodded in relief.

"Fascinating," Sam burbled, sounding exactly like a certain pointy eared alien from a classic TV show. "And Ray, you say this is at least five dimensional?"

"Has to be," Ray declared. "A Klein bottle requires four dimensions, and that thing is past a Klein bottle. Note that it's morphing, too, so it's probably transitioning through higher dimensional manifolds. Well," he corrected, "you could see that in the video, anyway."

"I wanna see the vid then, at some point," Sam declared in enthusiasm, waving the paper image.

"Can do," Skip grinned. "It IS pretty cool. But anyway, we think we can set up to look for the things coming and going now, at least."

"That's something," Sam agreed. "Now we," she indicated herself and Ray, "have to figure out how to react fast enough to use it to get a team on the scene."

"Wrong way 'round, honey," Ray decided, deep in thought. "What we need to do is anticipate where they're gonna be, then wait for 'em."

There was a long silence.

"Good point," Sam agreed.

"The question is, how?" Don wondered.

Chapter 6

Inside a bank vault in London's financial district, the air was growing warmer. Abruptly a brilliant blue-white light flared, filling the space until the very shadows fled–for a moment. When it faded, three men stood there with a dolly. Two wore masks, but the third blatantly and brazenly exposed his face. Blazing blue eyes were surmounted by spiky blond hair. His aquiline nose was slightly crooked, betokening the fact that it had been broken sometime in the past, but otherwise he appeared normal.

"Get going," he ordered the other two, curt. "This is the last of it. Then we can begin acquiring the equipment we need." He glanced at his watch. "We have nine minutes and sixteen seconds before the extraction point. And hurry–if you're not ready when it's time for the extraction point, you stay here. If they find you in here, you know what happens. And if they don't open the vault for a few days…" He grinned thinly, without humor, a disturbing expression on his face.

The other two scrambled to obey, tossing crates of stacked US currency—held for currency exchange—and boxes of sorted, interleaved gold coin onto the dolly. They both knew that failure to get everything their leader wanted meant death, either by dehydration in the vault, a shootout with the bank guards, or at their leader's own hands when he popped into their jail cells and killed them to prevent them from talking to the authorities. Periodically the leader would call out a countdown.

"Precisely five minutes to extraction point."

One of the henchmen grunted something disparaging under his breath. "Blasted countdown; don't need th' damn thing. He just does it f'r th' adrenaline…"

"What's that, Simons?"

Simons blinked in shock that his superior had heard the comment. "Uh, nothing, Drago."

"EXCUSE me?"

Simons paled under his mask. "Uh, nothing, BOSS?"

"That will do, I suppose. My name is Doctor William H. Drago. YOU may call me DOCTOR Drago. Is that understood?"

"Y- yes, sir."

"And the countdown most certainly IS needed; it is essential. We need considerable funds to support our efforts. I want all that money. You, therefore, need to know how long you have to obtain it. I will hear no more complaints. You do remember what happened to Roberts when he tripped the alarm, don't you?" The calm smile had a frightening aspect that Simons couldn't explain, but he understood its import well enough.

"Um." Simons went white. "Yes, sir. Y- you know we're on your side, sir. And we're... clean."

"Good. And yes, I know that. But I will not tolerate incompetence. That could lead to our utter destruction, and that, I cannot allow. Get moving. You just wasted one and a half minutes of time. Three minutes, twenty-three seconds until extraction point."

The two men increased their speed, loading heavy cases of gold coin onto the dolly as fast as they could lift them. They knew better than to fool with the gold bricks; Drago wanted viable currency, and the bricks would be impossible to do anything with, short of stealing a smelter and coin stamp to melt them down and cast them into counterfeit coinage. That would take time. And Drago was not a patient man—if he didn't have to be.

The pair lugged one last box of paper currency—large denomination—over to the dolly and sat it down. Simons' partner, having learned from Simons' experience, noted respectfully, "That's the last of it, Doctor. With an extra ten percent pad for good measure." He gestured at the last box.

"Excellent," Drago noted, glancing at his watch. "And with thirty-three seconds to spare. Very, very good, gentlemen. I'm quite pleased. Now we wait for the extraction point."

"It's getting warm," Simons realized.

"It is," Drago agreed companionably enough, seeming to have entirely forgotten his earlier fit of pique. "The extraction point grows near." He glanced down at his watch, and the two workers bent to the handle of the dolly, ready to push. "In three, two, one..."

A bright light flared within the vault for the second time within ten minutes.

When it was gone, the men, the dolly, and a significant amount of currency, were gone, too.

ಸಿಂಡಿ

They showed up in a bank vault in the States. The two men unloaded the money into a specific location while Drago looked on.

Then he tapped his watch, and they gathered together. There was a flare of light, and they had vanished.

ಸಿಂಡಿ

Landing back in a small, perfectly cubical room whose floor was thickly padded, Drago dismissed his assistants. They went, glad to go, as he turned and sauntered out the opposite door and down a short spiral stairwell. There, he entered his personal office and sat down at a laptop computer.

"Now, let's see," he said with a smile, beginning to hack into the accounts system of the U.S. bank they'd just departed. "I think Dragonfire Enterprises' worth just went up... substantially..."

ಀಬ

Later, Drago sat at the desk in his office. He picked up the phone, dialed a specific sequence of numbers, and then dialed another sequence. "Hello," he said brightly. "My name is Doctor William Darkman. I'm the scientific advisor to the Director of the Department of Homeland Security. I work for Dragonfire Enterprises, Incorporated, and I would like to order some very specialized equipment. Yes, it's DNA resequencing equipment, and you'll probably have to customize it. Yes, I'll hold."

Drago leaned back in his chair and put his feet on the dark oak desk, crossing his ankles comfortably.

ಀಬ

"...Yes, that's exactly what I want. Yes, we want to be able to manufacture counter-agents for any biological weapons that terrorists might release. You know how it is. Thank you for understanding. Of course it's classified, or I wouldn't be using this line. Need to know basis. As soon as possible. Really? That's great. Yes, ship it to Dragonfire's main office. I'll arrange the funds transfer. Thank you very much."

Drago hung up the phone and smiled to himself.

"'Just enough light for the step I'm on'?! Bah! Time for the next step," he said, grinning devilishly. He checked his watch. "Let me see... when is that extraction point...?"

ಀಬ

Sam was kicked back on the sofa reading the paper while Ray propped Abby in the corner to play ball. She glanced over the top of the paper and grinned to herself as Abby let out a particularly loud coo and Ray laughed aloud.

For such a tough warrior, he's got a heart like melted ice cream when it comes to that child, she concluded. She watched with fond amusement for several minutes before returning her attention to the newspaper. Suddenly she swung her legs around and sat up straight.

"Ray, listen to this," she said in a tone that immediately commanded her husband's notice.

"I'm listening," he said, rolling the ball absently toward Abby while focusing his attention on his wife.

"'Ground Breaking Geneticist Kidnapped,'" Sam read the headline. "'Doctor Felix S. Kato, of Case Western Reserve University, in Cleveland, Ohio, mysteriously disappeared from his campus office late yesterday afternoon. The department secretary reported a loud argument in his office, though she saw no one but Dr. Kato enter, and saw NO one leave. She also avers that the office phone did not ring, before or during the argument. When an abrupt silence fell inside the office, she went to check on Dr. Kato, but found the office inexplicably empty and all windows closed and locked from the inside.

"'Dr. Kato is the Nobel prize winning geneticist who invented the DNA nanoball, a method of compacting DNA into a particle about twenty-five nanometers across. A nanometer is one trillionth of a meter, or about four hundred-billionths of an inch.

"'He and his team of Case Western colleagues, along with contractors from Genetics Universal and Genetherapy Incorporated, have been hot on the trail of using the DNA nanoball to manipulate human DNA for therapeutic treatments, including a possible cure for cancer. An unnamed spokeswoman for Case Western, as well as the nanoball team, indicated that his disappearance was a grave setback for the program, as well as of deep personal concern for all of his colleagues.'" She paused, having reached the end of the article, then added, "Hm. Can't say as I blame the spokesperson for wanting to remain anonymous, under the circumstances." Sam looked up at her husband.

Ray was frozen in place, ball raised to roll to Abby, but he didn't move, even when Abby began to bounce and yell to get his attention. The hazel eyes were distant in thought. "Nanoballs," he muttered. "Nanoballs..." He held up Abby's red ball and stared at it.

"What?" Sam pressed.

"Nanoballs," he repeated. "I—there's something about nanoballs, something I should know. Recent," he added in frustration, turning the toy ball about in his fingers as he gazed at it. "But I can't remember."

"Well, it isn't like you didn't take a few cracks to the noggin the other day, sweetheart," Sam pointed out. "That'll affect the short term memory."

"Yeah, but… dammit! I just know it's important!" he exclaimed, as Abby let out an annoyed shriek. Ray jumped, returning his attention to his daughter, and rolled the ball to her, whereupon the shriek metamorphosed into a happy coo in mid-scream.

"What I noticed was the similarity to certain bank robberies of our knowledge," Sam observed. "Nobody goes in, nobody goes out, yet something—or, in this case, someONE—goes missing."

"Hmph. Yeah," Ray agreed, temporarily diverted from the nanoballs as he caught a toy ball instead. "Awfully coincidental, that."

"If it is a coincidence," Sam insisted. "I don't think it is."

"You think our anomaly kidnapped him?"

"You said yourself he got enough radiodurans for a hell of a lot of experimentation," Sam pointed out. She shook her head. "What if this is the next step?"

"GUPTA!" Ray shouted, so loudly he scared Abby, who began crying. "DOCTOR GUPTA at Columbia University! The guy who led us to our anomaly! He was working on protein nanoballs too! THAT'S where I remember it!"

Teresa ran into the room and scooped up the screaming, frightened baby, seeing the troubled look on the faces of Abby's parents.

"Shit," Sam declared.

ॐＣ

While Sam studied the robberies, Ray looked for any connection between their original target, Dr. Gupta, and the missing Kato. They spent the rest of the day with heads down over their computers in the basement.

At the end of the day, they tagged up. "Whatcha got?" Sam asked. "Any connection?"

"Hell, yeah, there's a connection. I got confirmation from Kato's colleagues that he and Gupta corresponded, mostly by email, for about a year before Gupta came from India," Ray disclosed. "In fact, Kato was the sponsor for Gupta's immigration. Gupta's specialty was buckyballs, and he wanted in on Kato's nanoball research. Kato felt he'd be an asset to the team, and agreed."

"OoooOOOooo," Sam said. "So we've got a CLOSE connection."

"Oh, hell yeah," Ray agreed.

"So what happened?"

"Gupta worked with Kato and his team for awhile, but then something happened. He got kicked off the team for reasons unknown, and which so far no one has been willing to discuss. Not with me, not with anybody." Ray shook his head. "Almost immediately Gupta showed up at Columbia University, although I don't think Columbia U. knew that he left his previous employment under... uhm, questionable circumstances."

"Where is he now?"

"Gupta? That's a good question. He apparently hightailed it after meeting our anomaly dude, remember? Nobody's seen him since."

"Oh duh, yeah. Robert told us. Which could be good or bad for Gupta, I'd think," Sam mused. "There are three options for what happened to him, as I see it: one, he's on the run. Two, mystery man warped him out. Three, mystery man offed him for leading your team to him."

"Yeah," Ray agreed. "My bet would be option three, if Dr. Kato has gone missing."

"Mmm. Because Santa needs another expert on nanoballs?"

"Exactly."

"Which can't be good."

"Nope. What did you find, hot stuff?"

"Nothing," Sam sighed disconsolately. "I did more statistics today than I've done since grad school, and I got nothing. Zip, zilch, crapola. My analyses of the robberies show they have no real centroid."

"Did you try a three dimensional centroid?"

"Honey, I tried every statistical analysis in the book, and even invented a few. Unless he's got a space station out there that NORAD hasn't spotted—and yes, I checked, and no, they haven't—I can't find a centroid."

"So..."

"Yeah," Sam agreed. "If I can't find a centroid, I have no way to determine where the robbers keep going to and from." She hesitated, then offered, "But if they're using some umpteen dimensional thingamajig, I don't think I'd be able to find a centroid anyway, would I? At least, not necessarily in our dimensions?"

Ray rocked back, realizing she had a point.

"Well, shit," Ray grumbled.

&ೞ೧ೞ

"So, Ray, give us the possibilities as you see them," the Old Man ordered as the team met in the conference room once more. "I'd like to know how this guy is getting himself and his men in and out like this."

"Well, sir, there are several possibilities," Ray offered. "Pretty much all of 'em are variants on either a wormhole slash warp, or macro-scaled quantum tunneling. So. Scientists have already succeeded in creating a 'transporter' effect at the quantum mechanical scale, effectively causing a particle's quantum state to disappear from one place and reappear—I forget; it was less than room distance, I think—in another place."

"Like the TV show," Jay interjected.

"Right. Only it was one particle, and a short distance. So if this guy has found a way to scale it up, and keep the shift coherent, he's effectively recreated the TV show's gizmo."

Kruger pondered this information for a moment, then nodded. "Go on."

"Spacetime warps." Ray shrugged.

"How?"

"Beats me."

"What?!" The Old Man stared at him in shock. He had never known Ray Brady to utter those words before. Ray shook his head.

"Right now the only known way to warp spacetime is through a concentration of mass," he explained. "It creates a curvature of spacetime that enables a kind of faster than light travel—at least it appears so to observers, which we currently are, to our anomaly. Do you know tensor physics? The Einstein curvature tensor... uh..."

Kruger scowled. Ray stopped, taking in the Old Man's expression.

"Mm. You probably don't want to take a quick lesson in it..."

The scowl deepened.

"Well," Ray continued, trying not to leap too precipitately into the awkward silence, "obviously we don't know how to compact that much mass and handle it with ease. That doesn't mean other entities wouldn't, but we don't have the science to understand it yet. Other warp theories include the use of dark energy—which we haven't yet even proved exists—and superstring manipulation."

"Damn technobabble." Kruger pulled a face.

"At any rate, it would likely take some sort of ship, or at least a compartment, around the traveler to make any of those work, and we know our guy doesn't use one. I've considered the subject pretty intensely, and I can't readily see a way around that. Possible, but improbable, I'd say."

"All right. Keep going. Next candidate."

"Boson manipulation."

"Say what?" Jay wondered.

"Bosons are kind of interesting particles," Ray explained. "For instance, unlike other particles, several bosons can occupy the same quantum state. They're often the particles which carry the forces of nature. Photons and gravitons, for instance, carry the electromagnetic and gravitational forces, respectively. If he's learned to harness bosons, he might be able to do things relativistically."

The Old Man's nonexistent eyebrow rose. He nodded comprehension and permission to continue.

"Now," Ray went on, "if we expand that concept, and start looking at bosonic string theory, we get into tachyon fields. Tachyons supposedly cannot travel slower than light. It has four space momentum and—get this—imaginary proper time. But this brings up all kinds of causality issues in special relativity. You know, going back and becoming your own father. Transmitting future information back in time and hosing up the timeline by changing events. Shit like that. So," Ray shrugged, "we treat them as a kind of an instability field, rather than as a superluminal particle. If he's managed to leash those, travel through space, and maybe time, would be possible. But we've seen no real indication of time travel, just very rapid space travel. So we can probably nix this one, too. I just can't see a race—or even a being—utilizing only one aspect of that technology without delving into the other."

Kruger leaned back in his chair and thought for awhile. Ray, Jay, and the others waited patiently. Finally the Old Man leaned forward.

"All right, Ray. I presume you've saved the best—and most mind-bending—for last."

"You know me well, sir," Ray murmured, grinning, a hint of sheepishness in his expression. "I have. M theory."

"Get on with it."

"Some of the guys here have already heard the condensed version of some of this, so bear with me, guys, 'cause I'm going into more detail now. Okay. When string theory was developed, it went off in five different directions," Ray began.

"Let me guess: by five different researchers," Kruger hypothesized.

"Right. Now, each theory could explain certain observations pretty damn well, but no one single string theory could explain them all. So they created an overarching theory, M theory. String theory—or theories, rather—require about the usual four dimensions, give or take. M theory is an attempt to unite all five string theories across ten or eleven dimensions. It involves another structure besides strings, though, called membranes, or just branes for short. The theory isn't anywhere near fully developed—at least, not by us—so we don't even know for sure IF it works, let alone how. But some researchers—though not all—in the field postulate that the membranes could comprise alternate realities, parallel universes, or simply 'elsewheres.' Like cosmic strings, they have vibrational frequencies, so it's conceivable that two or more parallel or nearly parallel membranes could touch at an antinode." Ray paused to give everyone time to absorb the flood of information. "With me so far?"

Nods went around the room.

"Good. Yell if I lose anybody. Now, what we've observed in visible and near infrared seems to indicate the presence of spacetime manifolds."

"What's a manifold?" Kruger asked. "Besides on my car."

Ray took a deep breath, thinking hard. *How do I explain this? Damn, I shoulda buried my face in more of the M theory papers, instead of trying to prove to myself that the other theories were out in left field for this.* Finally he came up for air, with words he hoped would suffice.

"Maybe the best way to say it is like this. In our normal Euclidean geometry, we have points, lines, and planes. A plane is a Euclidean surface."

"Okay."

"Non-Euclidean geometries have been known about for a long time, such as spherical geometry or hyperbolic geometry. In those geometries, instead of planes for surfaces, they use the surfaces of spheres or hyperbolic surfaces—saddle shapes—respectively. Whenever you work with world maps in their various projections and see all the different kinds of distortions of the continents they produce, you're encountering efforts at projecting a non-Euclidean surface onto a Euclidean one."

Nods went around the table, and several glances went to the Mollweide projection map on one wall of the conference room. Ray continued.

"Manifolds are non-Euclidean surfaces; in this case, specifically they are surfaces that comprise x dimensions, but require at least x plus one dimensions to manifest. A Möbius strip is an example. It has one edge and one side; to an inhabitant, it would appear two dimensional. But it requires three dimensions to be formed. The next step up is a Klein bottle. It seems three dimensional, but requires four to be constructed. Our IR cameras saw at least a five dimensional manifold, and part of a six-D one. Maybe seven-D, too, but we aren't sure. It gets really hard for the human brain to pull out and identify the shapes pretty quick at that level. And we haven't developed a computer program yet that can scan an image and figure it out, either. They can DRAW them, but not identify them."

"Shit," the Old Man muttered.

"I am therefore proposing that our mystery being is using M theory," Ray declared. "It is my considered conclusion that he is using manifold vibrational intersections to hop from point to point in spacetime."

"But how?" Kruger demanded.

Ray shrugged in frustration. "If I knew that, sir, we'd have caught him by now."

Chapter 7

In a little town in northern Alabama called Rogersville, Haley Allen was preparing breakfast for her family in the kitchen when she heard a horrible crash in the general direction of the living room. Shoving the skillet with the eggs and bacon off the stove eye, she threw her potholder and spatula at the countertop, turning in alarm.

"Joey! Pete! Stop your roughhousing! If you've knocked over the entertainment center, I'll have your hides on the wall!" she shouted, running toward the living room.

She froze in the door. "Oh, Lord. Oh, my dear Lord," she whispered.

Just before she started screaming.

೫೦೮೩

"Yeah," the local police officer called on his radio. "Weirdest shit I've ever seen. Pretty gross, too. Roger that; a Huntsville Crime Scene Investigation unit is a real good idea. Yeah, I'm the town technical officer, and I got NO clue." He paused, listening, as the trembling Allen family stood in the yard nearby, staring in shock at the hole in the roof of their home, directly over the living room. "'Bout an hour and a half? Copy; I'll tape off the scene."

೫೦೮೩

The crime scene investigation team out of Huntsville prowled the Allen's living room, searching. "Shit," Detective Ford said, staring around at the room, searching for something to garner his attention, not wanting to look at its central focus.

"You said it," Detective Richardson agreed. "Thought I was gonna hurl when I walked in."

"Me, too. Okay, let's get the data and get the hell out. I'm thinking the first thing we need to do once we leave is contact the airlines," Ford said with a sigh, forcing his mind into an emotionless, clinical state.

"Agreed," Richardson confirmed, photographing the scene in detail, including the hole in the roof. "Recorder ready?"

"Running."

"Case 11502. Wednesday the twenty-fifth, eleven a.m., Detectives John Richardson and Mark Ford reporting. We are investigating a death of unknown cause. Location: 121 Blue Hollow Road, Rogersville, Alabama; single family dwelling, one story. A hole was punched in both the roof and ceiling from above; upper hole in roof smaller than lower hole in ceiling. Attic was completely penetrated. The diameter of said hole in the ceiling is approximately six to eight feet and irregular. Roof hole is about four feet and more oval in shape. Several house rafters were broken due to the force of impact, which was apparently substantial.

"Subject was found directly beneath the opening, amid significant roofing debris, atop the remains of a glass and steel coffee table and its contents. Right leg of subject was thrown haphazardly across the seat of the sofa, apparently during landing; judging by position and angles, all bones of said leg appear shattered, as do all other limbs of subject. Reference in situ photography."

Ford tag teamed. "The subject is obviously dead. Cause of death to be determined by autopsy; the number and type of injuries are both greater, and significantly different, than a simple fall from height should have produced."

"Subject is male," Richardson continued, bending over the body and examining the skin of the face and hands with a lens, "possibly in his mid-thirties, and may be Middle Eastern in origin. Dressed in dark suit, dress shirt, tie, all of which are rather the worse for... whatever happened to him. Tatters along all loose edges of the cloth. Skin appears suffused, with multiple ruptured small vessels near the surface. Both eyes have also ruptured. Small amounts of coagulated blood in eyes, nose, ears, mouth. The suit collar, tie, and shoulders of the subject's garments appear to be covered in a fine spray of blood, but there is very little blood at the scene. This would indicate that death likely took place elsewhere, well before the victim fell onto the house."

"Evidence of some burns on skin and clothing," Ford added. "Multiple broken bones, likely caused from the fall. No sign of contusions, another indicator of death elsewhere; but several odd cuts in strange areas on the body." He tilted his head up and looked through the hole into the azure sky above. "You guys discover anything up there?"

"Aside from the fact that I should've worn jeans instead of a skirt today, no," a female voice grumbled. "Can we please keep the damn TV crews away next time until I've been up and back down?"

"Sorry, Nicki," Richardson chuckled. He pulled his radio. "Harper, this is Richardson. Get the news crews back behind the tape and keep 'em there. No, preferably all the way to the street. Yeah. Okay, thanks." He turned back to his partner. "Get a body temp reading on him."

Ford nodded. Extracting a special forensics kit, he pulled a scalpel with gloved fingers, then unfastened the victim's shredded clothing and cut a slit directly into his abdominal cavity, then gagged, nearly throwing up.

"Geez, John! Look at this!"

Richardson bent over, then turned pale. A small amount of partially coagulated blood speckled the bile and fecal matter that oozed up from the abdominal cavity.

"Ruptured internal organs?"

"That's my guess."

"I've seen a lot of shit in my time, but this…" Richardson swallowed. Hard. He shook his head. "Get the temperature and let's get this guy into a body bag and to the morgue so we don't have to look at him."

"Yeah," Ford agreed.

He inserted a thermometer into the slit, and they waited until it registered. Ford pulled out the thermometer and checked the reading.

"HOLY SHIT!" he exclaimed. "What the HELL?!"

"What?" Richardson wondered.

Ford handed the thermometer to him.

"Son of a bitch!" Richardson exclaimed. "Thirty-three point four degrees Fahrenheit?!"

‽ℂℓ

Frank let an excited Jay into the house.

"They're downstairs, Major," the guard told him as he all but fell over the threshold, carrying a file folder.

"Got it!" Jay said, scurrying for the stairs. In the basement, he twirled the combination, punched in his code, and entered what he jokingly called, "the home office."

Ray and Samantha were both bent over their computers, Ray deep in an abstruse article on M theory, Samantha using a spreadsheet to try to mine data from the series of bank robberies.

"Guys, we found him!" Jay exclaimed, and blonde head and brown shot up.

"Found who?" the married couple said simultaneously.

"Gupta! The dude from Columbia University!"

"Where?" Sam demanded. Jay shook his head.

"You're not gonna believe this."

"Try us," Ray insisted.

"Forensics lab in Huntsville, Alabama. They got positive DNA and dental matches on him. He crashed through somebody's roof at a pretty damned high terminal velocity; the forensics techs estimated a good two hundred fifty, three hundred miles an hour, maybe more, and basically splatted their living room—only he didn't bleed everywhere. His eyes and capillaries had been frozen—exploded—but there were burns on parts of his body and scorch marks on his clothes. The landing broke damn near every bone in his body, but the coroner says he was dead long before that." He tossed the file down on the small conference table between them.

"Cause of death?" Sam snapped, as Ray reached for the folder.

"Dual," Jay said. "Explosive decompression—and asphyxiation." He paused. "Wanna guess what his core body temp was when the CSI unit got on the scene?"

Sam and Ray waited expectantly.

"Just above freezing. Half his guts had ruptured from being frozen. His brain was almost mush from multiple embolisms. A good portion of his blood evidently sprayed out his orifices under pressure. He was apparently still at least partly frozen when he hit the house, because there were splits in the skin associated with solidly frozen flesh experiencing a heavy impact."

The three stared at each other for long minutes. Ray finally opened the folder and leafed through its contents, which included the in situ scene photos. His face remained neutral, but Sam, who was looking over his shoulder, paled slightly.

"Explosive decompression, asphyxiation, half frozen body, burns on skin and clothing, terminal velocity and one helluva landing," Ray enumerated grimly. "He was wearing?"

"Normal business suit. Same one the last people alive saw him wearing at the university," Jay elaborated. "Rather the worse for wear. You can see the tatters. Oh, and NO reports of aircraft losing a passenger, either. Anywhere in the world, in… a long time."

"It can't be." Sam looked at Ray.

"It has to be," he responded solemnly. "There's no other reasonable explanation. He fell from low Earth orbit. Our damned Santa Bunny popped this guy right out of his office and into space."

"Bloody son of a bitch," Sam said with a grimace of disgust.

❧☙

As the U.S. Army Missile Command was headquartered in Huntsville, it didn't take the Old Man much maneuvering to get the body and all other evidence into his control. The explanation given to the press and the family whose house had been hit was that a hot air balloon flight out of nearby Decatur, Alabama had gone horribly wrong. It had been caught in a powerful updraft, and the pilot had been trying to warm himself with the burner flame, lost his perch, burned himself, and then fallen from a considerable height. The remains of a hot air balloon were conveniently "found" in a remote mountain location just across the state line in Georgia a day or two later.

Fields took over the examination and confirmed the Huntsville team's forensic findings. "And the only real explanation," he reported, "is the one that Ray puts forward. Gupta—and it IS Gupta; aside from the DNA and dental records, I had a team reconstruct his face—was placed, essentially instantaneously, at a low orbital altitude, and promptly died of the exposure to vacuum. He was up there just long enough to freeze solid—literally—before re-entering and sustaining a few mild friction burns as he achieved terminal velocity. Think somewhere between two thirds and one half of an orbit, a sub-orbital trajectory, I'm estimating, although I'm certainly no orbital mechanic; it might have been more like a couple of orbits. And there wasn't anything on him that NORAD might have easily picked up, so we got no heads-up there. His momentum—what little he had—decreased from drag and he headed down. The mostly still frozen carcass then hit some poor family's house, punched through their roof, and literally shattered every bone in the body, as well as 'cracking' the frozen flesh."

"This anomaly guy is…" Sam began, horrified.

"Merciless," Ray finished for her.

"We have got to find out what he is after," the Old Man declared. "I want the whole team—at least the ones who are savvy in such things—looking for any indication of our anomaly popping in and out. The same things going missing in multiple places. Unusual patterns of standard acquisition, and unusual things being acquired. Unexplained murders. Even supposed paranormal stuff. We can't afford to miss anything."

"Yes, sir," Jay saluted.

"Now GO. You have three days to see what you can find before coming back to me with a report."

ⅎℂ₳

Three days later they all met in the conference room down from the Old Man's office.

"Okay, what have we got?" Kruger demanded.

"We already know about the gold," Ray pointed out.

"Right."

"Chromium, too, and some nickel," Sam added, shuffling through printouts.

"My old CIA contacts indicate several aircraft manufacturers have had structural aluminum go missing," Danny Wilson observed. "Boeing, Mc-Donnell Douglas, Northrop Grumman, and some others. Oh, and there was an attempt at... well, let's just say one of our nuke manufacturing sites."

"What were they after?" Kruger demanded.

"Not sure for certain," Wilson answered. "But it was in the area with the lithium and tritium storage."

"So they didn't get it?"

"No, sir. Security was too tight."

"Good. Any attempts elsewhere?"

"Not that we can find, sir," Wilson responded. "Seems like they changed direction after that; they went after mercury in significant quantities."

"MERCURY?"

"Yes, sir."

The Old Man sighed in annoyance. "I always did hate jigsaw puzzles. Next?"

"Graphite rods, some helium, and heavy water have disappeared from several nuclear plants around the world, according to my sources," Jay threw his contribution into the fray. "After that visit to Oak Ridge, I do NOT like the sound of this."

"All right," Kruger nodded grimly. "Observation noted. What else?"

Billy the Kid piped up just then. "NASA's missin' some spare centrifuge parts."

"Centrifuge?!" Sam exclaimed.

"Yep, boss lady, centrifuge parts. Oh, and paraffin."

"Paraffin," Kruger echoed.

"Paraffin," Billy nodded.

"And high precision detonators," Pete Hansen, their munitions expert, added.

Kruger shook his head.

Ray finally tossed a paper across the table at the Old Man. "Here's the fun stuff. Genetic equipment, lots of it. MNNG, a special chemical that can affect radiodurans. And the pièce de résistance. Environment suits. Out of China and Russia."

Kruger took the paper, studying it.

"Environment suits? Wait, you mean, SPACE SUITS?!" the Old Man asked, jaw dropping as he stared at the copy of an invoice.

"Yep."

"What the hell for?" Major Hansen was just as perplexed.

"Dunno," Ray replied. "What was all the stuff again? Gold..."

"Hold on a minute," Jay shuffled through the paperwork and began reading, scribbling a list as he did so. "Gold, chromium, nickel, mercury, maybe lithium or tritium, some aircraft aluminum, graphite, some helium and high precision detonators, paraffin, heavy water—which means deuterium, and NASA centrifuge parts. If he were going after plutonium or yellowcake I'd say he was building a nuke. But since he hasn't—"

"What about Hanford?" Billy asked.

"Huh?" Jay looked blank.

"Hanford, Washington," Kruger filled in the major. "Where they converted non-fissile uranium isotopes to plutonium back during World War II. Billy's right. There's tons of leftover radioactive crap there."

"Which is exactly why this guy wouldn't go there," Ray observed. "That shit is so radioactive—at least the stuff that might be useful to him—that I doubt his men could even get anything before they keeled over and died. Not to mention the purification it would have to undergo."

"What, then?" Jay demanded. "Gold, chromium, nickel, mercury, lithium, tritium, deuterium, helium, aluminum, graphite, detonators, paraffin, centrifuge parts... oh, and genetic equipment, MNNG, Conan the Bacterium, space suits... I don't get it. How the hell does it all fit together?"

"Wait... space suits... there's a shitload of tritium and uranium on the Moon," Ray ruminated.

"The Moon?!" Jay exclaimed. "You gotta be shittin' us, Ray. The MOON??"

"Yeah, Jay. Everybody hush and lemme think a minute," Ray protested. The room quieted, and he grabbed a pencil and paper and began doodling equations and drawings. Unobtrusively, Sam looked over his shoulder.

"Oh, no," she murmured after several silent minutes.

"Oh, yeah," Ray growled affirmation.

"What?" the Old Man asked, and even his voice held the barest hint of dread.

"Listen to this scenario," Ray said grimly. "Fissile material and detonators for a nuke. Tritium and deuterium—from the heavy water—for a hydrogen bomb. But tritium decays fast, and tritium and deuterium gas are hard to handle, so if you want to stockpile it, you store it as lithium-6 deuteride. When the nuke detonates, the lithium takes a neutron hit and splits into tritium. They couldn't get lithium-6, but they COULD get mercury. So they get regular lithium and use mercury to separate the lithium-6 from the lithium-7 isotope."

"How?" Jay wondered.

"Toxic little process where you mix a mercury and lithium amalgam with lithium hydroxide," Ray explained. "The lithium-6 preferentially stays in the amalgam, and the lithium-7 goes into the lithium hydroxide. You can do it safer with a vacuum distillation process, but not only is that inefficient, I'd guess he doesn't have the facilities for it if he's going after the mercury."

"But we haven't seen any sign of mercury toxicity anywhere," Wilson protested.

"On Earth, no," Ray pointed out.

"Space suits again," Kruger guessed.

"Right. Now, here's the fun part. Put 'em all together and use chromium and nickel for the x-ray mirrors instead of uranium and graphite, and what does that spell?"

"Neutron bomb," Kruger sighed, leaning back abruptly.

"Plural—in quantity," Ray added, "by the looks of the numbers."

"Wait, wait, wait," Jay interrupted. "How do you get neutron bombs out of all this shit? I can see nuke, or even thermonuke, but neutron?"

"How much do you know about neutron bombs, Jay?" Kruger asked.

"Not much," Jay admitted. "It was never covered in any of my briefings."

Ray drew in a deep breath, mentally preparing a technical lecture.

"A neutron bomb is a standard thermonuclear device that's been maximized for neutron emission," he explained. "It's all about how it's built. The basis is always a fission bomb. A thermonuclear, or 'hydrogen' bomb, starts off with a fission bomb as the trigger. The fission bomb uses either highly enriched uranium-235 or plutonium-239. The uranium is probably easier to get, especially in yellowcake form, but then you have to process it to enrich it. There's several ways to do that. Early techniques used diffusion processes. During World War II, the S-50 plant at Oak Ridge used thermal diffusion, capitalizing on the fact that U-238 and U-235 diffuse at different rates across a temperature gradient. It wasn't real efficient," Ray noted, "but it worked at the time.

"During the Cold War, they used the K-25 gaseous diffusion plant in Oak Ridge and I think a few other places," he continued. "Helluva big facility was in Oak Ridge, I know. The idea was to react the raw uranium with fluorine to produce uranium hexafluoride, then force it through a semi-permeable membrane. The U-235 hexafluoride was a marginally smaller molecule than the U-238 variety, so it passed through the membrane easier. But it's not a good system. Problem one, it takes six steps just to get from yellowcake to uranium hexafluoride. Two, uranium hexafluoride is corrosive as hell, and they were constantly having to change out parts in the gaseous diffusion system. Three, you get any water in the system and all hell breaks loose. Four, it's toxic as Hades. Five, storage of the waste product is a pain in the ass, both environmentally and safety-wise."

Ray paused to take a breath and gather his thoughts as the others listened.

"Of the more modern techniques," he continued, "you've got a buncha different laser techniques, none of which are actually in production that I know of, mostly due to inefficiency, I suspect. There's an aerodynamic technique which eats power like mad; some chemical methods that aren't in production either; plasma separation, another power hog; the old World War II Calutron electromagnetic method, messy and also requiring lots of power—and then there's centrifuges."

"Aaand we've got centrifuge parts stolen from NASA," Billy noted.

"Yup," Ray agreed.

"Okay, so we've got a standard nuke," Jay verified.

"That's only stage one," Ray elaborated. "The uranium decays naturally, but if you slap enough of the pure 235 together—or for that matter, the plutonium—the fission becomes self-sustaining, and you get the famous critical mass chain reaction."

"And a big boom," Dan interjected.

"Right," Ray said. "But the important part of the thing is that the chain reaction occurs due to the release of neutrons."

"Oookay," Jay said, nodding. "I'm startin' to see where this is going…"

"Now, we use it as a trigger for a thermonuclear bomb as follows: The heat and pressure immediately following the fission explosion is used to compress tritium and deuterium, which then fuse into helium… and release even more neutrons. And I've already explained that the most efficient way to store the fusion fuel is as lithium-6 deuteride. Further, the amount of fissile material can be reduced if a small amount of tritium is put into the fission bomb itself, because it will be forced to fuse and release neutrons, increasing the speed of the chain reaction."

"So why isn't every H bomb a neutron bomb, then?" Jay complained. "I'm not a physicist, Ray."

"I know, Jay, be patient; I'm getting there," Ray said, as the others looked on, interested. "The whole bomb is wrapped in a casing which is designed to contain the energy for the scant nanoseconds needed to maximize the pressures and temperatures, which reach levels close to those of the Sun—"

"Shit," the Old Man exclaimed, shocked. "I didn't know THAT."

"...And which is usually made out of depleted uranium, or U-238, because of its high density," Ray continued as if he'd not been interrupted. "Now, U-238 itself absorbs neutrons, and can be converted to fissile plutonium-239 if it takes a neutron hit. Maybe add some graphite or beryllium in there to aid the neutron reflections. Put it all together, and you've got a bomb that contains the neutrons long enough to maximize explosive force." He paused. "BUT–that is NOT what we want in a neutron bomb. We don't care about explosive force; we want radiation, and lots of it. We want to release the neutrons. So we replace the 'neutron mirror' of the depleted uranium casing and the graphite with something that's essentially transparent to neutrons–like chromium and nickel."

"So the pressure is maintained, but the neutrons get loose," Jay said.

"Right. Now the lethal dose we've been tossing around for humans is ten Grays," Ray elaborated, "because that's a sure-fire dose, but the LD50 is—"

"Da wha?" Billy interrupted.

"Lethal Dose–Fifty Percent. The dose that it takes to kill off half the population. The human LD50 dose is actually around SIX Grays. But the effect is delayed at that level; there's a 'walking ghost' phase. A neutron bomb will pump up the volume to eighty Grays, and will kill at up to twice the range of a conventional nuke. AND will kill INSIDE shielded vehicles and buildings. It can even make the local objects temporarily radioactive, especially if you're sitting in something like a tank with depleted uranium armor."

"But it would lose explosive power, wouldn't it?" Dan asked.

"It does," Ray admitted. "But the tradeoff is considered worth it. It isn't completely nondestructive to infrastructure, contrary to popular belief. It's just a lot more destructive to life than to infrastructure, especially if detonated at the right altitude."

"Dayum," Jay muttered.

There was a long silence.

"Neutron bombs," the Old Man declared solemnly and with conviction. "He's making neutron bombs."

"So how did you make the jump from neutron bombs to the Moon, Ray?" Sam asked.

"Well, I can't be for certain, honey. But we've known about tritium in lunar rock and soil samples since the Apollo program," Ray explained. "Harvard, and the Smithsonian Astrophysical Observatory, and a shitload of other research centers that study lunar samples have proven that. It's theorized to be produced by cosmic ray hits. We also know there has to be uranium, because they've detected radon gas and its daughter product, polonium, from the days of Apollo all the way up through the Lunar Prospector."

"What does radon have to do with uranium?" Billy wondered.

"It's close to the end of the natural uranium decay chain," Ray answered. "At least it is, time wise. In terms of the different elemental isotopes produced, it's probably closer to the middle. It's just that the last of the daughter elements have really short half lives, compared to the first ones." He considered for a minute. "And if he's taking the time to do all this, he needs something stronger than structural aluminum for some things, so I'd bet he's also scooping up ilmenite from the lunar maria, extracting titanium oxides, and refining them for titanium. Light like aluminum, but stronger."

"And ilmenite is?" the Old Man asked.

"Ilmenite is an igneous mineral generally found in alkaline basalts—just the sort found in the lunar maria," Ray added. "And a really good titanium and iron ore."

"Shit, how many degrees Ray got?" Dan muttered under his breath.

"Several," Kruger snapped off.

"Not enough," Ray sighed, rubbing his forehead.

"Okay, so he's what?" Sam got back to their problem. "Scooping up shit off the Moon and loading them into wheelbarrows, then warping them back to Earth?"

"Probably," Ray agreed. "Except for the really nasty parts, like the lithium separation."

"Why haven't we seen signs of lunar activity, then?" Kruger asked.

Ray shrugged. "Who says it has to be on the Earth-facing side of the Moon? Besides, do we even observe the Moon that much these days, let alone with anything of resolution sufficient to see a tiny refining setup? Not to mention the best place to look for some of this is in the polar regions, down in the deep craters, where it's all but impossible for us to see unless we send a probe flying directly over. That gives 'em a ready water supply in the ice there, too."

Shoulders slumped all around the table.

"But the genetic equipment?" Jay pressed. "What's that all about?"

Ray shrugged again. "To make a virus that makes humans more susceptible to radiation, maybe? Or weakens them? Or maybe just to have multiple technological fronts for his attack. Radiological AND biological."

"And the gold?" Sam wondered.

"He BOUGHT the space suits, honey," Ray explained. "And the genetic equipment. Legally. In cash."

"SHIT," Jay said.

℥℧

"So if he bought the suits," Kruger said, after a long silence in which everyone had a chance to absorb the dump of information that had just been presented, "can we trace him?"

"Not quite sure about tracing the man," Ray said, "but I've got the front organization, at least. Dragonfire Enterprises. Claims to work for—get this—the Department of Homeland Security."

"DAMN SON OF A BITCH!" Kruger shouted, half rising from his seat in his fury. His face turned a dusky red. "Under our noses the whole TIME?!"

"Looks like it, sir," Ray said, subdued.

"Calm down, Robert," Sam soothed, alarmed by the severity of the Old Man's reaction. "We found it. Now we'll keep track of it."

"Find out what they're up to, and see if you can get a leg up on 'em by finding or figuring out what's next," the Old Man ordered, curt. "Dismissed."

℥℧

Sitting in the home office with Sam and Jay, Ray suddenly sat up straight. "That's it!" he exclaimed, and the other two jerked upright, turning toward him.

"What's it, Ray?" Sam pressed.

"Detonators!" Ray noted. "Think about how many detonators they got, versus how much fissile material we believe they have."

"Ooo, shit, yeah," Jay realized. "He gotta have at least about twice as many detonators as he's got."

"Plus extras for however much more he plans to get," Ray pointed out.

Sam was already typing on her laptop. "Got 'em," she said. "There's only three real manufacturers of that type of detonator, because of its nature, and that work's classified. Let's go see Robert."

ಶಂಟ್ಸ

"Excellent," the Old Man said in satisfaction. "In that case, we will break up the team into three units. Sam, you'll head up Red Team; Ray, you have Green Team, and Jay, you'll head Blue Team. Choose your targets, lady and gentlemen." He put the page listing the three manufacturers on the table.

"Dibs on this one," Ray said immediately, putting his finger down on the last manufacturer, Sloika Demolitions Manufacturing, Incorporated, just outside Provo, Utah.

"Done," Kruger said. "Sam?"

She pointed at the first entry, Castle Munitions, in Albuquerque, New Mexico.

"Jay, you get Bassoon Industries, in Los Alamos, near the Labs."

"Yes, sir."

"I'm curious, Ray," Sam said, turning to her husband. "Why did you choose Sloika? You seemed really intense, and really specific."

"It's a simple matter of probability, honey," Ray explained. "Sloika is the biggest of the three, with the highest output of detonators of all types, so it's the most likely to get hit."

"Shit," Sam muttered under her breath. "Shoulda done more of the research myself."

"Look, Sam, we gotta stop 'em," Ray said earnestly. "Whatever our anomaly is up to, it isn't good. I don't want to see Abby growing up in fear—or worse, not growing up at all. I don't intend to die, but if it's a choice between me, and you and Abby, I'll take him down with me."

"But you'll be careful."

"He always tries to be careful," Jay vouched for his friend and leader. "Sometimes shit happens, ya know?"

"To Ray more than others," Sam pointed out, "because he jumps in with both feet where angels fear to even tiptoe."

Kruger sat and watched the ongoing discussion, which was becoming heated.

"What do you want me to do, Sam?" Ray asked, exasperated. "I'm doing the best I can."

"Only other thing he can do is command from the rear," Jay muttered in a low tone—one intended to be to himself.

"Not a bad plan, actually, for a change," Sam caught the mumbled comment. "Command from the rear. Hell, Ray, your nose still isn't completely healed! You just took the splint off this morning!"

"Get serious, Sam."

"I AM serious!"

Kruger broke in. "I'm afraid I have to agree with Samantha, Ray," he said. "If you were at a hundred percent, I wouldn't throw my weight into the argument. But you're not, so consider this an order, as I know your wife won't make it: You will command Team Green from the rear."

"Shit," Ray grumbled.

"Excuse me?" the Old Man raised that nonexistent eyebrow.

"Shit, SIR," Ray amended, still annoyed.

The Old Man snorted, letting it go. "Go get your teams ready. I want you on site by tonight, local midnight, at the latest."

ഇറ

They broke the relatively small DSRPO team up into three groups, each having SIGINT experts and medics, and filling in firepower with Marines recently recruited by the Old Man when they'd begun realizing what they might be up against. Doc Fields came along with Team Green. "After all, I gotta be there to patch Ray up after he manages to get the shit beat outta him again," he grumbled, good humored.

"Not this time," Sam had declared. "Robert's ordered him to stay in the back."

"Thank God," Fields said, eyes rolling Heavenward with gratitude. "I can concentrate on keeping everyone else together, for a change."

"Enough," Kruger had ordered. "Go."

They went.

ഇറ

By the wee small hours of the next morning, Team Green was in position inside the Provo munitions plant, with a complete battery of photon detectors ranging across the electromagnetic spectrum aimed at the warehouse stockpile. An impatient Ray tried to sit still and watch the monitors from the command center without pacing or fidgeting.

Team Blue was similarly ensconced in the plant in Los Alamos, New Mexico, Jay watching the monitors closely; and Sam had Team Red in place and watching the facility in Albuquerque.

The digital clocks on their apparatuses flicked the time by slowly.

ഇറ

"Ssst," Skip got Jay's attention. "Jay. Come look at this."

Jay leaned across and looked over Skip's shoulder at one of the monitors. "Shit. That looks like one of those manifold thingits that Ray was talking about."

"Sure does. And it's changing."

Jay keyed the microphone on his shoulder. "All personnel, ready weapons," he muttered. "Incoming bogeys."

ဆဩ

Josh Hamilton leaned over to tap Samantha on the shoulder. "Boss, we got something," he breathed in the dark.

"THE something?" Samantha whispered sharply.

"Manifolds forming, yeah," Hamilton verified. "Up from microwave and into near infrared now."

Sam hit the broadcast button of the mike on her shoulder. "Alert. Anomalies incoming."

ဆဩ

Don Donaldson turned to notify Dr. Brady of what he saw on his monitors, only to find the scientist operative right at his shoulder, staring at the changing images as microwave Möbius strip slowly twirled and re-sculpted into an infrared Klein bottle.

Ray tore his eyes from the displays long enough to meet Don's eyes; Ray's hazel gaze sparkled in excitement. He keyed the mike on his shoulder.

"Get ready, guys. We're about to have company."

ဆဩ

A bright, blue-white flare of light lit the inside of Bassoon Industries' warehouse. When it faded, a dozen men, dressed in dark jumpsuits of a thick material with an odd sheen, heavily armed, stood there. Several pushed hand trucks.

"Steady," Jay murmured into his mike, knowing his team's earpieces would prevent their targets from hearing. "Hold your fire. Let 'em tip their hands. I'll give the call."

Six of the men stayed at the point they'd arrived, while the rest took the hand trucks and headed straight for the stacked crates of detonators. As soon as the first crate of detonators had been loaded onto a hand truck, Jay flicked a switch. Instantly the entire warehouse was flooded with brilliant light. He flipped his microphone to loudspeaker mode.

"FREEZE!" he shouted through the mike. "YOU ARE UNDER AR-REST!"

႘൪ഃ

A bright, blue-white flare of light lit the inside of Castle Munitions' warehouse. When it faded, a dozen men, dressed in dark jumpsuits of some thick material with an odd sheen—which Sam recognized from the bank robbery videos—and heavily armed, stood there. Several pushed hand trucks.

"Easy does it," Samantha breathed into her mike. "Let 'em go for the goods."

Six of the men stayed at the point they'd arrived, while the rest took the hand trucks and headed straight for the stacked crates of detonators. They started loading crates onto the hand trucks, then moving them toward their arrival point.

႘൪ഃ

A bright, blue-white flare of light lit the inside of the Sloika Demolitions warehouse. When it faded, a dozen men, dressed in dark jumpsuits of some thick material with an odd sheen—which Ray recognized from the bank robbery videos—and heavily armed, stood there. Several pushed hand trucks.

"Hold your fire," Ray whispered into his mike. "We're recording. We want the evidence first. Follow my lead."

A tap came on his shoulder. Ray turned. Doc Fields glared at him. Ray keyed the mike.

"…Uh, that is, I'll give the order to take into custody."

Six of the men stayed at the point they'd arrived, while the rest took the hand trucks and headed straight for the stacked crates of detonators. As soon as the first crate of detonators had been loaded onto a hand truck, Ray nodded. Chief Master Sergeant Randy Holmes, by the wall, threw a switch. Instantly the entire warehouse was flooded with brilliant light. Ray flipped his microphone to loudspeaker mode.

"THIS IS THE POLICE! YOU ARE SURROUNDED! PUT DOWN YOUR WEAPONS AND PUT YOUR HANDS ON YOUR HEADS!"

Chapter 8

The group of six anomalies at the arrival area immediately dropped to the floor and targeted their weapons on the direction of Jay's voice. But instead of firing bullets, the large rifle style weapons fired some sort of energy beams. Loud, reverberating hums filled the warehouse from the weapons. "WHOA!" Jay yelled, diving behind a stack of crates as the wall behind him singed. "ALL PERSONNEL, OPEN FIRE!"

The Marines opened up on all twelve anomalies, and it became almost impossible to hear over the echoing din of hums and gunshot reports. One, then two, of the anomalies stacking detonator crates went down, riddled with bullets. But the six in the middle with the heavy energy weapons were, Jay realized, mowing down his troops. One Marine dropped right beside him, a cauterized three inch hole where his nose and eyes used to be. Jay looked down momentarily and saw the gray concrete of the floor through the hole in the man's head, just before brain matter began sagging into the opening. Ten yards away, another fell when his leg was instantly cut from beneath him. Ernie immediately began a combat crawl toward the man, intent on dragging him to safety.

Jay gestured to his top men, and they spread out behind the crates, slinking ninja-like, in an attempt to flank their opponents. Jay managed a shot that took the top of an enemy's head off in a spray of blood, bone shards, and clumps of brain tissue; the man crumpled like a rag doll. Jay ducked and dodged immediately, so that by the time the dead man's colleagues could target where Jay had been, he wasn't there anymore.

Skip and Danny took out a detonator retriever and a firepower, respectively; one in the groin, the other in the back. Both targets were knocked to the floor by the bullets' momenta. Scarlet pools spread around them as they bled out.

But the Marines were going down like flies. Holes appeared in torsos, limbs severed, and heads disappeared. Sometimes, if the anomalies happened to converge on the same man, he was cut in half–or worse. Ernie was kept busy retrieving wounded while their new medic, with little combat experience to speak of as yet, bandaged with all the speed she could muster–which still didn't seem to be enough.

Bullets fired from behind bulletproof barriers were evidently no match for whatever weapons the anomaly team was using. In some cases, if bullet trajectory happened to intersect beam line, the bullet simply evaporated. And transparent bulletproof barriers offered little to no resistance to energy beams.

Through the chaos, the men retrieving the detonators managed to fully load one hand truck, then another, and trundle it, under cover of fire, to the site of their arrival. Then they combat crawled back to their teammates, who were loading a third hand truck. One didn't make it; he lay on the floor in no man's land and bled out. "How long?" another shouted.

One of the anomaly troops glanced away from his rifle sights long enough to check his watch. "THIRTY SECONDS!" he yelled back.

It was the last thing he said, as Jay put a bullet through his eye. But it was enough. Throwing two more crates onto the hand truck, the remaining anomalies scrambled to get it back to their arrival point.

"Shit!" Jay exclaimed, feeling the heat emanating from the direction of the anomalies. "GIVE 'EM ALL YOU'VE GOT!"

A brief spatter of lead was met by the energy weapons, then followed by a retina-searing burst of blue-white light…

…And the anomalies were gone.

ಐംഗ

"How many dead?" Jay asked their new medic, Stephanie Walters.

Walters sighed. "Six enemy—fifty percent—but we got whupped, Major. We've got fifteen casualties, and three wounded, two of those critical. Nearly seventy-five percent of our force got taken down, or out. Whatever the blazes those weapons were, they punched the living daylights out of us. Literally." She paused, solemn. "And, Major… Ernie didn't come back. He's missing."

"Missing?!" Jay exclaimed, horror-stricken. "ERNIE?? No, no, no." He turned slightly, closing his eyes. Dread and pain etched his features.

"Yeah," she murmured. "I'm afraid so. The bad guys didn't seem to care much about this," she gestured at the large red cross she wore on her uniform. "He went in deep to get one of the Marines who got too close, and…" Walters shook her head. "I saw him get hit. It MIGHT'VE been an accident, but… I dunno. Then another Marine literally fell on top of me, and I lost track. I don't know where he is now."

"Probably either dead, or with… THEM. Six of one, half a dozen of the other, since we don't know where they are. Dammit, I can't even mount a rescue! And they still got away with the detonators," Jay grumbled, furious. "Or at least some detonators. SHIT."

"And between them and us, the warehouse inventory is pretty much scrap," Skip noted, gesturing around. Broken crates lay about, spilling their contents onto shelves and the concrete floor. Other crates were riddled with bullet holes, or contained three inch diameter burn holes all the way through. Jay took a look at one, inspecting it with curiosity, and realized he'd been smart to keep in motion. He sighed.

"The Old Man ain't gonna like this," he realized. "Not only did we not stop 'em, I got a big chunk of his new recruits turned into well done hamburger." He shook his head, sick at heart. "I didn't even have the chance to get to know 'em. AND we lost Ernie. ERNIE, of all people! Damn. Now I know how Ray feels about..." He broke off.

"About what?" Walters asked compassionately.

"Nothing," Jay answered somewhat brusquely. "Old history. And need to know."

"Ah," Walters said with understanding. "I'll shut up then."

"Thanks."

"Do you need anything, Major?"

"No," Jay sighed. "A drink, maybe. A stiff one. Are our three survivors patched up?"

Walters nodded. "As good as I can make 'em without a hospital, anyway. Straightedge is seeing to getting them aboard med evac choppers. I'll be going shortly."

Jay nodded numbly. "Guess we need to make like ghosts: clean up this mess as best we can, and disappear."

"What time will you be back at HQ?" Walters wondered.

"Um..." Jay glanced at his watch, then swept his gaze around the warehouse. Skip and the others had already started breaking down their equipment; other stealth choppers outside had dropped off an additional "cleanup crew," to handle body retrieval and blood removal. The damaged inventory would be removed as well, and scorch marks covered or cleaned away. A terrorist robbery would be the explanation; the company hierarchy and security had been clued in on the possibility, but not told its nature. *And I get to tell 'em the government failed to protect their critical equipment,* Jay thought soberly. *While mourning one of my oldest friends, who isn't likely to be coming home. Damn it all to hell and back.*

"We'll be done here in about three hours, then a couple hours to fly back to headquarters," he estimated. "Plus debriefing. Why?"

"I'll be waiting in your office, and we'll go out for that drink you mentioned," Walters elaborated. "In my professional opinion, you could use it. It's on me—medic's orders. Buck up, Major. We'll get 'em back for this."

Jay raised an eyebrow. She smiled at him, a deliberately encouraging expression, then turned and headed for the exit and the med evac chopper beyond. Jay looked her up and down as she departed, truly seeing her for the first time and realizing that she was a very attractive woman. Mentally he suddenly saw an image of Ernie, grinning from ear to ear, and giving him an encouraging wink.

Ernie always was a ladies' man, Jay thought. *The "Latino Lothario," he claimed. He'd... he'd want me to... not to dwell...* He shook himself out of his morose thoughts, and watched the helicopter take off.

"Hm," he said to himself.

૪୦୧୪

"Hey, look at it like this," Skip offered, consoling. "We nailed the site, and we nailed the incoming. They just had us outgunned. Until Ray manages to figure out how to build us shit like their rifles, that's the way it is."

"I know it, but I don't have to like it," Jay growled. "And you aren't the one to have to talk to Ray and tell him our oldest buddy went missing. Let alone report to the company president and head of security and explain that we 'screwed up.'"

"Nope," Skip said, manufacturing a cheerful grin that he really didn't feel. "Above my pay grade, man." He pointed. "Speaking of which..."

Jay looked in the direction Skip pointed and saw two scowling men in suits approaching.

"Shit. It's not even dawn yet." He turned and snapped off a smart salute to Skip, who goggled.

"Wha? You outrank me. What the hell was that about?" Skip wondered.

"'We who are about to die, salute you,'" Jay quoted, and went to meet the president and chief security officer of Bassoon Industries.

૪୦୧୪

"...And we weren't expecting them to have machine guns, let alone white phosphorus grenades," Jay explained, doing his best to translate what happened into something a reasonable layperson could understand and believe. "We got 'em, but they didn't care if they shot the shit out of your warehouse. I'm sorry, sir."

"What about our inventory?" the company president demanded.

"I've got a call—" Jay's cell phone rang just then, and he glanced at the caller ID. "Excuse me, gentlemen," he told the Bassoon executives. "This is precisely the call that should answer your question."

Jay turned away and popped his cell phone. "Major Sampson," he barked officiously. "Yes, sir. Yes sir, that's right. That's exactly the way it went down. Afraid so, sir. Yes sir, I'm sure they will. Thank you, sir. My report will be on your desk an hour after I get back to mine."

He closed the cell phone and turned back to the corporate officials. "I'm authorized to inform you that the U.S. Government will fully compensate your losses," he said. "Since most of your inventory was for us anyway, and since we cleared away the debris to avoid concerning your employees, we'll see what's salvageable and possibly arrange a contract for repair and refurbishment."

"Good," the president remarked gruffly. "Damn ragheads."

"Excuse me, sir, these weren't Middle Eastern," Jay corrected, then ad-libbed. "Homegrown neo-Nazi, we think."

"Oh," the president said, chastised. "Well, damned disrespectful, regardless."

"They are that, sir," Jay sighed, thinking of his dead team members—especially Ernie. "They are, that."

Chapter 9

The men in jumpsuits within Castle Munitions continued loading crates of detonators onto hand trucks. As each truck was loaded to capacity, it was trundled back to the guards. Each of the six workmen had two hand trucks, and each hand truck held five crates. They were getting a lot of detonators.

"Three minutes!" one of the guards called, glancing at his watch.

The workers speeded up. There were already eight full hand trucks ready for extraction, but three were only partly full, and one had just had the first crate loaded. And every one of them knew that if they didn't arrive back with the complete complement, there would be hell to pay.

"Two minutes!"

Two more hand trucks arrived, with a couple of grunts and groans, at the extraction point. The remaining four workers threw crates onto the last two hand trucks at breakneck speed, trying to be barely gentle enough to avoid damaging the contents–which should be well packed in any event. That meant they weren't too gentle.

"ONE MINUTE!"

The four men slammed the last crates onto the trucks and hauled ass over to the huddled group.

The room grew warm. "Mm, feels good," one guard remarked. "It's cold in this drafty old place."

"The hell you say," one of the workers remarked, wiping his sweaty face with his sleeve. "Trade with ya, next time."

His buddy with the energy rifle merely laughed.

There was a bright flash, and all twelve men—and all twelve full hand trucks, complete with sixty crates of detonators—disappeared.

೫೦೦೪

The violated warehouse of Castle Munitions stood black and silent for a full ten minutes. Then the soft sound of a clicking latch echoed from the front door all the way back through the cavernous building. The door eased open, disclosing only more dark, and two Marines slipped through. They disappeared into the dim stacks of crates before being followed by two more, then four. All eight vanished into the stacked inventory.

Two minutes later a radio sounded outside the door. "All clear, ma'am. It's safe to come in."

Samantha Brady strode through the door, munitions expert Peter Hansen at her side. "How many of 'em did they get?" she barked.

"Get of what?" one of the new Marine recruits asked.

"Hang on a sec, Boss, and I'll check," Hansen offered, flicking on a flashlight.

He darted into the depths of the warehouse, running from shelf to shelf, for about another five minutes. Then he arrived back at Sam's side.

"Every last damn one of 'em, Sam," he announced.

"One of what?" the Marine asked again. "Or is that classified, ma'am?"

"It isn't now," Sam grinned, turning toward the Marine. "Gather around, boys and girls, and let me explain what just went down…"

ଫ୦ଔ

The decimated "reclamation team" from Bassoon Industries had just managed to get themselves, the bodies, and their cargo clear of the landing pad when the second team from Castle Munitions, dubbed Beta Team, arrived, smirking from ear to ear.

"Looks like WE got the entire batch," one of the guards gloated, as the Bassoon team, bloody and limping, gladly vacated the landing room. "Not even challenged by the plant guards."

"As opposed to SOME teams we could name," another remarked, condescending. He hit a special button on his watch twice, then turned to the others. "Okay, the boss knows we got the shipment. Now let's get it into the storage room with the batch Gamma Team brought."

The guards shouldered their energy rifles, and each man took firm hold of a hand truck. They grunted and huffed for awhile as they worked the bulky trucks off the landing pads and onto the hard concrete floor. Suddenly one of them snapped his head up, looking around.

"Whose watch is beeping?"

Each man stopped right where he was and checked his watch.

"Not me."

"Me neither."

"Doesn't sound like it's coming from a watch," another decided. "Sounds like…"

"Oh, God," the first exclaimed, realizing. "RUN!"

But before they could do more than turn, the crates on their hand trucks blew up.

ଫ୦ଔ

"Ladies and gentlemen, this is how it's done," Sam smiled without humor. "We arrived early for a reason. We determined, as best we could, the most probable area for these guys to arrive, based on centrality and open space. I concluded that they'd want to have room to move and not well, I dunno if this manifold would, or could, land 'em in the middle of a structure or not. But we assumed they'd want to avoid any chances of same. So we picked the most open area of the warehouse. Then we replaced about a dozen crates of detonators in that location with... special crates. NOT containing detonators. Well, not THOSE detonators, at least." She smirked.

"What was in 'em?" another Marine wondered.

"Depends," Sam's grin grew deeper. "Some of 'em had conventional grenades in 'em. Some had incendiaries. All had mercury fuses that initiated a timer on the grenades. As soon as they moved the crate, the mercury sloshed and started the grenade's countdown timer. I had Pete set 'em for about fifteen minutes to make sure the crates got clear of the warehouse and through these guys' little manifold to the other side. And they should be going off..." she glanced at her watch, "about now." She looked up. "Mr. Marathon Man gets no detonators, and we get no bloodshed among our team."

"And probably none of their team left, either," Hansen pointed out.

"Probably not," Sam agreed. "Mr. Bad Guy, the times they are a-changing." Her entire team smiled wolfishly.

৪০৫৪

The landing pad for the extraction point turned into Hell within moments, as crate after crate detonated in sequence, some spraying jets and spurts of molten iron across the area, others simply exploding. In seconds the soft landing cushions were aflame; what crates contained legitimate detonators were either in splinters, or providing additional fuel for the fires. Beta Team, the unit that Drago had sent to Castle Munitions, dropped where they stood, sliced to ribbons, blinded, or maimed, and burned to death on the floor.

With the flip of a switch in the control room next door, the sprinkler system kicked in, spraying the area with cold water. Other workers hurried in with fire extinguishers and other fire suppressant mechanisms, but there was little that could be done until the oxidizer in the incendiary grenades was exhausted.

By that time, there were no survivors, and no detonators.

There was little that the pad personnel could do. They extinguished burning pads and crate fragments, venting the acrid fumes outside the facility as quickly as possible. Then they dragged out the bodies and debris, and studied the crackled, fractured concrete floor beneath, wondering how on earth they were going to repair it before Dr. Drago found out.

Chapter 10

At Ray's shout, the tightly grouped guards stepped apart, revealing a familiar tall man with vivid blue eyes and spiky blond hair in their center. A small box rested at his feet on a dolly. Crudely stenciled across it in black paint were the words, "ACME BOMB (Dirty)."

"Well, well, well," the blond man said in a voice heavy with sarcasm. "Why am I not surprised? You, sir, are becoming a positive annoyance."

"I could say the same of you," Ray responded in a similar tone.

"I suppose," Drago replied laconically, shoving the box toward Ray's group with his foot. It rolled some fifteen feet away and creaked to a halt. The men with the hand carts stopped dead in their tracks. "The difference is that I know what I'm doing, and you don't."

"I'm here, aren't I?" Ray pointed out.

"You are. And so is that," Drago pointed at the crate marked BOMB. To Ray, it looked like something from a Coyote and Roadrunner cartoon. "Which means I had more of a suspicion than you did." His watch beeped just then, and he checked it, then smiled. "Curious? That was my confirmation that your deductions are less accurate than mine. That was, in fact, my signal that I don't need anything here. I already have all the... supplies... I need." His smile turned into an annoying smirk. "And you are intelligent enough to deduce what THAT means, I expect."

Ray tried not to pale, but it was an autonomic response, beyond his control. *Hell, yeah. It means one of the other DSRPO teams failed. A team led either by my best friend... or my wife. It means they died. It means SOMEbody... died...*

"So." Drago's unnervingly bright blue eyes were fixed on Ray, reading his reactions. "There WERE other teams." He shrugged. "Emphasis on were. So I and my people don't even need to be here. We can just leave."

"I don't think so," Ray snarled, shoving the grief aside and allowing the anger to rise to the surface. He brought up his gun. Instantly all the Marines followed suit, and Drago and his team were encircled in rifle barrels. "I repeat, you're under arrest."

Oddly enough, none of Drago's guards raised their weapons. Instead, the workmen with the hand trucks eased backward until they'd rejoined their companions.

"Oh, I think not. If you knew we would be here, you know what's coming next," Drago went on, calm and unruffled. "We depart, and that," he gestured at the BOMB crate, "stays. And you—and half the city—die."

Ray snorted. "Old cartoon jokes don't impress me."

"Uh, Ray," Don, still at his instrumentation, interrupted. "It's no joke. I show radioactive material in there."

"Hell. No way he'd irradiate himself," Ray scoffed.

"I didn't say there wasn't shielding in there," Donaldson corrected. "I said there was radioactive material in there."

"Explosives?" Ray barked.

"Can't tell from here."

Drago's smirk grew broader. His eyes gleamed oddly. "And I set the timer via remote to go off three minutes after we extract, from my private office, before we ever left to come here. BUT..."

Ray stared holes through him.

"...If you let us go, I'll use the remote to shut off the timer." Drago made a show of patting his pockets down, coming up empty. "Oh, silly me. I left the timer control on my desk... in my private office." He grinned at Ray, raised his hands, and shrugged. "What can I say? We all get absentminded sometimes." He pretended to pause to think, while Ray stole a glance at Donaldson's readouts.

Damn, Ray thought, *Don's right. I can see the seams around the lid of the lead box. Whatever's in there is hot—damn hot.* He gave Don the high sign; Don immediately sent out a coded message to Dime.

"I'll tell you what," Drago spread his hands toward Ray in a placating gesture, still wearing his smirk. "We'll leave, and I promise I'll go straight back to my office and remote it from there."

"Do we have a choice?" Ray snarled, not trusting him for an instant. *But if he's outta the way, we stand a better chance of doing... something.*

"Not really," Drago replied smoothly. "Not unless you MIND dying with most of the city."

The room was getting warmer. Ray glanced at Don, who nodded.

"Lower weapons," Ray ordered the Marines. "Let 'em go."

"Smart man," Drago smiled his most maddening smile. "My comrades, gather yourselves."

The other twelve men huddled close around their leader.

"Here it comes," Don observed.

There was a brilliant flash of light, and they were gone—except for the BOMB.

"GET GOING!" Ray yelled, running for the dolly containing the radioactive material, which he still wasn't sure was really a bomb. And even if it was, the blond bastard might be a man of his word. But he couldn't take the chance. It could be a huge bluff; it could be a bomb that this man really would shut off; or he might shut it off now, only to reactivate it later. "EVACUATE! ALL NONESSENTIAL PERSONNEL OUT OF THE BUILDING IMMEDIATELY! Don, you got Dime standing by?"

"Yeah, and a demolitions team at the nearest abandoned shaft mine," Don verified. "Dime's hovering right outside with a hoist ready."

Ray shoved the heavy box toward the open door. Seeing the effort required, Don and Doc both ran to help him as the Marines filed out through the door as quickly as possible.

"How long we got?" Ray gasped.

"Two minutes, forty-eight seconds," Don panted, glancing at his watch without ever stopping applying his full weight to the dolly.

Twelve seconds later they had it outside in the pre-dawn light and Don was hooking it onto the helicopter's hoist. Ray gave Dime the rotor up motion, and Dime pulled away with the deadly cargo, throttle at maximum.

They watched as he disappeared into the scant twilight of the mountains just to the east.

"God, I hope he makes it," Doc whispered.

"Amen," Ray breathed, fervent.

ഇരുജ

By the light of a clear sunrise, Dime maneuvered deep down a canyon, then followed the slope of the mountain at its end, rising to half the mountain's height, where he saw the smoke from the flares. There, a Navy SEALs demolitions team had been deposited at the mouth of the abandoned Black Cat Mine, opened up the sealed, half-mile deep shaft, and now awaited him and his cargo.

They waved him down, as he delicately maneuvered the dangerous cargo below him, all the while keeping one eye on the 'copter's chronometer. *Already a minute and a half gone and I'm burning seconds lining up with the mine shaft,* he thought, frustrated. *Gotta get this right the first time, 'cause there damn sure won't be a second time. And not much time left.*

Looking down, he saw one of the SEALs give him the thumbs up. "Gah!" he instinctively cried, hitting the cable release. The helicopter immediately recoiled upward slightly as the crate with the bomb plummeted downward.

With great skill, Dime used the recoil to aid in maneuvering his craft away from any possible upward blast—which also gave him a clear view as the Looney Tunes crate vanished into the black opening of the deep mine shaft. Navy SEALs took to their heels, getting as far away as they could, vanishing into the underbrush. Dime counted down the seconds on the chronometer then, watching as they ticked slowly by.

At five seconds after the crate had vanished, an explosion rose from the upper mountainside, and the rock and dirt slumped down and inward, filling the mine shaft and burying the crate beneath tons and tons of rock. The side of the mountain kept moving until the mouth of the mine was completely hidden. Gradually the dust thrown into the air settled, and Dime could look down on the raw earth where scrubby vegetation and a black maw had been moments before.

Thirty seconds later, the still settling debris bulged outward slightly, as something buried deep beneath exploded.

Chapter 11

Drago—and his team—landed with an unaccustomed thud on crackled, scorched, pitted bare cement and looked around.

"What the hell happened here?!" he shouted in outrage.

"A trap, sir," one of the extraction point technicians explained, anxious. "The first team encountered heavy resistance and came back pretty badly shot up. They had some of the cargo, but weren't able to get all of it. They DID have a wounded hostage, the team's medic judging by the Red Cross insignia, but he died about five minutes ago despite medical attention. The second team brought back everything–except it was booby trapped. They didn't even get off the mats before all hell exploded out of those crates."

"What sort of hell?" Drago demanded.

"Incendiary hell," the techie sighed, paling, his eyes going distant.

Drago looked into those eyes, seeing their haunted expression, and eased his tone, but anger still raged within him.

"Send me the team leader," he ordered.

"I would if I could, sir," the tech replied, snapping back to the present and growing paler. Drago did not think the pallor was from fear of his superior, either.

"Dead?" he asked the tech.

"Yes sir. All of them, sir. The entire team. It was…" The tech suddenly went white, wheeled, and bolted for the bathroom, just off the landing pad control room. Drago watched him go.

"That bad, eh?" he asked the air.

"Yes sir. Really bad," another tech answered from the control room doorway. His tone, too, was very subdued.

Drago sighed.

"Darwin Awards," he muttered. "The lot of them. And that… MAN, that… infernal NUISANCE… still thwarted me! If no team successfully brought back a complete load, we are lacking sufficient detonators!"

"We have some, sir," the second tech offered. "Probably a good third of a load, maybe a little more. Maybe as much as half. That's enough to get started, with what we already had."

"True, Williams," Drago said, looking up. "Very true. Any indications of a nasty explosion in the industrial district of Provo, Utah? Or anywhere in or around Provo at all, for that matter?"

"No sir," Williams answered, "not that we've heard."

"I figured as much. He is crafty, that one. A worthy opponent, possibly one of Them—although his strength belies it. I shall have to devise another means of ridding myself of the nuisance. And in the meanwhile, I want you," he turned to his own retrieval team, "to debrief the team that brought back our hostage, and see what you can find out that may aid me in that effort. Anything you find, bring it to me immediately—my office will be open. I want That Man out of my hair—permanently."

"Yes sir," his team leader snapped off.

Drago spun on his heel, then turned back.

"Oh. Find something personal on the dead hostage and send it back through the extraction point to the warehouse he came from," he said. "If you can't find anything distinctive, cut off his hand and send it through. His fingerprints should be sufficiently... unique."

"Yes, sir," the tech replied through clenched teeth.

And Drago headed for his office.

ဿလ

"Look at this, sir," one of Drago's men said, coming into his open office a little while later. "I just found this on the body of the dead hostage the other team brought back. It was in his wallet."

Drago stared down at a photograph. It was an image of a tiny baby in a pink onesie with wide blue eyes, a blond fuzzy head, and an adorably big smile. "Hm," he said. "Relatively recent photo, too. Maybe... a year or so old?"

"Yes, sir, that's what we estimated. Could be his, could be a teammate's. Either way..." The man shrugged.

"Well, it's a starting place, I suppose," Drago decided. "I want this group—this MAN—out of my way once and for all. Get the computer people on this. Search every hospital obstetrics ward in the whole damn United States if you have to, but find this baby. From there, perhaps, just perhaps, we can trace her back to someone that will prove... useful."

"Yes sir." The subordinate shrugged. "Or... we could just snatch the baby and ransom it: the baby in exchange for letting us alone."

"Ha ha!" Drago grinned. "You, my boy, are going to go far in my organization. An excellent idea. By the way, has the hand—or any other trifle—been sent back to his teammates?"

"Not yet, sir. There's still some time to the extraction point, so we were doing a thorough search of the body and we found that," he pointed at the photo, "going through the dead guy's shit."

"Does he have a name, this 'dead guy?'"

"Staff Sergeant Ernie Travers, according to his ID. Looked to be a real medic, judging by all the tools and gauze and crap in his pockets. Initially we thought it might just have been a ruse, 'cause the other team said he was only getting the wounded and bringing 'em back to the other medic to patch up. But no, he was the real thing."

"And they shot a medic in cold blood? Usually such men are altruistic. Might he have actually been trying to assist one of ours?"

"No, sir. It was an accident, sir," the man reported. "He raised up into the line of fire–to tend to his wounded, we think. It was unexpected."

"Did they GET any of ours?"

"Alive? No sir."

Drago nodded in thought. Finally he looked up.

"Has he been tested?"

"No sir. Do you want that?"

"I do."

"I'll contact the sawbones and get him to come for a DNA sample, then."

"Very good. Make sure you have searched the body VERY thoroughly, keeping anything that may be of use to us. Then send it back through the extraction point to the warehouse. They should still be repairing the damage there, according to the debrief report from Team Gamma, and they can damn well clean up their own mess. No sense cluttering up our place with a useless corpse; we have enough of our own, after this debacle. Now hop to it. And don't forget the baby."

"Yes, SIR!"

୫୦୧୫

"Oh. What?" Drago had been deep in thought—the eyes of the baby in the photograph had been hauntingly familiar, and he was puzzling over whether she was whom he suspected—and hadn't realized that several hours had passed. That is, until his secretary gently tapped him on the shoulder and handed him a report, withholding another. He took the proffered folder and opened it.

"As I suspected," he murmured. "Contaminated. Just as well, then." He closed the folder and tossed it aside.

The secretary handed him the second folder, and he flipped through it nonchalantly at first. Then his eyes widened and an eyebrow raised.

"They've found the hospital where the baby was born, sir," she said. "Springfield, Virginia Memorial."

"Unbelievable," Drago exclaimed. "Not everyone here is a dunderhead after all. Excellent, Brenda. Have Barton assemble a little 'away team.' I'll lead it."

"Will do, sir," Brenda said, exiting the room.

"Now, Mr. Whoever-the-Hell-you-are, we'll see if we can't put a cramp in your style. Or at least slow you down." Drago kicked back in his chair, a pleased smile on his face, and hummed to himself.

୫୦୧୪

A bright light flared in the darkened archives room of Springfield Memorial Hospital, around two in the morning. Several men in dark uniforms and masks, and one blond man in trousers and shirt, stood in the room when it dimmed once more.

"Spread out and search," the blond—Dr. William Drago, of course—ordered. "Bring me anything pertinent you find."

They were there for an hour, half of the men searching the files, the other going through security videos. "Boss! Uh, Dr. Drago!" one of the video watchers suddenly hissed. "Over here! Look! It's the dead guy!"

Drago strolled over to watch the imagery of the DSRPO man—Ernie—walking cheerfully down a hospital corridor, carrying a soft plush teddy bear and a bouquet of flowers, then stop in front of a room and knock. Within seconds the door was answered–by the man that had been the thorn in Drago's side.

"It's him! The guy! The guy that Dr. Drago fought in New York City!" another subordinate exclaimed, looking over Drago's shoulder. "Got to be the ringleader! We'll get you, buddy!"

Drago smiled, a cold, malicious smile.

"Freeze image," Drago ordered. "Zoom in. Get the room number."

"Right, sir." The lackey did as ordered, and Drago read off the screen.

"Obstetrics ward, room 204," Drago read aloud. "September twenty-third of last year, by the video timestamp."

"Hold on juuust one minute, Boss." One of his men dug energetically through a filing cabinet. "Here we go, Baby Brady, female, born that day." He leafed through the folder he'd extracted. "Boss! Look at this! It's him!" He extracted a photo and handed it to Drago.

Drago looked down to see a family photograph of Samantha, Ray, and baby Abigail Brady, taken shortly after birth. Samantha was still in bed, swathed in a hospital gown, as she and Ray beamed out of the picture.

"Well, well, well," Drago murmured, smile widening. "What do we have here? Such a delightful little family scene. So much love. Don't you think so?"

His accomplice merely sneered. "You want us to kill 'em, Boss?"

"You can try," Drago shrugged, thoughtful. "Abigail Brady, you said?"

"Yes sir."

"ABIGAIL Brady. Now how about that? William, my boy, do you think... yes," Drago murmured to himself. "Yes, it makes a certain... sense. Abigail, soon we shall once again meet face to face. Indeed, little lady, time allows for things to happen, most unusual things."

Chapter 12

Ray had moved as fast as he could to get his mission wrapped up and then back to DSRPO headquarters. News of casualties had been filtering in throughout the afternoon but the news he'd be waiting for had yet to come. He strode in the lead of his team, head seeming to swivel nearly three hundred degrees as he scanned anxiously for two of the three people in the world he cared about most. Behind him, a member of one of the other teams came up to Doc, whispering something in his ear. The two headed off in the direction of Medical, at top speed.

Jay and Sam were standing together in an alcove, chatting quietly, looking solemn. The sight caused Ray's blood pressure to drop and his heart rate to slow slightly.

He ran to them, picking Sam up and swinging her around before planting a hard kiss on her lips.

"Oh, hot stuff!" Ray began, turning to Jay and giving him a man hug and slapping him on the back.

"He was there?" Sam queried sharply.

"Yeah, him and a Wyle E. Coyote dirty bomb," Ray growled. "He said one of our teams went down and he had everything he needed. He didn't even try to get any detonators."

"HA!" Sam exclaimed. "It worked!"

"What worked?" Ray wondered.

"Sam proved sneakier than any of us, Ray," Jay said soberly. "While my team was involved in a shootout, she just let 'em waltz in and take what they wanted, unmolested…"

"Except for the mercury fused grenades I had Peter put in the crates," Sam grinned.

"So they didn't get anything?" Ray asked hopefully.

"Not from Sam's team," Jay murmured, downcast. "They got maybe about a third of their intended load from us, judging by the equipment they had."

"How many?" Ray shot a keen look at his best friend.

"Eh, 'bout twelve, MAYBE fourteen. Not QUITE one third."

"No, Jay. I meant personnel. How many did you lose?" Ray's tone was gentle.

"About seventy-three percent, down or out," Jay said with a hang-dog expression, looking up to meet Ray's eyes, his own apologetic almost to the point of pleading. "Ray... one of 'em was Ernie."

There was a dead silence. Ray merely blinked, trying to accept the dreadful information that had just been so baldly presented.

"From what Jay's been telling me," Sam added, voice soft as she laid a hand on Ray's shoulder, "one of the new Marine recruits got too close to the main group of bad guys, and got himself popped. Ernie went in to get him—and got shot, too."

"Then," Jay said, voice raw as he tried to keep it from cracking, "when they all warped out, Ernie was within range and got taken with 'em."

"Oh, God," was all Ray could think of to say at first. Then he added, "We gotta find these bastards, fast! Don't worry, Jay. We'll get Ernie out!"

Jay shook his head, more downcast than Ray had ever seen him.

"He's out. While we were cleaning up the warehouse, the manifolds started forming again, so we got outta sight and waited. When the... thingamawhatchie... came and went, Ernie's body was lying on the warehouse floor. They... sent him back."

"His pockets had been rifled," Sam noted, "but they sent him back to us. I'm not sure what that says about 'em..."

Ray swallowed hard, but said nothing.

"We think cause of death was the original wound," Sam offered.

"Yeah. Looks like they actually tried to take care of 'im, 'cause he had a bandage on, but he was hurt too bad," Jay sighed. "No signs of further wounding. They didn't do anything else to him." He glanced over at Ray's team, milling about with the other teams. "I don't see Doc. He's probably off to tend the wounded and do an autopsy on Ernie, make sure they didn't actually..." his voice tapered off.

Ray's shoulders slumped.

Jay put a hand on one of those shoulders.

"I am so sorry, man," he whispered, contrite. "It's... it's all my..."

"No," Ray declared, in a voice stronger than either of them had expected. "No, it's not. Take care of yourself, Jay. I'm not going to lose you, too."

And he headed for the debrief, leaving Jay and Sam staring after him.

ജഇ

The debrief in Kruger's conference room was an odd blend of solemnity and exultation.

"Well, the good news is," Kruger decided, "by the sound of it, they didn't get all they needed, by a long shot."

Heads nodded in agreement all around the room, but no one said anything.

"The bad news is, we lost a lot of our boys and girls—including one of our oldest team members," he continued.

"I'm gonna miss Ernie," Doc murmured, sad.

"Cause of death?" Ray almost snapped, breaking the solemn mood.

"His one and only wound," Doc shook his head. "The energy ray blast seems to do a reasonable job of cauterizing, but when it nicks the descending aorta, well…"

Ray nodded without replying.

"I… I'm sorry, guys," Jay murmured into the silence. "I pulled an OK Corral and didn't even think about the Clantons being better armed than us Earps. I never once thought about doing it any other way." He glanced at Samantha with respect. "I… stand by to be relieved of duty, sirs, ma'am."

Ray waved a dismissive hand.

"Same thing would've probably happened with my team, Jay," he told the other man, "if this anomaly dude hadn't brought a bomb of his own and held us in a standoff with it." He glanced at his wife. "Sam was the only leader of the lot who thought 'outside the box,' as it were. Maybe… maybe it's time for me to step down as field leader."

Eyebrows shot up all around the room at that. Several jaws gaped.

"Why, Ray?" Samantha asked softly, as Kruger watched, one worried eyebrow knit with the scarred ridge where the other eyebrow should have been.

"You and Doc are right, Sam," Ray explained. "I lead with my face too much. If someone else were in charge, somebody who thought differently, whose tactics were smarter, less, I dunno, confrontational, maybe we'd still have a full contingent of new recruits. And Ernie."

"More likely," the Old Man stepped in, "we'd have lost most of 'em, instead of just part of 'em. You've got more field experience than anybody else in this room, Ray, barring me, and I can't do it anymore. Don't beat yourself up because you and Jay did exactly what I expected of you. Either of you."

"But Sam…" Jay began.

"Did something different because I DON'T have the field experience," Sam expostulated. "I had a field team leadership on my hands, and, while I know I can put up a good fight personally, ordering personnel around in a combat situation is NOT my forte. So when you guys went off to do your things, I decided to do what I know I do best—work behind the scenes to bollix up the machinery."

"Despite our losses," the Old Man declared, "which are many and painful, I must decree this mission a success, ladies and gentlemen. We successfully predicted their strikes, we observed their incoming blips—even when we weren't expecting another," he glanced at Jay with approval, "and we prevented their obtaining anywhere near the quantity of detonators they needed or wanted. Granted, they got some, and that IS a concern. Still, for a first go, we did well."

Ray, Jay, and Sam nodded in a discouraged fashion.

"No one will be relieved of duty OR reassigned," Kruger went on. "You did fine, all of you, and I expect you to continue doing so. In your own distinctive ways," he added. "Just learn from this and do better next time."

"Only try not to lead with your nose so much, Ray," Doc grumbled. Ray closed his eyes.

"Team dismissed," the Old Man ordered, and the group filed out.

ॐ

Ray and Sam trailed a depressed Jay back to his desk, determined to do something to cheer him up. The problem was, Ray wasn't in any better mood. Samantha decided she had her hands full.

"We lost one of the Musketeers," she murmured. "But at least my D'Artagnan still has the both of you to lean on."

"Porthos," Jay murmured. "'Cause he loved the good life, outside o' work. He just didn't live long enough to get fat."

Ray stopped dead in the corridor.

"Waitaminit," he said. "If Ernie was Porthos, and Sam is D'Artagnan, which of us is Athos, and which is Aramis?"

"You're Athos, Ray," Sam decided. "But Aramis doesn't exactly fit Jay, I'll admit."

"Does that make our Marathon Man the Countess de Winter?" Ray wondered, wearing a sour look. "Eiugh. I swear I've had nothing to do with the man, ever."

That got a chuckle out of Jay despite himself. Sam threw a triumphant glance at Ray, who returned it in a more subdued fashion. Then they noticed the young woman waiting at Jay's desk ahead.

"Who's that?" Ray wondered.

"Medic," Jay remembered. "I almost forgot. EMT Stephanie Walters. She was Ernie's second, and she said I needed a drink. Kinda..." He flushed slightly, and Sam and Ray managed to avoid raising eyebrows, "kinda 'prescribed' it." The trio walked up to the waiting woman. "Hi," Jay said.

"Debrief was a bitch, huh?" Stephanie said quietly.

"It was… rough," Jay admitted, "but not because anybody MADE it rough."

She nodded understanding.

"Ms. Walters—"

"Call me Stevie, please."

"Stevie, this is Dr. Ray Brady, and his wife Samantha Brady," Jay introduced his companions. "Ray, Sam, meet Stevie. She is a damn good EMT."

"Wow," Stevie murmured, shaking their hands. "The top dogs."

"Are we interrupting anything?" Sam asked. "We were just trying to cheer Jay up."

"No, no," Stevie said. "That was my intent, too. He was pretty upset by losing Ernie. I gathered he and Ernie go way back."

"Ray, Jay, and Ernie were the team's founders," Sam explained without going into detail. "They've been together… a long time."

"Oh," Stevie said, eyes wide. "Then why don't you guys join us? I was just going to take Jay—er, Major Sampson—out for a drink when he got off duty, help him get his head back on right."

"I'm off duty now," Jay observed, "and hell yeah."

"That sounds like a nice idea," Samantha decided, eyeing Ray.

"Great! The Marine units went to their favorite bar about an hour ago. Are there any others from the debrief that could use a drink?" Stevie wondered. "There's a nice little pub over in Del Ray called The Cherry Tree. That's where I figured to take Jay."

"Yeah, there are, yeah, I know the place, and I've got an idea," Ray said, extracting his cell phone. "Why don't we make this a wake?"

"Excellent idea," Sam agreed, as Stevie nodded vigorously.

ಬಂಡ

The core team took over the back room of the pub, ordered pitchers of beer, and sat around swapping stories about Ernie, mostly funny, some giving the measure of the man.

Ray and Jay managed to tell unclassified versions of their first meeting with Ernie, by way of leaving out all mission details, so Sam found out a little about the scar on Ray's right shoulder. Neither of them said anything about the Iranian mission, however.

Stevie, sitting beside Jay, commented to the others about how Ernie had made a gentle pass at her when she'd first come on board the team, not realizing that she WAS part of the team. Then he'd hastily apologized when he found out she was his new assistant, noting that he never mixed work and pleasure.

"It must have been a recent policy of his, then," Sam snorted. She proceeded to tell them all how, when she and Kruger were recruiting their first team members—Ernie, Jay, and Ray—Ernie, the first to awaken, had made a pass at her—with his face still completely covered in bandages. And tried again even after accepting the invitation to join DSRPO. "It was like having The Invisible Man flirt with me," she giggled.

Ray scowled briefly, a hint of possessive jealousy surfacing, and Sam pointed out, "Honey, you hadn't even woken up from the surgeries yet." That settled Ray, who didn't really believe Ernie would have tried to undercut him anyway.

"None of you newer guys really know this, but Ray didn't give me the nickname 'hot stuff.'" Sam continued sipping her drink. "It was Ernie. He continued to call me Hot Stuff from the first time we met and even after Ray and I became an obvious item."

"You know, Ray's been calling you that for so long that I'd forgotten about it," Jay added.

"Yep. Leave it to Ernie to give my wife a lover's nickname that stuck forever." Ray smiled and fought back tears.

To everyone's surprise, the Old Man walked in just then to join them. He mostly sat in the corner and listened to all the stories, but he did tell one revealing tale about the comrade they'd all lost.

"I'm sure you all remember a few years ago, that bad winter we had with the influenza epidemic," Kruger began, and the room fell silent out of respect for their top leader. "Back when we thought we had that anomaly in Brussels. And how I caught the flu, and—yes, Dr. Fields, I know I didn't slow down like I should have…"

"It's no wonder you picked Ray," Fields grumbled. "Peas in a pod. You were probably just like him, in the day."

"We are, and I was," the hint of a smile graced the Old Man's lips. "I sure as hell didn't lose this eye in a dart game. Anyway, you assigned Ernie to me, to ensure my resulting bronchitis didn't go into full fledged pneumonia."

"Yeah, I remember," Fields averred, as the others in the room nodded. "I had to get SOMEone to ride herd on you."

"It might have been a wiser decision to pick someone other than Ernie," the Old Man's ghost of a grin widened a bit. "He didn't ride herd quite as hard as you hoped he would."

"Oh? How so?"

"After work, instead of seeing me straight home through the snow and ice and into bed, I convinced him to go out for a drink with me," Kruger admitted. "It didn't take much twisting of his arm. He'd been on that task for a solid week at that point, and both of us were about stir crazy. So we went over to my favorite watering hole. I'm sure, judging by some of the stories already told, that everyone remembers how fond Ernie was of the ladies…"

A chorus of "yeah, uh-huh," went around the pub's back room.

"Did he find one?" Ray wondered, a wide smile on his face.

"He did, indeed," Kruger grinned back. "A lovely thing she was, too. Platinum hair so fair it was nearly white, pale blue eyes, porcelain skin, buxom, curvaceous, all the things Ernie liked in a woman. First he sent her a drink, then, when that was accepted and eye contact made, he moved to her booth in the corner. Oh, don't worry, John," he told Fields, who had scowled, "he kept an eye on me, too.

"Judging by her complexion and what tidbits I could overhear of what passed for a conversation—and there wasn't as much talking as I'd have expected, either, and you can draw your own conclusions about that— she was from one of the Scandinavian countries. I didn't hear enough to determine which one," the Old Man reminisced. "But they seemed to, er, get their meanings across well enough, if you know what I mean."

A laugh went up.

"Finally she passed a slip of paper across to Ernie, gave him a long, lingering kiss, and left the bar. Ernie all but floated back to my table and commenced to tell me how wonderful she was. 'We didn't speak the same language,' he'd declared, 'but the language of love knows no bounds.'" Kruger was doing an excellent job of mimicking Ernie's slight Latino accent. Ernie, the others knew, had mostly lost or ditched it over the years, especially after accepting the DSRPO offer and a new identity, but had never completely lost some of the consonantal rolls.

This time the gathered team guffawed.

"That is SO Ernie," Jay averred between fits of laughing.

"Then he informed me that he had found 'the one,' and that there was a torrid affair in the offing," the Old Man said, smiling gently. "His face— Ernie was a gentle man to begin with; most healers are—but I swear his eyes were glowing. 'I'm going to call her later,' he told me, 'and set up a little, er, meeting.'" Kruger shook his head and squelched a grin, knowing what was coming.

"'See? She gave me her phone number,' he told me, and handed me the slip of paper," Kruger continued the story. "I took the paper and looked at it, and... well..." he broke off.

"What?" Sam demanded. "What happened, Robert?"

"I looked at Ernie, as seriously as I knew how, and I said, very pointedly, 'Ernie, this isn't a phone number.' Ernie looked a little puzzled. 'What do you mean? Of course it is,' he vouched. 'And she and I will be having a little liaison later this evening, after I have seen you home and in bed.'"

"'Ernie,' I tried again, 'this is NOT a PHONE number.' He glared at me and demanded to know, if it wasn't a phone number, what the hell it was. Well, there was no getting around it at that point. I'd tried to give him a hint, but he wasn't taking it, so I had to tell him. 'It's her price.'"

The room exploded in laughter.

Ray lifted his mug of beer. "To Ernie Travers," he announced, "the Latino Lothario. May his memory remain ever green."

"Amen," the others chorused, and they drank.

℘ℭ℘

The Bradys had each had more than enough alcohol at the wake. Emotions of sadness and happiness filled them both. Ernie had been a good friend and colleague to them for years. Ray knew better than to drive at that level of intoxication but the two of them had gotten caught up in the evening. The traffic down the George Washington Parkway was minimal at that time of the night so at least they weren't likely to get into an accident, barring stray deer.

"Maybe we should've taken a cab," he half-heartedly told Sam.

"You okay?"

"Well, we're only another couple miles from home." Ray thought about it for a moment. "You know what?"

"What's up?"

"Abby is in good hands. Let's take a detour." Ray pulled the SUV off at King Street.

"Where we going?" Sam leaned her head over onto his shoulder, propping her elbow on the console and inadvertently setting off one of Abby's stuffed talking animated creatures.

"I can swing my arms, side to side..."

"Shit." Sam swatted at the little blue spotted dog and knocked it into the floor. It continued to sing. Her level of inebriation intrigued Ray.

"Hit it again, hot stuff, that'll learn 'im." He laughed as Sam fumbled for the thing in the floorboard and finally got it shut off. "Remind me not to let you disarm any improvised explosive devices after you've been drinking."

"Never was dexterous drinking," Sam smiled.

"Yeah? What are you good at after drinking?" Ray pulled the car into Jones Point Park and found a dark corner to park overlooking the Potomac River. Almost immediately Sam's seatbelt snapped free and she was crawling over the console onto his lap.

"I might can think of a few things." Sam pressed her lips against Ray's aggressively.

"I see." He slid his hands up her ribs underneath her blouse and then around her back to pull her closer to him. A second or two was all he needed for her bra to be undone.

"Now who's dexterous?" she said playfully and slid her bra out through her left sleeve.

"Mmm…" Ray groaned as she ground against him and he cupped her breasts in his hands.

Honk. Sam leaned back against the horn. The two of them laughed together like high school kids on a first date. Getting caught up in the moment was a very effective means of forgetting about nuclear terrorists, super bacteria, and dead colleagues.

"Shh. We're gonna wake up somebody." Ray laughed through kissing his wife.

Sam worked her hands down Ray's buttons, undoing them quickly. She then unbuckled his belt and zipper. Ray slid her skirt up above her hips, grabbing her buttocks as her chest heaved up and down in anticipation. Finally, Sam had him at attention and free of his underpants. She worked herself on top of him and slid her panties to one side, taking him into her. She sighed out slowly at first. Ray could feel her warm moist breath against his ear.

"Mmmm…" Ray groaned and thrust his pelvis upward into his wife's.

"I love you," Sam whispered into his ear as she bit it.

"I love you too, hot stuff."

Chapter 13

At some point the action in the car had settled down. Sam and Ray had held each other until they had almost fallen asleep when there was a knock on their window and a flashlight in their faces. Some fast talking to the Alexandria policeman and the rest of a short drive home left them exhausted and collapsing in bed. Ray would have been able to muster up the energy for another round but the two of them were tired. Not just physically tired, but deep down emotionally and psychologically tired. Following a quiet peek at their daughter, they drifted to sleep pretty quickly in each other's arms. And then, soon, Ray was fitfully asleep.

He'd known it would happen tonight, after the events of the day. After... Ernie. At least flashbacks only occurred in his sleep, now. He was back in Afghanistan again.

The CIA didn't normally send him in for missions of this type, but they were obviously concerned that Ibn bin Ibrahim had managed to get his hands on some serious munitions, and wanted to know what was going on. So Dr. Raymond Bradford, specialist in half the sciences known to man, had been put in charge. His liaison had been a capable young lieutenant just making a name for himself in military intelligence, if "making a name" was a phrase that was applicable in intelligence work: one Lieutenant James Samuels, "Jay" for short.

Up in the mountains, they hiked along in heavy disguise, which even included colored contact lenses, dressed in peasant garb appropriate to the region, rough homespun long, caftan like chapuls topped with pakul hats and lungee turbans, clandestinely scouting the area. Somewhere nearby, they knew, was bin Ibrahim's hideout—a network of tunnels and caves housing some one hundred men, with concomitant substantial weaponry. Their intent was to pass themselves as recent recruits to the jihad and infiltrate the group, determine what they had, then plant a homing device and slip out.

It had worked... almost.

৪৩

Ray stirred in his sleep, his dream memories disturbing his rest. He bumped Sam, and Sam merely sighed without awakening, rolling over to snuggle into Ray's side. The skin to skin contact soothed Ray, and he settled back down.

৪৩

They'd been there just over a week. They'd located the main munitions cache, schmoozed with the worker bees, and managed to get glimpses of bin Ibrahim and his lieutenants, huddled in conclave–which, the spies found out, they usually were, save for meals only.

Once everything was positively identified, they began planting the homing devices. Devilish little things, designed by some Army intelligence officer. That guy with the vivid blue eyes, Ray's dream self recalled… that had been why he was in the pre-brief… the devices looked like large granite pebbles, and operated in a hopping frequency spectrum that no one who didn't know what to look for would find. A couple in the munitions dump, a couple more in the cave reserved for bin Ibrahim's meetings—which was very nearly in the center of the complex, but near the surface—planted during mealtime, and they were done.

They'd been caught on the way out by the sentries. When the guards hadn't believed their explanation that they'd been sent on a clandestine mission by bin Ibrahim's second in command, Mohammar Muhammed Khurezi—an explanation delivered in perfect regional dialectic Afghan—and instead accused them of cowardice, there was only one thing they could do.

Ray had pulled out his gun and shot one of them.

The gun battle was fierce but brief. Ray took a hunk of lead in the right shoulder, but otherwise, they'd made it away clean, running like hell into the nearest ravine before the main camp could come after them, leaving three dead guards behind.

And they had kept right on running, all through the night, until they'd reached the extraction point. There, a Marine Osprey and two SuperCobras had awaited them. Out of breath, they called the code word even as they bailed into the Osprey, and the aircraft took off.

As the Osprey accelerated toward the border, the SuperCobras hesitated, turning. Dr. Bradford looked out the window even as the young medic he'd met for the first time seconds earlier, Ernesto Torres, treated his shoulder. He knew they were searching for the homing signal, which Jay had been careful to place on the largest munitions cache in the caves.

Abruptly, both helicopters unleashed every missile they had, then turned and followed the Osprey at top speed.

Behind them, it appeared as if a volcano had erupted, deep in the mountains of Afghanistan.

৪০০৪

Ray rolled over, this time to spoon against Samantha. He let out another sigh, and he was back in the Middle East with his original, pre-DSRPO team. But this time it had been Iran.

ঋৎওভ

Once they'd gotten close to the suspected nuclear weapons facility, they'd changed from mountain farmers to reasonably well dressed workers, complete with faked identification, thanks to some of Raymond's colleagues in the CIA. The clothing cache had been right where Ray's briefing had said it would be, completely undisturbed.

They'd slipped neatly into the facility during the dawn shift change, and each of them had taken up a different worker's position, tiny hidden button cameras and recorders gathering information. Ray's brain did considerably more of that than any electronic device could, however, and it didn't take him long to realize that not only were the Iranians working on nuclear weaponry, they had it in active production. Everything in the facility was highly compartmented, and nothing was labeled in such a way that the relatively uneducated workers could make anything of it other than a way to earn more money than a mountain farmer could. Still, for someone with Ray's high level of knowledge and extensive background, the clues he found were more than enough. He knew advanced missile guidance and homing technology when he saw it, and had been around the scientific block enough to recognize radiation shielding, too, no matter how carefully disguised.

'Shit,' he thought. 'An Iranian Manhattan Project. This is so not good for any American ally in the entire region.'

At lunch break, he'd given his fellow operatives the high sign. At sunset, they wandered out of the facility as if going to nearby farm huts, each taking separate routes. On the way out, Ray had bumped into a "co-worker" in the doorway. Their eyes met for a moment beneath their headgear; Ray wore a shearling cap, but the other man wore a turban, completely covering his head. Dark beards covered most of the rest of their faces. Both wore long embroidered tunics and loose pants, with woolen coats over all to protect against the cold of the mountain evening.

'Huh,' Ray had thought, 'odd for Afghanis to have such blue eyes AND pale skin. But that tends toward a recessive trait, so it's not impossible, I guess. Musta had an ancestor come down over the mountains from the north.'

After dark, the infiltration team met up at the cache site and changed back into farmer's togs, being careful to bring along the miniaturized surveillance equipment, and made for the extraction point.

෩ඏ

Ray squirmed a little, kicking off the covers. Samantha, cold, pressed against his muscular, warm body. He grew still again.

෩ඏ

He relived the mine field incursion, the bits of human flesh that had battered their humvee, the Marine sailing through the air. The call for the same medic who'd patched up his shoulder coming out of Afghanistan. The discussion of how best to retrieve Smith. And the failure of the resultant plan.

'Nightmare,' some part of his brain decided. And it had been, then, and now. But he'd survived it, and so had Jay and Ernie. But none of them were the same anymore. 'We all died that day,' his subconscious realized. 'Bradford, and Samuels, and Torres. All dead.'

Because that had been when Sam and the Old Man had shown up.

෩ඏ

"Hello there, Doctor," the Old Man had said. "My name is Robert Kruger, and this is my second, Agent Samantha Waters. We have a proposition to put to you."

"And what would that be?" Ray had asked.

"We're starting a new division of Homeland Security," Samantha had explained. "Some… anomalous… events are beginning to come to our attention, and our division has been formed to look into them. We want to ensure we don't have a threat to national security. And now we need a team for that division. A man with your background on that team—even helping lead it—would be a great help."

"What's this organization, and what precisely are you investigating?"

"Anomalies involving spacetime," Sam had said simply, and laid a file folder in his hands.

Ray had flipped through it a bit awkwardly; several of his fingers were still bandaged. But Sam had kindly assisted him, and he couldn't help but think, looking at Kruger's missing eye, 'There but for the grace of God…'

Soon he realized the nature of what he was reading: they were protocols designed to handle the event of a first contact from either an extraterrestrial source, or a future source. And there was data in there to back up the need, hard data. He looked up at the two.

"You're serious? This stuff is legit?" he asked.

"More serious than you can imagine," the Old Man said.

"Okay, you've answered one question, assuming I believe you. Now the other."

"The organization is the Directorate of Special Research Projects and Operations," the Old Man said.

"We call it DSRPO, or Dee-surpo, for short," Sam had added. *"We're under the auspices of DHS, but we're all but independent of... well, of anybody. Plausible deniability combined with really HIGH level national security. We have the approval to do whatever is necessary to protect the United States against any spacetime threat. Carte blanche. Only about twenty people other than members of the team know that our organization exists."*

"We are far beyond top secret," Kruger put in. *"You can ask the President about us, but the Vice President has no need to know."*

"Who then?" Ray had raised an eyebrow.

"President, Sec Def, National Security Advisor, Director of National Intelligence, Director of Homeland Security, the chairpersons of the House and Senate intelligence committees, the Joint Chiefs, and a few others. You'll be briefed more later," Sam told him.

"Pretty deep hole," Ray mused.

"The fact that you've had to essentially be given a new face proves convenient in this case," Kruger had noted. *"Combine that with a new name, and we have an excellent new DSRPO operative. If you're willing, and interested."*

Ray considered for a moment. Then he gave Kruger a hard look, and Sam a once-over. He remembered Kruger smiling to himself just then, and shooting a glance at his attractive companion, who didn't notice either man's scrutiny.

"One stipulation, first," Ray had said.

"Name it."

"James and Ernesto come along if they're willing."

"You mean 'Jay Sampson' and 'Ernie Travers'? They're already on board," Sam gave him a brilliant smile, nearly causing Ray to melt into the bed. *"They've been waiting on you. Seems like the three of you bonded pretty deeply, with the kinds of missions you've been doing. That's a good thing."*

"Then I'm in."

"Congratulations, Dr. Reagan Brady, and welcome to DSRPO."

"Reagan? Brady?"

"Yes. You. Dr. Reagan Brady." Kruger smiled sardonically. *"I'm sorry to say that Dr. Raymond Bradford didn't make it out of Afghanistan."*

‚ò∩‚

Ray's dream flash-forwarded to his somewhat turbulent and frequently interrupted courtship of Sam—*damn inconvenient missions,* his subconscious thought in humorous annoyance—and Sam's ultimate agreement to take his new name. He'd been a little bit old for her–she'd been twenty-eight, he'd been ten years her senior. But it never seemed to matter. They were just... matched. Mentally, physically, and emotionally, they couldn't have made a better pair. And Ray suddenly understood why no one else had ever succeeded in getting his attention: in his mind, and in his heart, there was no one to compare with Sam.

The wedding with Sam had perforce been small, with only the team in attendance. The Old Man had walked her down the aisle, in lieu, Ray supposed, of her father; and the wedding night had been... glorious. He nudged Sam's hips with his groin as he slept, remembering how he'd discovered her decidedly unbusinesslike side on their wedding night–she'd insisted on waiting until then to sleep together, for reasons she never told him. His new wife displayed, it turned out, extremely wanton behavior in bed. And Ray couldn't have been happier. Or so he'd thought.

Another leap forward in time—just a couple of years—and Sam had been giving birth to their daughter.

"*C'mon, honey... push... that's it... push... now breathe...*"

"*Huh... huh... Ray... I, I can't...*"

"*Yes you can, honey. And I'm right here. Breathe... breathe. It's okay. C'mon. You can do it.*"

"*UUNGHH!*"

"*PUSH! One more time, Sam! I can see her head! PUSH!*"

And Abigail Sarah Brady had slid out of her mother's exhausted, trembling body into her father's waiting hands.

The doctor and nurse had quickly cleared the infant's breathing passageway. Seconds later, the little voice was crying out lustily. "Huh-hAAAIIIIII!"

℠ℂℂ℀

"Hi... Hi..." Abigail's high pitched little voice penetrated into Ray's dream state, waking him. Ray rolled over and saw the lights on the acoustic baby monitor as he forced himself out of his dream. It was Abby's first, and only, word to date; a little premature, the doctors had said, but since much of the rest of her development had been held back by her frequent infections, one that Ray and Sam had been glad to accept. Except at the moment.

"Shit, Abby, go back to sleep!" Ray groaned and looked at the alarm clock on the nightstand. "Two-thirty in the morning! Christ, Abby."

"We should be happy, Ray—her first words."

"I know, hot stuff, but couldn't she have chosen the daytime to have a little conversation with herself? Damn!"

"Just let her be for a few minutes and see if she goes back to sleep on her own," Sam said, without budging.

"*Hi... Hi...*"

"Good idea," Ray rolled over and spooned his wife closer to him, hoping to go back to sleep himself.

"*Hi... Hi...*"

"'*Hello, I'm Alphabet Pal... A says aaa. A says aaa. Every letter makes a sound. A says aaa.*'"

"What the...?" Ray sat straight up in bed. "You didn't leave that damn toy caterpillar in her crib, did you?"

"No!" Sam replied, startled.

"*Ow... Shit!*"

"Even if somebody taught her to say shit," Ray declared, flinging back the covers, "that's NOT Abigail's voice. And it sure as hell isn't the toy!"

"Someone's in Abby's room!" Sam cried. "And I did NOT recognize that voice!"

Ray and Sam leaped out of the bed simultaneously, both of them instantly wide awake. They grabbed their pistols from under the pillows and headed in a full sprint to the nursery.

೮೦೦೪

They met Teresa in the hall, also armed, and all three burst into the nursery. A strange man bent over Abby's crib, reaching for her. He was dressed in a jumpsuit identical to the ones Santa Bunny's assistants seemed to always wear.

"Freeze, bastard!" Sam snarled like a tiger, bringing her Glock to bear. "Back away from my child!"

Teresa and Ray spread out, weapons aimed.

"What the lady said," Teresa growled. "Or you're gonna get lead poison. Lots of it."

"Ha ha ha." The intruder laughed without humor. The sound was cold as ice. "You would actually shoot? So close to the baby? Now, now, what irresponsible parents." He leaned further into the crib, making it impossible for them to use their weapons.

Ray let out a primitive howl of rage as he tossed his Ruger aside. A high kick knocked the man backward, away from the crib, as Ray stepped in to grapple the man. Samantha ran over and scooped up Abby;

all the while, Teresa tried to keep her sights trained on their home invader, backing up Ray. She managed to pump out a round or two, but they didn't strike their intended target, merely flying into empty space where the man had been.

Ray soon found that this man, while no Santa Bunny, was no slouch, either. Ray's palm heel strike/throat jab combination was countered by a hard outer block, and followed up by a punch to Ray's solar plexus. It never connected, as Ray swung one arm down and around in a circular low outer block, and brought the other fist in for a potentially fatal punch to the right side of the man's ribcage. But the man shuffled backward, out of Ray's arm length.

In response, Ray spun into a tornado roundhouse kick. The first narrowly missed taking the man's head off, only failing when he leaned backward in a move that could almost have come from the movie, The Matrix. Ray used the momentum, pulling his leg in to spin even faster, and thrusting it out at the last second.

But somehow the intruder was ready for him. Even as fast as Ray's foot was moving, the man still managed to grab the scientist operative by the ankle. Then he took advantage of Ray's high angular momentum to lift him off his feet and spin him around once, before letting Ray go, a nude human missile aimed at a glass window.

Ray had just enough time to fold his arms over his head as he hit the window and glass splintered everywhere.

‼۞&#x3;

Ray found himself flying head first through the air as thin pieces of broken safety glass moved in slow motion around him. The bedrooms were on the second story of the house, and it looked like a helluva long way to the ground. Utilizing all his high-dive training from years of swim meets when he was younger, he did his best, with what time he had, to aim for some thick landscaping shrubs, and was more or less successful.

Thank God I talked Sam out of planting roses around the house, he thought ruefully as he rolled out of the arborvitae and onto his feet. His naked body was cut up enough as it was from the window and the foliage. He didn't want to think what flowering thorn bushes would have done.

Looking up at the window, he could hear gunshots and Abby shrieking and crying. Suddenly a high pitched scream from Teresa rang out, followed by a long string of expletives from Sam. There were more gunshots, then Sam's fierce, "Kieee-YAH!" followed by several meaty thuds.

"Hold on, Sam, I'm coming!" Ray shouted up at the window as he started to run for the nearest entrance, which happened to be the back door. He rounded the corner...

... Just as the house exploded.

The blast wave threw him back a good thirty feet. Ray smelled singed hair and felt airborne debris adding to the lacerations on his nude body. Dimly seeing a wisp of smoke drift by his eyes, he reached up and smacked a hand down on the smoldering lock of his own hair, extinguishing it. *So much for my "Superman curl."*

Slowly he picked himself up from the grass in the back yard and stared in stunned horror at the structure before him that had been his home, the refuge he shared with the love of his life and their child.

The wood frame structure was splintered and twisted. The entire top floor was gone, and at least half of the first floor. "S- sam?" he whispered, then his voice grew stronger. "SAM! ABBY! TERESA! *SAM?!* WHERE ARE YOU? *ANSWER ME!!*"

A groan sounded from somewhere in the wreckage, and he ran, heedless of bare feet on splintered debris. He tripped and stumbled over something bulky and soft, sprawling onto the grass. As he gathered himself back up, he looked down to see what he'd tripped over. Frank Grayson's pale white face stared, glassy eyed, at the sky. The guard's back was sharply bent at an abnormal angle, and one arm was gone, the stump lying in a puddle of blood in the grass. "Shit," Ray whispered, horrified. He turned back toward the wreck of his house, desperation and fear battling hope and love.

Entering the creaking, unstable structure, he watched his footing carefully. Aside from the risk of structural collapse, stepping on a nail barefooted was entirely different from stepping on wood splinters. "Hello?" he called again, and another muffled groan sounded nearby, beneath multiple layers of sheet rock and broken two by fours. He grabbed the detritus and began pitching it aside.

By this time, several neighboring houses had lights on, with faces peering out of windows and doors. Emergency sirens sounded in the distance. Carl, his next door neighbor, emerged in pajamas and robe, carrying a spare robe, and came toward Ray, who was still digging desperately.

When he got the dust covered human dug out, he realized it was Teresa in her shredded, bloody pajamas, and she'd been shot in the chest. "Oh, dear God," he whispered. "Teresa, are you... is it...?"

"Been… better," she panted in a whisper. "Think I… got a punctured lung. Maybe busted some ribs. And… and the fall didn't… didn't do me… any good."

"Don't move. Help is coming. I can hear the sirens."

"I know better 'n that, Dr. Brady. I'm a nurse, remember? I ain't goin' anywhere 'til the paramedics get here. Frank?"

"Dead. Sam and Abby? Are… are they…?"

"I dunno, Dr. Brady. I'm sorry. I just… don't know." She began to cry as Carl draped the robe over Ray and called for his wife to bring a blanket for Teresa.

ဆာ

Jay and the rest of the team mingled undercover among the emergency workers. Fortunately the blast hadn't really set anything on fire—a benumbed Ray was glad they'd opted for electricity instead of natural gas, in that moment—but it was still one hell of a mess. Jay and Doc attached themselves to Ray and stayed with him, Doc working on his lacerations, as Stevie Walters rode away in the ambulance with Teresa–to a hospital that the Old Man had designated. Jay had draped a blanket over Ray's shoulders, atop Carl's spare bathrobe, as soon as Doc had finished treating the cuts and scratches on Ray's torso from the relative privacy of Ray's backyard shed, and Ray cinched the robe closed. Then Doc started on Ray's arms and legs. As per usual, a cold pack went on the lump on Ray's head; he'd taken a whack from flying debris. But his nose was still intact, as Doc pointed out with rather less than his usual acerbic tones. Jay's arm stayed across Ray's shoulders for several minutes, offering silent male comfort and companionship.

By this time, Jay had the whole story in private from Ray in the shed. "Damn, Ray, I'm so sorry," he whispered, horrified. "I'm so sorry."

"About what? We can rebuild the house."

"About the boss and the baby."

Hazel eyes flashed gold sparks. "You think they're dead?!" he demanded, numbness and shock falling away. "Hell, no! He TOOK 'em! HE'S got 'em, Jay!"

"Calm down, Ray," Doc said softly, "and be reasonable. No one survived that blast."

"Teresa did," Ray snarled. "Find the bodies, then. You find one piece of tissue with DNA that belongs to either Sam or Abby, and I'll believe they're dead. No, Doc. HE got 'em. That's who was in the nursery–him, or one of his lackeys. Lackey, I think, unless he was in disguise, which given his ego, wouldn't fit his M.O. The doors and windows were locked, Frank was on duty, and the security system was on. And the guy was wearing one of the robbery uniforms."

"Why, Ray?" Fields asked, gentling his voice, concerned for his friend and colleague.

"Huh?"

"Why would he kidnap them?"

"Hostages," Ray said bitterly. "Something to force me to cooperate. Judging by his comments at the munitions factory, Marathon Man takes this personally—me specifically. I'm a nuisance, and I keep getting in his way. So he goes after my child as a bargaining chip. Sam probably was a bonus."

Doc and Jay exchanged glances behind Ray's back. The look said, *He's got a point. If we don't find any bodies or body parts, maybe he's right.*

"Listen, Ray," Sampson said gently, "I've gotta go play my game of police spokesman for your neighbors and the press. I'll make sure everyone on the team knows to look for... forensic evidence, or lack thereof."

"Okay. Good," Ray said gruffly. "Thanks, Jay."

"No problem, pal."

"What's the story?"

"Home invasion by a gang, you guys surprised 'em, you got flung out the window, they got the wife and child as insurance and booked it, blowing the place up with a pipe bomb or some shit like that. Forensics is lookin' for the 'some shit' now. Got the brother in law, wounded the nanny. Status of wife and child not known at this time."

"Okay. I'll stick to it, then. Is the basement—"

"Secured," Jay reassured him. "Nobody gonna find nothin' down there."

He exited the shed and became an 'official spokesperson,' calming the neighbors and giving out their cover story to the press. Ray sighed in a pain that was more mental and emotional than physical as he watched. He didn't recall ever feeling so helpless in his life.

"C'mon, Ray," Doc offered, leading him out of the shed and guiding him with one hand on his good arm as they managed to run the gauntlet of neighbors and news media without having to say anything, and avoiding cameras whenever possible. "Somebody's gonna take you someplace safe."

"I'm not sure there is such a place, Doc," Ray muttered under his breath.

ఴఴ

Doc led Ray over to a large dark car parked down the street and opened the rear door. Ray eased in and Doc closed the door behind him before turning back to help Jay. Ray found himself sitting beside the Old Man, as the driver—behind a glass wall—pulled the car into the street and accelerated away. "So."

"So," Ray sighed.

"You don't think they're dead, do you?"

"No, sir." Ray's voice was steel.

"You think Mr. Santa got 'em?"

"YES, sir."

"Me too," Kruger nodded.

"Glad somebody believes me."

"Yes, I do. All right," he patted Ray's shoulder as if to tell him to settle down. "Let's see what the team finds. Meanwhile, I'm taking you to a safehouse, you're taking the meds that Doc slipped into the pocket of that robe, and you're getting some sleep whether you want it or not. Tomorrow we'll talk."

ॐ

Kruger was sitting by his bedside in the safehouse when Ray woke. He sat bolt upright instantly.

"No bodies except Grayson's," Kruger said crisply, "no body parts, no blood except Teresa's–AND someone else's, NOT connected to you. No sign of Samantha and Abigail."

"I told you," Ray said in a low voice. "They're not dead. He's got them."

"I know. And now I am about to give you some very private, very personal, but no less official, orders."

"Yes sir?"

"Listen to me closely, Ray." Kruger straightened up in his chair and scowled. "Do whatever it takes, but find my daughter and my granddaughter, and bring them home alive and unharmed no matter what is required."

Ray's jaw dropped. Then he recovered.

"Yes, SIR," he growled.

Chapter 14

Ray, clad in the DSRPO team's black BDUs, sat alone at the conference table, surrounded by stacks of files–the various data they'd gleaned on the Santa Bunny anomaly. He sighed, despondence in the sound. *I already know most of this shit by heart*, he thought. *I gotta find Sam and Abby, which means finding this bastard. But where in the name of all that is holy do I start?*

His eye was drawn to a photograph. He picked it up. It was the very first enhanced image of their target, the one that Sam had pulled from the security camera in the Y-12 plant.

Ray stared at the image from the video, of the man with the spiky short blond hair and vivid blue eyes–the man who had had his wife and daughter either kidnapped or killed. The more he stared, the more convinced he was that the face was familiar.

I've seen him before, Ray decided. *Someplace before New York City. Someplace…*

He allowed himself to drift into a light reverie, almost an altered state of consciousness, staring at the eyes in the photograph, letting his mind drift through years of memories, sifting, sorting, in an attempt to locate the desired recollection.

Blue eyes… blond hair… bright blue eyes… under… under something… a hat brim…? Something about… last night's flashbacks… Shit! In all of the excitement, I forgot all about it! Suddenly a flood of memories hit him, many of which had been in his dreams in the moments before his home had been invaded. *The Army officer in the pre-brief for my Afghanistan mission, the one who designed the homing devices*, Ray realized grimly. *The guy I ran into in the door of the conference room, on the way out. And I think… I THINK… he was in a turban in the caves, too.* Another flash of memory hit. *The eyes–the same ones that had looked out at me from under an Iranian turban as we exited a certain nuclear facility. Dark beard–but those can be faked. The turban would cover the blond hair nicely, though. And… oh, dear God… the Marine squad leader in Fallujah.*

Ray shook his head. "Every time there's been major bloodshed around me in the last decade and a half, I've seen this guy," he realized. "I wonder…" He paused, trying to think it through, before giving up.

"Am I finally going nuts? One way I know of to find out." He reached for the phone. "Jay? Get your ass over here, and bring Danny and Billy the Kid with you. Now."

ഗരു

"Son of a bitch," Jay growled, as he recognized both the Army major and the Marine squad leader in the photograph of their suspect. "You're right. It IS him. Both times."

"So where else has this guy been that nasty shit has been going on?" Ray demanded to know.

"I take it that's what Danny and I are here for?" Billy Hargrove, their IT expert, asked cheekily.

"You got it," Ray all but barked. "We're getting our leader, and my wife and daughter, back if it's the last thing we do." He corrected himself. "If it's the last thing *I* do."

"WE," Jay corrected him firmly.

"All over it, Ray," Dan declared, voice determined. The other men's eyes immediately hardened. "Billy, you and I need to get on this sooner than yesterday. What's the best way to do a massive media search?"

"Hmmm," Billy shrugged. "Gimme the best photo images you've got of this guy. I'll scan it all into my system and get correlating points on the face from several different angles, then turn it loose in a web search."

"Here." Ray shoved a stack of imagery from Oak Ridge and the bank robberies at Billy. "All you could possibly want. What else do you need?"

"Time," Billy said.

"Sam and Abby don't have forever, Billy."

"I know, Ray. My part won't take long. It's the search that I don't know about."

Ray nodded as Dan and Billy left to begin their work.

ഗരു

Drago stared in a blazing fury at his assistant, who stood there awkwardly, a profusely bleeding scratch just below his hairline, the side of his face and his collar dripping with blood, juggling a howling, squirming one year old in his arms, with a naked woman unconscious at his feet.

"What in the bloody HELL did you do?!" Drago screamed. "What is SHE doing here?!" He pointed at Sam's unconscious, unclad body.

Jones, the henchman, executed a kind of shrug crossed with a flinch, then snatched at Abby as she tried to crawl up his shoulders, screeching and clawing at him in anger and fear.

"I couldn't help it, Doctor. There was a baby monitor in the nursery, and the baby woke up—I think it was the flash from the extraction point that did it. Anyway, both parents AND the nanny ran in, loaded for elephant. I barely managed to throw the father out the window—he is a

DAMN good fighter—shot the nanny, and tossed a grenade at the mother as the extraction point arrived. But the mother dove at me. I punched her lights out, but her momentum carried her through the door with us."

Jones hefted the child to elaborate. Abby promptly bopped him in the nose. He winced, eyes watering.

The reasonable explanation calmed Drago, who realized his man had, in fact, done extremely well to take on all three adults—especially considering who the father was—and still get back with the baby, let alone relatively unharmed.

"Never mind, then," he said, thinking furiously. "This may prove to our advantage. With baby AND wife, surely their leader will talk. Or at least negotiate."

"What do you want me to do with them?"

"Take them to the lab and have them tested for infection," Drago ordered. "Then put the baby in the nursery we've prepared, and the woman in a holding cell. And get yourself cleaned up." He waved a finger at the forehead cut. "You're bleeding all over everything."

"Yes sir." Jones nodded. "I'll find a coverall that will fit her."

"No," Drago barked. "Just as she is. I WILL break this family, once and for all, regardless of what it takes."

"Whatever it takes?" Jones leered in understanding. "First dibs?"

"Since you brought her back, of course. Start slowly, though. A little roughing up should do nicely as an opening salvo," Drago decided. "Let her... anticipate... the main event."

ဆာၵ

Sam woke up, still naked, in a tiny room made of concrete, with no windows and only one—very solid—metal door. Abby, Ray, and Teresa were not to be seen. The room was chilly and somewhat damp, and she stood, wrapping her arms about herself and pacing to keep warm.

She had no idea how long she'd been there, but the stiffness of her body and her hungry insides told her it was morning, and well past breakfast. There was no sign of food or water, and no noise audible past the sturdy metal door. Samantha looked around the tiny cell, but there were no furnishings whatsoever, and her bladder was beginning to make a fuss. She eyed the corner of the room.

No, better wait, she decided. *Obviously the guy got Abby and me. And since they haven't given me clothes, I've got a really bad feeling about this.*

ဆာၵ

"So, Dr. Brooks, what were the results?" Drago asked as he entered the genetics engineering lab.

"Pure," Drago's team physician replied, looking up from his work. "Both the baby and its mother. Although the child likely has cystic fibrosis according to a sweat test I performed, it isn't contaminated."

"Really?" Drago raised an eyebrow. *But the father... Hm. Here is significant food for thought.* "Are you absolutely sure?" he pressed. The baby was sleeping in a playpen nearby, and he wandered over to look at the young one. A fuzzy blonde head tossed for a few seconds, then Abby settled back down.

"Positive," Brooks said confidently, pausing to get a folder from his desk and hand it to Drago. "Here, see for yourself."

"No infection," Drago murmured and studied the lab results. His attention quickly wandered back to Abby. "No sign whatsoever. In either of them."

"And the tests went through completely clean. No problems, no question of the results, beyond the usual error bars."

"Which we've refined to infinitesimal ridiculousness. Very good, Brooks."

"Thank you, sir."

Drago left the medical lab, deep in thought.

∞❧

Jay and Ray were still poring over the data when Billy and Dan returned late that night. "Got 'im," Billy declared. "Boy, did we got 'im."

"Whatcha mean by that?" Jay said, looking up.

"Well, let's see," Danny said. "He was in the background of a TV shot after the Oklahoma City bombing–apparently one of the investigators, by the looks of his clothes."

"He was one of the paramedics doing triage after the collapse of the Twin Towers on 9-11," Billy added.

Ray blinked.

"And," Billy continued, "you're not going to believe this. The photos were black and white, of course, so I can't be one hundred percent. But I've got matches for his features at Los Alamos, during Manhattan Project days; in the background of a group picture at Princeton, with Einstein; at the University of Paris, beside the Curies; at the Muséum National d'Histoire Naturelle with Henri Bequerel... Do you want me to go on?"

"How... how far back does this guy GO?" Ray gaped in shocked astonishment.

Billy shook his head. "I'm not sure. Daguerreotypes get kinda difficult to match. They have a different perspective and resolution than modern photography, not to mention essentially being negatives."

"DAGUERREOTYPES?!" Ray expostulated. " But... those were invented in 1839!"

"Yep," Billy confirmed. "But look at this." He tossed over a printout of a painted portrait. "You recognize one guy."

"Dammit," Ray breathed, hazel eyes wide as they focused on the bright blue eyes of one man in the portrait.

"Do you recognize the other guy?" Billy wondered.

"That's... that's Faraday," Ray stammered, not sure he could be any more shocked. "Michael Faraday."

"Circa 1818," Billy elaborated. "I've got him traced back to at least the late seventeen hundreds, alongside somebody named Hans Christian Ørsted."

"An early researcher into electromagnetism, and the first to specifically describe the 'thought experiment,'" Ray mused. "Or did he?"

"What do you mean?" Danny wondered.

"Einstein, with his theories of relativity, popularized the concept of the thought experiment, or the 'gedankenversuch,' as he called them," Ray explained. "What if our anomaly actually taught that concept to Ørsted, rather than Ørsted developing it on his own? A deliberate introduction of the notion into our scientific process? Then he guided its development until it saw full fruition in Einstein's work?"

"Why would he do that?" Danny asked, puzzled.

Ray shook his head. "I dunno. All I know is that, if it's really him—"

"I've got better than ninety-five percent probability on the features recognition algorithm," Billy interjected.

"...Then he's following the development of branches of physics leading to both nuclear energy and multidimensional physics. Following—or guiding?"

"Shit. Easter bunny," Jay said, eyes practically bulging from his head.

"Mm. Sure looks like it," Danny agreed, shaken.

"I dunno. I'm STILL not convinced," Ray muttered. "There's DEFINITELY an element of Santa in there, too. The guy is way the hell too strong and fast for any normal human. I'm REALLY starting to think Santa now. You know, if he's an alien from an advanced culture, with an amazingly long lifespan relative to ours, he doesn't need to travel in time. He's already got the technology, and all the time he requires to manipulate us."

"Well, we got this much," Jay noted. "Now we gotta figure out where he took Ray's girls."

"Amen, brother," Ray agreed vehemently.

"You know, we GOT fingerprints," Jay noted. "On Mr. Marathon. From the fire escape, back when we first encountered him."

Ray spun. "We WHAT?? Why in the HELL didn't someone tell me that before now?!"

"Uh, Ray, I think we did. You kinda got knocked for a loop, remember? Like, a couple times?"

"And what have we done with 'em?"

"Dunno, but I'll check."

"Damn straight you'll check! I want those prints run through every database in the book, and all the ones that AREN'T in the book. I want to know who the hell this man is!" Ray ordered.

"On it," Jay said simply and without rancor, rising and leaving the room.

⁊β

After much consideration, Drago decided to make a little visit. Little Abby's arrival had raised a certain idea in him. He checked his new watch, then left his office, headed down the hall. He took an elevator up a couple of floors, wandered down three doors, and into the manifold room. He moved to the portal area and waited patiently.

He was abruptly engulfed in blue-white light. When it left, he was standing in the semi-darkness in a nursery. He moved to the crib and looked down at a small form, perhaps two or three years old, with pale yellow, almost white, hair lying in the bed. The normally hard expression he wore softened, the eyes going distant; he reached down and caressed a tiny back with infinite tenderness.

Simultaneously, he and the child inhaled, then let out a sigh, tension leaving both bodies.

"Hello, little fellow," he breathed, voice soft and gentle, even tender. "It's still hard for me to believe that it all began here. Such a long, long road..."

⁊β

He'd been something of a child prodigy, to put it mildly. Reading at three, graduating from high school at fifteen, a doctorate by age 20. DAR-PA, for whom he'd been a co-operative student employee in college, had snapped him up as soon as he had completed his Ph.D. He had immediately been dropped into classified projects—like the membrane intersect program.

It didn't take long before he'd superseded the current project scientist; his comprehension of the physics was far greater than any of the others on the project.

But that had been when he'd run into the other side of government research programs, the side that had become the bane of his existence–the politics. For something as important as the potential ability to warp an entire platoon into an enemy headquarters, the pressure to show demonstrable results was tremendous. And the project was already far behind schedule and greatly over budget.

Never mind that the project essentially dated back all the way to World War II and the Philadelphia Experiment–with that event's dreadful, eerie aftermath. Possibly, he'd suspected, even earlier than that. But new science had been developed since then, and DARPA wanted results; or rather, its Capitol Hill bosses did. And preferably the day before yesterday.

"Doc Billy," as the young scientist had been affectionately dubbed—a title he'd always considered rather demeaning and disrespectful—was all too well aware of the possibilities of the thing. After all, transcending physical space, space the size of a planet, was the least of it. Drago knew very well that the membrane intersect had the capability to traverse the very cosmos itself–past, present, and future. And altering the natural vibrational states of the n-dimensional branes with merely three dimensional tools was asking for trouble.

But it didn't matter. Results they wanted; results they were determined to get. The highly volatile situation throughout the Middle East only added fuel to the fire raging under Drago's feet.

A deadline had come down for the first test: brane a one kilogram cube of lead from one side of the lab room to the other, then back. And do it by the end of the quarter. Or funding would be pulled, and the project would be declared a failure and cancelled. And if that happened his young career would be finished before it had even gotten well started.

But it had worked, sort of. The block vanished in a flash of light, right on schedule. Only it didn't appear on the other side of the room. A search of adjacent rooms was made with no more luck. Yet the cube returned on time to its origin in a blaze of glory, apparently unharmed.

Personally and privately, Drago dubbed it a complete failure. His superiors had deemed it a partial success sufficient to continue the program, and ordered the experiments to go on with an eye toward doing the same thing with a lab rat inside a year–six months preferred, if possible. They were magnanimous and allowed Drago's team a little wiggle room on that, recognizing that living organisms were somewhat more complicated than a block of lead.

Drago and his hand picked team worked night and day, literally, in shifts, until they could get the lead cube to appear and disappear on cue, on mark.

Then it was time to up the ante: live animal testing. Drago himself personally placed a small white rat in a cage, then sat the cage at the extraction point. Then he stepped back and waited.

There was a flash of blue-white light—and the rat, with its cage, was gone. And didn't come back.

At all.

ঙ৩৪

Drago came out of his reverie, not quite ready to follow his disturbing thoughts further, and looked down at the toddler in the crib, an uncharacteristically soft, regretful look in his eyes.

"I am so sorry, little one," he murmured. "Sorry I allowed it to happen, and sorry I cannot stop it now. For if I did, I should never have learned the truth. And, brief though it was, I should never have found... HER."

He slipped back into memory.

ঙ৩৪

The animal experimentation was the stuff of nightmares—literally. Indeed, it caused a high turnover rate among Drago's hand picked team—but still it continued. Eventually they had been able to bring the rats back—but not in their original condition. Never in their original condition. Some came back horribly deformed, body parts and internal organs completely rearranged. Others came back with entire sections missing. Sometimes the cage came back, sometimes not. Sometimes it was ALL that came back. And sometimes cage and rat came back in what the sickened scientists euphemistically reported to their superiors as "an integrated unit."

Those rats that weren't already dead upon return were swiftly and humanely euthanized. Dissection of the remains revealed nothing to explain the nature of the malfunction; it only depicted sometimes-dreadful rearrangements of internal body structure, at times even when external appearances were normal.

Drago sent his stressed, exhausted team home for a short hiatus. He himself sat alone in his office all night, debating the wisdom of continuing the project—or at least, continuing ON the project, as it seemed obvious that the project would go on, in some form or fashion, whether he was there or not. After all, how many decades had it been going on already? When-

ever a team failed, the government simply canceled the current contract, renamed the program, and put out another call for proposals. 'The names were changed to protect the innocent,' he thought in distaste.

But that was the consideration that made up his mind for him. He knew who his replacement would be on the program should he leave, and deemed the man, though hardly an imbecile, nowhere near up to the task. In addition Calvin was a "yes man" to the hilt, with little backbone for standing up to the high brass, even if something wasn't right. Drago didn't resent his bosses; they were just doing their jobs. But he considered it HIS job to tell them when things weren't right, or weren't ready. Calvin, on the other hand, was apt to get someone killed.

Drago had opened his safe and pulled out the documentation detailing the mathematics of the program. He sat back down at his desk, his only illumination his desk lamp, and ran back through the derivations.

Suddenly he saw it—the term that was in error. It was, of course, in the section of calculations done by Dr. Calvin, he noted, face twisting in something near disgust. Perhaps he needed to re-evaluate his opinion of the man's competence. Years after, he had. Unfortunately, in retrospect, that had been far, far too late.

He scribbled down the correct term, and galvanized into action. In his haste to correct the apparatus to meet the program schedule, he didn't stop to translate the mathematics into the physical ramifications. Instead, he leaped to his feet with an exclamation, and headed for the lab, picking up a caged rat on the way.

Plunking the cage on a nearby table, Drago dove under consoles and inside electronics, ensuring the entire configuration met his critical eye. Then he fine tuned the settings on the vibrational inducer for what he swore was the trillionth time. A quick check of the chronometer had him hurrying to place the rat's cage on its mark.

Moments later he noted for the first time that the room was growing increasingly warm. There was a dual blue-white flash of such intensity that the young scientist was temporarily blinded. When he could see again, an agitated but healthy and intact rat was scrabbling and scampering inside its equally intact cage...

...On the other side of the room.

৪০৩

Within a couple of weeks, animal testing had successfully progressed from rats all the way up to chimpanzees. The team was ecstatic; morale had risen by an order of magnitude.

Then the word came down that Drago had been dreading: Time to do a test with humans.

"Oh, dear God," Drago had murmured to himself—or the Deity he wasn't sure existed, he didn't know which—in the privacy of his office, "I hope we're ready."

The team went over the apparatus with a fine toothed comb. Somewhere in the midst of that—he knew now; he hadn't known then—Calvin had tweaked the settings on the vibrational inducer back to their previous values. It hadn't been a malicious act; the idiot, Drago had concluded, had simply noticed the difference, didn't ask why, and "fixed" it. Then the volunteer soldiers filed in, Colonel Black, the program's military liaison, at their head.

"Here you go, Doc Billy," Black boomed cheerfully. "All the lab rats you could possibly want."

In the idealism of youth, Drago stepped forward then and did something he would never do again.

"No, Colonel," he'd said. "I won't send another man to do something I won't do myself."

Failing to note that the room was not warming as the extraction point approached, Drago jumped onto the mark—

—And vanished in a blaze of light.

He didn't come back.

Chapter 15

The transition had been... odd. Like some strange drug-induced hallucination, perhaps, where one smelled colors and tasted sound. Drago had spent long, long years seeking to describe the sensation of that journey, and failed. He had finally concluded that no Earth language contained the words to do so. Perhaps, somewhere out there among the stars, existed a race with the language to express the feeling; he didn't know.

But he knew an entire lexicon of words to describe its end, and many, many of them were curse words. For Drago had suddenly come to an abrupt understanding, in a very tangible and personal fashion, of the physical meaning of that mathematical term he'd found: It corresponded to the passage of time and the rotation of the planet. And to his horror and agony, he now found his lower body had materialized in the aged stone wall of his office building, as the planet had rotated past him in his traverse. His body and the rock wall were now an integral unit, molecule by molecule, atom by atom, perhaps even down to the quantum level, merged beyond all hope of separation. It was by sheer luck of miscalculation that he hadn't ended up in deep space. As the galaxy had rotated and the Earth had moved there was little likelihood that he should have ended up on Earth, especially not in the same building across the room. He later realized that there was a quantum entanglement aspect of transporting through the membranes that he hadn't even considered. He was damned lucky. Or maybe not so much. Materializing into the vacuum of space would have been much less painful and much more merciful.

The pain was instantaneous and excruciating, and he had instinctively screamed with the full power of what was left of his lungs. He watched as if from a distance while red blood—his own—pulsed from the pores of the granite itself with each heartbeat, and flowed in delicate, scarlet rivulets to the polished floor of the lobby, like some garish spring risen from the stone. 'A literal wellspring of life—my life,' passed through his shocked mind, dazed by the surreal horror and pain. And that life spring was ebbing away.

Unable to withstand the shock of the transition, he passed out.

That was the last thing he remembered for a long time.

ʚ◦ɞ

When he finally started returning to consciousness, he realized two things. One, he was no longer in pain. Two, he was free to move again—with what was, apparently, a whole body. Shortly thereafter he comprehended that he was lying comfortably in a bed. Opening his eyes, he scanned the room—a hospital room. Whipping the covers off, jerking the hospital gown away, he scanned the length of his nude form, noting each idiosyncrasy of detail. 'Intact,' he thought, confused. 'No sign of scarring. No artificial limbs. But how...? It WAS real, wasn't it...? Or have I...'

The door started to open, and he quickly whipped gown and covers back into place, closing his eyes. After a moment, a very feminine chuckle sounded. "You don't have to pretend, Dr. Drago. I know you're awake. Welcome back to the land of the living. Oh, and we got your name from your badge, so no, I'm not psychic." He heard the hint of another chuckle threatening to escape in her voice.

Drago had opened his eyes to gaze into the most vivid, lovely green eyes he'd ever seen, vaguely realizing that the chestnut brown hair and curvaceous body attached to them was clad in a spotless white cat suit covered with a long lab coat.

⁚C⁛

She'd been his physician. She hadn't gone into the details of how they'd rescued him from the wall, but she did explain that he was in his future, along with several of his lab rats—those that hadn't ended up in the same granite walls he had. It seemed the people of Earth's future were familiar with brane intersect devices, the program he'd worked on having eventually perfected them. So he assumed certain aspects of technology—including rescue operations—were more advanced. It wasn't until the physical therapy began that he realized HOW advanced.

"I have a good five times the strength I did," he observed in surprise, as he hoisted a mammoth cabled weight. "How the hell did you do THAT?"

Dr. Amelia Huggins had merely smiled. "Perhaps I can explain it to you sometime," she demurred. "And yes, you're approximately five times stronger now. With much greater healing abilities. Since your time, we've learned how to make ourselves virtually immortal."

"How?"

"Later."

"But I have to figure out how to go home soon," he said softly, a pang striking his heart.

"William... you know you can't."

"But I already know you have the technology," he'd protested. "And have it far more perfected than I did."

"I know, but you still can't go BACK."

"But..."

"You'd affect the timeline, William. You're a physicist. You know how that works, what it means." Dr. Huggins sidled well within his personal space; the attraction between them had been almost immediately apparent, but up until then she'd conducted herself with admirable clinical detachment. "You'll be released from medical care soon. Then I won't have to worry about breaching doctor/patient ethics. If... you know what I mean. And I promise I'll try to help you come up to speed, and... settle in."

He'd smiled and nodded. "That's... better than going it alone, I suppose," he murmured, heart torn. Then he mentally shook himself. His parents had died in an automobile accident the year before he'd made himself a guinea pig; he had no close family, no significant other, few friends, and none of those close. 'What do I have tying me to that past now, anyway? There's far more here to explore, to learn. And a beautiful someone who wants to be at my side in learning it. William, my boy, you nearly killed yourself, but I think you ended up winning the lottery.'

It wasn't until much, much later that he'd learned the rest of the truth.

೫ಂ೮ೊ

They were lovers by then. He'd moved into her condo, and for the time being at least, become a househusband, until they could find a place for him in society, or bring him up to speed on the science so he could resume research. Much to his surprise, he found himself enjoying it. There wasn't that much to do in the daytime, admittedly. But at night... ah, God in Heaven, how he looked forward to the nights. Amelia might be highly clinical at the hospital, but in the bedroom it was an altogether different matter. And Drago loved it—and her.

By this time he'd learned that he was some two hundred years in his own future, give or take, and that the human race had advanced considerably, using the extraction points to navigate space the way people in his day moved around a building. Amelia had even introduced him to a friend, someone she considered a brother, from another planet: a seven foot tall bipedal reptilian with yellow eyes whose name was, as near as Drago could wrap his mouth around it, Sslph. It seemed Earth had become part of an interstellar culture, a kind of coalition of stellar systems. And Sslph had offered to take them off Earth, to let Drago explore the cosmos. He was thrilled.

Until, late one night, Drago had broached the subject of children with Amelia. And she had started to cry.

೫ಂ೮ೊ

"WHAT?" Drago blurted. "You're... you're a what?!"

"Alien. As in extraterrestrial. Sslph really IS my brother, William," Amelia explained. "I'm... I'm human, but I'm not..." She paused, trying to meet the shocked blue gaze of the man she loved. "Remember your history, William? The Spanish Influenza Pandemic. 1918. Right after Comet Encke?"

"Yes," Drago dredged his memory. "Yes, I remember. There was some scuttlebutt when I was a child about organics in the comet tail producing viral-like components in our atmosphere that then interacted with native viruses to mutate into the pandemic. But it was never proven."

"That's exactly what happened," Amelia admitted, shamefaced. "But it wasn't natural, and it wasn't accidental. My people, the Ssliths, use that method to expand their empire."

"Your PEOPLE??"

"It's... sort of like the opposite of terraforming. Instead of adapting the planet, we arrange to... to make ourselves... compatible with the planet. First we find an inhabited planet. Then we... we bioengineer materials to do exactly what you described, and we insert them into cometary nuclei with timed release mechanisms. It injects the chemicals into your atmosphere, and the result is that whoever is infected and survives is... is genetically changed. It weeds out those who are incompatible with our lifeform, and forces the DNA of the survivors to begin mutating. With successive 'pandemics,' and natural breeding, over time the species changes. Once it has changed enough to reach a... a kind of critical mass, I suppose you'd say, we're able to manipulate the quantum foam and... well, the end result is that we download ourselves into the new, modified bodies. The woman who was born with this body—her mind died when I was transferred into it. It's like... like reformatting a computer. The old programming gets overwritten. Deleted. She doesn't exist anymore." By this time Amelia was crying openly. She clutched at Drago's hands.

"You have to believe me, though. I didn't choose to do this. I WOULDN'T choose to do this! NEVER! But sometimes, even in us, things go wrong with our bodies. I had a very rare disease where my healing ability was running amok. I was growing extra limbs, extra eyes, fingers, toes, I had THREE TAILS! You've seen Sslph—Ssliths don't even HAVE tails! My body was going mad, and I think my mind would have soon followed. It became impossible to do for myself, then impossible to walk—how can you walk when you have five legs, seven feet, and a brain programmed for only two? I turned into a complete invalid.

"I was never given a choice, William. They put me under deep anesthesia, telling me they were going to try an experimental procedure. When I

woke up, I was in this body! I never... I NEVER..."

She crumpled on the bed, sobbing brokenheartedly. Despite his revulsion, Drago put out a hand and stroked her chestnut hair, soothing. "So... this really isn't the human race I'm living among."

"Mostly, no."

"Mostly?"

"There are a few that have... resisted. They didn't catch the virus, or maybe somehow their bodies rejected the mutation. We don't know. I can't say I blame them; I never cared much for the Sslith government's expansionary politics. Especially being a physician myself. The knowledge that I... killed a sentient being... in order to live... An innocent person... and she had no choice! Oh, great Creator!" She closed her beautiful green eyes, in pain that, Drago suspected, was every bit as deep as when he had become embedded in that wall. 'But there is no way to heal her pain,' he realized.

A sudden thought had hit Drago then. "Amelia... how did you fix me? I should have died..."

"You WERE dying," she admitted frankly, opening her eyes and meeting his adored gaze. "And I fixed you the only way I knew how. We had to cut you out of the wall, William. There wasn't a whole lot of you left after that. So I spliced that section of our genetics that was coded to regeneration into your DNA, and kept you on massive life support until it had a chance to 'take' and grow the rest of your body back. I... forgive me. I thought if I... that it would somehow atone..."

"So... I'm no longer human, either?"

"Not... entirely, no."

"Like you?"

"No, not like me. Or, not like this body, I guess I should say," Amelia sighed. "You're not changed enough for a Sslith to download into you. But you're not human anymore, either. And that's why we can't have a baby. We're... we're genetically different enough to be two separate species. And now you hate me for being a... an alien... THING. When I love you more than life itself." She buried her face in the silken bedclothes as sobs shook her lovely, voluptuous body from head to toe.

Drago dragged his hand over his face. The only thing he could think of to ask was, "What was your name?"

"Wh- what?" Amelia raised her head. Her flushed face was covered in tear stains.

"What did your name used to be? Before you... before they moved you?"

"Ssaree," she murmured, dragging the backs of her hands over her wet cheeks. "My name was Ssaree."

He nodded thoughtfully. "Ssaree." He tried the name on for size. It fit. "Ssaree, I... I don't hate you. YOU didn't kill anybody. The ones who 'downloaded' you did that. And you saved my life the best you knew how. You... regardless of what you are, I love you for WHO you are. I'm a scientist. I'm open minded. But that doesn't mean that what your people—your government—are, is, is doing to my people..." Realizing he was stammering, he paused, gathered his scattered wits, reined in his anger, corrected himself. "What they DID to my people, Ssaree... is not right. Not at ALL."

"I know. I don't particularly appreciate what was done to me. But I suppose the doctors were in the same situation with me that I was with you."

"I see." Drago nodded again, thinking fast. "Do you know where this resistance is located?"

"No. But I may be able to find out how to contact them," she confessed. "I'd been thinking... before you even came..."

"Do you want to try?"

"Do you want to?"

"Yes."

"Then I'll come with you, William. I love your body, love your touch, but I love your mind and heart more. The essence of you, that is what I love. I'll fight for your people because they are YOUR people."

"Then, Ssaree, we truly are mates," Drago had declared, cupping her face in his hand just before he kissed her tear-wet lips.

℘☾☪

Jay returned a couple of hours later. By this time it was past midnight, but he had news.

"You're not gonna believe this one, Ray," he said, shaking his head and sitting down across from his team lead.

"Try me," Ray said bleakly. "At this point I'll believe just about anything."

"We found a match to the prints," Jay averred, and Ray sat up straight. "WHERE?!" he barked. "Give me an address to find this bastard!"

"Whoa, whoa, whoa there, boss man," Jay calmed Ray down, putting out a warning hand. "Settle down there. It ain't what you think. Ain't nowhere even close, trust me. We ran criminal records through the FBI, DoD, Interpol, police networks, you name it. Nuthin'. Then we started on DoD employees, school teacher certifications, all that shit. Still no joy. What we finally GOT... is an FBI record... in the children's anti-kidnapping files, of all places. They're a lot tinier, because the kid is only about four years old, give or take. But little Billy Drago's prints are a dead ringer in every single point for the latents we pulled off the fire escape. There's no mistake. Look." He tossed down a color printout of the dossier.

Pale blond, almost white, hair and big, luminous blue eyes in a toddler's happy face gazed up out of the photograph on the form.

The two team members gazed at each other.

"Easter bunny," Jay added, and Ray nodded agreement.

"Where?"

"About an hour from here. Got a vehicle waiting. Figured you'd want to go see right away."

"You figured right. Let's go."

ഇരുള

They'd located the resistance, and both of them had joined it, although it had taken quite a bit of doing to convince them that Amelia—Ssaree, Drago corrected himself—was legitimate and no spy. In the end they'd been placed in a resistance ring under the ultimate command of one General Abigail, the regional commander. Elsewhere on the planet, the rumor mill in their unit averred, Abigail's father and mother also commanded regions, assisted by two others: one sometimes respectfully addressed as Odin, and believed to be part of the commanding family, though the family neither confirmed nor denied it. The other was known only as The Dragon, rumored to be as ruthless as his namesake, although affiliated with—or at least connected to—the commanding family in some fashion. Last names weren't used, and often code names were employed in order to hinder traceability in case someone was captured.

Ssaree was to return to her job at the hospital as usual; since that was where downloads tended to occur, she would be the unit's mole. Drago would be the courier, bringing Ssaree's information to the unit. It all worked fine for a few months–until Ssaree got caught.

ഇരുള

Jay and Ray finally arrived at the Drago residence and knocked at the door. It was just past midnight, but the man of the house was still up. He cracked open the door, chain still attached. "It's late. What do you want?"

Ray held out a badge; it was legitimate, as well as most—if not quite all—of what he was about to say. "Homeland Security, sir. Do you have a child named Billy?"

"Why?"

"We have a concern about kidnapping, sir. Some recent home invasions have resulted in child, and even child/mother, kidnappings. It appears to be the work of a gang of terrorists after so-called 'Aryan' children. We have reason to think Billy may be a target."

"Oh, dear God," the senior Drago said, turning pale, immediately releasing the chain and opening the door. "Come in. I'll show you to the nursery and get my wife."

He led them up the stairs, ducking his head into the master bedroom. "Jeanie, wake up, honey," he said. "Put on your robe and come on. You were right about doing the FBI registration. These men are with Homeland Security, and they think terrorists in the area are after Billy."

Within seconds a petite blonde woman, swathed in a terrycloth bathrobe, had joined them and the four headed down the hall toward the nursery. Mr. Drago opened the door...

...and Dr. William H. Drago straightened up from where he leaned over the crib, spinning to face them.

‘’

Instinctively, Ray lunged forward, pulling his pistol. But to his surprise, Drago turned toward a window of the nursery and leaped through it, shattering the glass and sending a shower of shards in his wake—outward, away from the nursery.

Jeanie Drago cried out, rushing over and scooping up her sleeping child, cradling him close, as her husband inserted himself bodily between them and the window.

"SHIT!" Ray exclaimed, and he and Jay whirled, sprinting down the hall and taking the stairs in two bounds. In seconds they were out of the house and around to the side.

‘’

"Peter," a frantic Jeanie asked, "what do we do?!"

"Those men are trying to protect him, Jeanie," Peter William Drago replied. "They're after that man who tried to harm Billy. Grab the pistol, take him into the cellar and stay there until I tell you. You'll be safe there, and I'll get the shotgun and try to help 'em catch this guy."

Jeanie turned toward the door, little Billy in her arms; then abruptly turned back, grabbing her husband's arm. "Don't kill him, Peter."

"What?! He tried to hurt Billy!"

"I..." Jeanie shook her head. "Something isn't what it seems, honey.

That man… he wasn't trying to hurt Billy, he was patting him on the back. And did you see his eyes?"

"No…"

"They're the spitting image of Billy's. And so soft–until he saw us. Or them, rather. He… he isn't a bad man, Peter, not really; he's fighting desperately for… something. I dunno. Call it women's intuition. I just have this feeling, Peter. Almost like… like he IS Billy, or maybe, more like who Billy might become like, some day. Maybe… maybe he's not the man the police are looking for. I can't explain it; I just know: Don't hurt him if you can help it."

Peter stared into his wife's eyes for a long moment, seeing the plea there. Finally he capitulated. "Okay," he agreed with a nod. "He could be family or something, and it was a case of mistaken identity. Maybe he's actually on our side and trying to protect a young cousin. Now get downstairs with Billy. I'll try to sort this out without anybody getting hurt."

Jeanie nodded and hurried for the basement as Peter ran for the gun safe.

‘’…

In the side yard, Drago was picking himself up–as well as picking the odd shard of glass from his shoulder.

Huh. Doesn't have quite the high dive training I've got, Ray thought absently as he confronted the man.

"Billy Drago?" Jay called, and their opponent instinctively looked up.

"Where's my wife and child?" Ray demanded, gun targeted on Drago's chest.

All he got was a soft, maddening smile.

"I SAID, where are my WIFE and CHILD?!" Ray repeated, depressing the trigger on his Glock past the safety.

Drago cast a surreptitious glance at his watch, then turned his bland gaze back on Ray. "What makes you think I'd know?"

Ray growled like a rabid wolf.

"The presence of one of your men in the nursery," Jay answered for an enraged Ray. "Dressed the same way as your men in the various bank robberies you've organized, per security video. Some of which YOU appear in."

"Not to mention the… shall we say, unusual mode of entrance?" Ray snarled, finding his voice again through his fury.

"Ah, well, now that is a bit unique, isn't it?" Drago remarked calmly.

"Brane manipulation? Or boson?" Ray queried, and Drago raised an eyebrow.

"Impressive," he mused, "that you should even be aware of either possibility."

"No shit," Jay growled. "You got no idea who you're messing with."

"Nor, apparently, do you," Drago fired back. "But you do know you dare not use your weapons, lest you lose all trace of your precious family."

Ray threw a sharp glance at Jay, and both men lowered, then holstered, their weapons. That proved to be Drago's cue.

A sudden leap into a handspring brought Drago caroming into the pair before they could react. Jay sidestepped backward, avoiding part of the blow; Ray threw an upper block with one arm, an outer block with the other, and a front kick with his right leg, which connected with Drago's chest, knocking him out of his handsprings.

But Drago landed neatly on his feet as Ray aimed a jump kick at his head. Drago ducked, and Jay aimed two solid blows at his face—only his face wasn't there when the punches were. Instead, Jay staggered back from a heel striking his solar plexus, landing hard on his backside on the ground, trying to get his breath.

Ray had regrouped and threw a flurry of side kicks, knife hands, and palm heel strikes at Drago's head and torso. Some connected; but Drago retaliated in kind, and even faster, and within seconds Ray himself was staggering, suddenly remembering that his brain pan had been rattled a few times too often of late.

Drago freed himself of the men as his once and future father came around the corner of the house, armed with a shotgun. Drago Senior moved to Ray's left, standing between Ray and the wood frame house. Jay, still on the ground and only mildly breathless, retrieved his pistol from its holster and took aim at their anomaly.

Unexpectedly Drago broke into a run, directly at the senior Drago. This prevented Jay from opening fire for simultaneous fear of either hitting the innocent man or penetrating the house. Connecting well before the other man could react, Drago threw his father to the ground without harming him.

೮೦೧೩

Drago didn't stop. He kept running, around the corner to the front of the house, hearing the scuffle of feet behind him as the two DSRPO agents ensured his father was okay before all three men charged in pursuit. A single leap took him to the low porch roof, and he clambered swiftly to the nearest window, easing it up silently, knowing it had no lock or even a latch; he'd used it to escape too often in his youth not to be aware of it. He crouched, still and silent, in the cloaking darkness for a moment as the men scouted the yard. As soon as their footsteps hit the porch stairs, he slipped through the window.

Once inside, he was back in the nursery, his childhood bedroom, now empty. He could hear running footsteps spread out downstairs as they searched the house for him. Drago checked his watch, and smiled as he felt the room grow warm.

A blue-white light flared, and he was gone.

Chapter 16

"Mrs. Brady?"

The disembodied voice emanated from somewhere near the ceiling of her tiny cell, and Samantha looked upward, searching.

"A little to your right. Over in the corner. That's it. Do you see it now?"

A highly miniaturized camera and speaker hid in the corner's shadow. "Yeah, I see it," she nodded. "Can you hear me?"

"I can."

"Where's my baby?!"

"Safe… for now."

"What do you want?"

"Cooperation."

"To do what?"

"Perhaps I should be more specific—I desire your HUSBAND'S cooperation. I want him to work for me, or at the very least, to cease hindering me in my work."

"What's your work? If you're the one that broke his nose—not to mention had him flung through our second story window and my nanny shot—I can't see that you could be doing anything he'd want to cooperate with."

&OCB

On the video monitor, a nude Sam stood defiant, in all her glory, hands on hips, blonde hair tousled about her bare shoulders, blue eyes blazing. *A veritable goddess of a creature,* Drago thought with sincere admiration. *What a pity that I… but that is not the point of this conversation. Still, she may prove useful as breeding stock. Even if my heart did not belong to…* He broke off his thoughts before they could turn morose. After all, he had lived many long years since Ssaree's death. Years in her past, true; many years nevertheless.

"My work," he continued, "is to purge humanity of a curse."

&OCB

"I don't see any curse around here except you," Sam snarled. "You stole my baby, you hurt—maybe killed—my husband and my nanny. I think my house blew up…"

"BE QUIET! If you want to see your precious infant alive again, shut up, woman."

Sam silenced.

"Good. Now, what I want you to do is very simple. I want you to read a prepared statement during a video recording. The recording will be sent to your husband. Yes, he is alive. Meanwhile, you and your baby—little Abigail, isn't it?—will be held here, safe. Once he responds in the desired fashion, you will both be released unharmed."

"I have your word?" Sam asked, suspicious.

"My word, upon my honor, milady."

Sam raised an eyebrow. *Interesting turn of phrase,* she thought. *Very... archaic. And he obviously doesn't realize that Ray ISN'T the team leader, I am. Wonder how I can play off this? Hmm?*

"Let me see the prepared statement and I'll tell you."

"Very well. I had half anticipated such a request, and prepared for it. After reading it, if you so desire, a word here and there may be changed to make it more... comfortable... for you. I am sure, for instance, that you have a special name for your husband, which you prefer instead of his formal given name."

A scratching sound came from the bottom of the door, and a sheet of paper worked its awkward way through the narrow slit. Sam went to the door and picked it up, beginning to read.

ೞೞೞ

"Reagan, it's Samantha. I'm okay, honey, and so is the baby. Dr. Drago is our host, and he's taking good care of us. He wants you as an ally, Reagan. He's doing a really good thing, trying to rid humans of a terrible plague, and he wants your help. The species has to be purged of the infection, purified. There is no hope for those that are already infected. There is simply no way to remove the plague from their bodies. They will have to die.

"He's already had medical tests run, and the baby and I are free of the plague. That means you are, too. So if you cooperate, or at least refuse to interfere, he'll release Abigail and me, unharmed. Please, honey. Help him. What he's doing is right. Besides, I want to see you and the baby soon. Do what he says.

"I love you."

ೞೞೞ

Sam looked up from the paper. "You're Dr. Drago?"

"I am. Dr. William H. Drago."

"You call cold, naked, hungry, and thirsty 'taking good care of us?'"

"The baby—for whom we planned—is in a proper nursery, Mrs. Brady. We did not anticipate YOUR arrival. Agree to do the video, and you will be provided clothing, food, water, and a suitable living space. Perhaps even allowed to care for the child yourself."

"And if I don't?"

"If you do not, matters may not go so... well."

Sam understood the veiled threat in Drago's words. She waved the paper.

"This sounds like you're planning to kill everyone that's infected with this... plague."

"There is a reason for that. I am."

Sam scowled. "Then... not just no. HELL no."

ಬಂಗ

Drago sighed silently, betraying an inner weariness with the whole matter, but neither his stance, nor his expression, weakened. *She is going to be stubborn, it would appear. I really had hoped it would not come to this. But if she is who I think she is, she must be toughened up, in any case.*

"Very well. It be on your own head, Mrs. Brady."

He flicked off the vid comm and hit another communications switch. "Jones?"

"Yes sir?"

"You have the details of the plan?"

"I do, sir."

"You may proceed."

"Thank you, sir!"

Drago walked out of the room, headed for his office to devise another means of communication with Dr. Reagan Brady.

ಬಂಗ

"All right," Ray concluded, as they sat in Kruger's office, debriefing to him. Ray found the debrief helped keep his mind off what might be happening to Sam and Abby, and he concentrated on his train of thought, trying to ignore his voice when it cracked despite himself. He knew he looked haggard; he hadn't even bothered to shave. He didn't care—there were other things more important at the moment. The Old Man, his father in law, merely leaned back and listened as the others talked, and Ray briefly wondered if he were really as calm as he looked. "The guy can teleport—or whatever you want to call it—to and from just about any place in space, at least on Earth."

"Why not off?" Jay wondered.

"Gotta know where to go, I'd think," Ray postulated. "Ain't like we know a whole lotta habitable planets."

"Mm, good point," Danny agreed.

"On the other hand," Ray pointed out, "if he's a Santa, then maybe he's COMING from a habitable planet." He shook his head gingerly. The blast thirty-six hours prior had not done anything for his multiply concussed noggin, he decided. Neither had the most recent fight. He sighed. *Damn, but it would be nice to get a chance to actually heal up before getting into another fight.* Then he mentally shook his head. *Not until Sam and Abby are back. Whatever it takes, Ray. You do—endure—whatever it takes.*

"Ray," Jay pointed out logically, "we found him as a kid. He was LOOKING AFTER himself as a kid. Think about it. Instead of having it out with us in the nursery, like his dude did at your house, he immediately dove out the window—knowing we'd go after him—to take the confrontation outside, away from the kid. And did you notice, he never once attacked the kid's father–because that's HIS father, too. He ain't no Santa, Ray, he's an Easter Bunny."

"Then explain his strength, Jay. His quickness. He took you down before you could even blink."

"Yeah," Jay admitted, flushing. "Somethin' obviously happened to the dude, to ramp him up like that. But I still say Easter Bunny, maybe with a Santa component. Or maybe cyborg Bunny."

"Ugh," Danny muttered. "There's a mental image for kids' nightmares."

"Maybe his parents are Santas, too," Ray argued.

"Maybe. But they ain't doin' nothin,'" Jay riposted. "No sign of them bebopping around spacetime. And I already thought about that and did some checking, back when I first matched the kid's fingerprints. I got birth records for 'em, and genealogies going back a good ways. No time loops, no sudden appearances, nuthin.' Besides, it'd be kinda dumb for Santas to register their own Santa kid with the government they're trying to hide in. But him, you got all over the place for the last... how many centuries?"

"Jay does have a point, Ray," Billy the Kid agreed. "Even without all the other shit I found, you got two of him existing here at two different ages. That's gotta make for some time travel in there some damn place."

"Anyway," Ray continued with a weary sigh, waving away their comments to stop the argument he was too tired to continue, "this isn't getting us anywhere in finding my girls. What we have to look at are the common denominators, the common factors in all these appearances. I see two."

"And what are they?" Danny asked shrewdly.

"Major terrorist events–both sides," Ray observed, "and the development of nuclear physics."

The others thought for a few moments.

"Makes good sense," Jay finally agreed. "I can see it. Where does it take us?"

"Not sure yet," Ray admitted ruefully, as his voice cracked, "but I sure as hell don't like where it's pointing."

"Nuclear terrorism," Billy opined.

"Right," Ray confirmed.

"Against who?" Jay demanded. "I thought he was the one that made the homing devices for us in Afghanistan. AND he was the Marine unit leader in Fallujah."

"And was part of the rescue and investigation teams at Oklahoma City and 9-11," Billy pointed out.

"But he was also inside the nuke plant in Iran as one of the workers," Ray observed. "And I think he was in the caves in Afghanistan, too."

"Maybe he was doing the same thing we were," Danny suggested. "One of the good guys, in a different group from us. Lord knows, if we're as deep under cover as we are, we likely aren't the ONLY group. Maybe he's even with a deep six police unit, trying to see what WE'RE up to. Policing the police, as it were."

"Maybe," Ray said, "but if he's one of the good guys, why is he STEALING money all over the globe? Why is he swiping material that goes into making neutron bombs? What kind of genetics is he doing with radiodurans? Why did he have Teresa shot, Frank killed, and kidnap Sam and Abby? Hell, why'd he try to take me out in the first place?"

"Perhaps," the Old Man interjected then, "he has been playing sheep dog."

"Sheep dog?" Jay echoed.

"Yes," Kruger answered. "You know, herding humanity in the direction he wants it to go, to serve whatever ends he has in mind. And any branch away from that direction is being pruned, if you'll excuse the mixed metaphors."

"Maybe," Ray decided. "But what are his ends? Why is he doing it? What does he hope to accomplish?"

Kruger shrugged.

"You're right. This doesn't make sense," Danny complained. "We're missing some major puzzle pieces, here."

"Don't I know it," Ray sighed, hoarse. "Okay, enough with me blundering my way through this. The lives of my wife and child are on the line; innocent civilians around the world could be in danger. I'm beat to hell and back, with a badly rattled cranium into the bargain. I need help. Time to get serious."

He reached for the secure phone and dialed a series of numbers, then waited. "Paul? Yeah. This is Ray. Yeah, THAT Ray. Uh, not exactly. Yeah, um, well, not anymore. Listen, you're about to get pulled onto another project. Yeah, I know what you're working on out there is important. But this is an emergency. Homeland Security. Yeah. My boss will send the orders through. Hope you can pack fast. See you in about six hours."

"Who was that?" Jay asked.

"My old graduate advisor," Ray explained. "Dr. Paul Allen. No, not THAT Paul Allen," he added, seeing eyebrows rise. "He works for Lockheed Martin Skunkworks, in... a nondescript location in the desert, in Nevada," he finished with a sheepish grin. "He's an expert in this shit, and probably should have been recruited for DSRPO instead of me."

"Not necessarily, Ray," Kruger remarked. "Does he have your... 'field experience?'"

"No sir."

"Then we got the right man. But you're right, you need help now. You're beat to hell and back, exhausted, and emotionally torn to shreds, and not a man of us blames you. I'll get on those orders pronto."

ಸಃಚ

Sam paced the small cell, mentally measuring it off. It wasn't perfectly rectangular, she discovered. The wall that the door was in was about a foot or so shorter than the opposite wall, which appeared to her eye to be slightly curved. She frowned, trying to puzzle out her location.

Suddenly a scream came from the speaker in the ceiling. Sam recognized it instantly, and she spun toward it. "ABBY!" she shrieked. "Abby, can you hear me?! It's Mommy! It's all right, darling! What the hell are you bastards doing to her?!"

"She can't hear you, Mrs. Brady," a different voice sounded, and she recognized it as the man who'd invaded Abby's nursery at home. "But I can. Your little darling is fine—for now. She only wants the toy I'm dangling juuuust out of her reach. Would you like for her to have it? I can give it to her. I can have the nurse feed her. All you have to do is get your husband to cooperate."

"Eat shit and die, asshole," Sam snarled.

"Suit yourself. But now we have little Abby's screams recorded. We can play them day and night, whenever we like, and you'll never know if it's really Abby screaming, or the recording."

Oh, God, Sam thought fervently, horrified. *Please don't let them hurt my baby.*

The screams went on for the next three hours.

ഇൽരു

At the end of that time, when blessed silence fell, Sam couldn't feel her bare feet against the cold concrete floor. Yet she still stumbled about in an effort to keep warm. Suddenly the metal door flew open and an intense gush of cold water, like that from a fire hose, knocked her hard against the far wall, bruising her back on the rough concrete. She slid to the floor, scraping back and elbows in the process, and huddled there, face averted and forearms in front of her head, until the water shut off and the door slammed closed. Then she staggered to her feet.

Dripping wet, hair streaming water, she padded through the puddles of water in the room, shivering as she tried valiantly to stay warm.

ഇൽരു

"You know," Jay remarked, "if this guy IS a Santa Claus of some sort, it would sure be nice to know what the hell he is, if you know what I mean."

"If only we had a sample of the guy's blood," Danny agreed. "That would tell us for sure if he's a Santa or a Bunny. Or a cyborg Bunny."

"Yeah, 'cause we could get the forensics boys to DNA type it," Jay noted.

"Wait a minute," Ray paused. "Blood! Shit! Sam, baby, I hope you haven't done the laundry!"

"Get real, man! Laundry?!" Jay stared at Ray as if he'd lost his mind, wondering if their leader had finally reached his breaking point. *After all, he's been going for damn near forty-eight hours now, had that noggin clocked again, and is stressed out as all hell. The man gotta have a shutdown button hidden someplace. And this might have just tapped it.*

"Yeah! Remember our first encounter with the guy in New York? And how I had blood all over my shirt?" All signs of exhaustion had fallen from Ray.

"Yeah…"

"The blood on the back of the shirt wasn't mine! I busted his nose, between an elbow and a head butt to his face, and his nose was bleeding like Niagara!"

"And the shirt is in the laundry," Kruger observed.

"But the house is blown to bits, Ray," Jay protested.

"Aha, therein lies the rub," Ray grinned. "The laundry's in the BASE-MENT. Right behind the 'home office.' Let's go."

"Get to it!" The Old Man reached for the phone. "I'll have Fields standing by."

෧෬

An hour later the screaming started again. Sam strained to listen to the minutest nuance of sound, a gasp, a wail, a repeated noise in the background, any potential clue, in an effort to determine if it was a looped recording or fresh, live screams from her baby girl. *God help me, if this keeps up, I'm going to become immune to the cries of my own child,* Sam thought in anguish. *Assuming Abby and I survive this, what kind of mother will I be?!*

After two hours the speaker went quiet, and Sam was left in an eerie, dead silence. Her skin had dried, though her hair was still damp and lay, chilly, against her head, neck, and shoulders, and her feet were turning blue. Hypothermia might be a problem if she didn't manage to get warmer soon. Sam did her best to warm herself by crouching on her feet and hugging herself.

The door opened, then closed again, and Sam rose and turned to see what the play was going to be this time—more of the same, something new, or would they up the game and get more serious?

The man who'd invaded the nursery stood looking at her naked and chilled body, grinning. The cut she'd put on his forehead right before he'd decked her had been cleaned; two stitches closed the deepest part, and steri-strips held the rest shut. The smile on his face wasn't one of a happy man. It was the smile of a crazy son of a bitch about to do something bad. Very bad. Sam knew that smile. She'd seen it before. *Serious, then.* She braced her mind for more pain.

"Hi there," he said with a leer, scanning her up and down slowly, noting her goose bumps and the way her nipples had hardened in the coldness of the cell. "Remember me, doll?"

"Hell, yes. Your face is one I'll never forget." Warily, she sidestepped as he penetrated deeper into the room. *More pain coming.*

"Oh, ain't that the truth, babe." He lit a cigarette. Sam eyed it warily, knowing. "Every night you'll see me in your dreams."

"You wish." *Ready for the pain.*

"Oh, trust me. I'll have you screaming before I'm done with that sweet ass of yours." He moved close, puffing the cigarette. Suddenly his hand swung away from his face. There was a sizzling sound and the stench of burnt meat as the lit tip of the cigarette contacted Sam's side.

Sam didn't even flinch. *Pain.*

"Ooo, tough bitch," he said, smirking. "Bet you get off on pain, don't ya?"

Another burn, this time on the side of her breast. Her breasts quivered, but otherwise Sam remained motionless. *That's not the worst of it.*

Jones threw the cigarette aside and backhanded her in the face in one move. She tried to roll with the blow and come back around, but she slipped on numb feet, stumbled and fell, cheek already bruising. Before she could recover, he was on her, handcuffing her with her hands behind her back. Her blue eyes glared.

She never said a word. But she had thoughts. She thought about her husband who would be coming for her and her baby girl. She thought about her baby girl who was somewhere close by, scared without her mommy or daddy. She thought about her own father who would move Heaven and Earth to find them. *Oh, yes, there is pain coming. Nothing like the pain this idiot thinks he can inflict. I'll endure it. Then. HE. WILL. FEEL. PAIN!*

He pummeled her breasts and kneed her in the groin, causing her to double over and heave, her empty belly trying to purge itself from the impact and the pain. Then he forced her to keep her head down and slapped her ass until it was bruised red and sore, periodically pounding his fist into her ribs. When he finally released her and she tried to straighten up, he shoved her into the concrete wall and let her slide roughly down it onto the cold, wet floor. She left more skin on its coarse surface.

He laughed, a cruel sound, and turned toward the door. "This was only the foreplay, babe," he grinned. "I'll just let you lie there and anticipate the… 'main event.' I'll be back later."

"Looking forward to it, you fucking coward." Sam glared at him from her crumpled, twisted position on the floor as he walked out. "I am SO going to kill the shit out of you."

"Sure, baby, sure. That's the attitude. Love the spunk."

And the door closed. A click told her it had locked securely. *Pain. Let your mind go. Let the pain calm.* She focused her mind and tried to recover. Then she rolled onto her belly, her handcuffed arms still awkwardly restrained behind her.

Letting her hands go as limp as possible, Sam gradually worked them through the rings of the handcuffs. She pushed as hard as she could, feeling the skin tear as she did. She bit at her swollen lip as she grunted through the pain. Fortunately for her the asshole that cuffed her had done it hastily and didn't slam them completely tight. Not that it mattered much anyway; Sam had learned long ago how to dislocate her thumbs to get out of virtually any set of shackles she was faced with. *All part of the training.* She grunted and forced the cuff on her left hand over it, taking most of the skin on her knuckles with it. Then repeating the process on her right hand was easier, as she could sit up and bring her hands around in front of her to see what she was doing. Finally, not too much the worse for the wear, she was free of the handcuffs. She snatched them up and flung them into the corner, ignoring the *splash* and *clank* as they skipped across the puddle in the corner of the concrete floor. Sam rubbed her scraped, raw hands and licked the wounds on her knuckles. She inspected her ribs and didn't think any of them were broken, but there were a couple of them bruised. The cigarette burns were the worst, but they'd heal. She'd be fine.

Sam paced for another half-hour, like a caged tiger, trying to keep warm, before exhaustion caught up with her.

Too tired, stiff and sore to care any longer, Sam found the driest patch of floor she could and curled up on it, trying to rest. The baby screaming started back up five minutes later. She put her hands over her ears and closed her eyes, praying for forgiveness. She needed to regain some of her strength or she would be no good to her little girl. In her present state even ten minutes of sleep would make a difference.

෫෮෪

Drago watched the woman in the cell pacing back and forth. *She is an amazing creature,* he thought. *So determined, and yet so loving and tender. So like my Ssa…*

He broke off that thought quickly and reveled in the fierceness this woman had. It reminded him of times when he'd seen similar acts of ferocity. Similar heroism. Perhaps, he considered, toughening wasn't needed in this case. Still, if it caused her to become willing to contact her husband, it would be worth it.

Despite himself, the comparison continued in his mind—the comparison of this woman to one he had known and loved with all the passion of his being, long, long ago in the future.

Besides, there was something he needed to know. So, steeling himself, he let the memories flow.

৪৩৫৩

Drago had arrived for their lunch date at the restaurant and found Ssaree waiting with another person. "B- bill," she said, trying not to stammer, "this is my colleague, Hsthys. I haven't seen him in ages, so I thought I'd invite him along to meet you."

Her beautiful green eyes were dilated, and Drago instantly knew something was wrong. "Bill" was their secret alert code; she always called him "William" in private. But he barely had time to register the fact before he felt a weapon pressed into his ribcage from behind.

"Bring her, Hsthys," the man behind him ordered. "This ought to provide us some of the information we want."

৪৩৫৩

But it hadn't. Ssaree and Drago were too new to the resistance to be able to provide much information at all, even had it been useful, even had they wanted to. Unfortunately the agents of the Sslith Empire didn't believe them. Torture was an acceptable means of extracting information to that political entity, and it was used freely and often.

Drago had been through more pain embedded in the granite wall, however, than any torturer could ever inflict, and he withstood the assaults reasonably well, considering. It was watching what they did to Ssaree that seemed to turn him wrong side out. The rapes were the worst. And knowing the relationship between them, they always raped her in his presence. He was imprisoned, of course; some sort of advanced bonds contrived of—even he, as a physicist, wasn't sure. A localized graviton field, perhaps. All he knew was that his body was plastered firmly to a wall while his beloved, the one and only true love of what had since become an exceedingly long life, was gang raped and beaten repeatedly in front of him. And he was helpless to stop it.

৪৩৫৩

Eventually they decided that Ssaree was useless; as she'd said again and again, sometimes screaming it, she knew nothing. Therefore they concluded that Drago must be the key, and that he'd somehow convinced her to go along with him because of her love for him. It was obvious, however, that the love went both ways, as he cursed and spat and struggled to free himself whenever they "went to work" on her, as the Empire operatives put it.

As the two of them managed to hold on, leaning on their love for each other even as it was used against them, it only enraged their captors, encouraging them to adapt their techniques. Finally, after one of the gang torture sessions where Ssaree had been beaten and raped so hard that blood flowed down her poor trembling legs, they started something different.

"You used to have too many of these once, didn't you, Ssaree?" Hsthys said, picking up her limp hand and spreading her fingers. "I wonder how it would be to have too few. Want to find out?"

Too weak to cry out, Ssaree only whimpered in fear as Hsthys pulled a large knife and placed her hand on a stone block. Drago cursed at the top of his lungs, his roar of rage almost drowning Ssaree's scream as Hsthys callously lopped off two of her fingers. Even as they began growing back, he moved her wrist onto the block.

ಎಃಇ

By the time they hacked off her left leg at mid-thigh, the end was in sight. They were working faster than her healing ability could keep up, and the blood loss had already been severe. The femoral artery had been severed when the leg was cut off, and blood poured freely onto the floor, spurting with every beat of her valiant, loving heart. Ssaree was bleeding out, and Drago could only watch as those adored green eyes faded and grew glassy. When her body sagged limp in the restraints, he knew she was gone.

He let out a howl of agony as something within his chest shattered and something within his mind snapped, and he lurched against the invisible restraints with all the power he could muster, more strength than he had ever even imagined he possessed. It was only then that he discovered they'd assumed him to be pure human, and set the restraints appropriately: he felt his torso move. Not much, but it moved.

'Not in bloody time,' he thought, enraged and grieved, 'but I'm damned if she won't be avenged!'

Summoning everything he had, adrenaline surging wildly, he tore himself off the wall. One wrist snapped loudly, and a rib cracked, but he barely felt it; it would be healed soon anyway. Before the two Ssliths could move, he was on them. He broke both necks quickly. Then, before they could heal, he took the same blade that they'd used to hack Ssaree apart and gutted them, heedlessly flinging entrails across the floor in his mad rage to reach their hearts and aortas—or the Sslith equivalents, whatever they called them.

He found them.

He slashed the essential little organs to bits and strung them around the room. A delicate, lacy necklace of cardiac tissue adorned Ssaree's lifeless throat when he'd finished, an adornment at once beautiful and garish; and the agents' blood joined Ssaree's on the floor. He wiped his feet on the absorbent matting by the door, put there for the purpose.

Then he ran.

೮つᏟᎧ

He wasn't sure how they'd managed it, how they even knew, given the heightened security after his and Ssaree's arrest, but his resistance unit was waiting for him in the tertiary rendezvous point in an alley two blocks down from the hospital. A strange woman was there also, waiting with them. She had long, medium blonde hair with random, cherry red streaks, in the style that in Drago's day would have been called cyberpunk. Her skin was deeply tanned; her deep blue irises surrounded by red brick-toned whites; her fingernails a deep henna color.

"Follow me," she said, without introductions. "Quickly. There is little time to waste."

He did—into the sewers, along maintenance tunnels, and up into a lab building. There, they were met by two human Ssliths who were evidently moles like Ssaree had been. They skipped introductions and hurried into what Drago took to be a laboratory.

Inside, Drago was faced with a familiar apparatus. It was decidedly more sophisticated than any he'd ever seen before, but he still recognized it instantly.

"A membrane overlap!" he exclaimed. "An extraction point!"

"You should not be here now." The strange woman nodded at the device.

"Are you some other kind of alien?" he asked.

"No. I'm human, just enhanced."

"Enhanced? How?"

"You will figure it all out in… time."

"Time?"

"Go home," she said. "This is not your time. Maybe you can stop all this. You and Dad say you can't, because of the physics, but I figure it's worth a shot. Who knows? The two of you might be wrong."

"Me and your dad?! I don't know you. What the hell are you talking about?" Drago began adjusting settings as fast as he could.

"Personally, I like paradoxes. It keeps you on your feet. Makes you twist your brain around something hard to believe in. But paradoxes require multiple timelines. You and Dad both agree that there is only one." She paused briefly. *"Just because you believe something is impossible doesn't make it so. Do something. Make humans smarter. Give us a chance to beat the bastards. Find a cure for the flu or a way to kill them without killing us. The first chance you get, cause a paradox."*

"I... I don't know what you mean."

"Neither do I," she replied. *"Just do something to give humanity, to give us, more time. Time always allows for things to happen."*

"What does that mean? Time always allows for things to happen?"

"You have to do something whether it works or not. If you do nothing then what was the point of you coming here? Of... sacrifices we've all made?"

"...I see."

"I've said too much already. Go back. Prepare. Stop this."

"Thank you. I'll do my damnedest. Ma'am, your name, if you don't mind?" He stepped onto the extraction point.

"We'll meet when the time is right." The woman smiled. *"Just know for now that you can call me Abby. And I forgive you. I forgive you for everything you have, uh, will do. I know now that you must do one thing from here on out."*

"What is that?"

"You must be ruthless and bloody. You MUST get it done. No matter what it takes, you must find a way to save humanity," Abby said, just as a blue-white flare of light overtook him. *"And don't forget. I forgive you."*

⁍⁃⁎

But he'd miscalculated in his haste to escape. Or maybe he hadn't accounted for the quantum uncertainties properly. Or maybe the girl form the future messed with the controls somehow before he'd used them. Or maybe it was damned luck. Instead of landing in his own time, he overshot, by several centuries. Drago came up in the middle of Europe—literally in a hayfield—in what he soon discovered was the early 1700s. With no way to return, let alone reach his own time.

The post-traumatic stress disorder that had begun when he'd materialized in the stone wall, and been shoved roughly and rapidly along in the past week of torture, culminating in Ssaree's horrible death, gained full hold on him then. All control vanished from his psyche as surely as everyone he'd ever known had vanished from his life. He shrieked and screamed like a maniac, throwing anything he could lay hands on at anything—or anyone—he could see. He ran madly through the woods and the fields, heedless of brambles and briars, clothed or not, as if all the hounds of Hell pursued him. He sat in the pouring rain and cried, howling for his Ssaree, keening for *everything he'd lost. It didn't matter if his flesh tore, or his body chilled; he healed within moments, and his immune system seemed impervious.*

Eventually the acute phase faded and he came to his senses. He found an empty crofter's hut and moved in, living a hermit's life, scavenging his food from the land around him, no longer wanting contact with anyone. He needn't have worried. The few neighbors he had considered him a raving madman and avoided him—like the plague, he thought in black humor.

A few years thereafter, he discovered that he wasn't aging like those around him.

That had been the beginning.

ও৪৫ও

Doc Fields was just finishing the DNA analysis from the back of Ray's shirt when the Old Man came in with a visitor. Ray looked up and gave a wordless exclamation, hurrying over to greet the older, brown haired man with the smile crinkles at his gray eyes. "Paul!" he said. "Good to see you again!"

Paul Allen, Ray's graduate advisor and mentor, shook his head. "Mr. Kruger here briefed me, Ray, but I swear I still wouldn't have recognized you."

"Yeah, well, and I thought you were a billionaire," Ray said, making the same old joke they'd used when he was younger.

"I'd swap with that Paul Allen anytime he's ready." Paul smiled. "Somehow, I don't think it's gonna happen anytime soon, though. So why am I here?"

"Hit a couple of rough spots and my brain is getting tired." Suddenly Ray looked more exhausted, more battered, than any of them had ever seen him. The others—even Doc—paused what they were doing, worried, to watch. Within seconds, however, a beep from his equipment drew Fields' mind and gaze back to his work.

"With good reason, if I understand Mr. Kruger, here, right."

"Afraid so."

"Wife and baby daughter?"

"Yeah."

"Damn," Allen drew a deep breath. "Maybe I can help. I'll do my best, anyway."

"Hey hey, how about this?" Fields got their attention as he scanned the DNA results. "Major Weird Shit, reporting for duty. Hey, guys, c'mere, I got something. I dunno what I got, but I got something."

Everyone gathered around his workbench.

"Now this," he laid out a chart, "is the full genome sequence of an ordinary human. In this case, it happens to be me. It was handy."

"Typical baseline human." Paul nodded.

"Almost up to average," Ray goaded, trying to drag his morale back to normal by his own bootstraps.

"Right." Fields laid out another chart, ignoring the good natured barb by way of considering the source. "This, however, is the genome sequence I just made from the blood of our anomaly on Ray's shirt." He gestured at several points on the chart. "Note the completely different structure here, here, here… and here."

"Sumbitch," Jay murmured, intrigued. "But Doc, they're pretty much exactly the same everywhere else."

"You noticed," Fields remarked dryly. "Yes, everywhere else except those snippets are totally human in appearance."

"So…" Ray studied the genetic sequences, "is he human or not?"

"I honestly don't know how to answer that question, Ray," Fields admitted. "Part of him appears to be, yes."

"But not all of him," the Old Man finished for Fields.

"Uh, yeah," Fields agreed reluctantly. "I don't know whether he's a human mutant, an alien mutant, or a human-alien crossbreed… or something else entirely."

"Is it safe for us to assume he's a Santa Claus of some sort?" Ray wondered.

"By definition, I'd say so," Fields agreed. "He's not fully human, anyway. From what I can tell, and what we know of the human genome, this," he tapped their anomaly's genetic sequence, "explains how he beat the shit out of you, Ray. Speed, strength, and proprioceptic capabilities are all found in these two sections here. And here," he gestured at another section, "he's missing the p21 gene."

"Say what?" Jay asked, puzzled.

"That's the gene that, when absent, enables regrowth of limbs and such in animals like salamanders," Fields explained. "The cells in the area of the injury become like embryonic stem cells, and each one will develop into whatever kind of cell is necessary to grow back the missing part. When p21 is present, scar tissue grows instead. HE hasn't got it. At all. Research has been going on, but hasn't progressed nearly so far as human test subjects yet."

"Which explains why the black eye and broken nose healed so fast," Ray mused.

"Yeah, I'd think that would be a correct assessment, Ray. So he ain't one of ours. He could be, I suppose," Fields hypothesized, "a UFO abductee that was experimented on, or some such shit."

"Human once, but no longer," Paul summarized, closer to the truth than he knew.

"Right. Assuming we had proven any abductions to be real. I dunno about that, though." Doc gave Dr. Allen a sharp, querying glance, silently inviting him to elaborate.

Paul discreetly maintained silence.

"Mmph. That does explain a lot. At least I know it took something other than normal human to beat my ass." Ray was satisfied.

Dr. Allen snorted. So did Fields.

"Make you feel better, big guy?" Jay patted his shoulder—the one that had been shot. Ray winced, and Jay smirked.

"And here's where it gets even MORE interesting," Fields continued. "The p21 gene is somehow involved in preventing the formation of cancer cells by cells with damaged DNA—such as from radiation. It doesn't PREVENT the DNA damage, it just prevents runaway replication. We're not quite sure how, yet."

"But radiodurans outright repairs the damage," Ray mused.

"Exactly," Fields agreed. "I'm thinking now maybe we have some idea of why he wanted Conan the Bacterium."

"And I don't like the sound of that," the Old Man interjected. "Not at all."

"Hell no," Ray averred. "Call it a hunch if you like, because we sure don't have the complete picture yet, but I don't think this is good."

"And," Fields threw out one more fact, "it gets weirder. The only animals I know of in which p21 is naturally NON-occurring... are amphibian, and maybe a few reptile, species."

The room became dead silent.

"Now I'm more confused than ever," Jay finally admitted. "What the hell have we got hold of? He's human, but he's not human? He's been around since the late seventeen hundreds? Is he a Santa Claus, or an Easter Bunny? Or both?"

"Whatever these modifications are could mean he's extremely long lived," Fields noted. "It may not be necessary to invoke Easter Bunny, given the Santa Claus evidence. He may have simply lived that long here."

"That's just what I said," Ray agreed.

"But there was that little kid version of him we found," Jay reminded them in protest. "With him as an adult IN THE SAME ROOM with the kid. That says Easter Bunny."

"Jay's right," the Old Man pointed out. "Dr. Fields, possibly you might pop out to the Drago residence and collect some DNA samples from the family? The ENTIRE family? That should at least tell us what we're starting off with."

"Good point," Doc murmured, gathering equipment. "And if they refuse?"

"Then we've got our answer," Kruger noted. "Don't press it, and don't get yourself in trouble if you can avoid it. But take your weapon."

"On my way." The others watched as Fields headed out.

"My head is spinning here," Paul raised an eyebrow and a hand. "Gentlemen, let's go find a room and sit down. I think we need to have a long talk."

&OCR

Drago emerged from his reverie with a sigh that might have contained a hint of pain, having found and confirmed the memories he wanted, which in turn seemed to verify what he suspected to be true.

"Abby," he murmured. "She said her name was Abby. And her father... must have been a scientist. General Abigail? And her father, General...? Hm. I wonder..."

He wandered out of the observation room and down the hall, in the general direction of the radiodurans lab. The words "bloody" and "ruthless" rang in his mind, but not as much, or as loudly, as the words, "I forgive you."

&OCR

Sam lost all track of time. Cold, hungry, thirsty, and in pain that was physical, mental, and emotional, she simply lay there, trying to blot out all sensation. She could not have told whether she was there a day or a year. Nor did she care. It seemed an eternity, regardless. *Ray's time dilation must be in effect*, some part of her brain thought whimsically. *But am I traveling at the speed of light, or are they?*

After awhile she mustered the strength to get back on her feet. She stretched carefully, then bounced from foot to foot trying to loosen her stiff and protesting muscles. She eventually decided she was maneuverable, if still cold. There was still plenty of pain but it was dull.

The door opened again.

Jones stood in it, leering.

"Ready for the main event, baby?" he asked, closing the door.

"Hell, yeah," Sam muttered. *Time for the PAIN.*

☙☞

Outside, three more men in jumpsuits waited their turn. One was already aroused in anticipation.

"Damn," he muttered, "wish I was goin' first. Suck-up Jones gets all the fun."

"Slow down," one of the others said in a thick accent, with a grin. "Trust me. Better Jones goes first."

"Why?" his companion demanded.

"You have never done this before, eh?"

"No…"

"Newbie." He responded with a leer. "After the first man, the woman is all soft and bloody from being forced. Believe me, blood and semen make a lubricant like nothing else."

"You ex-military?"

"Yes. Let us say… the Cold War did not end everywhere."

"Oh."

"Exactly."

"Jones is inexperienced, too, then."

"Yes. I could tell: He demanded… how is it you say? First crack at her. You and I and Marcos here are the ones that will have the fun, though. All the fight will be out of her, and it will be as smooth as silk. And just as good."

The crotch of the first man's jumpsuit swelled even further.

His companions laughed.

☙☞

"Hello there, little one," Drago told Abby in a friendly, affectionate tone. Abby was now awake and playing with blocks in a corner of her playpen. *Had I had my wish, this might be my child*, he thought, studying the toddler's features, fair like his own. *Mine and Ssaree's. But no. This is the real world, William. Wishes won't do here.*

"Hi." Abby looked up and said her one word. Then she repeated, "Hi."

"Hi," Drago smiled in gentle amusement at the rather one sided conversation. "I have the feeling we've met before," he murmured then, sobering. "Although perhaps 'before' is not quite the right term. Your daddy is very intelligent, isn't he?"

"Hi. Da. Hi."

"Yes, your da. Dr. Brady. And quite an excellent fighter. I recognized some Marine techniques among his repertoire."

"H- hi," Abby hacked a bit as she said the word, then coughed.

"Oh dear. The cystic fibrosis seems to be acting up again. It IS a trifle damp and cold in here, I'm afraid. Perils of the construct, I suppose. But I'll have the laboratory and nursery temperatures adjusted, a dehumidifier added, and see to it that Dr. Brooks monitors you very closely for respiratory infection. It simply won't do for you to get sick. You have far too much work ahead of you. And I think I have something in the works myself that will help a great deal. Don't worry, little one; I'll see to it that you're ready when the time comes." He smiled. "Goodbye for now, little Abby dear. Or perhaps I should say, General."

"Hi."

Drago couldn't help but chuckle at the incongruity of her farewell, as he departed the lab in search of Brooks to ensure the child's continued health.

ഇന്ദ്ര

Jones maneuvered Sam into a corner, where he proceeded to massage her breasts roughly, pinching her nipples—still erect from the cold—hard. Disgusted, Sam nevertheless permitted it, biding her time, noting the crotch of his jumpsuit starting to bulge, as she waited and watched for some chance—any chance—to prevent what was about to happen. He reached for the zipper pull at his throat and unzipped the entire front of his jumpsuit, letting it drop to the floor around his ankles. *What is it with men and commando?* Sam wondered, mentally shaking her head. Jones pinned her arms to the walls, nudging her thighs open with his knees.

"Whaddaya think, sweet cheeks?" he murmured into her face. His breath reeked of stale tobacco smoke. His teeth were yellowed.

"Ha ha!" She glanced down, trying to appear defiantly bemused. "I've seen bigger in a high school locker room," she informed him calmly. *Boy, is this guy a neo. Left my feet free.*

"Smile while you can," Jones snarled. "You're gonna think big in a minute, bitch!" He shoved his engorged groin between her thighs.

"Nope. Don't think so." *Bringing the fucking PAIN now, asshole!*

Sam released her poor aching bladder, emptying it all over the man's erection before he could get close to her entrance. Startled and angry, he jerked his hips backward with a curse, which was just what Sam wanted.

She brought her right knee up with all the force she could muster, straight into Jones' unprotected—and by that time, highly sensitive—groin. He screamed like a girl, and Sam followed that up with a hard head butt, then a swift kick to his left inner knee. The knee bowed outward, accompanied by sickening pops and snaps as the tendons and ligaments in the joint tore. This time the sound that escaped him was more like a shriek. Sam didn't bother with planting her feet again before pushing another sidekick through the loosened knee. This time bone cracked free of the skin.

Jones toppled onto his side, left knee destroyed and useless, ankles tangled in his jumpsuit, still seeing stars, and screaming in pain. His right hand groped blindly for the pockets in his twisted, rumpled jumpsuit, looking for his sidearm.

"You want some more, 'bitch?'" Sam was already on top of him, reaching for his right hand. Grabbing his fingers in both her hands, she yanked backward and apart, and he screamed again as the tendons—and some of the skin and muscle—in that extremity gave up the ghost. She forced the bloody, maimed hand back and around, driving him to roll onto his stomach, where she put her knee into his upper back, just below his neck. He now lay face down in a puddle of her urine and his blood, and he gagged briefly at the ammonia smell. She let her shin follow his spine down and leaned her entire weight on that leg.

"No, no!" He squirmed in pain, but her weight was far too much to lever off in that position, especially with one knee out of commission and his shredded hand pinned behind his back. There was another pop as his right shoulder dislocated, and he howled.

"Does it feel like I'm killing the shit out of you now?" she growled into his ear, grinding his useless hand beneath her knee. "Does it?"

"Oh, God," Jones whimpered. "Don't! No more! Please! My card key is in my chest pocket. Don't do it!"

"Thanks for the information. Too little, too late, fuck you and die! Emphasis on die!" Sam said as she grabbed his forehead with both hands, making sure her knee pressed down hard on the base of his neck. Jerking back as hard as she could, she heard and felt the loud snap. Jones sagged to the floor. Then she spat on him.

Quickly Sam stripped him, donning his jumpsuit and boots—which were rather too large, a fact that concerned her—and using the velcro adjustments on the uni-size garment to cinch it around her smaller body.

Looking in the multiple and quite capacious cargo pockets, she found a comb, which she used to detangle her damp hair, a Glock 18 full auto with two extra thirty-three round magazines, fully loaded–and the card key to her cell.

~~~

The three outside heard the high pitched screams, and leered at each other. The room fell silent shortly thereafter.

"There we are," the experienced soldier said to his companions. "She is ready for us."

Just then they heard the click of the door lock. "I shall let you go first," the seasoned man offered generously. "Enjoy."

"Thanks, buddy," the first said gratefully as the door swung open.

They didn't even have a chance to register the fact that the person in the uniform jumpsuit was female. One had his nose driven through his brain by a palm heel strike, the second had a thumb thrust through his eyeball, and the third's trachea was collapsed with a knife hand to his throat. Seconds later the three of them were crumpled on the floor of the corridor, very, very still. A few minutes after that, and Sam was standing in the corridor outside, with four bodies locked inside her former prison. Fortunately for her, one of the men waiting outside had had smallish feet. She'd found boots that were at least not too big to move around in.

"Time to find Abby and get the hell outta here," she muttered to herself.

Chapter 17

Sam began a frantic search for Abby. In her stolen uniform, the few soldiers—at least that was how Sam had begun thinking of them—that she encountered paid her no mind. Whenever no one was looking, she tried her key card on various doors.

The first room she entered was evidently a laboratory of some sort. There were workbenches covered with glassware, laptops scattered about, and what looked to be some analysis equipment. Sam recognized a gas chromatograph, a mass spectrometer, and a few other things. No people, and definitely no baby. She ducked back out, passing by a row of what looked like propane bottles. Upon closer inspection she discovered that indeed they were propane bottles, but she had no idea why they were there. She scanned the area and noted a large picture frame window across the way leading to another room full of equipment. Above that room she could see a catwalk. Where it went, she wasn't certain, but she decided to go around the room and work her way through her present floor and then find a way to the next one. She'd search every inch of the place if that was what it took to find her daughter.

The next room she opened… was macabre. Metal shelves lined the walls, and on the shelves were tubes and jars. On one side of the room were what appeared to be normal rats, but as she progressed along the shelves, the rats appeared more and more abnormal.

"He's mutated 'em," she decided, studying a rat with three tails and twice as many digits on each foot as normal. By the time she reached the other side of the room, she was growing nauseated. The animals had progressed to higher and higher mammals, and now contained various small primates: macaques with double hands, capuchin monkeys with abnormally large heads and missing patches of fur; and squirrel monkeys with brain cases larger than their limbs could carry. Some evidenced signs of irradiation.

Sam backed out once more and hurried down the oddly curving corridor to the next door. Opening it quickly, she stepped inside and closed it behind her, looking around. But this time she turned into the corner of the room and retched. There was nothing in her belly to come up, however, and she looked up to survey large cylinders containing… mutated humans.

Row upon row of dead, twisted men and women, some lacking limbs, others without faces. Still others had huge, abnormal eyes without irises. One child appeared to have no brain case. Spines contorted in horrible ways. All appeared to have been exposed to either extreme heat, or strong radiation.

Sam swallowed hard and left the room as quickly as she'd entered it. *What are they doing to MY baby?!* she wondered in desperation. *I have to find her before they do something dreadful!*

But when she opened the next door, there was someone inside, working at a laboratory bench.

"Oh, pardon me," she said, starting to back out rapidly.

"No, no, come in, and hurry," he urged in a whisper, gesturing frantically. "It is all right; I am a friend. I know who you are, and I know where your daughter is. My name is Dr. Felix Kato, and I was kidnapped much as you were. Perhaps we can help each other."

"Kato?" Sam's eyes widened. "Case Western U.?"

"That's me." Kato nodded.

"What the HELL is going on, then? Do you know?"

"Unfortunately, I do," he admitted. "How much do you know about gene manipulation via viral recombination?"

"About enough to be dangerous," Sam confessed, "and what do we do if someone comes in?"

"As long as no one comes in who recognizes you, I called you in for assistance," Kato brainstormed.

"Okay. The only person left who'd recognize me is some Dr. Drago."

"And he is precisely the most dangerous man in this place, wherever it is," Kato informed her. "He is the one in charge. He is creating a very specialized gene therapy, for what reason I do not yet understand, and he is forcing me to do it." He saw the confused frown on Samantha's face. "Let me explain. Have you ever heard of a bacterium called Deinococcus radiodurans?"

"Yup. 'Conan the Bacterium.'"

"Right. Now, this Dr. Drago—and he is a scientist, by the way, many times over, though not a physician—has taken the radiodurans DNA and cut and spliced it with a particularly virulent influenza virus. Then he will try to have the virus infect a person. He wants to be able to take the radiodurans' ability to resist extremes and implant them into human genetics. But simply replacing out the flu DNA with the radiodurans' DNA is insufficient, as he has discovered the hard way."

"Yeah," Sam said, her stomach lurching despite herself, "I think I saw that, down the hall."

"Mm. Yes. You probably did," Kato agreed. "The problem is that for some reason the spliced DNA never survives passing through the cell membrane. We don't know why just yet, but I have developed a technique that appears to circumvent that problem altogether."

"Nanoballs?" Sam wondered.

"Amazing." Kato raised an eyebrow at her knowledge. "Yes."

"My husband figured as much," Sam deferred.

"Ah. Yes, 'the Nuisance.' I have heard Dr. Drago speak of him. Oddly, Drago seems to admire him and despise him simultaneously. He must be a very intelligent man, this Dr. Brady of yours."

"He is."

"So," Kato returned to his subject, "the trick is to wrap the DNA in carbon nanoballs so that they survive the implantation through the cell walls initially. Passing through the membrane destroys the nanoballs and the virus starts using the cell as a replicator factory. Thus, we begin replicating the radiodurans mutated flu. The infected cell has its DNA changed, and as the flu moves through the body's systems—amazingly rapidly, it appears from my tests, as it uses multiple vectors—the cells are mutated. The additional hurdle was to prevent further infection of others in contact with the test subjects, so that only those specifically dosed by the mutated influenza—and any offspring they may have—are affected, and that was evidently accomplished before my advent."

"So have you done this yet?" Sam asked.

"Oh, yes. His research was already sufficiently advanced that it took little other than the implementation of the nanoball technique to complete it. The laboratory is mass producing the serum even now, and when there is enough, Drago plans to hold the world hostage with the threat of nuclear attack from anywhere to anywhere via his very unique transport system."

"But WHY?"

"His plan, as best I understand it, is to use the gene therapy serum on his own army and then irradiate the rest of the world. The flu virus and the nanoballs transport the genes of the radiation resistant bacteria to the human cells and then the human cells rewrite the genetic code, making the resultant human much more resistant to radiation by many thousands of times. My research indicates it may enhance considerably more, as well—he calls the result Homo Sapiens Extremum."

"Dear God. He's a madman."

"I believe so," Kato said solemnly, "but a madman with a purpose, which is the most dangerous kind. As yet, however, I have not been able to discern that purpose."

"He wanted me to read my husband a prepared statement saying that there was a plague," Sam recalled. "Could he believe that humanity is infected with this... plague... and he's going to pull a Noah's Ark?"

"I cannot answer that." Kato shrugged. "It makes a certain amount of sense, based on what we do know. I am afraid I don't know any more than you on that matter. Since I came here... under duress, shall we say... he only trusts me to a point. I suppose you could term it 'need to know.' And in his eyes, I do not. But I do have an important answer for YOU."

"What?" Sam's stomach rumbled loud enough for both of them to hear.

"Where your baby is."

"Has she been harmed?" Sam's face grew grim.

"No. At least, not yet. She is being very well cared for–surprisingly well cared for, in fact. He even provided care for her cystic fibrosis. This Drago seems to consider her extremely important, almost to the point of affection, an emotion I have never seen him show to anyone else. I seriously doubt he would actually physically harm her, though I have no doubt but that you have been terrorized with such threats. Experimentation, however, is a different matter. I know that her genetics have been provided to me—as have yours—and that I was to test the latest serum on the two of you." He nodded at an apparatus in the corner. "That's the batch just finishing up."

"Are you on his side?" Her stomach growled again and Sam was beginning to realize how long it had been since she had eaten or drunk anything.

"HELL, no." Kato paused as Sam's stomach let out a prolonged howl. "You need to eat something. Hold on."

"No time. We must find my baby!" Sam said defiantly.

"If you must fight for her you will need some strength. And that talking stomach is a dead giveaway, in any case." Kato rummaged through the lab refrigerator and dug out a can of soda and a pizza box from a famous New York pizza restaurant. "It's cold, but still very good. I can microwave it if you'd like."

"No." Sam grabbed the coke and the cold pizza and devoured them both, fairly bolting it all down. "Are we in New York?"

"I doubt it. We get stuff in here from all over the world. A side effect of Dr. Drago's transport system."

"I see." Sam finished off the last of the food and then patted the pistol in her pants pocket for reassurance. "You coming with me?"

"Right." Kato nodded.

"Then let's find Abby and get the hell out of here before the batch finishes."

"You have the key, Mrs. Brady. I'll lead you to your child and then follow. You are obviously very capable."

ଞଓଔ

"Now," Dr. Allen began, as they all got comfortable at the conference table, "Mr. Kruger has shown me the videos you got of the... doors, for want of a better term, that your 'Santa Claus' is using. I took the liberty of running a little transform computer program on 'em, one I ftp'ed from the Skunkworks, and I was able to pull out some more information–particularly shapes. Shapes that I recognized. Those higher order manifolds you've got are Calabi-Yau manifolds, Ray."

"No shit. So we're definitely working with at least a version of string theory," Ray concluded.

"We are. And I suspect you're correct in that we're actually looking at membrane vibrational intersection points," Allen agreed. "Mr. Kruger tells me you've already given the team a rundown on M theory."

"More or less," Ray shrugged, as the others watched and listened. "Not as detailed as I'd like, though. I've been pretty busy in recent years, but I've tried to keep up with the research, especially in the last few weeks. Besides, they don't understand the math anyway."

"And that's reasonable; they aren't trained to. Now, let me throw some stuff out on the table so that you guys can sort through it and pick out the pertinent puzzle pieces," Allen offered. "You've already determined your 'anomaly' is a 'Santa Claus,' or at least in some part partakes of alien genetic material. Right?" He nodded at Kruger, who nodded back. "And we now know that we have definite string, possibly superstring, and likely M, theory in operation, as the means by which your anomaly gets from place to place."

"Right," the Old Man confirmed.

"And, while it may be entirely possible—probable, actually—that your anomaly's genetics give him an incredibly long lifespan relative to our own, the mere presence of the technology he's using does not—repeat, NOT—require that."

"I... do not like the sound of that," Jay muttered.

"Why not?" Kruger demanded of Allen.

"Okay, let's look at time travel for a minute," Allen dropped easily into teacher mode. "We know that one way time travel is possible, in a manner of speaking, due to the Theories of Relativity, both special and general. This is because the relativistic traveler, as a result of time dilation effects, will experience perhaps two years elapsed time, whereas outside his particular reference frame, several hundred, even a thousand, years may have gone by.

"With me so far?" Allen watched as heads nodded around the room. "Continuing on that note, the Gödel metric, and certain other, solutions to the General Theory permit something called 'closed timelike curves' which at least theoretically allow for time travel into the past. However, these solutions require that the universe take on characteristics that we haven't observed, and very well likely don't exist. So scratch those." Allen watched as frowns and pursed lips moved around the room.

"Then there are things like wormholes—but we'd have to find one, or make one using a black hole—and a spinning Kerr black hole becomes a possibility, assuming we could build a spacecraft that could withstand the tidal forces around a black hole. A Tipler cylinder would work in a somewhat similar fashion, but then we have the problem of finding materials to withstand the spin. In essence, a Tipler cylinder would be an artificial cosmic string." He paused to let that sink in.

"A singular problem with most time travel methods that we might devise is that it would be impossible for the time traveler to travel back in time further than the creation of the device," Allen noted. "And he generally requires some sort of ship in which to do the traveling."

"Dr. Who's Tardis," Ray mumbled under his breath with a grin.

"Exactly," Paul grinned back, having caught the remark. "Now, it's patently obvious that our guy here," he deliberately phrased his statement to put himself on their side, and thus a team adjunct, "doesn't have a ship. He jumps off the sides of buildings, pops into and out of vaults, and the like."

"Yeah," Jay agreed, "but what's that got to do with time travel? This guy's beboppin' around the planet."

"But you have evidence that he has appeared in history for the last couple of centuries," Paul pointed out, "and that he has not significantly changed in appearance. Even a long lived race ought to show SOME signs of aging. And consider this," he added. "If we are indeed dealing with M theory, then we are dealing with eleven dimensions—"

"But why don't we perceive them? I know what Ray told us, but I always thought we just had four," Jay wondered.

"Because the other seven are condensed into manifolds," Ray explained.

"Correct," Paul agreed with his former pupil. "Imagine each point in spacetime with an eleven dimensional coordinate. Only, seven of those eleven are compressed, hidden, like when you hide rows of data in a spreadsheet." Eyebrows went up around the room.

"And then unfold them when you need them," Kruger said slowly, as the idea took shape in his mind. "Like when you need to look at the data… or go to another place in spacetime."

"Exactly," Paul's smile grew wider. "Which is why you see the progression of manifolds as these 'doorways' appear. The coordinates are, literally, unfolding."

"Extraction points," Ray suddenly made the connection. "Jay, just like when we infiltrated—er, those places—and we had specific locations we had to make it to in order to be extracted at the end of the mission. He's using these things as extraction points."

"Ooo," Jay said, leaning back and whistling. "That's why he led us on that hairy wild chase through New York. He had to reach his extraction point."

"Exactly. Which means he has some control over them, but that control is limited," Paul elaborated. "Study the robbery videos. Notice how each one has a different duration. Some are short, some are relatively long. And it makes sense, if you're talking about controlling something like a brane."

"Which would be damn hard, with our technology and hardware," Ray realized.

"Yep. He's gotta be brilliant to be doing this at all, let alone with the precision he has."

"But IS he using our technology?" Jay asked.

"You tell me," Allen replied. "If he has his own source of technology, why is he stealing all these components from around the world to build his nukes?"

"Shit," Jay muttered.

"But you still haven't explained the time travel thing," the Old Man complained.

"I'm getting there, sir," Paul said patiently. "Of those eleven dimensions, more than one is timelike."

"Yeah," Ray mumbled thoughtfully.

"Which means," Paul concluded, "that it is as easy to 'brane' from one TIME to another, as it is to 'brane' from one PLACE to another."

"So… the Boss and the baby could be anyplace, and anyWHEN," Jay said slowly.

"Yes," Paul replied with a solemn, if regretful, nod.

"Paul," Ray groaned, "you just made my job infinitely more difficult."

ℴ❧

"Wait here." Three doors down, Kato stopped. "Let me do the talking."

"What is it?" Sam asked, her pistol at the ready.

"Play along, and keep your hand near the pocket with your weapon as if guarding me. Whatever you do, stifle your maternal instincts until we get well away."

"Understood." Sam nodded, and unlocked the door.

Inside were two guards and a nurse. The nurse had just finished feeding and changing Abby, and was putting her back in the crib.

"The serum is complete," Kato declared. "I will be keeping the baby in the lab for at least the next twenty-four hours for testing, to monitor the progress of the transformation. I will require formula, food, diapers, and anything else the baby will need."

With a heroic effort Sam restrained herself from snatching up Abby and merely nodded sternly, in confirmation of Kato's statements.

The nurse gathered up the requested items and placed them into a diaper bag, handing them to Sam, who slung the bag over her shoulder.

"Anything else?" the nurse asked.

"Yes." Kato thought quickly. "The baby will have to remain in a specific position for extended amounts of time. My… assistant…" he let his face twist into an aggravated scowl, as if Sam's presence were an intrusion, "here will be required to carry her for long periods while still helping me. Do you have a baby carrier?"

"Yes, we do." The nurse nodded affably enough, and pulled out a strap-on baby pack. "Back or front?" she asked Sam. Sam pretended to consider.

"Front, for now," she concluded, "but show me how to switch it around if I need to."

It proved quick enough; the pack was designed for simplicity and ease of use. The nurse demonstrated, helped Sam into the baby carrier, then fetched Abby and slid the sleepy infant into the pack.

"All right," Kato huffed, making himself appear annoyed at the prospect of having a baby underfoot for the next day and night, "let's go and get this over with, already."

He and Sam left the nursery.

80CB

"Not necessarily, Ray," Paul soothed. "One of the things my supervisor at the Skunkworks authorized me to tell you guys, once he got the orders from Mr. Kruger, was about a particular project I've consulted on."

"Yeah?" Ray wondered.

"What if I told you that DARPA has a new—well, maybe not so new, depending on how you look at it—top secret special access program to develop quantum teleportation concepts?"

"The Defense Advanced Research Project Agency would of course have such a program," Ray grinned thinly and nodded at him. "You're shittin' me, aren't you, Paul?"

"No, old friend, never, at a time like this."

Ray perked up.

"So... is it functional?"

80CB

Outside the nursery, Sam closed her eyes for a moment. The feeling of her child so close to her bosom, as she was supposed to be, brought a newfound energy to her. Abigail was safe in her arms again.

"We must keep moving," Kato nudged her.

"All right, let's get out of here," she declared in a low tone. "Do you know where there's a way..." she pondered the lack of windows for a moment, "out? Down? Up?"

"Up. Stairs or elevator?"

"Elevator is easier, but more likely to get caught. Stairs." Sam sighed. "This way."

80CB

"Through here. There should be no one inside." Kato stopped in front of a door.

Sam swiped the key card and two adults and one toddler slipped through the door.

Inside was a massive power substation.

"What the hell?!" Sam wondered, as Abby cooed softly, waking and recognizing her mother's scent, before snuggling in to sleep deeply.

"I don't know everything Drago does here by a long stretch, but I do know he draws a tremendous amount of power," Kato noted. "Where he's pulling it from, without anyone noticing, I have no idea." He began leading her on a circuitous and somewhat dangerous route through transformers, cables, capacitors, and circuit breakers. Instinctively Sam wrapped her arms around Abby as she followed, still looking around. Suddenly the light dawned.

"Of course!" Sam exclaimed. "The teleportation system must draw tons of power! And you're right, there's no way he could draw it from outside without someone noticing. He's gotta be generating it somehow. At least part of it." She paused, staring at a massive transformer. "Boy, would Ray love to get a look at this."

"This way. Hurry."

On the far side of the room, in the direction Kato was headed, Sam could see another door.

೮ುಗ

"Not... exactly," Paul's face twisted wryly. "Close. But maybe with what you guys have gathered, combined with what we've already got, we can MAKE it functional. Fast."

"What have WE got, other than manifold evidence?" Ray wondered.

"We've got several dead bodies from the anomaly's followers–soldiers, I suppose," the Old Man pointed out, "complete with articles of clothing, personal effects, and energy weapons. I've had an inventory made, but no one's had time to look at the stuff yet. We'd only just gotten the messes cleared up when your house... when..." Kruger broke off at the expression on Ray's face.

೮ುಗ

Jay saw it too.

"Then what say we get that inventory up here and take a look, see what we've got," Jay averred staunchly. "We're gonna find Ray's girls. I swear to you, Ray, we'll find 'em."

"I just hope we don't find 'em too late," Ray said hoarsely.

೮ುಗ

Five minutes later two adults and a child were hiking up a long, winding staircase that seemed to curve in a great spiral upward, with landings occurring periodically. Sam shifted Abby to her back, handing the diaper bag to Kato, who slung it across his back and shoulder.

After three and a half flights of stairs, they had to pause for Kato to catch his breath. Samantha began realizing the truth of Ray's assertions that she was in excellent shape, vastly superior to most other people.

Abby whimpered, having just awakened, and Sam shushed her urgently. Kato fished in the diaper bag and produced a pacifier. Sam accepted it with gratitude and stuck it into Abby's mouth, clipping it to the baby carrier. The little one settled down to suck on it, and they began another upward trek.

"This place is cylindrical," Sam decided after a few more flights of stairs.

"I believe so, yes, but again must plead ignorance," Kato confessed. "I have seen most of the floor we were upon, but little of anything else, save a large room with a kind of portal in it—through which I was brought—a tunnel, and an elevator."

Periodically they had to stop to allow Dr. Kato to rest, but Samantha made sure it was never on a landing, just in case someone decided to take the stairs. It was obvious the stairs were only a kind of emergency exit, but she wasn't willing to take chances, not with Abby on her back.

After nine floors, they reached the end of the stairwell. No door out– just the end.

"Well, shit," Sam grumbled.

℠∙℠

They ended up backtracking to the last door they'd seen and going through that. The top floor proved to be storage, of all things.

"Who the hell puts their stored stuff in the top of a high rise building?" Sam wondered, annoyed. "This is not helping us get out."

"Consider, Mrs. Brady," Kato murmured in the lowest tone he could manage, never knowing where a listening device might be. "I know the floor we were on. It was on the bottom, for the stairs started there. There was no exit. We had to climb. You yourself suggested we might go up; I merely confirmed it. What was your basis for that suggestion?"

"Uh, lack of windows," she noted. "But I figured we were in a basement."

"I can vouch for the fact that we were not. Think about the radius of the spiral stairs."

"Just larger than that first floor. It goes *around* the structure. So... we aren't in a high rise," Sam reasoned. "And as cold as it's been, and still is... and with few indications of air conditioning vents... we've been underground the whole time." She thought for a moment. "I wonder..."

"Wonder what?"

"I'm going to play a hunch," Sam decided. "Come on. We're going back down another floor and see what we find." She paused, eying her companion from head to toe, scrutinizing him and sizing him up. "Listen, it might get hairy, scary, and deadly."

"Er, well..."

"If things get bad, get out of my way and take cover," Sam grinned thinly. "Can you stand killing? If you can't, then don't watch 'cause I'm about to do some."

"Uh..."

"Just do the best you can to keep up, and stay behind me. And try not to get in my way. Let's go."

༄ༀ

The second floor down seemed to be some sort of automated equipment; judging by what she saw, Sam suspected it was the facility maintenance level. Water pumps, a few air conditioning units, and the like filled the area.

Unfortunately, there were also several maintenance people there, working on various malfunctioning items.

"Shit," Sam muttered without moving her lips, "get ready, Dr. Kato. We aren't waltzing through here with a baby on my back."

"Understood," Kato murmured in reply. "Play it casually and let us see how far we can get, though. Think extremophile testing."

"Oh, okay. Gotcha." *I like this guy. He thinks fast on his feet. Wish we had him in DSRPO. He'd come in handy. Assuming we get outta here, maybe...*

Sam roughly shoved Kato in front of her and marched him across the room as if they belonged there and she was simply "escorting" the prisoner. One of the maintenance workers looked up.

"Hey, what's going on?"

"Trial run with the brat," Sam responded laconically. "Doc here—or rather, I think Dr. Drago, since THIS guy is a total loser—wants to see how the kid handles cold, heat and light. Lots of light. Oh, and dehydration."

"Shit. What's he gonna do, turn the kid loose in the middle of the prairie?"

"Essentially, yes," Kato confirmed with a regretful sigh. "And... see how long it survives."

"Cold, man."

"Has to be done," Sam barked. "You know it, I know it, and Dr. Drago knows it. C'mon, you, let's go." She shoved Kato's shoulder.

They made it through the facilities floor with no further incident.

ൟൟ

"Yeah," Sam nodded as they entered a tunnel, right where she expected it to be. "I knew it."

"Knew what?"

"I think I finally figured out what this thing is. And from here on out may not be pretty. Or easy."

"What is 'this thing,' then?" Kato wondered.

"An old Cold War era missile silo. You can buy 'em online these days. Millionaires turn 'em into houses, storage units, whatever. We're headed through the tunnel that leads out of the silo proper into the adjacent launch control complex."

And as Sam unlocked the door at the end of the tunnel, they found themselves staring at eight armed guards.

"Hey, that's the brat the boss wanted brought in, isn't it?" one asked, pointing at Sam.

"Yeah, and we got no orders for it—or that doctor guy," another pointed at Kato, "to be comin' through here."

"It is necessary to test the child in the environment," Kato protested, trying to continue their bluff. "Why ELSE do you think we would have a guard with us?" He jerked an annoyed thumb at Sam.

"Pete, check the latest orders," the first said. "Make sure there's something we haven't missed. One way or the other, we don't wanna screw up. You know how Dr. Drago can get."

"Yeah, let's look…"

As the guards began checking the computer console for new orders, Sam and Kato locked eyes. Each knew what the other was thinking: *We've only got a couple of seconds before they realize we're lying. What do we do?*

Sam raised an eyebrow, concerned. Kato nodded slightly, but that didn't reassure her much. *Get ready to protect not only your baby, but this guy, too,* she told herself, mentally steeling herself for what was about to happen. She surreptitiously tightened the straps on the baby carrier.

ൟൟ

Fortunately, the guards were still intent on the orders roster; they hardly knew what hit them. Sam instantly waded in, both hands and feet flying, every protective maternal instinct she possessed fully engaged. Surprisingly, Kato was right behind her, guarding the rear and helping to protect the child on her back.

Sam took out the first guard with a single, hard palm heel strike to the nose—the same move she'd used on one of her intended rapists. The second fell when a high front kick took him in the face. Kato dropped the third with a combination of multiple lethal punches to the right side of his rib cage that stopped his heart from shock.

By this time Abby was awake and crying in fear, but there was nothing Sam could do except keep going. Guard number four went down when Sam drove her fist into his solar plexus, then head butted him with all the force she could muster. Number five went airborne over Kato's shoulder into number six, thence into the concrete wall. Number seven aimed at Kato, and shot number eight when Kato wasn't there anymore. Sam supplied seven with another hard kick to the head, and they heard his neck break.

"Damn," a surprised Sam remarked between gulps of air to Kato then. "You CAN fight."

"I am third generation American," Kato declared with pride. "My grandfather was a seventh dan shotokan sensei. My given name may be Americanized, but certain... traditions... were passed on." His grin was as close as it was possible to come to a smirk without actually being one. "You are with Master Kato's son and therefore I will do my best to honor my father's heritage."

Sam grinned back, and opened her mouth to say something. But the approaching pounding of feet gave warning that reinforcements were on the way.

"Run!" Sam urged. "Stairwell should be near the center! Tight spiral! Two stories, and we ought to end up on ground level!"

They ran. Abby cried, loudly and hoarsely, with the occasional choking cough caused by her cystic fibrosis; Sam recognized the signs of another oncoming infection, likely abetted by the cold damp environment of the silo, despite any so-called "care" by Drago. By the time they reached the ground floor, which was encased in what appeared to be a ranch house, her screams had brought another guard contingent. But this time there were twenty.

"Shit," Sam muttered, "James Bond never had to get away from Blofeld carrying a fourteen month old baby! Hush, Abby! Oh, the hell with it! Stay behind me, doctor!"

Sam extracted the Glock auto from her pocket and simply mowed down the guards, locating the exit and running as she went. A couple more bursts from the fully automatic pistol outside the door took care of the last of the guards. Sam hit the release on the gun and let the empty magazine drop to the ground, extracting the second from a cargo pocket and slapping it home. Kato scavenged three fresh magazines from a downed soldier, appropriated a weapon of his own, and handed two of the magazines to her as they took off at a dead run, shoving the third in his shirt pocket. Sam stowed the fresh ammo in the same cargo pocket she'd just used as she sprinted as hard as she could go. They ran well away from the building before pausing barely long enough to look around them.

It was open prairie. Other than the immediate complex, there was nothing but gently rolling grasslands as far as the eye could see; definitely nothing in the landscape to provide cover for them. "Where the hell are we?" Sam puzzled, as Abby settled down in the presence of warm sunshine. "We could be in any of a dozen or more states. Or another country. We need to get an SOS out, fast, or else get the blazes outta Dodge."

"I would opt for getting out of Dodge," Kato suggested. "I see a parking lot to our left."

Quickly Sam and Kato shifted the baby carrier to Sam's chest, so that Abby would be protected by Sam's body as they fled. Then they took off running again, headed for the vehicles. "Do you see one that looks old enough to hot wire?" Sam wondered, as they sprinted.

Kato, even with his adrenaline up, was just barely able to keep up with the lithe blonde, even burdened with the baby as she was.

"N- no," he panted. "All late model. Anti-theft system, probably GPS locators..."

As they got past the building, Sam's eyes lit up.

"Planes," she said in delight.

Abby cooed.

৪০৪৪

The trio clambered into a Cessna Corvalis with Sam in the pilot's seat, and Sam started the engine, warming up the plane to taxi out. Kato unbuckled the baby carrier around Sam's movements, strapping the baby carefully into a passenger seat before taking the copilot's seat himself.

Sam scanned the cockpit, briefly familiarizing herself with the controls.

"There," Kato indicated. "The radio. Call for help."

"Won't do any good," Sam pointed out, "until we get airborne. No telling where the nearest airport is that could hear us—probably a hell of a long way away, for these guys' security purposes—and the higher we are, the better our chances of line of sight comm."

"Then get going," Kato urged, "because the cavalry isn't here, and the entire tribe is on the warpath after us." He waved a hand at the side window.

Armed soldiers in black jumpsuits were pouring from the silo building.

Sam released the brake and nudged the little aircraft forward, taxiing at maximum speed for the runway. Behind them, the soldiers—a good forty or fifty in number—ranked themselves, the first row dropping prone, the second row to one knee, the third standing. They all took aim at the fleeing aircraft as it began its race down the runway.

Just then the radio spoke.

"Mrs. Brady, you are most impressive, and obviously a very devoted mother. However, I now have what I need from Dr. Kato and I am perfectly willing to have my men open fire and riddle your craft with energy pulses, bullets—oh, and white phosphorus grenades. Did I mention those? And your aircraft with a full tank of aviation fuel. Such a fireball; very messy. I'm quite certain no one aboard would survive. And you do have dear little Abigail with you, don't you?"

Sam went white.

"He's bluffing," Kato protested. "He has to be. I've seen the way he takes care of that child."

"I can't take that chance," Sam murmured.

She throttled the plane back, letting it slow to a stop on the runway, her shoulders slumping in defeat.

Chapter 18

First, Ray and the team watched all of the videos again, this time with Paul providing commentary. Soon they understood the sequence of events, and what it represented in spacetime, in much more detail.

By that time, Fields had returned from his DNA sampling run, having encountered nothing but cooperation from the Drago family, and the data all indicated that the family was completely normal. Moreover, little Billy Drago's DNA precisely matched, in every detail, that of Ray's assailant–save for the non-human aspects in the assailant.

"It's him," Fields had noted, "but something major happened to him between toddler and mature adult. What exactly, I can't even begin to say, but I'd hazard an educated guess that he's been... 'tinkered with.' Free will or not, I don't know. Maybe," he hypothesized, "it's the reason he's acting the way he is now."

"What do you mean, Dr. Fields?" Paul wondered. "'The reason he's acting the way he is now'–would you mind elaborating?"

"Well," Doc shrugged, "if it wasn't his choice, there might be some mental trauma there—even PTSD, maybe—that's pushed him over the edge. Or, whether it was his call or not, the process may have caused mental instability. Brilliant though he appears to be, you gotta admit some of his actions haven't been exactly... rational. Let alone humane."

"True," the Old Man agreed with his chief medical officer.

"Either way, Santa Bunny," Jay nodded.

"I'd say so," Fields agreed. "Ray?"

"Looks like it," Ray admitted reluctantly. "And it fits with Paul's hypothesis, too. Dammit."

"Calm down, Ray," the Old Man offered, in a more soothing tone than any of them had ever heard him use before. "We ARE going to find them and bring them home safely. Let's move on."

Then they began going over the inventory of personal effects that had been taken from the various dead soldiers of their anomaly. They pored over the information until late into the night.

"Protective jumpsuits, not unlike partial MOPP gear," Fields noted, "standard handguns, a mask in the case of the bank robbers, extra ammo and magazines..."

"Multi-tools, wrist watches, the odd knife, and not much else," Jay finished. "Except for the two guys we got back from the munitions factory, and they had those ray gun rifles."

"Which we need to take apart and retro-engineer," Paul pointed out.

"Shit, guys, I'm brain dead," Skip protested. "What the hell time is it?"

"About two o'—" Kruger started to answer, glancing at his watch.

"That's it! That's IT! Gimme those videos again!" Ray exclaimed, and a startled Paul handed him the remote. Ray keyed up the normal black and white sequences and looked back through the videos. After viewing only a few, he growled, "I knew it."

"Knew what, Ray?" Paul pressed.

"Look," he pointed at the video still playing. "In all of the scenes, every single one of the henchmen are wearing watches that are all the same. And the Santa Bunny was looking at his watch the night he jumped off the building in the Big Apple! And HE had TWO! Get me one of those watches!"

The Old Man reached for the secure phone.

⃝⃝

Sam was back in her cell again, dressed this time, but alone. She was pacing the floor when the door opened.

Two brawny, heavily muscled men, with faces that didn't look like they'd ever attempted a smile, and might crack if they tried, entered the room.

"Time for a lesson, lady," one of them said, scowling. He flexed thick, stubby fingers on meaty hands.

"Yes, I rather think so," Sam agreed calmly.

⃝⃝

A box full of watches was presented to Ray. He fished one out and began studying it, then handed the others out until they were all gone. "Okay, guys, have a look at these and let's see what we can come up with. Especially you, Paul," he added. Paul nodded.

Everyone bent their heads over the devices, studying readouts, poking buttons, trying sequences of buttons. Little shrill beeps sounded frequently.

"Well," Fields concluded, "it ain't like no watch I've ever seen. It's got more screens than I ever saw, short of in a newspaper comic strip."

"But each screen looks, more or less, the same," Paul mused. "Seven numbers, and a time countdown."

"Yeah..." Jay agreed. "But what do they mean?"

"Hold on, I found something," Ray said. "Mr. Kruger, sir, do you have the detailed reports on our New York outing?"

"I do, but I'll have to go back to my office for the hard copy file."

"Would you mind, sir? It may be very important."

Without another word, trusting his chief scientist's instincts, the Old Man rose and left the room.

ꕥ

The first ham-fisted swing at Sam connected nothing but air. The second struck a powerful forearm outer block–and stuck. Before the thug could think, his nose had been broken with a palm heel strike, Sam's favorite fatal strike because it was so quick and easy. But not this time. This time, she would TAKE her time. *Pain. Lots and lots of pain.*

Sam maintained her grip on the man's wrist, crouching to step easily under his arm, elbowing his floating ribs hard enough to hear them snap and using his body to shield her from the second strongman. A rock hard hammer fist into her assailant's groin nearly doubled him over and left him howling, especially when she grabbed what she could and brought it back with her. The big man let out a high pitched, falsetto shriek as her long fingernails dug in through his jumpsuit and left his manhood slashed and bleeding.

Grabbing his wrist in both hands, she pulled down at the same time she stood up forcefully. His elbow bent drastically the wrong way, accompanied by the sounds of mayhem on the tendons contained in it. Sam sidestepped behind him, dragging his shattered arm with her, which forced him to double over in pain. Then she drove her elbow down hard on the base of his neck. He collapsed on the floor, unmoving, with no sign of respiration.

The whole thing had taken under a minute.

Sam looked up at the second man, a wolfish grin on her face, a look of shock on his.

"Your turn," she said.

He stepped back.

ꕥ

"Here you go, Ray," Kruger said, handing the scientist a file folder. "That's everything."

"Thanks, Boss," Ray smiled. "I think..." He put the folder on the table and began flipping through it. "Now let's see. GPS coordinates and..." He looked quickly between the report and the device he held. "There we go," he said in intense satisfaction.

"What?" Paul wondered, leaning over his shoulder.

"Look, Paul," Ray said. "Here..." he pointed at the report, "and here."

"Ooo, bingo."

"Right."

"Fill us in, please, doctors," the Old Man said crisply, but his lone blue eye betrayed excitement.

"Seven numbers and a countdown clock," Ray pointed out. "And it so happens that I lucked across the screen corresponding to our first encounter with the Marathon Man in New York. The first three numbers are latitude, expressed in degrees, minutes, and seconds. The second three are longitude, also degrees, minutes, and seconds. The seventh is—"

"Altitude!" Jay guessed. "I get it! I get it!"

"Right," Ray grinned. "'Cause our anomaly jumped off a building to get to the right altitude!"

"And the time?" Fields asked. "Countdown to the—what did you call 'em? Extraction point?"

"Right," Ray confirmed. "Only this one is counting up, because the window has already passed."

"But we've got countdowns set for coordinates all over the globe," Paul noted. "No wonder the bastards got around so fast."

"What was the deal with the main anomaly guy wearing TWO watches, though?" Jay wondered.

Ray and Paul exchanged a long look.

"'Cause unlike the robbers, the anomaly wasn't AT the extraction point," Paul said, "was he, Ray?"

"No. We chased him all the way there. It must have been some sort of navigator, to tell him how to get there from where he was."

"Bingo," Jay said, sitting back in his chair, satisfied with the answer. "THAT makes PERFECT sense."

"So we have the locations right here to brane doors all over the world," Paul added. "But why didn't he think of that? Why do we even have access to these watches? I'd have thought he'd have arranged to pop in and get 'em all back."

"He's cocky," Jay interjected. "I could tell that from the get go. He doesn't know Ray, doesn't know you, and doesn't know how determined this team is. He's smart, and he knows it, and he let his ego get in the way. He underestimated us."

"Exactly," the Old Man said in satisfaction.

"Ah," Paul said, a grin spreading across his face.

"Everyone check and see what's the shortest time to the next extraction point," the Old Man ordered.

Beeps sounded furiously in the room as everyone checked their chronometers.

"I got five hours," Dan noted. "Then the next screen has the same coordinates, but is about five minutes later."

"In, then out," Paul murmured. "For ongoing operations."

"Yup," Ray agreed. "And the 'out' almost certainly takes them back to their headquarters."

"Anybody got less than that?" Dan wondered.

A mixed chorus consisting of variants on "nope" sounded around the room.

"So we need to find the location of that extraction point, and use it to send a force through," the Old Man decreed.

"It's not far," Dan noted, studying the coordinates and mentally referencing them. "It's in D.C."

"Good," Ray said. "So we—"

"But it's… up in the air…"

That gave Ray pause, and he glanced over Dan's shoulder.

"Ah," he said, in sudden recognition, then grinned. "Okay. Here's the plan…"

℘ℭ℥

Strongman Number Two exercised all the stealth and craft he could manage, watching Sam as they stalked each other around the room, looking for a momentary diversion, a temporary weakness, something out of position. Sam was unnervingly calm.

Just then, the sound of Abby screaming issued from the speaker in the corner near the ceiling. In an instinctive reflex, Sam's head jerked around toward the sound, distracted.

The man took that opportunity to lunge. Sam barely glanced in his direction as she jabbed her stiff fingertips into his windpipe. The man made a sound like, "Gaagk!" and collapsed. Moments later he had asphyxiated from a crushed larynx.

Sam grabbed the large man by fistfuls of jumpsuit at the waist and neck, slinging his two hundred pound girth over onto the other dead man like a bale of hay. Then she turned back to the camera and speaker.

"Next?" she said calmly.

℘ℭ℥

"Are you sure about this?" Kruger asked. "Your nose may have healed—"

"More or less," Fields muttered.

"—But you're still pretty beat up, Ray…"

"I'm sure," Ray said, in a low, firm voice. "They have Sam and Abby. Adrenaline will more than make up for any residual injuries. Besides, Doc there is gonna shoot me up full of all sorts of stimulants and pain killers. Right, Doc?"

"Now, I don't know about…" Fields stopped with that line of thought once he looked up at Ray.

"RIGHT, DOC?" Ray said, staring and glowering all the way through the physician, who in that instant, swore the man had x-ray vision.

"Right," Fields agreed reluctantly.

"We've got the jumpsuits, we've got the energy guns, and we've got their weapons. I'll dress like one of them, load for grizzly, then go through the extraction point. If we've got it figured like we think, I'll end up in their headquarters. Which, if my research on Dragonfire Enterprises is right, is very likely in the middle of the Dakotas, but I can't be totally sure of that. My GPS locator should give you my position immediately, but I'll still try to send a covert message you can home in on to help speed things up. Then the rest of you guys," he looked around the room, including Paul in the glance, "come after, as fast as you can. You'll be airborne already and ready to drop."

"Like all the bats of Hell were behind us, pal," Paul murmured. "I'm not losing an old student and friend again."

"But what if this door goes into, like space or something? You said they had space suits and were probably doing stuff on the Moon," Jay protested. "Not to mention what happened to Gupta."

"Because I checked," Ray said. "It looks so much like all the other extraction screens it's not even funny. If I was him, I wouldn't have a Moon door or a space door just any old place. I'd want it someplace safe, where I was the only one who could access it. More than likely, that means there's only one extraction point—maybe two—between their Earth headquarters and their Moon base. Besides, I'm willing to take the risk."

"Sam wouldn't be," Kruger pointed out quietly. Ray turned and looked at his secret father in law, seeing the concern in that lone eye.

"I know," he said softly. "And if you don't like it, say the word now."

The others watched, mystified, as something unspoken passed between their chief scientist and their top leader.

"You're sure?" Kruger pressed after a long, silent moment.

"As positive as it's possible for me to be," Ray said with confidence.

"Go, then."

Ray was outfitted and loaded with all the weapons he could carry without looking obvious, a full hour before the extraction point. He was dressed in one of the unisize jumpsuits, with the appropriate watch, a pistol, an anomaly energy rifle, a DSRPO comm unit, and several other DSRPO classified weapons hidden in the plentiful cargo pockets of the jumpsuit.

Meanwhile, Jay was having the precise location of the extraction point—which happened to be in the Mall, next to the Washington Monument—cordoned off. This perimeter included the Monument itself, as the extraction point had an altitude above anything they could readily reach. The cover story was that a bomb threat had been called in, and a special bomb team was responding to the potential terrorist event, activating the District Response Plan. The entire Mall area was being cleared per the Plan to facilitate the cover story.

"It's EP minus fifty minutes," Ray said, as the van carrying him, Kruger, Allen, and Fields, arrived at the base of the monument. "Let's get going."

Jay joined them, and they entered the monument, going into the elevator and riding up to the observation platform inside the top.

There, they found Holmes' part of the team delicately removing the window and its reinforcements, so that Ray could exit through it.

"Ray, you better be damn sure of this," Fields grumbled, worried, as he shot Ray up with a full hypodermic of stimulants and pain killers. "Wish the cover allowed for an air bag, just in case. I can repair a lotta shit, but if you're wrong, ain't no way in Heaven or Hell I can repair a greasy spot on the ground."

"If I can't find Sam and Abby, Doc, I'd as soon be a greasy spot on the ground," Ray replied absently, watching his special chronometer. "Hurry up, guys. We got ten minutes."

"Why in the hell would they put an extraction point up here?" Jay wondered.

"Who knows? Maybe they can't control where they go precisely?" Ray mused.

"I don't buy that. They went in and out of banks and such pretty damned accurately," Jay argued.

"Good point, Jay." Ray nodded. "Something to think about."

"Putting them in hard to reach and unexpected places might keep people from stumbling across them?" Paul added. "Or through them?"

"Or…" Jay broke off, a frown on his face as something occurred to him. But before he could voice the thought, it was interrupted.

"Done," Holmes declared, removing the window framework and setting it aside.

Jay and Paul helped Ray clamber into the window, his legs dangling outside. "First point coming up," Ray noted. "In three… two… one…"

A light flared about halfway down the side of the monument. In broad, clear daylight, it was far less noticeable than the one in New York had been.

They waited impatiently for four minutes and thirty-seven seconds. "You got the fall time calculated, pal?" Paul asked.

"To the tenth of a second, Paul," Ray answered. "Here it comes. And here I go—in three, two…"

Ray pushed out of the window and began to plummet Earthward.

Halfway there, a light flared…

…And Ray vanished.

Chapter 19

"Oomff," Ray grunted under his breath as he hit what felt like judo mats. He rolled over quickly, onto his feet and into a crouch, bringing the energy weapon to the ready, but nobody was there. He felt to make certain the nine millimeter handgun with the silencer was still in place on his chest webbing holster. It was. The other one was in place on the other side. He was good to go. *Why WOULD anybody be guarding the transport room? After all, to their knowledge, who could use it other than Drago and his henchmen?* Ray thought to himself.

Keep moving. He wasn't sure he was buying his own theory about nobody guarding the room and the hairs on the back of his neck stood on end from that unknowing fear. He shuffled quietly across the mats to the door leading from the room. He scanned around trying to get some idea of where he was, but the room was very nondescript. It had a tall ceiling about five meters high with padded walls and floor. The padding was a cream colored leather-like material similar to some of those Ray had seen in karate dojos, and looked new. He had expected to see all sorts of weird equipment that belonged in a cheap 1950s era science fiction movie. But there was none of that to be found. The closest thing in the room that suggested anything unusual going on was the fact that there were bright green glowing bulls-eyes on all six walls. He also realized that the room seemed to be perfectly cubic—five meters tall, deep, and wide.

The lighting came from fluorescent strips above and through the one large window on the other side of the room across from the large double doors. The window was at the eight o'clock position of the big green bulls-eye on that wall. Through that window appeared to be where Drago had hidden the scientific "doohickeys" and "thingamajigs." The scientist in Ray wished he had time to take a look in there. But he was there to find his wife and daughter, liberate them, and kill every last rat bastard that got in his way. As pissed as he was, he might kill a few of them for the hell of it even if they weren't right in his way.

There was also what appeared to be a three meter wide garage door on the adjacent wall to his left, at the four o'clock position of the bulls-eye on that wall. Ray opted for the standard double door. He tested the push bar and found that the door was unlocked, so he slipped through into the next room and then checked his team phone. *No signal. Shit.*

The team phones were the state of the art and could roam on any network undetected as well as use any wireless network connections to get a signal out. But even the global positioning receiver was getting nothing. Ray set it to vibrate if it picked up a signal. He also set his Maps application to link his and the rest of the team's phones so they could all see each other's global position. If the phone got any signal at all, the team would immediately know where he was. He then slipped the phone back in the pocket on his sleeve. He did a quick scan around him and kept moving.

Quietly Ray scouted from hall to hall of the facility and several times he had to take hiding places as Drago's men passed by. After more than ten minutes of slinking through the building, or whatever it was, given Ray couldn't figure out the reason for the circular architecture quite yet, he heard a baby crying.

The sound came from just down the hallway and to the left. Ray crouched in the corner behind a line of flammable liquids cabinets and a couple of wheeled trash cans. He watched patiently, resisting the urge to go guns blazing and burst into the room with the crying baby. But Ray had been to more than one dance and he knew that patience would pay off. Seconds later he found he was right.

Four men, each carrying handguns at the ready, approached the door. One of them swiped a passkey on an electronic lock. The door hissed open with a *click*. The four men eased cautiously through the door, covering each other in standard military stack and entry posture.

"She's a wild bitch, be ready!" the man in the back ordered.

"Can't believe she took down Cobb and Rayez!"

Sam! Ray understood what had happened immediately; his chest swelled with pride as a wicked smirk spread across his face. *That's my Sam.* He held his pistol in his left hand and the energy weapon in the right, fully prepared to go all "two gun mojo" on them. Double tapping, some called it; whatever, he was more than capable.

The men passed through the door one at a time. The fourth, and what appeared to be the leader, did not enter, but merely stood in the doorway. His back was to Ray and that was good enough for him. Still in a crouch, he eased the pistol up and took a bead on the man in the doorway. *Schpatt!*

The round hit at the base of the man's skull, moving upward, severing the brain stem and blowing gray matter out the front of his forehead. The man slumped over and fell to the floor like a rag doll. Ray was already behind him and firing at the man just inside the door and to the right, before swinging the silenced gun to the man on the left. *Schpatt. Schpatt schpatt!*

The last man standing was startled by his colleagues falling around him, and that was all the diversion Sam needed. One second later, she had snapped his elbow upward and into two pieces. A fraction of a second following that, she pulled the handgun from his hands and hit him in the face with the butt of it—twice. By the time two seconds had gone by, Sam was behind the man, twisting his neck with all her strength. By the third second the man lay paralyzed and dying on the floor. Ray pumped a round into him just to be sure.

"I had it under control." Sam wiped blood that wasn't hers from her face. "Eyes are on us!" she pointed at the cameras in the corner by the ceiling. Ray turned and put a couple of rounds into the sensors.

"Not anymore. Move!" Ray urged. "Get their weapons."

"Right." Sam picked up the dead men's weapons and extra magazines and stuffed them in pockets in her unisex jumpsuit as fast as she could go, which was pretty damn fast. She checked that there was a round in the chamber of the weapon she carried and dropped in behind Ray.

"You okay? Looks like you had some trouble." Ray motioned to the other two dead bodies in her cell.

"Peachy," was all she said, so Ray left it at that.

"Where's Abby?"

"That son of a bitch has her somewhere in this rat warren," Sam spat. Ray turned and could see the concern in her eyes. "God, I'm so glad to see you."

"I KNEW you were both still alive. I love you, Sam!" Ray led her around the corner and backed against the corridor wall. "Shhhh."

"What's our situation, Ray?" Sam breathed the query to her husband. She might be the boss, but field ops was Ray's bag. Ray was glad she knew when to relinquish authority.

"We're alone. I teleported in, hoping to get out a signal to the team, but so far I'm not getting any tower, wireless, or satellite reception," Ray whispered.

"That's because we're in the bottom of a missile silo somewhere in the Dakotas, I think." Sam kept her back against the wall but looked in the opposite direction from Ray.

"Okay. Then we have to assume that there will be no backup. It's all up to us. If we can move upward we might get some signal out." Ray paused for a brief second. "Listen Sam, we shoot everyone in our path and we shoot to kill. Got it?"

"Damn right!"

"Then let's move." Ray nodded and stepped around the corner with his pistol ready. A team of Drago's henchmen was headed that way fast. Ray didn't hesitate and neither did Sam. The two of them charged at full speed and started firing into the oncoming team. The charge startled the men at first, giving Ray and Sam all the advantage they needed. Ray dove into a belly slide as if he were stealing home plate, all the while pumping out blasts from the energy weapon. Sam stayed close to the wall at first and continued to fire. A few rounds zinged off the wall near her head, so she turned and ran across the corridor and up the wall on the other side, using her speed to carry her a full two steps up the wall. She then pushed hard off the wall with her legs into a sideways dive back over the top of her husband; the whole time she fired a continuous stream of 9mm bullets at Drago's men. She rolled to her feet and never stopped moving. Ray turned over onto his butt and then up onto his feet. They ran past the dead bodies, slowing just long enough for Sam to pick up one of their energy weapons.

"Now this is more like it," she said. "Two flights up the stairwell and we'll be at the nursery. Don't know if they are still keeping her there or not, but it's our best shot. Ray, if you see a slightly older oriental man, not wearing a jumpsuit, don't shoot him. He's a good guy. He's that missing Dr. Kato. I don't know what they did with him after they put me back in the cell."

"Uh huh," he grunted. Ray pounded the stairwell door open with a booted foot and dropped to a crouch with the energy weapon moving through potential aim points, stopping, and then moving to the next one. "Clear!"

"Clear behind us," Sam replied.

"Up we go." Ray bolted up the first flight of stairs and didn't have to wait at all for his wife. "Second floor, you said?"

"Yes. Go!" She nudged him.

Ray and Sam made the second flight of stairs in no time and took up positions on each side of the door.

"Ready?"

"Ready."

Ray kicked the door open and backed away quickly as Sam dropped to knee level and looked for targets. There were six knees in the henchmen jumpsuits so she opened up on them. Ray rolled back around into the doorway and fired several shots of the energy weapon himself, but they hit the wall on the other side because Sam had already incinerated the men from the knees down. The three of them were screaming in pain, so Ray shut them up quickly, but the jig was up anyway. An energy bolt danced across the gray metal door behind his head, only inches away, singing his hair. Ray ducked back through the door, pulling Sam through the door with him by the back of her jumpsuit.

"Down!" he shouted as several more energy blasts vaporized metal and concrete around them.

"Ray! Below us!" Sam shouted just as several automatic weapon rounds pinged the metal staircase near them. Sam held her weapon over the rail and fired a couple of random shots in that general direction. A scream told her she'd got somebody. But it also triggered a fresh barrage of lead.

"Shit! Up! We've got to go up, Sam!" Ray shouted and then pumped a few energy bolts of his own down the stairwell.

"Then go already!" Sam fired a round over her shoulder and down the stairwell as she bolted up the stairs ahead of her husband. Ray turned behind her and followed suit as fast as he could manage. Each of them fired behind them whenever they got the opportunity.

"Third floor!" Ray kicked the door open and there was nobody there. He fired a round of the energy weapon through it just in case. Sam did likewise. "Must have beat them up here. Keep moving. We'll look for another way back down to Abby. If nothing else, we'll try using the energy rifles to cut through the floor. From what I've seen, that should work pretty well."

"Right." Sam slammed the door behind her and Ray jammed it with a metal chair's leg. Then he pushed a bookshelf over onto it.

"That won't hold them for long," he said.

"Not with these energy weapons, it won't," Sam agreed.

They turned down the hallway past several laboratories and then Sam seemed to recognize where they were.

"Any ideas, Sam?"

"Yeah. I think this is not too far from the Resident Evil lab."

"The what?"

"There's a lab in here with all these mutated creatures in chambers. It is seriously creepy bad, like out of a movie or a video game, only it's real. Then through there down the next hallway and there is another stairwell on the other side." Sam seemed pretty sure of the layout.

"How do you know all this?"

"I made it all the way out with Abby once already and got caught on the aircraft runway up top." Sam noted. "That was when things got ugly."

"I see," Ray replied. His wife never ceased to amaze him. Then his phone vibrated against his arm three times. "Yes!"

"What is it, Ray?"

"My phone just got a signal. The team knows where we are."

"So... where are we?"

"Hold on." Ray whipped out his phone and looked at the map application. Sam was right. They were in—or rather, some ten miles outside—Devil's Lake, North Dakota, almost halfway between Grand Forks and Minot. "Well, we're a long damned way from Virginia. Couple hours at the least. You were right, it's North Dakota."

"We do it ourselves, then," Sam said, expression grim.

"Yes. We do it ourselves, or at least buy time until backup can get here." Ray knew that the team was already loaded and in the air orbiting outside of D.C., but even in the team's very fastest jet, they were still a couple of hours away. Maybe they would have the presence of mind to get a team from Minot Air Force Base, which was only a few minutes away.

Then a voice over the PA system in the silo sent chills up his spine.

    ⁖⃣₧

Drago had found his encounters with the man from the government to be a nuisance, and to be more than just interesting. He was getting tired of that nuisance always showing up at just the wrong time. Apparently he was quite a considerable foe. Drago stood and walked to the large window of his office overlooking the high bay area not far from the extraction point room. He only wished there was something he could do that would allow him to change how things were going to be. He also realized that his present foes would have to become his allies or get out of his way.

"It is time, Dr. Brady, for us to change the playing field," he muttered to himself. Then he keyed up the security cameras of the complex and watched as the Bradys devastated his henchmen, his highly skilled and well paid henchmen. He plopped himself back into his chair, only partially watching the firefight taking place throughout his complex. He couldn't kill them now. He was pretty sure of it. It didn't matter if he wanted to or not–he couldn't. History wouldn't allow it.

He had resolved himself to win the future for humanity even though centuries earlier he had decided he could not change the future. God knows he had tried, and tried, and tried. Every time he had attempted to change the future, his actions, in fact, were the very things that triggered the events that history had recorded occurring. He contemplated the conversation he had with that strange resistance leader woman from the future who sent him back in time, Abigail. He was virtually certain now who that girl was. How she could be the little sickly child he held captive in his complex he had no idea, but somehow she would manage to live for centuries to help lead the resistance against the aliens. He had always assumed that their paths would cross again–that they must cross again sometime in the distant future. Drago had no idea that his path and hers were so intertwined. But he was beginning to figure it all out.

He remembered, when he first realized what timeframe he was in hundreds of years before, that it had taken him more than fifty years to truly grasp what Abby had told him to do.

"Create a paradox," she had told him.

But how? How could he create a paradox? Drago of course understood what a paradox was, but how to create one was a whole other matter. Although he had been a very studious physics student in college, he had done like most scientists and did just what he needed to get by in his other classes, such as history. History was of little interest to him when he was younger. But now, history was all important to him.

He knew of certain events and his knowledge of the future should have been detailed enough to immediately create a paradox. Or so he had thought. It turned out to be much more difficult than he had ever imagined. It appeared that history was what it was. For some reason, it kept ending up the way it always had.

ഇൗൽ

The first real opportunity he had was after he had first ventured back to the Americas in the early 1800s. Being so much more educated than the general populace, it was very easy for Drago to position himself as a wealthy individual and even in some cases as a medical doctor. He knew more about the human body and how it functioned than any human on the planet at the time, so why not call himself a medical doctor? He made himself a sought out scientist and professor of medicine. And somehow or other he managed to find himself as an advisor to John C. Calhoun, Congressman John C. Calhoun, of South Carolina, in 1814. It was just after the end of the War of 1812 that they had crossed paths.

Drago only vaguely recalled that Calhoun had been involved in the early interests of the South seceding from the Union of the United States of America based on what he recalled from his high school and undergraduate school history. His thoughts were that he might hurry the Civil War along thirty or more years prior to its original start, hoping to spur the technology growth that war causes by decades. Drago wasn't completely certain about the history but his theory was that humanity's technology must have grown by leaps and bounds during the Civil War. He certainly recalled the Manhattan Project of World War II and he had plans for that when the time came. But in 1815, his sights were set on the Civil War.

To Drago's surprise, Congressman Calhoun was much more of a nationalist than he had ever expected. In fact, Calhoun had every intent of supporting national tariffs, public works efforts, a national bank, and a public infrastructure to support a better War Department. None of these things seemed to be in line with the "secessionist hero" Drago remembered from high school history. Granted, it had been centuries since that time, but an interesting side effect of his alien manipulated DNA was that he had damn near total recall of his memories—what memories of history class he had, anyway.

Drago took it upon himself to advise Calhoun and push him as much as he could toward the philosophy of "state's rights." It was Drago who brought to then Vice President Calhoun's attention various works by Jefferson discussing the states' rights to resist federal law. He urged Calhoun to take it further, and triggered his writing the *South Carolina Exposition and Protest* opposing the Tariff of 1828, which forced the farmers of the South to buy from industries of the North instead of cheaper suppliers from outside the United States. It was at this moment that Drago thought he could spark a war. He created street protests and rallies. He wrote letter after letter to politicians and media alike. He even went so far as to go door to door in some cases to drum up the secessionist fervor. Drago had more than five thousand copies of Calhoun's protest document printed up and passed them all around Washington D.C.

He continued to support Calhoun and push the argument that the states could veto any law written passed by the federal government until it became too much for President Andrew Jackson to take. In 1832 Calhoun resigned as the Vice President and went back to South Carolina, deflating a lot of the fervor for Civil War that Drago had managed to stir up. In 1833, Senator Clay came up with a compromise that cooled Calhoun, then-Senator Calhoun of South Carolina, to the point where secession was no longer the only solution. Had it been a hundred years later when Drago had evolved to the realization that he had to be "bloody" on occasion, he would have simply killed Clay before he came up with that damned compromise. But Drago hadn't become that person, not yet. In the end, he had spent thirty or so years involved in American politics to no avail. No paradox followed and things happened the way they happened. It had been an extreme amount of effort for naught.

As paradoxes went, starting a war early, assassinating somebody famous, or changing the outcome of a major sporting event never seemed to pan out. There had been so many other instances where Drago had wandered through history attempting to improve mankind's chances to defeat the future aliens. But in no cases was he able to create a paradox. In fact, in one attempt in 1912 during a visit to Austria to visit a young Albert Einstein he actually triggered events, purely by accident, that led a group of people known as the "Black Hand" to plot to kill the Archduke Franz Ferdinand just two years later. That assassination, he recalled, was often considered to be the event that sparked World War I.

Even when he wasn't planning on intervening in history it always turned out to prove that history was what it was. His last attempt to create a paradox was in 1963 in Dallas, Texas. Drago tried to prevent the assassination of a president and ended up being captured in a photograph on a grassy knoll with a rifle. Meanwhile, the President was still assassinated right before his eyes. Nothing he could do about it.

ଛଠଓଃ

Later in early 1970 Drago needed reconnaissance information of the Moon as he was formulating his current plan against the aliens. He developed a small sensor based on future technologies and wireless communications capabilities that were undetectable by the technology of the 1970s. He positioned himself working as an engineer on the United States space program for NASA and manipulated events enough so he was a flight hardware engineer. Drago had every intention of placing his payload on the mission of Apollo 12, but due to last-minute changes beyond his control it actually ended up as a component on Apollo 13.

Drago wasn't quite sure how but he was pretty sure that his sensor had managed to drain too much power from the stirring fan in the cryogenic oxygen tank. This in turn melted the insulation off the wires inside the tank. As soon as the stirring fans were turned on, sparks were generated between the bare wires, which then led to the explosion that created the

Apollo 13 malfunction. NASA would blame a thermostat wired for the wrong voltage but Drago knew better. He had caused the problem.

For centuries everything that Drago did seemed to be only a part of history. From these experiences he concluded that there was only one timeline and that he could not change the future. He was just as much a part of history as anybody else—an anomaly that wasn't an anomaly. Therefore, he decided to plan to prepare for the future and be ready when the alien invasion began. He was beginning to understand what Abby had told him when she said that HE didn't believe in paradoxes. His experience was leading him to a point where he was certain paradoxes could not be created. And he was also concluding that somehow in the future, he was allied with this Abigail and whoever her father was. He was pretty certain about who both of them were at this point, though his future with them still seemed quite hard to grasp. Reaching an alliance with them considering their present status seemed, well, unlikely. The ramifications of his conclusion were quite mind-boggling and Drago had taken over two centuries to reach this point.

He looked across the security screens once more and decided that enough was enough. His men were not going to stop the Bradys. History assured that. No need in wasting more lives that were not infected. He keyed the microphone on the complex intercom system.

Chapter 20

"Hello Dr. Brady. It is so good to meet you... again." Drago's voice pierced through the air. "Perhaps we can do it more formally this time. Proper introductions and all that. The social graces are so important, wouldn't you agree? Now, I think it is high time you put down your weapons and come to me. We have very much to discuss. Otherwise, your charming daughter might come across some very unfortunate mishap."

"You leave her alone, you vile piece of shit!" a venomous Sam spat.

"Ah, now now, no foul language in front of the baby! Don't worry, Mrs. Brady. If you put down your arms and come to me now, your daughter will be fine. Isn't that right, Abby?" Drago sort of laughed, and Ray could hear his daughter coo at him. "Besides, I don't need you killing more of my men for no reason."

Ray raised an eyebrow. *He can't be mistreating Abby too badly if she's cooing. What the hell is going on here? Only one way to find out, at this point. Don't trust him any farther than I can throw him, anyway. And he's got Abby, regardless.*

"All right. Where do we go?" Ray scanned the room for cameras but wasn't having much luck finding one. Drago could travel through time and space with what appeared to be ease. So Ray figured the man could hide video cameras pretty much anywhere he wanted.

"Very good. I'm so glad you are such a smart fellow. Back down to the bottom floor on the elevator in the center of the building. I will be waiting for you there. Hands up. No guns," Drago ordered, then followed with, "or something... unfortunate... might happen."

Sam and Ray emptied their pockets of weapons, leaving them on the floor of the corridor where they were certain Drago could see through his video cameras, wherever they were.

Ray and Sam carefully but hastily made their way to the elevator and spent the eternity it took to travel down three floors. Once the elevator door opened, Ray's heart pounded with excitement, fear, and anxiety as he saw his little girl in the clutches of the man he'd seen act as such a ruthless killer.

"Hello, Dr. Brady. Mrs. Brady." Drago didn't move a muscle as he stood stiff and menacing. Somehow at the same time he managed to hold Abby in his left hand firmly but, oddly enough, gently. "Dr. Brady, my name is Dr. William H. Drago."

The husband and wife ignored Drago, focusing on their child. "Abby," Sam said. "Mommy's here, baby."

"Hi."

"Hi, Abby, princess," Ray added.

"Hi." Abby reached out for them, but Drago pulled her hands back. "Well now, Abby, my dear. Your parents are being quite rude; ignoring my formal introduction and such. We shall hold off on the reunion for a moment." Drago motioned to the nurse behind and to his left. The nurse stepped in and took the baby from him, turning and heading down the corridor. She disappeared around its curve.

"Let Abby and Sam go, Drago. I'll stay behind and we can work this out." Ray started to shuffle his feet slightly to adjust his weight. If he needed to spring into action he was going to be ready. He scanned the room and only counted fourteen weapons pointed in his general direction. No, the numbers were too great to go head on. He'd have to talk his way out of this, or hope for a miracle—or backup. He didn't care which one got there first.

"I'm sorry Dr. Brady, but that will not be happening today. I think it is time to get the entire family in for consultation." Drago grinned at them, an odd, fey gleam in his eyes. "What do you know about paradoxes, Dr. Brady?"

"What? Paradoxes?" Ray wasn't expecting the conversation to take this type of turn. "I know that I like them only slightly more than I like you. They hurt my head. You, well, you just piss me off."

"Ha ha, very good." Drago laughed. "You see, I am faced with a conundrum of Biblical sorts here. The balance of humanity might well weigh heavily upon what we do here in the next few minutes."

"A bit overly dramatic, don't you think? You crazy sonuvabitch!" Sam spat at him.

"Now Mrs. Brady, please. No need for name calling. You see, I could kill you both now. I could even kill little Abigail. But I made a vow to myself long ago not to kill a human if he or she is not infected. And then there is the paradox. If I kill either of you now I certainly will not meet you in the future. That tells me that I don't kill you... or I do, and somehow you come back to life. But it doesn't matter. None of you are infected so I do not desire to kill you. But don't get me wrong. Give me reason and I most certainly will."

"Infected by what?" Ray shuffled the weight on his feet again. Scanning the room looking for an edge or a crack in somebody's attention, he prepared himself for the smallest opportunity to strike if it came. His muscles tensed as his jaws clenched tighter and tighter. *Infected? The future?* he thought. *What the hell?*

"By THEM! The infection has been going on for more than a century now. If humanity is to survive, I must stop it. And you, Dr. Brady, keep getting in my way and meddling with my plans!" Drago said. "You must stop this! Humanity is at stake here!"

"Meddling with your plans, yeah, I'm kinda funny that way. When assholes start stealing the stuff to make neutron bombs it rubs me the wrong damned way," Ray replied.

"Yes. I gathered that about you. I should kill you now, but that would violate my personal vow. And to top it off, I strongly suspect you must join me in the future if we are to stop what is coming. So I could not kill you if I tried."

Ray could see a real look of confusion on Drago's face for a brief moment.

"Join you! Ha. That's never gonna happen," Sam added before Ray could respond. "Now I know you're nuts."

"Oh, but you will, unless there is a paradox. And there will not be one. Over the last couple of centuries I've come to understand that temporal paradoxes do not exist," Drago said. "Ergo, you will join me."

"So how do you know you don't join us?"

"Interesting point, Dr. Brady. It would make no difference in either case, I suspect."

"You're not making sense," Sam complained.

"Indeed. Forgive me," Drago began. "I have the full time upon which to draw, but you—"

"Okay, seriously, let Abby and Sam walk out of here," Ray interrupted. "They'll walk until somebody comes and gets them. You and I will stay behind and talk this out." Ray hoped to continue to buy time until he could think of a plan or reinforcements could arrive. "If we're to join you, we should start with some gesture of trust now."

"No. Nobody is leaving. And the gesture of trust, as you suggest, is me not killing you where you stand. You must all stay and join with me. There is much work to be done," Drago replied.

"Tell me about this infection you keep talking about," Ray queried. "Where does it come from? And who is infected?"

"Humanity is infected! At least a large portion of it is. It started with Comet Enke. Oh, I know it is hard to believe, but I was in Tunguska and found the fragment of that comet long before any Russian expedition made it there. I needed an electron microscope or an X-ray diffractometer to be sure, neither of which existed then, but I kept samples. I isolated the strain. It took me years to convince Crick and Watson what to look for! Those two moved so damned slowly and methodically and far too cautiously for my needs. Were it not for my pushing and cajoling them I think they would never have gotten to where they did! And Franklin and Gosling took so long in developing their diagnostic capabilities that I almost left them and did it myself. Were it not for me, I wonder where humanity's level of science would truly be. The short answer is that the samples from the comet fragment had more than just influenza in it, and whatever else was there had DNA that was clearly not human."

Ray watched as Drago continued to monologue. As fascinating and insane as the story sounded, as much as it seemed to validate his and his team's work, he had to set it aside for the time. He had to focus on his wife, his daughter, and the fact that there was a madman in front of him who had no telling how many neutron bombs at his disposal. Buying time was never a bad idea. Time always allowed for things to happen. It was something he had always observed and learned, in many cases, the hard way. It was something that one day he intended to teach his daughter. It was something that he hoped soon he was going to teach the crazy bastard in front of him, with extreme vengeance.

"Not human? You mean alien then? Like you?" Sam interjected.

"Ha, I'm human! Dr. Brady, you met me as a child! I'm human," Drago replied.

"But you aren't fully human, are you?" Ray asked. Still no break he could see. *Keep him going, something will happen.* "We examined the, uh, your blood from our first encounter. It has been altered from the child's."

"Ah yes, you did manage to make me bleed, didn't you? I should have considered that. No matter. I'm human. I find it quite intriguing how time always allows for things to happen in the most peculiar ways. Don't you? There was an unfortunate accident at DARPA, oh, about thirty-five years from now when I first tried the Membrane Extraction Point." Drago smiled at Ray, studying his expression. "Aha, you figured it out?"

"You invented the technology, right?" Ray asked. He hated that Drago could read him so easily.

"Yes, I do, did, will, whatever. Time traveling really does confuse the tenses."

"You mean senses?" Sam quipped.

"No, he really does mean tenses, Sam."

"Yes. I found myself far in the future and fatally injured and dying. The aliens in the future rescued me and cured me with some sort of reptilian alien gene therapy. A very long story," Drago said, as if it annoyed him that Ray questioned his humanity. Then he added, "But suffice it to say I met a charming lady who rescued me from the alien scourge. That lady was a general and went only by the name Abigail."

"Abigail?" Sam and Ray both mouthed simultaneously. "What the..."

"Yes, it is intriguing, isn't it? Hundreds of years in the future... and there she was. She didn't look more than late twenties or early thirties. Though there were some abnormalities in her appearance. Slight skin tone changes, some sort of red streaks running across her face, and eye color oddities, but it was her. Our little Abby." He nodded down the corridor in the direction the nurse had gone.

"Bullshit!" Ray replied.

"Maybe so." Drago nodded. "But there are no paradoxes. And I've seen stranger things happen through time."

"So you keep telling us. Then what? Where does that leave us now? No matter what you say, you have neutron bombs, and I can't let you keep them." Ray had had enough. It was time to take action to get his wife and daughter to safety. And then...

"Boss!" a voice from behind them shouted. A man rushed into the room. He had headphones and a microphone on as if he were a radar controller at an airfield. It turned out that was exactly what he was.

"What!" Drago spun on him, annoyed.

"Boss, I've got inbound aircraft moving fast. Looks like fighters from Minot Air Force Base."

"What?!"

₧◊₧

"What?" the Old Man shouted from the cockpit to the back of the plane at Jay.

"Sir! I've got the feed now. The fighters have lifted off and are inbound for Ray's location. I'm pulling it up on the screen now." Jay fiddled with the controls of the classified Google Earth platform and brought up the latest, most detailed information on the area. "Clearly an old missile silo with a small airstrip on it. Looks like the airstrip was added recently."

"Fighters? At Minot?" Kruger asked.

"Yes sir. There just happened to be a squadron of six F-18s there doing a B-52 escort training mission. I have co-opted them," Jay replied. He continued tapping at the keys of his console and pulling up more data screens to analyze. "They were more than happy to have a more aggressive training mission."

"Uh-huh. I guess so. So what are we going to have the fighters do, exactly?" Kruger settled in behind Jay. "And how long until we get there?"

"Not sure about the fighters yet, sir. The helicopters and the strike team, if you can call it that, will be there momentarily. The fighters are for cover or maybe a Hail Mary play if we need one." Jay turned back to the console and tapped furiously at the keys. "We're about ninety-seven minutes out, sir."

"Dammit all to hell! I hate being late for a fight," Kruger replied. Jay could see the man's jaw was clenched tighter than his fists. "Stay on top of this. This thing will be over in twenty minutes or less."

"Yes sir."

Jay sat back from the screen long enough to take a sip of his coffee and glance out the window. The DSRPO team was on-board their modified Gulfstream 5 and were cruising at maximum altitude and speed. It wasn't fast enough to get them in play for Ray, Sam, and Abigail. Jay hoped that calling the shots from afar would keep them in the game enough to give Ray an advantage at the right moment. Jay had been working with Ray for the better part of his career now and he knew that sometimes all Ray needed was a pin to drop, causing someone to flinch, for him to make a move. Jay was planning on dropping some pins and three whole choppers full of security from the nearby Air Force Base. Hopefully, some of that would make somebody blink just long enough to give Ray time to do something.

"I'm switching the comm channel on now," he said as he flipped a toggle on the upper left side of the console. Instantly, flight chatter could be heard.

"...roger that Kitten Two, you are to cover the air for the ground units and hold fire unless fired upon or given other orders. Also be advised that we have ears in the sky that will be hot from here on in. It is their asset on the ground and we are taking direction from them—call sign Big Ears."

"Uh, understood, Big Ears are hot and calling the shots."

"Minot, we've got the choppers now. They are in-bound and moving into position...HOLY SHIT! What was that?" the lead pilot shouted.

"Son of a bitch, was that a SAM!? Somebody down there just set off a load of stingers. Evasive! Evasive!"

"Kitten One, what's your status, over! Repeat, what's your status, over!"

*"We are under heavy surface to air fire and trying to gain some altitude.
Choppers Two and Three are hit! Chopper One is under heavy fire."*

"Repeat that, Kitten One! We show Chopper One track still good."

*"Look out, guys! Negative, negative! More stingers. Chopper One is
down. Control, the Spittin' Kittens are requesting to go hot!"*

At this point Jay grabbed the radio and keyed it open. Kruger reached
across him and took the mike. Jay didn't flinch or mutter a sound.

"This is the Big Ears in the Sky. You have permission to go hot but do
not hit that silo directly. I repeat, no direct targeting of the silo facility."

"Roger that, Big Ears!" the pilot responded and paused only briefly.
"You heard the man, boys. It is time to go hot."

"Hail Mary, sir?" Jay looked at Kruger.

"Hail Mary."

"Ray, old boy, be ready, somebody is about to flinch." Jay whistled as
he shook his head. Kruger nodded in agreement.

☾☥

Ray eyed Drago, wondering if this was the moment he'd been waiting for. The henchmen were still surrounding them but were distracted.
Drago had stopped his monologue and was shouting into a radio.

"We've got all those surface to air missiles! Use them!" he scolded one
of his men.

"Yes sir. Jackson and Taylor are already on it."

"Good," Drago replied. "I shouldn't have to do everything myself!"

A few tens of seconds later, there was an explosion above and outside
somewhere. Then there were two more. Then another.

"Somehow, you have alerted the outside world to our whereabouts. I
should have foreseen that. It will only be in vain, though!" Drago snarled
at Ray and Sam.

Ray didn't like it. Then the complex shook violently.

"There are NO paradoxes, dammit!" Drago added.

Ray could feel what seemed like a squishing or bouncing undulation
from the floor. Then he remembered that some of the old silos were
actually built on spring systems to dampen out the force from explosive
attacks. Then the place shook again and again, causing an equipment rack
to rattle and roll across the floor on its casters. Almost all of the men in
the room glanced at the free rolling rack of controller equipment.

That was all Ray needed.

He slipped directly backward and spun into the man behind him and
Sam. A fraction of a second later he had the man's gun and was firing it

madly at the other men in the room while ducking behind the rolling equipment rack. Sam hadn't missed a beat of it and as soon as Ray had made his move she dropped to the floor, going after the kneecaps of the man to her right.

The building shook again. The henchmen and Drago had become slightly discombobulated, but neither Ray's nor Sam's rhythm was off. The two of them moved swiftly and deadly, like a beautiful, violent dance. Both of them were in the zone where time slowed down for them. They made things happen when it did.

Ray looked up, searching for Drago, and pumped a couple of rounds in his general direction, but Drago was moving fast—too fast for Ray to hit and still keep from getting hit himself. Then the weapon's slide clicked open and empty so he threw the gun at the head of one of the remaining standing guards.

By this time Sam had managed to commandeer two pistols for herself and took up where Ray left off. Rounds from the pistols pinged around the room, throwing blinding sparks and shards whenever they hit the walls of the silo. Most of the occupants of the room had scattered to whatever hidey-hole or bit of cover they could duck into or nearby.

"Sam, on your right!" he yelled, then rolled over and belly crawled to the nearest downed body to find another weapon. This time he found an energy weapon. He worked the safety into the on position and rolled on his back, throwing an energy bolt across the room that released a puff of pink steam as it vaporized the midsection of one of the men. He continued to fire the weapon with surgical precision.

"Sam! Keep on the offensive and attack," Ray shouted to her. "We go on the defensive and we're dead meat."

"Don't wait on me! You're the point man! Point!" Sam replied as she pulled magazines from one of the dead henchmen's webbing and reloaded her pistols.

"Right. Go, go, go!" Ray pushed the rolling computer rack like a running back pushing his lineman through a seam in the defense. Sam followed behind him, blocking for the sack from the rear.

"Ray! Up there! Drago!" Sam nodded toward a catwalk leading to a spiral stairwell off the side of the room.

"Got it! Move!" Ray pushed the rack until it fell over and crashed through a large picture frame window looking into the membrane control room's antechambers. There was a doorway there leading into the extraction point room. From the looks of the architecture of the place, the catwalk was a shortcut, bypassing the stairs on the far side of the EP room. "We go through there and up the stairs on the far side. We're cut off this way anyhow."

"You da boss," Sam replied with a smile as she leaped through the broken window head first. Ray was right behind her, blasting away with the energy weapon.

The two of them backed against the wall on either side of the exit door and then Ray jumped and kicked it open, all the while preparing to fire cover as needed. Sam kept their backs covered.

"Clear!" Ray shouted and burst through the door and bolted across the room to the base of the staircase. He could hear pistols firing on the other side of the door he'd just come through and paused almost long enough to consider going back. "Come on, Sam!"

"Get down!" Sam burst through the door opening in a dive. Just behind her, and before Ray could truly take cover, there was a huge explosion on the other side of the wall. Fire and debris flew through the doorway. Ray shook his head and worked his jaw to relieve the ringing in his ears.

"What the hell was that?" he asked. He then scanned around for survivors, and as far as he could tell nobody was going to come running through that door. The fireball still engulfed most of the outer room. Then the sprinklers went off, dumping water on them like a torrential rainfall.

"Propane cans. Saw them earlier and knew they'd come in handy at some point." She smiled at her husband as he helped her up. The two of them wiped water from their faces. "What next?"

"Where's Abby?"

"Up!" She pointed up and to their right.

"Through this door and up, then." Ray checked the charge meter on his weapon and guessed it was somewhere around half full. He really had no idea what that meant. If he had known for sure that it was fully charged when he had started firing it willy-nilly then he could reverse calculate how many it had taken to drain it to half. That is, had he been bothering to keep count of how many times he'd fired it in the first place. He decided just to keep moving and firing until it looked close to being out of gas. If he got the chance, then he'd kill somebody else and take their weapon. At least that was his current plan.

The two of them moved swiftly but cautiously up the stairwell. It was like déjà vu all over again and neither of them liked being in a situation where they could get boxed in from the top and bottom so easily. At least this time they knew that they had already taken out many of Drago's men, there was some sort of air cover happening above, Drago seemed flustered, and water was pouring out of the sprinklers on all of the floors as best they could tell. It was perfect conditions for being outgunned and on the offensive.

Once up the first level they burst out onto the catwalk where they had seen Drago zip off in such a rush. The building continued to shake with explosions from outside, on the surface, but the explosions seemed to be much fewer between. Drago and his men must have been fighting back. Ray figured that somehow Jay and the Old Man had arranged this diversionary attack to buy them some time. He hoped that it would be enough time for them to get to Abby and then to someplace safe. Then they needed to figure out how to stop Drago's plan—whatever that was.

෴

"Sir, it has to be six F-18s. Didn't know they had those over there?!"

"It doesn't matter where they came from or what they are. Shoot them down!" Drago ordered.

The longer range and faster fighters executed evasive maneuvers from the shoulder launched surface-to-air missiles, making it harder for Drago's men to bring them down. Several of the men fired with the energy weapons but had little luck targeting the swift moving fighters.

"They can't be loaded with too much ordnance, sir. They will run out of missiles before too much longer anyway," the radar technician explained. "Sir, I'm picking up a much bigger radar track moving in fast."

"What is it?" Drago fired off a stinger then dropped the shoulder fired system on the ground and walked over to the radar truck. "That isn't a fighter plane."

"No sir." The tech looked up at the sky as a screech of engines picked up. "I think it is a B-52, sir."

"Damn! Take cover." Drago grabbed the headset from the radar tech and punched in the PA and general communications frequency. "Bomber incoming! Take cover."

Drago turned back to his crate full of surface-to-air missiles. He'd stolen them years before and had been hoarding them. He had more than enough to fight a small revolution. He threw one of the systems over his shoulder and activated the seekers. The bomber was flying way out of range of the stinger missile but he let it fly anyway.

"I've had enough of this. Those bastards could sit up there and do this all day!" he shouted to nobody in particular. Then he keyed the microphone again. "All hands inside to the lower floors. In approximately one minute it is going to get extremely hot up here."

Drago tossed the mic down, picked up a handheld radio from the radar truck, and headed for the silo entrance. The airstrip behind him began exploding in a bright orange fireball from one end to the other as the roar of the B-52 zoomed overhead. The concussion from the blast nearly knocked him off his feet but he managed to maintain his balance as he backed through the doorway. Several of his men weren't as agile and strong as he and weren't as lucky.

Drago passed through the upper levels of the passages and looked at his wristwatch. He did some quick calculations in his head and then he pulled a cell phone from his pocket. The number in his address book simply read 'silo.' He tapped the number and pressed dial. He listened for a second to make certain he got a signal and the phone began to ring. On the third ring it picked up.

"Hello, this is Dr. Drago. If you intend to activate this function press star now."

Drago pressed star and then hung up the phone with a slight laugh to himself. Of course he didn't have to wait for the message to play out or even for the instruction to press star. He simply had to dial the number. The computer knew it came from his phone and only he had that number and direct encryption to give the order. A simple few keystrokes on the phone and the command could be sent. But Drago had to find humor somewhere in his crazy predicament.

A countdown timer started on the phone's screen. It started counting down from one minute. Drago picked up the pace to the lower floors. He thought it would be best if his men did too. But he really didn't care, since most of them were expendable.

Drago pulled his pistol to the ready. He wasn't sure what had happened with the Bradys. He hated leaving them to his men but he had to take care of business up top.

"What is with the damned sprinkler system?" he called into the silo command center on his radio.

"Sir, it's the Bradys. They have taken most of the first two floors and set off some sort of large explosion there. The sprinklers went off then. We have them locked out, I think. They're not getting above the seventh floor."

"Gentlemen, I suggest you leave the seventh floor quite abruptly and make your way for at least the fourth floor or lower. Bradys or no. On your way out, somebody shut off the damned sprinklers."

"Sir?"

"Suit yourselves, but it is going to get very hot in there in about a minute. Unless you like temperatures above a hundred and twenty degrees Fahrenheit and lethal doses of radiation, I'd start evacuating the higher levels immediately. Return to base if you can get to the teleporter. Drago out."

He took a turn through the labs toward the nursery and picked up Abby along the way. By the time he got to Abby, the sprinklers had stopped and the clock on his phone had made it to ten seconds and counting. He listened to the radio chatter and could tell his men were evacuating down the back staircase to the lower levels. It sounded as if the Bradys were on the front staircase nearest the teleport room and the catwalk. That meant that his people were cut off unless he could lure the Bradys upward and away from there. Good thing he had just the bait he needed.

"Well, general," he mused at Abby. "Plug your ears in three, two…" he held his hands over the baby's ears and held her close to him. The building shook violently and it erupted with a noise that sounded like a plane crashed on top of a train wreck in the middle of a twenty car pile up just outside the silo. "That, my dear, was a neutron bomb exploding. I don't think we'll have to worry with our Air Force friends any longer today."

Abby looked at Drago playfully and pulled at his hands. She didn't seem to mind the noise too much. It mostly died away fairly quickly. Drago noticed that the temperature was really starting to pick up though. The radiation levels were probably rising quite rapidly as well. The two of them had probably better keep moving lower for now.

"I think we might need to get something else from the lab," Drago smiled. "I hope the good Dr. Kato has been as successful as we think he has been."

೮೦೦೪

"What the hell was that?!" Sam grabbed the wall to support herself as the entire silo bounced like a Cadillac hitting a speed bump at fifty miles per hour. Ray caught himself and offered his wife a hand to steady her legs. She waved him away. Ray nearly laughed at her headstrong independence.

"That, hot stuff, was a thermonuclear device exploding. Probably one of Drago's neutron bombs if I had my guess." Ray frowned. They knew now that Drago was smart enough to make a real nuke. Ray also started thinking about radiation doses. "It's gonna get real hot in here pretty soon. Too bad somebody shut off the sprinklers, that might have helped. We'd better start moving back down soon."

"Not without my baby," Sam said and turned up toward the third floor just as the door flung open.

"Down!" Ray grabbed his wife and pushed her against the floor. A spray of bullets bounced off the wall above them and an energy blast vaporized part of the hand rail attached to the wall just behind Sam's head. That was too close for Ray's comfort. "Move!"

The two of them bear crawled down the stairs and underneath them at the next landing using the stairs themselves and the railing to the catwalk for cover. Both of them returned fire as best they could. For a moment or two it looked like they were done, but then the shooting stopped from above.

"I'd suggest the two of you stop shooting or you might hit your darling daughter," Ray heard. He immediately recognized Drago's voice. Ray and Sam stopped firing and began to slowly back down the next flight of stairs.

"We're backing down," Sam shouted. "Don't you dare hurt her."

Chapter 21

Drago sneered at the two of them from one level above on the cat-walk. Ray was doing dose calculations in his head as fast as his brain would work—which was considerable—and glancing at his wristwatch. Abby should be fine as long as he didn't go any higher with her. That was, if he had done the numbers right in his head. The math was making him more than a little queasy just thinking about how near the danger zone they were. The radiation from the neutron bomb fallout was now most likely everywhere up top and was penetrating layer after layer of the silo. As a secondary effect, some of the metallic materials like the iron rein-forcements in the concrete were being knocked into a radioactive decay isotope chain as well.

So the silo itself was becoming more and more radioactive. It would take a day or two for it to decay down to safe levels. That meant that Ray, Sam, and Abby were trapped there unless they used the extraction point device. It also meant that there would be no help on the way for a couple of days. And to top it off, Drago was using the radiation, Abby, and a handgun to create a Mexican stand-off with them. They had played a bit of cat and mouse with a couple of Drago's henchmen trying to get the drop on them from behind but Sam and Ray had dispatched them quite handily. As far as Ray could figure, the rest of Drago's men had made it behind them to the teleporter and were gone. It was just the three of them, the baby, and probably the kidnapped scientist still there in the facility.

Drago had been slowly, threateningly, and very calculatedly making his retreat up the stairs. The closer he got to the top, the more radiation they were all getting bombarded with. Ray was concerned about the dosage already.

"That's as far as you can go! Any higher and you're gonna be hitting a lethal range! For God's sake, let's back down a level and talk this out!" Ray shouted.

"Now, Dr. Brady. I'm sure you realize that little Abby might already be close to maximum exposure for long term effects. But if you will put your weapons down, we will come down a bit more."

"As soon as we put our weapons down she's as good as dead anyway," Sam shouted.

"I wouldn't hurt her," Drago replied.

"What do you think you're doing now?" Ray grunted. "Besides, I'd rather her die with me than live with you, you crazy son of a bitch!"

"Come down or I'm gonna shoot anyway," Sam threatened.

"I don't think that is truly an option. Do you? Neither of you could hurt your precious little one. And since I don't want to see her harmed either, and I can't give her up to the two of you and surrender, then..." Drago did an overly dramatic shoulder shrug and pulled an injector gun from a velcro pocket in his pants. He made no hesitation in placing the thing against Abby's neck and pulling the trigger. The injector made a snapping hiss sound. "I do hope the radiodurans serum has a positive effect on you, Abby dearest. After all, it's hot out there. And we need to get out of here."

"Stop!" Sam shouted and rushed up halfway to where Drago stood and drew a bead on him with her pistol.

"NO! Not my baby! Take the shot, Sam!" Ray pleaded with his wife.

"Ray, it's too far! I might hit Abby! And it's too late—he already shot her up with that shit!"

All three adults watched as a flush flooded little Abby's skin, a bright berry red spreading out from the injection point. Abby let out a surprised gurgle, then a lusty yell of anger that turned her face an even duskier red. Only then did Drago respond.

"Oh, come now, Dr. Brady. I'm not so daft. We all three know that Mrs. Brady is out of ammo. And the general here seems to be doing just fine, as I expected, so..." Drago smiled knowingly, held the injector gun against his own neck and snapped the trigger. The blue-green liquid in the serum vial sloshed as he tossed it to the floor, clanging against the metal gridwork. "Care to join me? I'm going to take Abby outside for a stroll. It's a lovely day for it, don't you think?"

Drago sneered one last time and turned up the stairwell of the missile silo. Ray was pretty sure that he could see bright berry red, almost glowing, patches and vein lines streaking across the crazy bastard's face, a sure sign of radiodurans. He was more concerned about the effect it was having on his baby girl. But he held his ground and watched as the son of a bitch turned and sprinted full speed up the last three flights of stairs and turned out of sight down the exit corridor. The sound of a large metal door cycling open in the distance echoed off the metal and concrete silo cavern. That was followed closely by a powerful *clang!* as the door was slammed shut—but not cycled. Drago continued to tease them to follow. They had little choice.

The fact that Drago managed to open and then close the door was key. They both knew what that meant. Drago hadn't weakened from the radiation. The serum had worked–at least for him. They hoped it had done the same for Abby.

Sam was already halfway up the stairs before Ray could grab her by the arm. "We can't go any higher than this next level, Sam. It would be lethal. If it isn't already."

"He's got Abby! I'm going!" Sam tried to pull away from him but Ray held her firmly.

"I know you are, Samantha. So am I. But neither of us are going without this. We'd never make it another fifty feet otherwise." He bent over and picked up the injector gun and snapped it to his neck. "You know he left this here on purpose, I think. He knows we're coming after him. Hell, he invited us. Sam, listen, you don't have to go. I'll do this."

"That is a HELL of a thing for you to say to me, Reagan Brady!" Sam yanked the injector from Ray's hand and snapped it to her neck before he could stop her. "She's my baby too! And you KNOW we stand a better chance if we stick together!"

Ray could feel his entire body stinging and burning and could see his wife's face turning alternately pale and red. Spider veins of brilliant claret coursed across her face, spreading out from the injection site on her throat.

"Let's go get that bastard."

"You da boss lady." Ray grinned, a tight, humorless expression.

Sam returned the expression, a wolfish light in her eyes. "You Goddamned right I am. Now let's go get our baby back from that psycho son of a bitch!"

As they thundered up the stairs after the man who held their baby prisoner, who even now was carrying their child into a nuclear wasteland, they began to change. They could both feel it. Muscles were stronger, swifter; respiration and pulse slowed relative to their degree of exertion.

Ray glanced aside at his wife, who was easily keeping up with him. There were berry red blotches and spider veins all over her skin; but her skin was darkening. *Like a deep tan*, he thought. He glanced at his own hand as they ran–it, too, was a dark bronze color. *Melanin*, he realized, *to protect against the electromagnetic radiation. And who knows what else? We're… we're extremophiles now.*

The upper levels were still thermally hot in areas from the residual heat of the blast, as well as, Ray suspected, from fires outside. The dead bodies of Drago's own men lay scattered here and there, those few that hadn't gotten deep enough into the silo in time. Some appeared parboiled, and a couple were partly charred; most simply appeared to have dropped in their tracks.

"The cold bastard didn't even give all his men time to get downstairs," Ray noted. Sam just grunted acknowledgement as she leaped one of the bodies without stopping, but her newly enhanced physique threw her off, causing her to go farther than she had anticipated. She slammed into a metal wall, bracing herself for the impact with her left arm and shoulder. Ray heard a sizzling sound, and as she cried out in pain, jerking back, the stench of burned meat reached his nostrils.

"Oh, dear God! SAM!" he cried, immediately beside her. She was cradling her left arm against her body, rocking slightly and staring down in shock at the horribly charred flesh. "Oh, God, Sam, it isn't... but it should've... it didn't..."

Sam's beautiful blue eyes, whose whites were no longer white but a dusky reddish brown, lifted to meet his.

"It didn't work," he whispered, gazing at her in sorrow. "We're both walking dead. And Abby..." his voice cracked and died. Dark hazel eyes watered, narrowed in an agony of expectation, as he waited for the first of the radiation symptoms to begin on his wife. *Abby's already gone,* he thought, horror stricken, *and Sam's enough smaller than me that the lethal radiation dose will be less. I'll get to watch her die before I die myself. It's over. I've lost. I've lost... everything.*

"Wait, Ray," Sam said, glancing down at her arm. "It's kinda... stopped hurting."

"Yeah, the nerves are fried, bab—" He broke off, staring at the flesh of her wounded arm...

...Even as the dead tissue sloughed away, debriding itself, and the fresh, raw wound underneath knit itself back together at an incredible speed. She gave a cry of pain as the dead flesh fell to the floor.

"GO!" Sam shouted, shoving him with that same arm. "It's working! Hurts like hell, but it works! We've gotta stop him before he can get away with Abby!"

ꙮ

Outside was devastation on a level with the aftermath of the historic Mount Saint Helens eruption combined with Hiroshima and Nagasaki.

The prairie grass was completely gone as far as the eye could see over the gently rolling landscape; not even root tufts were left. Little but bare ground lay underfoot. Bare, charred, and highly radioactive ground. Dust still swirled in the residual wind gusts from the shock waves.

Outbuildings were shattered and strewn about; automobiles and airplanes tossed about like a giant's discarded playthings, crushed and smashed. What little landscaping that had been put in before Drago acquired the place was so much kindling, the twisted trunks of trees protruding from the ground, splinters and sawdust everywhere, some of it still smoldering. Twisted metal and bits of charred wooden boards lay everywhere.

Further out, past the no man's land of the blast centroid, a circle of fighter jet wreckage encircled what was left of Dragonfire Enterprises' headquarters. Still further out, there were smoke clouds roiling up from beyond the hills. Any settlers for several miles would be dead, burned, or dying.

Drago froze for a brief moment, disoriented, getting his bearings and staring around him, as tiny Abby wailed for her parents. As Drago paused to pull together a semblance of a plan, neither adult nor child noticed the changes in their skin tones, or that their blond hair was rapidly bleaching white in the radioactive environment.

"Hush, little one," he murmured absently, and the child quieted. "You have a new daddy now, one who will introduce you to wondrous things. One who will teach you the ways of the warrior, the rebel. One who will teach you what it is to be tough, to ignore pain, to mete it out instead. You are invincible! You will be my little angel of vengeance, dear child! Merciless in your pursuit of justice! As merciless as–them!" He juggled the child in order to glance at his old watch. "Still over eight minutes left," he snarled. "Dammit, I hate improvisation!"

Abby began to cry again as radiation burns appeared on her little body. Her soft skin blistered, then the blisters popped. Almost immediately it began to peel, exposing new healthy tissue beneath, skin tissue that was darker than before. The effect was something akin to a snake shedding its skin. Drago took the time to glance at his own skin that was similar in appearance now, although the rash didn't appear to be as bad. The alien DNA and healing factor he already possessed now combined with the radiodurans serum factor made him even more invincible. His skin didn't blister like Abby's did. He showed little more than a bad sunburn, which soon peeled and then grew new skin. The process continued to repeat as the neutron radiation bombarded him, causing new damage. He barely noticed the pain. Abby, on the other hand, seemed to be in severe pain and was crying and screaming.

Unheeding and callous, knowing she would heal almost instantly, Drago immediately instituted his plan to toughen Abby. He had other things to tend to, anyway. He tossed the child to one side, and Abby landed on the ravaged ground with a thud, scraping her tiny knee on a rock and bumping her head pretty hard. She screamed in pain, then stopped in surprise as the scrape immediately commenced mending itself. Her little mind, however, only knew that she had fallen and been mistreated by a big man who was holding her, and she screamed even louder in fright and with her feelings hurt.

"Momma ma ma," she cried for the first time.

Meanwhile, a deeply tanned Drago, oblivious to the child's cries, searched about them, bright blue eyes—surrounded by brick colored "whites"—darting about. He found the broken empennage of a dismembered Cessna about ten feet the other side of the silo's hatch. "Yes!" he hissed in glee, madness taking him again. He grasped a protruding strut and dragged it to the side of the silo door, heedless of burning debris.

Then, with superhuman strength, he hefted it over his head with little more than a grunt, and waited.

&OCS

Ray reached for the hatch but Sam smacked his hands away. "WAIT!" she cried. "That'll hurt like hell. TRUST me. Use this like a potholder."

She grabbed a nearby packing blanket—evidently, Ray decided, this had been where certain equipment was delivered to Dragonfire Enterprises—and handed it to him. He wrapped his hand in it and opened the hatch, lunging through ahead of Sam.

As soon as he cleared the door, smoldering blanket still in hand, something HARD hit him squarely over the head, too fast for him to even crumple to his knees. Somehow his head punched all the way through several layers of hard. Hunks of scalp peeled off to hang down his face and neck even as something liquid gushed all over him.

The plane's empennage wedged firmly around his body, pinning his arms to his sides. Blood poured from his shredded scalp, his mangled face, his deeply sliced shoulders and arms, while the smoldering blanket in his hands, joined by several firebrands on the ground at his feet, ignited the aviation fuel from the punctured fuel tank. Within seconds, he was trapped in a blazing inferno, feeling his skin and the flesh beneath it searing away.

OH GOD! he thought in a panic, flashbacks of Iran and Iraq ripping through his brain like bullets, *I'm gonna die this time! In front of Sam and Abby! NO!*

He screamed, a high pitched, male falsetto expression of pure agony, twisting, writhing, trying anything to get free of the deathtrap that was burning him alive, slicing into his charring flesh. A lump of his cheek fell off, landing on what was left of the horizontal stabilizer, and he watched in a kind of detached shock as it sputtered, fried, and turned to charcoal in the raging inferno about him.

But it still hurts, he thought, tortured scream after scream issuing from his throat. *Dear God, burn the nerves away! End it!*

The reason for the continuing pain reached his conscious mind even as a blur leaped over his head and landed in front of him. Sam tried desperately to find a way through the blaze to rescue what was left of her husband.

"NO!" Ray gurgled through a seared throat, managing to twist enough to free one mangled, bloody, charred arm. "Find Abby! ABBY! No! DUCK!"

An agonized Sam didn't question: She ducked just as an aluminum strut whistled through the space her head had occupied fractions of a second before. Then she disappeared from Ray's view.

೮ა೦ყ

Drago drew back with the strut and hurled it, javelin-like, after the woman, then cursed and returned his attention to Ray. For Ray had finally managed to free himself of the small plane's tail section, and it fell at his feet. His clothing had burned away, and his naked body was raw and seared, gashed to the bone in places. He wobbled unsteadily as he stood. Drago gazed at him, grinning balefully, a wild, crazed look in the glowing blue eyes, like a rabid animal whose mind had lost all focus save the kill.

"One down, one to go," he gloated. "And then your precious little Abigail is mine."

"Don't think so," Ray panted, stepping free of the aircraft's remnants. Dead flesh was still falling from his body; a shoulder bone showed, and the top of his skull was bare of scalp. But with an effort borne of pure willpower, Ray stepped forward on pulpy, bare feet. Drago raised a surprised eyebrow—

—As Ray ripped loose the vertical stabilizer in hands that were already whole, and swung it at him.

With preternatural reflexes, Drago leaped back, but not in time to avoid a deep slice across his abdomen. Warm blood flowed over his belly as he realized that had he not moved at the last possible second, he would have been disemboweled.

Issuing a snarl of anger from deep in his throat, Drago snatched up a nearby two by four, one end still blazing, and cracked it over Ray's head, which hadn't healed completely yet. A fracture promptly formed on Ray's skull, and he crumpled to the ground.

೮೦೧೪

Sam turned and spotted Abby instantly—or perhaps heard was a better way of putting it; the lusty howls coming from the baby were such as Sam had not heard from her child since birth. Without another thought, she obeyed her husband and her maternal instinct and scooped her daughter up, sprinting away. *Maybe I can't save Ray*, she mourned, *but I can save our child. He'll live on through Abby, I swear.*

She heard a swishing sound, and dodged on instinct as an aluminum strut embedded itself in the ground behind her. Sam glanced at a white haired Abby, who was pressing close to her mother's breast in fear, and noticed her darkened skin appeared… scaly. *What the hell?!*

A large chunk of Abby's skin peeled away and drifted off on the wind, exposing new, smooth skin beneath, which in turn blistered and peeled. A light bulb went off in Sam's head. *Constant radiation burns and healing! Abby's entire body is doing just like my arm did.* Sam glanced at her own arm, to see the same scaling, like a video of reptiles outgrowing skin after skin in fast forward. Each newly formed layer was darker in color, melanin forming profusely in response to the radiation around them.

"Abby!" she said, as she spotted her target: a lone, partially wrecked plane some distance away. "You were crying so loud!"

"Momma ma ma." Abby looked up into her mother's intense face and smiled.

"That's right, mommy is here, baby." Sam thought that Abby's cries before had been the loudest the little darling had ever managed. They were much louder than Sam had ever heard. *No cystic fibrosis!* Sam hoped. *My baby's gonna live!*

At her current pace it hadn't taken long to make it to the twisted-up airplane she'd picked out as a temporary shelter. It turned out to be familiar; it was the same plane in which she, Abby, and Dr. Kato had tried to escape. The key was still in the ignition, for all the good it did. The door was gone, blown off in the nuclear cataclysm, and the landing gear was likewise demolished. Windows and the windscreen were broken out. Wings had been ripped away to join the debris field around them, but the fuselage was at least upright and intact, if decidedly battered. Sam set Abby in the pilot's seat and strapped her in.

"Don't move, baby; I'll be right back. Mommy's gonna go kick this bad man's butt."

An enthusiastic Abby clapped her hands. "BUTT!" she exclaimed and despite the dire situation, Sam tried not to laugh. "Momma ma ma ma." *Her third word, and what is it? It's 'butt.' We're gonna have to watch our language around her now,* she realized. A smiling Sam turned from her child in time to see Ray go down beneath Drago's club. The smile vanished.

She broke into a sprint. She had run competitively in college and it was clear to her now that she was running much faster than she ever had, much faster. She covered the distance in no time.

⁝⁝

Ray sprawled on the ground, seeing stars. He wasn't sure if his eyes were open or closed, but it didn't matter, because those damn stars were everywhere. Ray finally just decided that seeing all those stars was hellaciously annoying, because he couldn't see Drago for shit. He tried to shake his vision clear and began forcing himself up.

But suddenly he heard something make a titanic *thud*, followed by a grunt that sounded suspiciously like Drago. Unfortunately, this was accompanied by an unseen, but very sharp and painful object, pinning Ray's shoulder to the ground by going clean through it. Still dazed, he let out a cry of pain.

"Sonuvabitch," Sam's furious voice declared. "Not this time, you bastard! No way in hell!" Another meaty *thud* sounded, and Ray's eyes finally cleared.

Sam stood over Drago, who was on his hands and knees. As Ray watched, Sam swung a mammoth chunk of metal—obtained from where, Ray couldn't guess—at the man's head with all her strength, sledgehammer style. It immediately flattened Drago to the ground. That wasn't enough to stop the inhuman scientist, however. He clambered to his feet, ripping the thick metal bar—which Ray finally concluded had been one of the steel supports for the hangar all the wrecked private aircraft had been in—from Sam's hands and drew it back for a swing. Realizing Drago was about to take Sam's head off with it, Ray managed to muster all the strength his body had left along with some sheer will, piss, and vinegar, and pulled himself to his feet, ripping the broken aluminum strut in his shoulder free of the ground. Ray growled with a guttural sound that seemed to help him to his feet.

"Holy shit!" He growled again as he tore the strut out of his flesh using his good hand. It hurt like blazes, but Ray had hurt like blazes before, and now he knew that no harm would come of it, fear fell away as his clothes had mere moments before. Ray took a baseball bat swing at Drago's head before he could hit Sam, and the anomalous scientist went airborne, flying out into the prairie from the force of the blow, flipping feet over head like a rag doll and flinging up a tail of dust as he skittered across the ground. Ray, now almost healed, charged after him like a raging bull.

Behind them, Sam pulled something out of her pocket. She'd managed to grab one of the dead soldiers' pistols on their way out of the silo, and now she checked it swiftly to ensure a round was chambered. Then she ran after Ray.

There was little in the way of debris where Drago had landed. It was in no man's land, between the debris of Drago's complex and the wreckage of what had been the Minot military forces, so neither man had a ready weapon to hand. But both were skilled in martial arts, and the hands and feet of both men blurred with the speed and frenzy of their fighting. Drago, however, still had the advantage over Ray. Ray had the radiodurans serum, but after Doc's blood analysis, Ray knew Drago had both it and the alien reptilian DNA. Slowly Drago was wearing him down. But somewhat to Ray's surprise, Drago was also gradually retreating. No matter from what angle Ray approached the other man, Drago sidestepped, backed up, slipped past, leaped over—all in the same general direction.

Extraction point? He's leading me just like the first time we met in New York. Yeah, that's gotta be it. Gotta stop him. Can't let him get away again.

"RAY!" Sam's voice shouted from one side. "GET BACK!"

Acting instinctively on his wife's order, Ray fell back, rolling over and away from Drago just as Sam opened up the automatic pistol. Lead riddled Drago's midsection, sending him staggering back... and back. He fell to the ground, sprawled awkwardly, as blood flowed from the wounds in his belly and back; he'd been shot clear through. Only seconds later, however, he began to crawl, and Ray and Sam noted the hot air was growing even warmer.

"GET HIM!" Ray roared, lunging toward the center of the warmth, Sam right behind.

Drago smiled, tapping a few keystrokes in on his cell phone and then looked up at them with a maniacal smile. Ray certainly didn't like that look. It was the same one he'd had before he injected Abby with the serum. It was the same one he'd had when he'd jumped off that building in New York City.

"I don't think so," he said, voice still gurgling slightly from his punctured lung. "I just dropped a neutron bomb in the center of the Capitol Mall in Washington. Choose. Me—or D.C.? This extraction point forming now will take you to D.C."

The Washington Monument! shot through Ray's mind. *THAT'S what that extraction point was for!* Just then, both Drago's and Ray's wristwatches began beeping simultaneously.

"SHIT!" Ray exclaimed. "Not Washington! Millions of people are there! I thought you wouldn't kill uninfected people?! C'mon, hot stuff, we've gotta MOVE!"

"Most of D.C. is infected. Some are not. You, Dr. Brady, can save them if you choose to." Drago paused and laughed out loud. "Only time enough to do one or the other. Me or D.C.?"

Just then, behind them, they heard a sputter, followed by the sound of a propeller. Almost immediately the propeller started beating against metal and stalled, and a loud "FWOOMP!" reached their ears. This was followed by an ear splitting, childish wail of pain. Glancing over her shoulder, Sam screamed.

"ABBY! NO!"

Ray spun. The old plane had been made of stern stuff and the electromagnetic pulse from the nuke had apparently not killed the ignition system. And somehow, Abby had evidently managed to switch on the ignition of the plane out of childish curiosity, and whatever fuel was left in the lines had allowed the engine to start. The engine stalled out almost as soon as it started. But before the engine could fail completely, the propeller firmly wedged on the nose of the plane and the still molten asphalt of the taxiway—what hadn't burned away—grinding against it, sending sparks flying into the spray of aviation fuel and hydraulic fluid that spewed from the engine compartment. Now Abby was sitting strapped down in the middle of an inferno as far as Ray or Sam could tell.

Ray snatched the gun from Sam's hand as she started to run back for their baby. He whirled, took aim at Drago, and opened up, spraying the man's already healing body with more lead, emptying the nearly full magazine into the mutated madman. Drago gave an inadvertent cry of pain and slumped back to the ground.

"That ought to take care of you, until I can get back and finish you off!" Ray snarled, then spun and started to sprint after Sam.

"NO, RAY! I'VE GOT HER! WE'LL GET UNDER COVER, I SWEAR! YOU GO TAKE CARE OF THE CAPITOL!" Sam screamed back, already halfway to the blazing aircraft. Ray instinctively nodded in agreement.

He spun about and spotted the hint of what looked like a Klein bottle taking shape from the corner of his eye. *Damn. Infrared vision. Couldn't do THAT before.* He leaped toward it, and vanished in a blaze of light.

                                    ಐⵒೞ

Behind them, Drago, driven by the desire to avenge his Ssaree, by the realization that the Ssliths were still working to take over his world, by the knowledge that his plan was not finished, began to drag himself with his arms, heading for his own extraction point. Within seconds, he'd gotten to his hands and knees, starting to rise despite the copious trail of scarlet blood left behind him. He was made of sterner stuff than could be stopped by mere bullets. His will had been tempered by the horrors of near death, love, torture, loss, centuries of a madness driven vengeance, and the goal to save humanity's future. It would take a lot more than this to stop him.

There was a brilliant, blue-white flash of light, and he too was gone.

                                    ಐⵒೞ

Abby's little blouse was just starting to burn when her mother arrived at the flaming wreck. Without hesitation, Sam reached into the flames and grabbed the seat belt strapping the little one in. Her face contorted in fierce rage and determination, and she ripped the seat belt loose, then scooped up her screaming baby girl.

A twist, a leap, and she was lying on her back on the ground, Abby in her arms. Sam snatched the burning shirt from the child's body and flung it aside as she rolled in the dirt to put her own clothing out. Then Sam did something only a mother could do. She held her child against her breast, smothering the flames with her own body.

Dead, singed tissue sloughed off mother and daughter, as little Abby continued to scream in pain. At last the healing began, and Abby settled down. Sam turned toward where Drago had been, then spat a curse.

"Shit. He's gone. Next time. Abby, princess, we need to get back inside for now."

She trudged back through a scorched wasteland toward the metal door, still holding Abby. As they neared the door, a persistent beep made itself known. The female operative glanced around, then started searching for the sound.

Underneath the singed remains of the empennage that Ray had thought would claim his life lay the tattered, mostly molten remains of the jumpsuit he had worn. But in the sleeve pocket was his DSRPO phone. And it was beeping.

"Huh," Sam said in surprise, extracting it. "These things are a hell of a lot tougher than I thought. Then again, Ray did design 'em, and he needs something designed like a bull elephant, if it's gonna last with HIM carrying it." She pressed <on> and held it to her ear. "Samantha Brady."

"Sam, this is Jay," the voice on the other end replied. "You guys okay?"

"Uh, yeah, Jay, for certain values of okay, I guess," Sam answered, wondering how in the hell she was going to explain this one. *At least Ray was here with me. I don't have to explain it to HIM. Only the rest of the team—and Robert. Robert,* she sighed. *At least it isn't Quebec.*

"Everything under control?"

"Pretty much. Uh, listen—"

"We just arrived on site—er, rather, as close to the site as we dare get, and it's going to be a couple of days before we can come down. We saw the mushroom cloud on the way in, and the area looks like Hell dropped from the sky. Which I suppose it kinda did," Jay remarked. "We'll have to go set down at Minot Air Force Base and wait it out. Anyway, in a couple or three days it should have died down enough to get you guys out of there, unless Ray can figure out how to run the extraction point gizmo."

"Um, I doubt it. Ray's not here."

"Not there? But... Oh, my God... but you have his phone..."

"Oh! No, no! It's okay, he got here fine, he just... Drago sent a bomb through to the Washington Mall, and Ray went after it. Drago got away."

"The WASHINGTON MALL?!"

"Yeah."

"Son of a bitch! I KNEW IT! I KNEW it had to be something like that!" Jay spat. "Only reason for a 'door' being THERE!"

Sam overheard a flurry of conversation in the background, and something about 'I was right,' and 'getting Hansen over there pronto, if he isn't there already.' Then Jay came back online.

"Is this Drago dude Mr. Marathon Man?"

"Yep."

"Mr. All The Way Through The Last Several Centuries Man?"

"Uh, that I don't know about. But I'm betting so, from what I know."

"Okay. We're circling overhead and… my God! Is that you, standing by the silo hatch?!"

"Uh, yeah."

"GET THE HELL INSIDE, RIGHT NOW, CRAZY WOMAN!" Doc's voice took over the comm. "BEFORE YOU SUSTAIN A LE-THAL DOSE!" At that point the screen on the phone went black and it ceased to function. The radiation had finally proved too much for it. Sam popped the back off of it and pulled out the sim card. Then she dropped the phone and stomped on it.

"Get inside," she repeated. "A lethal dose?" Despite herself, Sam started to laugh.

Abby just giggled and clapped her hands.

′′′

Sam first stopped on the upper floor locker room and showered Abby and herself, then tossed all of their clothes and metals away. She wiped down the phone's sim card but wasn't sure about what she should do with it. She bent a metal filing cabinet door around it several times and then dropped it in an ammo box she found. Then she and Abby walked naked down four or five flights of stairs.

"That is probably far enough," she told Abby. She found a safety shower on that floor and then bathed them both once more. If there was anybody inside the place, she didn't want to kill them with fallout. She then rummaged through some lockers and cabinets and found some clothing for herself and a towel she could wrap Abby in. She picked a couple of weapons up off of dead henchmen along the way as well.

"We'll get you some clothes and a diaper from the nursery when we get there, baby. You're getting hungry, I bet." Sam hugged and kissed her daughter. Then she searched for Dr. Kato, and was surprised, during that search, to find nothing left of Drago's henchmen but dead bodies, which she scavenged for weapons. She discovered the reason when she reached the bottom floor, where his laboratory was, and which was, so far, relatively safe from radiation.

The entire corridor was filled with the remaining soldiers, fighting to get into Kato's laboratory. Periodically one of them would come flying out over the heads of the others, to either land on top of the crowd, or smash against the far wall of the corridor and slide to the floor, unconscious. No one paid any attention to the new arrivals.

"GIVE US THE SERUM!" one of them yelled.

"YEAH! GIVE IT TO US, OR WE'RE ALL DEAD!" another shouted.

"DAMN CRAZY, DOUBLE-CROSSING BASTARD DRAGO NUKED THE SURFACE AND THEN RAN! WE GOT NO WAY OUT!"

"Shit," Sam muttered. "Confined riot situation here."

Sam had scavenged a spare jumpsuit—its owner didn't need it anymore—and ripped and knotted it into a passable semblance of a baby sling, which she had used during the search for Kato. Now she squirmed it onto the back of her left hip, and drew her pistol.

But instead of pointing at the crowd and opening up, Sam aimed at an angle toward the ceiling. One quick burst splattered the crowd with concrete chips and sent ricochets caroming down the far hall. The crowd silenced immediately, spinning to see from where the shots had come.

"Hi there," Sam said, lowering her weapon into a nonthreatening, but still ready, position. "We're the new proprietors of this establishment. We just came from the surface and dealing with your Dr. Drago. Listen closely, because I will only say this once. Withdraw from the lab, place any weapons you're holding on the floor here in front of me, and get in single file. I will then take you and place you in individual rooms until you can be... debriefed."

"The hell you will," one of them said with a snarl. "I know you. And the brat. Dr. Drago will be looking for you."

With that, he whipped out an energy pistol and shot Sam in the chest.

Sam staggered back with a gasp of pain, but did not fall. She deliberately unfastened the top of the jumpsuit, pulling it down to expose her bare chest and the two inch diameter wound that penetrated it; Drago's soldiers could see completely through Sam's upper right breast to the wall behind her.

But even as they watched, the dead tissue sloughed away and the hole knit itself closed. Within seconds her full, lush breast was intact once more. They gasped as Sam slipped her arms back into her sleeves and zipped up the jumpsuit. Sam's blue eyes grew hard as diamond. Then she raised the pistol and shot the man square between the eyes dead. He slumped and fell with a *thud*.

"Satisfied? See these?" She fingered the red stains on her face and neck. "That's what enabled me to heal after you shot me. It's what enabled me and my husband to battle your precious Dr. Drago to a standstill, at least until he tried to bomb DC. Notice my child has them too? It's the serum. Drago is gone. He took the serum himself and deserted you. I'm sure most of you recognize me by now. Good luck trying to take US out."

There was a clattering sound as weapons dropped to the floor. Then everyone moved to the far side of the corridor, forming a queue beside their dead comrade.

"Wise decision."

୨୦୯୨

As it turned out, Kato, though a little banged up, was not much the worse for wear.

"I guessed what had happened as soon as I felt the structure shake," he informed Sam, after she had gotten everyone locked into rooms to wait for interrogation. "Drago had already come for Abby and enough serum for him, her, and perhaps a few more people, but he left the rest here. I suppose he expected to come back later and get the rest of it. But I destroyed it all," Kato declared. "As soon as he left, I dumped the entire batch into the chute that leads to the power incinerator, along with all of my research notes and anything else I could get my hands on. Then I sterilized everything in the autoclaves. It might not have gotten all of the radiodurans, but it definitely got all of the serum—AND how to make it." He sat down, rubbing the back of his neck.

"Then I was going to barricade the door, but it was too late. That... mob... was already out there. And didn't believe that I didn't have the serum."

"So you fought them off?" Sam queried.

"As best I could," Kato nodded. "Given that they could only get in the door by ones and twos, it wasn't too bad." He looked her up and down. "I see you have taken the serum."

"We had to, to get our little girl back," Sam said quietly.

"We?"

"My husband managed to brane in, and we almost fought Drago to a standstill, although it took both of us together to do it. But Drago forced us to split up while he got away. Ray's gone to Washington to defuse a bomb."

"You are a brave, loving woman," Kato responded, intense respect in his tone. "And a very wise and intelligent one, from what I have gleaned." He rose, standing straight, and slapped his hands lightly against his thighs, then bowed. "My compliments, Sensei Brady."

Chapter 22

Ray found himself in mid-air, dropping rapidly down past white mar-ble blocks toward a device caught in a net on the plaza below. Fortu-nately the area was still cordoned off and guarded by the same troops Jay had brought in, recruited by the Old Man. They had all turned, and were staring at the device in shock. One had the presence of mind to be on his radio, reporting in, Ray noticed, as the tableau grew larger, rushing at him. Unfortunately he, being lighter, was more prone to the effects of errant winds than the bomb had been, and he WASN'T headed for the net. *Shit. PAIN.*

He landed hard on the stones of the plaza, hearing multiple bones break; in excruciating pain, he spent precious moments simply lying there, allowing the healing process to begin. When his skeletal structure was sufficiently repaired to allow him to stand, he found himself sur-rounded by weapons, all aimed at him. It suddenly occurred to him that he was stark naked, his clothing having been burned away at the door of the silo, and covered with freakish blotches and veins of purplish pink into the bargain. He held his arms up, palms out, in a placating gesture.

"Ray Brady! I'm Ray Brady! Stand down! No, don't stand down—get out, and take as many people with you as you can!" he cried. "Drop a tool kit for me on your way! This is a neutron bomb from that shithead we've been chasing, and I'm gonna try to defuse it!"

They didn't look as if they believed him. *Shit, not good. This thing could go off any minute, and then the whole leadership of the nation is dead.*

Just then a hummer screeched up. Lieutenant Major Peter Hansen, DSRPO's resident munitions expert, bailed out before the vehicle had even come to a complete halt.

"RAY!" he shouted, managing to recognize his colleague by his posture and stance despite the change in his appearance. "That you?! What the hell happened? Where's your PANTS?!"

"Long story, Pete."

"Later, then. After you left, Jay anticipated something coming through the manifold thingy, put the Old Man on notice, and they had me stay behind. We've got the central city cleared and cordoned, for the most part. CINC is in the bunker; the others in the chain of command are in the air, outbound. What have we got?"

"Neutron bomb. Just like we figured."

"SHIT! Stand down, troops! He's on our side! Now clear out, look for stragglers, and evacuate the biggest area you can manage!"

As the Marines surrounding the base of the Washington Monument obeyed orders at top speed, Hansen joined Ray at the bomb. They both scanned it rapidly.

"Dammit to hell and back," Hansen murmured, "it must be on a timer, and we won't know how long we have until we get inside. How much do you know about the guts of nukes?"

"Plenty," Ray replied, voice hard. "Get out the tools and let's get going."

&∞જ

They decided, based on the apparent construction of the bomb, to do a two stage disarmament. First they would attempt to shut off the timer, then they would disconnect the high explosives—or rather, their detonators—from the electronic firing system.

It wouldn't be possible to remove the exploding bridgewire detonators without seriously irradiating themselves–or at least seriously irradiating Pete, who was already taking a certain degree of dosage just by being there, according to instruments.

But if the detonators weren't hooked up to the electronics, they wouldn't blow anyway. And if they didn't blow, none of the rest of the device would. So they set to work.

"Titanium casing," Ray noted as they removed bolts.

"Yeah. You were right about the Moon, I'm thinking."

"Or he got titanium from someplace we missed."

"You realize there's a certain probability he set the thing so that, if we disconnect the timer, it automatically blows?" Hansen pointed out, busy removing one panel of the titanium outer casing, with Ray's help.

"Yeah," was all Ray said. Pure radiation, he wasn't worried about anymore. A nuclear explosion was another matter altogether. *Somehow I doubt even the radiodurans is capable of putting me back together after being at Ground Zero of a nuke. Better hope Drago didn't get the equipment to do that, or Sam's gonna have to raise Abby without me.*

Lifting the panel aside, the two men looked into the guts of the bomb, experienced eyes scanning the interior, tracing wiring and identifying key components.

"Shit," Hansen said, spotting the timer. "We got about three minutes to do this thing."

"Then let's get with it and quit jawing," Ray retorted, adrenaline kicking in as his brain went into hyperdrive, searching the interior of the nuclear device.

"Okay, there's the case," Hansen declared, staring inside. "The... the detonator wires are ... that's not... Ray, this doesn't look right."

"Yeah, I know. The timer isn't right, either," a grim Ray noted. "Who drops a bomb on a nation's capitol that has a timer on it? You just bomb it and that's that. It's a diversion, maybe. That, or sloppy workmanship, thinking... No. It's a diversion. I have no doubt he planned to do this in reality, but THIS one, he set up just in case, to keep me busy. If I fail, he still gets his total destruction. If I succeed, he gains... something else." He glanced northwestward, worried. "Sam, hot stuff, be careful. Get in the silo and stay put."

Together the two men traced wires, periodically glancing at their watches. Ray temporarily forgot his regular watch had burned away, but noticed the tough little brane watch, charred and somewhat worse for the wear, counting down again, and puzzled over the matter briefly before his thoughts were interrupted.

"HERE!" Hansen cried, grabbing a wire between index finger and thumb. "This should cut the circuit between the timer and the ignition system!"

Ray slapped a wire cutter in the man's hand.

Hansen reached into the opening with the wire cutters. Delicately fitting them around the wire without dislodging it, he snipped the circuit. The two men glanced at the timer.

It was still counting down.

"That's... not good," Hansen murmured.

"Gimme!" Ray jerked the man out of the small opening, snatched the wire cutters, and lunged forward, getting his head and right arm inside. He started snipping every wire he could reach, as fast as he could, which was now damned fast. Within seconds, all of the visible wires were cut to pieces.

The timer was still counting.

"SHIT!" Ray exclaimed. "This crap was a decoy! The electronics are all internal! We can't get to it without going through the casing and into the nuke itself!"

"And the casing is solid chromium! We can't cut into it without risking setting off the high explosive!"

"Can't be," Ray determined. "They'd never have gotten the explosives in to begin with. There's a hatch somewhere…" he glanced at the timer, "…but we don't have time to find it!" He pulled back, glancing at his wrist, where the tough little brane door counter still ticked down. "Pete, get outta here! I got one shot at this, and you need to be far, far away in case it doesn't work!"

"What the hell can YOU do, ALONE?" Hansen asked, horrified.

"GO!" Ray shouted, crouching down and getting a good grip on the large hunk of deadly material with its ancillary devices. "More than you think!"

Hansen jumped into the humvee and sped away. He glanced back…

…just in time to see Reagan Brady heft the neutron bomb—pushing a half-ton weight, by Hansen's estimate—up in both hands, then suspend it over his head.

"Oh. My. God," he murmured in astonishment, then hit the accelerator, tearing up the turf of the Mall.

&OCB

Ray shifted the bomb in his hands, getting it well balanced, before stepping back with one foot, removing one hand and drawing the thing back like a baseball pitcher preparing a strike. With considerable effort, he held his position, waiting. It hurt like hell, and he could hear—and feel—tendons and muscles in his arm, chest, and back beginning to tear. *Dear God, let 'em hold on long enough. And please let Sam and Abby be outta harm's way. Ten… five, four, three…*

The brane watch began beeping.

Like a ghost, or a shimmering mirage, Ray saw the Klein bottle form about halfway up the side of the Monument, and a good twenty feet out.

He flung the neutron bomb at it with all the force of his newly enhanced body.

A blue-white light flared…

…and it was gone. Ray fell to his knees and then sat with his back against the monument wall.

"What a freaking day!"

&OCB

In North Dakota, about halfway between Grand Forks and Minot, a good ten to fifteen miles outside a small town called Devil's Lake, a bright blue-white light flared some hundred or so feet in the air, in the midst of what looked like the aftermath of a volcanic eruption. As it faded, a dark metallic object began to materialize inside it.

But before the bright light could flicker out, within a fraction of a second, the metallic object exploded in hellfire.

A shock wave swept over the decimated prairie, knocking half molten automobiles and shattered aircraft remains about like hay in a dust devil. What little combustible material that still remained incinerated into ash and blew away on the winds of the blast.

‽⃝

In the genetics laboratory of what had been William Drago's missile silo headquarters, Samantha Brady and Felix Kato felt the structure shake violently. There was a titanic concussion wave with it. Kato covered his ears, Sam grabbed her nose, and Abby buried her face in her mother's breasts. They were deep underground but the events of the day had softened the old silo a bit and as the shock wave passed overhead there was a slight bit of overpressure seeping through the structure of the underground facility. Sam noted that the pressure wave managed to penetrate into her sinus cavities with just enough force to feel like descending rapidly in a plane, making her ears pop. It was over in seconds. She worked her jaw to relieve the pain.

"Oh damn," Sam murmured, bouncing Abby as the frightened little one began to scream, "you don't suppose the insane idiot just nuked off the top of the silo, do you?"

Kato shook his head, then shrugged. It was the universal 'I don't know' gesture. Sam handed Abby to him.

"Here," she said. "Take Abby, and I'll go see. I think I'm the only one here remotely suited for it, anyway," she added, rueful.

"Be careful, nevertheless," Kato said, as Sam exited the lab.

‽⃝

The elevator was still working, which led Sam to conclude that the top of the silo was intact after all. Having loaded herself with as many weapons as she could reasonably carry from the confiscated pile outside the lab, she moved up inside the silo, floor by floor, checking everything out.

When she got to the control room that operated the brane door, she looked through the observation window and noticed the pads were on fire. Finding the sprinkler system specifically for that room, she initiated it, but did not go inside. The lone control panel in the room with her sparked once or twice, massive arcs that looked like a fireworks display, and she snatched the fire extinguisher from the wall and unleashed it upon the panel, pulling off a hatch to allow the foam to get inside. Glancing at her forearm, she saw no sign of scaliness, blisters, or snakeskin shedding.

"No radiation here, at least," she muttered to herself. "Something musta come through that was unpleasant, though."

Next door she found the room which contained the actual brane mechanism.

Or what was left of it.

ഇൗരു

After it became obvious that the neutron bomb was no longer a threat, Peter Hansen came back, this time with a set of black BDUs in Ray's size. Ray, still nude, gratefully donned them, after sprawling rather limply on the stone plaza for a few moments to allow his overexerted body to heal. Hansen also brought a couple of sandwiches and several liter bottles of water, which Ray consumed in short order, guzzling the water like a man who had been in the desert for several days.

Which, in a way, drifted through his mind, *I have, more or less. The serum's changed my metabolism, somehow. I can stand the dehydration now, thanks to the radiodurans, but it sure tastes good, all the same.*

Then Pete handed Ray something else. Ray examined the contents of the plastic bag he'd been handed and found gloves, sunglasses, and a balaclava.

"Huh?" Ray wondered, taking the items and staring at them, then giving Hansen an odd look.

"Your skin, Ray," Hansen explained, sympathetic but blunt. "We're gonna have to drive through the cordon to get back home. I can't black out the windows in the hummer. After what just happened, people will either think you're an alien, or that you've been irradiated. Even if they think you're a normal human, we don't need 'em seeing… this. Judging by the Geiger, you need decontaminating anyway."

"Oh, shit! I got fallout all over you, Pete!"

"It's ok. I already deconned. Get a move on, though, or I'll have to do it again."

"Oh," Ray said, sliding the balaclava over his head and pulling on the gloves. "Damn hot this way." He shoved the earpieces of the wraparound sunglasses through the eye openings of the balaclava, and he was covered from head to toe.

"Sorry," Hansen apologized. "Now hop in and let's go."

Chapter 23

"Well," Sam remarked, when she and Abby had been enthusiastically reunited with Ray in the conference room back at their office building, amid many hugs and kisses, "my skin is shot to hell and back. So much for a 'peaches and cream' complexion."

"Yeah, more like raspberries and cinnamon, hot stuff," Ray observed, studying her face intently. "I kinda like it."

"Yiecch."

"Er…" Ray suddenly realized he might have put his foot in that one. "Seriously, anything looks good on you."

"Speaking of raspberries…. Ppbbblltt!" Sam gave him one, eyes twinkling. He relaxed.

"Pink always did look good on you," Ray grinned then. "Your hair is white, though."

"So's yours," she retorted. "But the roots are already turning back to… well, not brown, it's turning black. We look… really weird." She studied him, thoughtful. "You don't look like you anymore. Or maybe it's the other way around, and this IS the real you."

"What do you mean?" Ray wondered.

"You haven't taken a look at yourself yet?"

"No time. Been trying to locate where Drago went. And—"

"Ooo. Any sign of him?"

"No. Near as Paul and I can figure, he must have had a backup brane system. I saw your report about the one at the silo."

"So he's gone."

"For now. He could be anywhere in space or time. Somehow I have the feeling he's not down for the count, though," Ray mused. "I'm going to look into getting us a way to get recon of the Moon. Maybe we need to figure out a way to go there."

"The Moon? Really, Ray?"

"Yes. It would be the ideal place for Drago to hide. He'd be the only person that could get to and from. We need to look into recon of it at a minimum. Maybe NASA needs to do a Moon orbiter sometime soon. And I've had more other stuff on my mind than looking into mirrors and contemplating my navel."

"Enough about that fruitcake. *And* what 'stuff' has been on your mind?"

"And… waiting for you and Abby to get home has been on my mind. I'm so glad to have you both home alive and well," Ray felt himself flush.

Sam gave him a tender smile at that.

"So you haven't bothered to look into a mirror. Yeah, now that you mention it, you've got about a twelve o'clock shadow. Have you slept, at least?" she wanted to know.

"Not really. Jay's pretty good about bringing me something to eat, though."

"C' mere. There's a bathroom down here," Sam said, leading the way. "You need to see yourself."

৪০৫৪

Soon the little family stood in a spacious, unisex handicapped restroom, and Ray stared at himself in the mirror for the first time since injecting the serum. It was true; his hair had bleached white from the radiation outside, just as Sam's and Abby's had. But the color was already starting to return in the roots as the hair grew out–his, being darker, was just more noticeable. He DID observe that the colors were deeper than they had been, however–his dark brown hair was now black. Sam's and Abby's platinum blonde shade was coming back in as a darker ash blonde. There were places, though, where their normal colors weren't growing in at all–instead, their hair was developing streaks of the odd, red wine color that marked the influence of Deinococcus radiodurans, the "terrible little berry."

Their skin tones were now a deeply tanned shade, also blotched and veined with the berry red, and as best Ray could tell he had no tan lines, and assumed Sam and Abby were the same. He could also see that the whites of their eyes were no longer white, but a brick red. Their irises were rimmed with a darker shade of their natural colors. Their fingernails and, Ray had noted before donning clothes at the Mall, his toenails, were a deep henna color, and they seemed to grow fast as shit. He was already thinking he needed to trim them.

All natural modifications of the human body in response to radiation, he decided. *An increase in melanin and other pigments in every external tissue. Probably something similar going on inside, too. And the berry red is from the radiodurans, for some reason. Maybe… maybe clustered around the lymph system? I dunno. Doc will sure want to look at this. I'm surprised he hasn't jumped my case already–oh duh. Time, Ray, time. The man only just got back with your wife and daughter. Give him time.*

But it was the contours of his face that drew his attention the most. For the face he'd seen in the mirror for the last few years, the face he'd grown accustomed to as Dr. Reagan Brady, was not the face he saw now, not the work of plastic surgeons. For the first time since Iran, Dr. Raymond Bradford stared back at him in the mirror.

"Damn," he said in surprise. "I hadn't even considered that."

୫୦୯ଓ

As they moved toward Fields' medical facility, a tense, concerned Ray quizzed Samantha about his appearance.

"No, I do not mind it," she told him, blunt and firm. "I knew what you looked like before your surgeries, Ray; Robert—"

"Dad," Ray corrected, glancing about to ensure they were alone in the corridor.

"Da," Abby piped, and both parents stopped to stare at their little girl, smiles of delight on their faces. Then Sam resumed.

"Robert showed—"

"He told me, Sam. In private. I know. He's your dad, Abby's grandfather, and my father in law. I haven't told anyone else, and I won't. So don't worry."

Sam paused, shifted Abby to her other hip, and stared at Ray, who returned the scrutiny calmly, confidently. Finally she nodded.

"Okay. Good. For what it's worth, I came up through the ranks on my own. My maiden name was really Kruger, not Waters. Waters was my grandmother's maiden name. I wanted to tell you, but Daddy was worried it would either look like nepotism, or make somebody a target."

"It made somebody a target anyway, and Drago didn't even know," Ray shrugged. "He thought I was the ultimate team lead, I'm guessing."

"Yeah, he did."

"So what did your dad show you?"

"Daddy showed me your files before we came in to recruit you. I felt so bad that your handsome face had had to be reconstructed. But they did a really good job. And it doesn't matter either way, Ray. I love YOU," she said, putting her free hand over his heart, "the guy in here, and I think I'd have loved you even if they hadn't been able to put your face back together at all."

"I love you, too, hot stuff," Ray murmured, sucking in a deep breath as he relaxed. *All I could want, all I could ever ask for, and more.* He put his arm around his wife's shoulders and squeezed lightly, then released her.

"Da," Abby said again, looking up at Ray, recognizing his voice. "Da?"

"Yes, honey," Sam told the girl. "That's Daddy. I know he looks a little diff— um, I know he looks kinda funny, but it's Daddy. Do you want to go to him?"

Ray held out his hands, tentative, prepared for rejection. But Abby went to him without hesitation. She buried her little face in his chest, wallowing around for several minutes, breathing deep and recognizing his scent; then she looked up at him and smiled.

"Da," she declared, certain. A tiny fingertip ran along a berry vein on his cheek, and she laughed, then clapped her hands. "Da! Da da!" And she giggled.

"That's right, princess, Dada," Ray beamed, feeling like his chest would burst.

Once again her hand covered a patch of berry on his skin, her other hand reaching up to fist in his white hair with black and wine roots. Then she laughed until she doubled over in his arms. "Dada!"

Eyes twinkling, Ray looked at Sam.

"I think she finds the, er, additions, amusing," he decided.

"Yeah, I think you're right, sweetheart. She's been fingering my spider veins too, while I carried her."

"Dada! Hi! Butt!"

Ray's white eyebrows shot up. "WHAT did she say?!"

"Uh-oh," Sam said in dismay, as Ray looked askance. "Lemme explain…"

"I'm listening," Ray said, looking at his wife with an odd glint in his eyes as they started down the stairs.

꧁꧂

"Well, it's the damnedest thing I've ever seen," Fields finally expostulated after a couple of hours in the medical lab. He'd run every test on them he could think of, and all had come back within reasonable norms–except for the exceptional amount of melanin present and a high number of cellular proteins that weren't normal in humans but WERE normal in D. radiodurans. Their DNA, however, was another story. It had been modified slightly.

"In what way?" Ray wondered.

"Well, among other things, it's that p21 gene again," Fields remarked. "The one that causes scar tissue if it's there, and regeneration if it's not. It's not that it's not there anymore, 'cause it is. It's just… different."

"Different how?"

"THAT... is gonna take me awhile to figure out," the specialist admitted. "But evidently it's been modified to allow for a certain level of regrowth—okay, a HUGE level of regrowth—instead of scarring. And I might add that that also seems to be affecting the aging process. I don't know for sure yet, but I'd say you guys are gonna outlive the rest of us by a substantial margin."

"Immortality?" Ray said, in shock.

"No, no, not immortality," Fields corrected. "Just a much extended lifespan. Couple centuries, maybe? I don't get it. But I'm gonna keep workin' on it 'til I do. I'll let ya know then." He shrugged.

"What about our speed and strength?" Sam, ever practical, wanted to know. "I can run almost twice as fast as I ever have."

"Oh, that. That's a simple matter of training," Fields explained. "When you train, whether for running, weight lifting, or whatever, you're damaging muscle fibers, stressing bone and tendons, and those muscles and bones and tendons respond to the stress by getting stronger. That's one of the reasons why you get sore afterward. It's just a natural function of the body. But now, every cell of your body, including every muscle fiber, every tendon, every bone, is what could be termed an extremophile. So the stress response, instead of taking days, weeks, or even months, is virtually immediate. Ray, remember when you hefted that neutron bomb, so I'm told?"

"Yeah?"

"Hurt like hell, didn't it?"

"Oh SHIT, yeah," Ray agreed, wincing at the memory. "I could feel the stuff tearing in my back and chest. I was only praying my muscles would hold out long enough to chunk the thing through the extraction point."

"Not surprising. And then, per the report I got, you laid down on the ground and rested until everything healed up?"

"Yup."

"Smart man, for once. The x-rays show you had stress fractures all over your skeleton, too. Well, next time you ever have to pick up and throw a neutron bomb—assuming there IS a next time, and I pray God there won't be—that won't happen. You'll just jerk it up and fling it. Your body has now adapted to that kind of stress. And unlike the standard bodybuilder, YOUR body will maintain the ability without the need for continued training, although training is still good."

"No shit?" Ray's eyes widened.

"No shit," Fields replied with a grin. "We'll probably have to come up with a special gym for you and Sam, but it's there, and pretty much there to stay. I'm still trying to understand the way you generate energy. You should've been burning calories like mad, but... I dunno. Give me time. Meanwhile, you're all about as healthy as you can possibly be. And I mean that in every possible way."

"Human?" Ray pressed.

"Uhm, not... not exactly. Yes and no. The genetic changes are... too fundamental. A subspecies, maybe? I dunno. It's too soon for me to say." He ran a distracted hand through his hair. "Damn, what a ton of stuff to analyze..."

"What about our children?" Samantha asked, practical nature coming to the fore.

"Abby? Abby's fine. As good as you two. Her cystic fibrosis is gone, but then we pretty much already knew that. Whether she'll be able to have children, given the lack of others like you three, I can't say yet."

"No, I meant siblings for Abby."

"Um," Fields hedged, "I'm not sure about that. It could go either of two ways."

The Bradys stared at him, waiting.

"Well, either you'll have another version of Abby, as it were—Homo sapiens radiodurans, let's call it for now, 'cause I don't like Drago's 'extremum' bullshit—or..."

"Or?" Sam pressed.

"Or you won't have any more," Fields said, solemn. "It's possible that Sam's body may interpret Ray's sperm as invaders, and fight 'em off. Which, I suppose, could make for one helluva cellular battle, given the regeneration capability. Or it could interpret a fetus as a tumor and destroy it. I... just can't say, yet. And we may not know until you try."

Sam and Ray exchanged worried glances. *I knew I had a bad feeling about it, way before Sam was ever kidnapped,* Ray sighed to himself.

&OCR

"As for Ray's appearance, it looks like all the plastic surgery got undone, and he went back to his original, genetically programmed, looks," Fields continued, after some more tests. They were sitting with several other members of Medical in Fields' consultation room. "I don't know how that's going to affect the cover story. But frankly, I don't think there's anything we can do about it. Judging from my tests as well as discussions with Dr. Kato, I think any attempt to surgically reconfigure Ray's features is just going to end up with his body rejecting the modifications and healing back into its genetic configuration."

"So I got my old face back and there's nothing anybody can do to change it," Ray verified.

"Yup. That's your mug and you're stickin' to it, I guess you could say."

"You've still got your 'Superman curl,' though," Sam noted, eyes rogueish.

"Yeah, and I don't get that," Ray remarked. Fields shrugged.

"Who knows? Maybe it's just the way you style your hair now. Before joining DSRPO, you always wore military short cuts, didn't you? Well, so maybe it was there all along, you just never grew it out long enough to notice."

"What about the pinkish red marks all over? And our eyes?"

"They're part of the configuration now," Kato, who had come back with the rest of the team from North Dakota, and was now part of DSRPO, answered for Fields. "They are part of you, and they will not go away."

"And as far as I can tell, Ray, your hypothesis is right," Fields tag teamed. "While the radiodurans type proteins are distributed throughout your bodies in each and every cell and membrane, there IS a concentration of them in the lymph system and the circulatory system, enabling them to get to wherever they are needed as fast as they can."

"There may even be a lesser concentration in the nervous system," Kato added. "But what we SEE through the skin is definitely due to the lymph system. The patches correspond to the lymph nodes, and the veins to the lymph ducts. You will have to cover them up in order to go out in public, if you desire to maintain anonymity."

"Hell, maybe you ought to just get a bunch of damn tattoos," Jay laughed.

"Never was big on tattoos," Ray responded.

"It is likely the skin would slough it off and heal anyway," Kato added. "I don't know if tattoos would even work on you. That might be an interesting experiment."

"I don't want tattoos. I'll cover up if I need to go into public."

"Ray's gotta use makeup," Sam began a singsong chant, teasing her husband.

"Shit," Ray muttered. "And I guess we'll have to get used to contact lenses, to cover up the 'whites' of our eyes. Or maybe that should be 'browns' now. This is not gonna be fun."

Sam instantly silenced, a grimace forming on her face.

"Oh, Abby is so NOT going to like that," she murmured. She glanced down at the child in her arms.

"We'll figure it out," Fields offered staunchly. "Somehow we'll get you three looking normal in public. Personally, I think there's something kinda... kinda cool about it. And I DON'T HAVE TO SET RAY'S NOSE, EVER AGAIN!"

The physician all but skipped in place, and everyone chuckled... except Ray, who scowled. Samantha elbowed him in the ribs, then gave him a 'lighten up!' look—so he stuck out his tongue.

Abby let out a loud cackle, doubling over, and everyone burst into laughter.

☙❧

"...So if that's what he planned to use it for, why the hell did he have another one forming there just minutes after?" the Old Man wanted to know in the debrief.

"You mean the extraction point in the Mall?" Ray verified.

"Hell yeah."

"Well, there's only so much control he can maintain over the membrane intersections, from what I could tell," Ray answered. "They seem to mostly COME in pairs. Probably a resonance thing."

"I think Ray's right on that," Paul agreed. "I bet if we go back and look at all the location data we took on the extraction points we will find a duality within or near them somehow."

"And maybe he planned on dropping bomb after bomb," Jay suggested.

"That doesn't make sense, Jay," the Old Man pointed out. "The brane doors alternated directions."

"I have another idea," Dr. Kato interjected. The room quieted, waiting for the team's newest member to speak. Kruger nodded permission.

"I think," Kato began, "that the particular extraction point through which Dr. Brady flung the bomb was not intended either as a second bomb drop, or as an unavoidable resonance. I think Drago intended it as an escape route for Dr. Brady."

Jaws dropped around the room.

"Why would you think that, Dr. Kato?" Fields wondered.

"There is something about the Brady family that Drago considers special," Kato said, shaking his head. "I do not know what. But I know that it would have been easier for him to kill Mrs. Brady and her child, and lie to DSRPO about it, than to maintain the level of activity around them that he did."

"He sure tried it with me," Sam growled. "And Ray, too, after that first nuke."

"No, he did not," Kato corrected. "He attempted to force you into submission, true. But had he wanted to kill you, you would never have awakened in the first place. In fact, the physician was instructed to ensure that your kidnapper had not caused serious damage to you when he knocked you unconscious. And by your own narrative, Dr. Brady had already taken the radiodurans serum before exiting the silo. Drago knew that the only way to kill him at that point was to essentially disperse his body, or overload the healing factor–neither of which he had the capability to do."

"What was it all about, then?" Ray wondered. "You believe his story about us being allies in the distant future? About Abby being some resistance movement general?"

"As I said, Dr. Brady—"

"Ray, please."

"And I'm Sam, or Samantha," Sam added.

"As I said, Ray, I am afraid I do not know. But I did overhear a conversation I do not believe I was meant to hear. And in that conversation, he spoke of 'toughening up' Mrs... er, Sam, ensuring that little Abigail was prepared for 'what was coming,' and figuring out a way to ally himself with you."

"Yeah, he pretty much told us that much, too," Ray expostulated, shocked. "With that homicidal nutcase? What the hell?! Somehow we need to find out if there is anything to this alien infection he kept going on about. And what about Comet Enke and Tunguska was so important?"

The members of DSRPO merely stared at each other in bewildered puzzlement.

"Time will play out soon enough and we will figure this out." Ray wasn't sure he believed Drago's story, but it was a compelling one nonetheless.

ಬಂಗ

There was no question of going back to their home in Kingstowne outside Alexandria; there was very little in the way of "home" left to go back to. And with Ray's new—old—appearance, and the berry blotches all over the entire family, which so far no amount or variety of makeup Sam could find had been able to sufficiently cover, the neighbors would certainly look askance.

"I'm thinking we're gonna have to try theatrical makeup, Ray," Sam finally gave up, shoving the various foundation samples back into the shopping bag from whence they came, along with assorted sponges and application brushes.

"What, greasepaint?" Ray wondered, using a disposable wet wipe to remove the latest failed makeup attempt on his cheek. He tossed it into the wastecan in the same unisex bathroom in which he'd seen his new, old face.

An impatient Abby grunted, then whimpered, and Ray dug around in the diaper bag, extracted the pacifier, and poked it in her mouth. The toddler promptly settled down in the baby sling on his chest.

"Yeah, or one of those special concealers designed to cover scars," Sam decided. "In the meantime, until we can find something that'll hide this bright berry shit, we're gonna have to be careful and stay... well, hidden."

"Damn."

"I wonder if we could just be like George Hamilton?" Sam pondered.

"What do you mean?"

"Could we get so tan that the berry splotches would be harder to notice?" she asked.

"We should try it."

𝜚𝒪𝒸𝒮

So the Old Man took them home with him to his house in Rosemont until other arrangements could be made. Teresa was still in the hospital, but she would come to the Kruger house to finish her recuperation when she was released in a few days.

"It's not like I don't have the room, son," he noted to Ray, as the little family moved into the bedroom wing of the rambling old house and deposited what personal possessions the Bradys still had in two of the rooms, one already provided with a crib and baby monitor. "And a basement setup not too dissimilar from yours. With a few modifications, we can make it work. We can even make it permanent, if need be and you're willing."

"Stands to reason," Ray smiled at his father in law, catching the male endearment and seeing the invitation implied in the older man's remaining eye. "I hate barging in on you, though. We'll talk about it. And... thanks—for everything."

"Thank YOU," Robert Kruger said softly, taking Ray's hand and shaking it. "You're all I could ever ask for in a son in law. You love my daughter and my granddaughter with everything you've got, and you're willing to risk everything for 'em, too."

"Damn straight, Dad," Ray averred, then embraced the older man, as unaccustomed tears sparkled in Samantha's eyes.

ൠ◌ൠ

Later, when they'd put Abby to bed, Sam grabbed Ray by the arm and tugged him along the hallway to Kruger's study. Knocking on the door was followed by a grunt from within, which somehow Sam interpreted as "come in." *Must be a father-daughter thing,* Ray decided. *I couldn't make heads or tails outta that sound. Then again, I understand Abby's least coo, so... yeah, I guess so.*

Sam slipped inside, towing Ray along for the ride, and eased the door closed. Kruger looked up from his leather easy chair, then put aside the book he'd been reading. The dark paneled room, walls lined with full bookshelves and the odd painting here or there, exuded cultured masculinity. The lights were off, save for the reading lamp on the end table beside the Old Man's chair, and a small fire in the fireplace; though the days were warming, the nights were still a little chilly.

"What's this about?" he wondered. "Samantha, you look like the cat that ate the canary."

"I... well, I..." Sam started, suddenly unsure.

"Spit it out, Samantha."

Sam reached into her pocket and pulled out a hypodermic pistol. Ray instantly recognized it; it was the same one Drago had used, the same one he and Sam had used, to shoot themselves and Abby up with the radiodurans serum. And it still had a small amount of blue-green fluid in it.

"This," Sam said.

The Old Man's nonexistent eyebrow went up, stretching his scar. Simultaneously, Ray's jaw dropped.

"May I presume that is what I think it is?" Kruger wondered.

"Yes," Sam said. "It's the last dose. I thought... well, I thought maybe..." She waved a hand over her eye, the same eye that corresponded to the one her father lacked. He understood immediately.

"Instead of giving it to Fields to study and duplicate?"

"I offered. Neither he nor Kato want to go there." Sam shook her head. "And I don't blame them at all. We're... Ray and I... we're not entirely sure we're human anymore, Dad. Poor little Abby didn't even have a choice. And that isn't something to shit around with. But... but I remember when you came back, and you'd lost... and how hard it was for you at first. Hard for you AND Mom. I don't really know if it'll work for that or not. Ray's face didn't change immediately, after all, and... and we don't quite understand why. Ray thinks it was because his face got hurt so bad in the fight and when it healed, it went back to its old shape. Doc Fields disagrees. He thinks it was just a matter of the time it took to recognize the different configuration and bring it back to genetic normal.

"But I wanted to give you the chance. It might work, or it might not. You don't have to if you don't want to. Here. It's your call. If you don't want to, throw it in the fire." She handed him the syringe.

Kruger sat there with it in his hand, staring at it, his one eye glazed over in thought. Ray and Sam merely stood there, watching him. Finally, without a word, he jabbed the hypo against his neck and pulled the trigger.

There was a snap, and a hiss, and they watched as Robert's eye grew wide with the sensations coursing through him. Berry colored spider veins raced out from the injection point. Behind that wave, melanin suffused his skin, darkening it. The white of his lone eye slowly turned a deep brick red. Suddenly he reached up with henna colored fingernails and scratched his scalp.

"Damn, you didn't say it would itch like hell," he complained.

"It... didn't," Ray murmured, stunned and concerned. "Tingly hot and kinda flushed, yeah, but I didn't itch." He leaned over the older man and studied his scalp, which like many men Robert's age, didn't contain nearly as much hair as it once had. In fact, he was essentially bald on top. "I'll be damned."

"What?" Robert demanded.

"Dad, you got hair," he said in surprise. "That's what's itching. Your hair is growing back in. There's a fine, like, I dunno, yellow peach fuzz up here now. The follicles must've regenerated."

"What the hell..." Kruger muttered. He rose from his chair, initially intent on finding a mirror, and his eye widened further in surprise. "The arthritis is gone."

"I didn't know you had arthritis, Daddy," Sam blinked at the unexpected revelation.

"In my knees, yeah, baby, because of some of the punishment they took jumping out of planes back in the day," he admitted. "I've just never been one to let it slow me down. But it was starting to get to me. Now..."

"It's gone?" Ray asked.

"Completely."

But there was no sign of an eye rejuvenating itself. Samantha threw her arms around her father.

"I'm sorry, Daddy," she whispered, near tears. "I hoped…"

"It's all right, Samantha," Robert murmured soothingly, hugging his daughter. "It seems maybe Ray was right, and it would take an injury to that part of my face to cause it to redevelop. Given the way I feel right now—even with the damn purply-red shit all over me—I might just give Ray a run for his money in the field, get myself popped in the face, and then, who knows?"

Kruger held out one arm toward Ray, and Ray stepped into the familial embrace.

262 Travis S. Taylor & Stephanie Osborn

Chapter 24

Midnight found the DSRPO team in Arlington Cemetery. For the first time since the founding of the team, they had come to bury their dead, but their dead were already "dead and buried." So they were here to exhume the empty coffins, place the bodies within, and inter them properly—all without leaving traces.

The last to be interred was one of the first members of the team, Staff Sergeant Ernie Travers, aka Ernesto Torres, medic. Ray stood silent as the body of his old friend was placed in its coffin, and the coffin sealed. Then he stepped forward.

"Ernie... Ernesto, I should say... was a good friend," he said into the darkness that enveloped them all. "A good friend, and my personal hero. You see, if it hadn't been for him, I wouldn't have lived to be here. I'd have died in a mine field in a hell hole of a valley in Iran. Or if not there, in the mountains surrounding it. You all know I have a habit of going into a fight leading with my chin. Most of the time I come out of those fights on top, mostly due to good training and experience and a heavy dose of old fashioned luck. Occasionally the other guy cleans my clock. More often than not, the face I saw when I woke up after getting the shit beat outta me was Ernesto's. Sometimes, when that happened," Ray admitted, "I'd get a flashback to Iran, and... well, I'm sure Ernie knew my waking up to see him wasn't always the comfort it should have been. I only hope and pray he understood. I think he did, because he never stopped being there." Ray paused, trying to swallow a lump in his throat.

"Somehow I got this stupid, subconscious notion in my head that, Ernie and Jay and me, well, after Iran, we just couldn't be hurt anymore. Not seriously, anyway. I guess... I guess now, I really can't, at least not without some SERIOUS bad shit happening. Sam's teased me about my 'Superman hair' for years. But I never thought my invincibility would come at the cost of Ernie's life." Ray's voice cracked, and he stopped. Jay stepped up beside him, putting an arm across his shoulders.

"It didn't," he told his field team leader. "I've come to terms with it, Ray. You have to, also. Ernie... well, he was just being Ernie. We all know how he was. He'd never leave a man down if he could help it, especially not one of the team."

"Don't you think," Kruger noted into the silence that followed Jay's remark, "that it's time you let that burden roll off your shoulders, Ray? You don't carry the lives of everyone on the team, and you never have. You couldn't, even if you tried. Nobody can except the One who made 'em. You weren't responsible for putting a minefield in the path of that convoy in Iran. You weren't responsible for the bad intel that never spotted said mine field. You're not responsible for the deaths it caused. And you're certainly not responsible for Ernie's death. You weren't even in the same state at the time." He looked around at the rest of the team.

"Ernie, and these other fine men and women, died because they were heroes," Kruger declared. "They believed in something bigger than themselves, and they believed it was worth pledging… I believe a very wise gentlemen once put it, 'their lives, their fortunes, and their sacred honor,' to paraphrase the Declaration a bit." He looked around. "I don't see anyone here who doesn't believe the same, or you wouldn't be here. You're all heroes and heroines in my book." He turned back to his son in law.

"So let it go, Ray. Leave it here, in Arlington with your friends. It's past time. You have a team to lead, and a daughter to raise. I think you'll do a lot better without carrying around a shit load of baggage that isn't yours. Don't you think, Samantha?"

"I do, Robert," Sam agreed, coming to put her arm around her husband; her other arm held their child, who reached for her father, hugging his neck. After several moments, Ray nodded awkwardly.

"Now, let's put Ernie to rest for the final time," Kruger said, solemn.

As the casket was placed into the vault in the mausoleum, all saluted. Since they could not afford to have a bugler play it lest it be heard, male and female voices alike lifted softly in the seldom heard lyrics of "Taps."

"Fading light dims the sight
And a star gems the sky, gleaming bright.
From afar, drawing nigh,
Falls the night.
"Day is done, gone the sun
From the hills, from the lake, from the sky;
All is well, safely rest;
God is nigh.
"Then goodnight, peaceful night,
'Til the light of the dawn shineth bright.
God is near, do not fear.
Friend, goodnight."

As the door clanged softly closed on the final vault, the remaining members of DSRPO faded into the dark.

Epilogue

Drago, almost but not quite healed of the gunshots, clothing tattered, burned, and smeared and soaked with blood, stepped through his brane door, and stumbled to a stop on the cushioned floor. He nearly fell before he was able to catch himself. Resting his hands on his knees, he stood in a half crouch, panting, as sweat dripped from his nose and chin.

A man with a patch over one eye—a man that Samantha Brady would, perhaps, have recognized—hurried to Drago's side, staring in shock at his superior's appearance. "Sir? Dr. Drago sir, do you need help?"

Drago shook his head, straightening his back and stretching against the last twinges of pain as he raised himself to his full height. He turned to his subordinate.

"I'm fine. Continue your duties. And have this landing pad decontaminated."

"Yes sir." He departed, leaving William H. Drago alone with his thoughts.

Drago checked his watches, then cursed under his breath—one of them was functional, the one that had brought him here. But the other showed only blank screens. *So. They have managed to either take down my system, or destroy it. In any case, I can no longer access it.*

However, the original extraction point test apparatus had worked as a perfect, if limited, backup system escape, and for that he was thankful. Reagan Brady had proven to be a unique opponent and had caused him to lose more than two hundred seventy years' worth of work, planning, and development of the brane transporters. *Dammit. Two hundred seventy YEARS! All shot to hell thanks to HIM. And yet... Reagan Brady was a worthy adversary. That, I must admit,* Drago realized. *If Brady is pure... and given his daughter's absolutely pure genetics, and that of his wife's, he almost certainly has to be... And if their daughter is who I believe HER to be... I think that perhaps I should devote some considerable effort to turning him to the cause. Father AND mother. They have the radiodurans now, in any event. That would match with what I know of the timeline, also. Well, time to regroup and expedite the alternate game plan. It will happen. After all, there are no paradoxes. So I must turn them to help me.*

Drago had no way of getting home since he had, once again, been banished to the hell hole backwaters of spacetime, where he had spent most of the past 300 years or so.

But he still had the original, working brane intersection prototype. Granted, it only had the power and control system for one door between two locations, but that was a start. *And I have the radiodurans serum, despite that meddling fool of a researcher,* he thought, pulling several large metal vials, intact, from his pocket.

And if Drago couldn't escape his hell, then he would… HE WOULD… conquer it! Some, he knew, including the Bradys, considered him crazy. Crazy mad, perhaps. But furious determination viewed in the absence of understanding, he considered, was hardly insanity. *They do not understand! But they MUST!*

Drago pounded his fist against the wall in a rage of frustration, disappointed in his progress, but then he began to smile. An almost maniacal laugh rang out, echoing eerily, as he scanned across the huge open high bay filled with advanced mechanics and armored space fighters and the hundreds of soldiers working diligently on them. *Soon, my friends, you will be superhuman!*

He turned and peered out the window and laughed again as the Earth's light rose over the lunar landscape outside. *Two hundred seventy years— bah! What is that to me?! A drop in the ocean of spacetime! No matter how long it takes, I WILL stop those menacing creatures from conquering humanity!*

Dr. William H. Drago turned from the window and headed for his old, original office, there to begin implementing his alternate plan of salvation. He knew just where to start. First was to co-opt the Brady family. And to do that, he had a plan.

Drago sat down in his office chair and looked at the cell phone and two small vials sitting before him in clear Dewar type containers. One container was labeled as "Child's DNA" and the other "Present Day Secretary of the United Nations." Drago took the two bottles and placed them in a special shipping container. Then he dropped in a letter he had fashioned and wrapped up the package and filled out a postage form for it.

I'll need to adjust the brane location, he thought.

ꙮ

Two weeks later Ray received a nondescript package in the mail. Upon opening it he looked at it cautiously and then scratched his head.

"What the hell?" he said.

"What is it, Ray?" Sam looked up from playing with Abby in the floor. "Who's it from?"

"Here, you read it yourself," Ray handed Sam the letter. "Dad, I think you want to hear this, too," Ray nodded to the Old Man who was also playing in the floor with his granddaughter.

Sam looked at the note and then started to read it aloud.

> *"Dr. Brady,*
>
> *I hope you and the wife and daughter have found yourselves well after our recent encounter. I am sending you this care package because you should really take a look at it. The containers are active DNA of the same person as a child and as an adult in present day. You look at it. Study it. I'm sure you will figure it out. When you do, use the cell phone in the box. It can only call one number, mine. But don't waste your call before you look into this DNA. Oh, and don't worry about how I got it. It is real, but I'm sure you will have to verify this for yourself.*
>
> *Once you do figure it out you will realize, as I have, that it is inevitable that we join forces. We must, as there are no paradoxes in time. I know you think we have had our differences and that I am mad. All of that might well be true, but in the end, time will allow for things to happen. And happen they will.*
>
> *Regards,*
> *Dr. William Drago"*

"What the hell?" Sam and Kruger said simultaneously.

About the Authors

Travis S. Taylor

Travis S. Taylor—"Doc" Taylor to his friends—has earned his soubriquet the hard way: he has a Doctorate in Optical Science and Engineering, a Master's degree in Physics, a Master's degree in Aerospace Engineering, all from the University of Alabama in Huntsville. He also has a Master's degree in Astronomy from the University of Western Sydney, and a Bachelor's degree in Electrical Engineering from Auburn University. Dr. Taylor has worked on various programs for the Department of Defense and NASA for the past sixteen years. He's currently working on several advanced propulsion concepts, very large space telescopes, space-based beamed energy systems, and next generation space launch concepts.

In his copious spare time, Doc Travis is also a black belt martial artist, a private pilot, a SCUBA diver, races mountain bikes, competed in triathlons, and has been the lead singer and rhythm guitarist of several hard rock bands. He currently lives with his wife Karen, daughter Kalista Jade, son Jase Lucas, two dogs Stevie and Wesker, and his cat Kuro, in north Alabama.

http://www.doctravis.com

Stephanie Osborn

Stephanie Osborn is a former payload flight controller, a veteran of over twenty years of working in the civilian space program, as well as various military space defense programs. She has worked on numerous Space Shuttle flights and the International Space Station, and counts the training of astronauts on her resumé. One of the astronauts she trained includes Kalpana Chawla, who died in the Columbia disaster.

She holds graduate and undergraduate degrees in four sciences: Astronomy, Physics, Chemistry, and Mathematics, and she is "fluent" in several more, including Geology and Anatomy. She obtained her various degrees from Austin Peay State University in Clarksville, TN and Vanderbilt University in Nashville, TN.

Stephanie is currently retired from space work. She now happily "passes it forward," tutoring math and science to students in the Huntsville area, elementary through college, while writing science fiction mysteries based on her knowledge, experience, and travels.

http://www.stephanie-osborn.com

Don't miss any of these highly
entertaining SF/F books

➤   Burnout: the msytery of
Space Shuttle STS-281
(1-60619-200-0, $19.95 US)

➤   Corruptor
(1-60619-233-7, $19.95 US)

➤   The Focus Factor
(1-931201-96-X, $18.95 US)

➤   The Melanin Apocalypse
(1-933353-70-8, $16.95 US)

➤   Warp Point
(1-933353-94-5, $16.95 US)

Cresperian Series

➤   Human by Choice ~ Book 1
(1-60619-047-4, $16.95 US)

➤   The Y Factor ~ Book 2
(1-60619-089-X, $18.95 US)

➤   The Cresperian Alliance ~ Book 3
(1-60619-087-3, $16.95 US)

Twilight Times Books
Kingsport, Tennessee

Order Form

If not available from your local bookstore or favorite online bookstore, send this coupon and a check or money order for the retail price plus $3.50 s&h to Twilight Times Books, Dept. LS511 POB 3340 Kingsport TN 37664. Delivery may take up to two weeks.

Name: _____

Address: _____

_____

Email: _____

I have enclosed a check or money order in the amount of

$_____

for _____ .

If you enjoyed this book, please post a review
at your favorite online bookstore.

Twilight Times Books
P O Box 3340
Kingsport, TN 37664
Phone/Fax: 423-323-0183
www.twilighttimesbooks.com/